SAPPHIRE

SAPPHIRE

Heather Burnside

An Aries Book

First published in the UK in 2022 by Head of Zeus Ltd
This paperback edition first published in 2022 by Head of Zeus Ltd,
part of Bloomsbury Publishing Plc

9 7 5 3 1 2 4 6 8

A CIP catalogue record for this book is available
from the British Library

ISBN (E): 9781838939625
ISBN (PB): 9781801108188

Typeset by Siliconchips Services Ltd UK

Printed and bound in Great Britain by
CPI Group (UK) Ltd, Croydon CR0 4YY

Head of Zeus
First Floor East
5–8 Hardwick Street
London EC1R 4RG

WWW.HEADOFZEUS.COM

For Pascoe and Kerry

Author Note

Dear Reader,

Writing this book has opened my eyes to the plight of many women in Britain today. Often, they do not choose sex work as a career option. In most cases it is a decision that is forced on them for various reasons.

A range of circumstances can push people into working the streets. Older women could be living in poverty and have no other means with which to provide for their children. They may be stuck in violent or abusive relationships where they are coerced into sex work.

Often, younger people have come from broken homes or spent time in care, their parents may be addicted to drugs or alcohol and have been incapable of looking after them or they may have become addicts themselves. Again, this is not always a conscious decision and can be influenced by many factors in their lives.

Without guidance from a responsible adult, it is easy to become led astray and drift into a world of drug and alcohol abuse. Many young people from these backgrounds have limited opportunities to succeed.

There are overlaps with street workers and homelessness

too since many homeless young women become sex workers in order to earn money with which to provide food and shelter for themselves or to feed their addictions. Once a young person has taken this course, they can become trapped and unable to find a way out.

I believe that everybody deserves a decent chance in life. Fortunately, there are specific charities that work tirelessly to help working girls and the homeless to rebuild their lives. Two of the charities I visited were particularly helpful and informative and I was amazed by the good work they undertake. With the help of these charities, some people go on to lead more fruitful lives and make a valuable contribution to society.

I would therefore like to give these charities (and the staff members who helped with my research) a special mention. They are:

Judith Vickers
Lifeshare
1st Floor, 27 Houldsworth Street
Manchester
M1 1EB
Website: https://www.lifeshare.org.uk/

Janelle Hardacre
Manchester Action on Street Health (MASH)
94-96 Fairfield St
Manchester
M1 2WR
Website: http://www.mash.org.uk/

If you would like to help unfortunate young people who find themselves on the streets, there are many ways in which you can do so. Both charities offer a range of opportunities from donating to volunteering. You can find out more on their websites.

Yours sincerely,
H Burnside

Prologue

2006

In a state of slumber, Sapphire snuggled deeper into the sleeping bag and pulled it tightly around her shoulders, trying to block out the biting wind. She had placed her makeshift bed as far back in the shop doorway as possible, but the chilly night air still found her, and her bones ached from the hard tiled floor.

Despite the cold and discomfort, she was having a lovely dream. It had taken her back to the time when she was still known as Sophie. She was thirteen years old and lying in bed at home, her sister Kelsey in the bed over from hers. It was the weekend and they had stayed up late watching the final of *Popstars* after having a chippy tea as a weekend treat. They were fired up from all the excitement of the final and still not ready for sleep.

'Who's your favourite from Hear'Say?' Sophie had asked.

'I like Noel,' gushed eleven-year-old Kelsey.

'No, I mean the girls. Who do you like in the girls?'

'Suzanne,' Kelsey replied. 'She's really pretty.'

'Not as pretty as Kym. When I get older, I'm going to have hair like Kym's. I'm going to dye it black.'

'Ew, no. I like blonde hair.'

Sophie enjoyed these chats with Kelsey. It was great having a sister who she got along with so well. Someone who she could share everything with, not only material things but opinions, hopes and secrets. Although they didn't always agree about everything, Sophie knew there was nobody else in the world who she would rather have as a sister, not even Kym Marsh.

Dreaming about her lovely sister gave Sapphire a warm glow. It started in her tummy and spread throughout her body, giving her a feeling of serenity. The warmth became hotter before cooling again. But as the cold hit her, Sapphire noticed something else. She was wet. It was a chilly dampness that seeped through her, destroying the dream and jolting her awake.

For a few seconds, her eyes flitted around the space, confusion crowding her mind as she took in the shop doorway and the man standing in front of her zipping up his flies. With wakefulness came clarity and she realised what had happened at the same time as she noticed the putrid odour of urine.

'That'll teach you, you fuckin' dosser,' he said scornfully as his mates sniggered and jeered in the background.

Sapphire tugged open the zip of the sleeping bag and shot up, too incensed to be cautious. 'You dirty bastard!' she yelled, stepping menacingly towards the man.

'I think she's a bit *pissed* off, Chris,' shouted one of his friends as Chris stepped away from Sapphire and joined in his friends' laughter.

Sapphire dashed towards Chris and lunged at him, but he dodged the blow from her clenched fist as he jumped back again. His hands were raised to the sides of his head, the fingers splayed as he taunted her by feigning fear. She knew he was probably more afraid of the humiliation of a female attack in front of his mates than by any damage she could do. But she didn't care. She was furious!

Sapphire was about to lash out again when she felt a sharp tug on her coat and heard a voice, pleading with her.

'Leave it, Sapphire. They're not fuckin' worth it.'

For a few moments she flailed wildly, determined to exact her revenge. But she was unable to connect. Chris stood back but she couldn't move forward as her coat was held in a tight grip. When the frustration became too much she spun around and turned her anger on the man who was pulling her back.

Jake, the convenient boyfriend. One look at his anguished, drug-ravaged face brought her crashing back to the present and she realised all her struggles were futile. Not just the struggle for revenge on the youth. But the struggle of life.

The dream was long gone, just like her childhood. She was in the real world now. Homeless. A junkie. A 'fuckin' dosser'. Someone to be taunted and ridiculed. And as the laughing youths walked away, leaving her with sodden clothes and the stench of urine, she resigned herself to facing another day of desperation.

PART ONE

FAMILY (2001–2005)

I

January 2001

Sue checked her bank statement one more time and did a quick calculation. She was perturbed by the result. Almost half the money was gone already. If she carried on spending at this rate, she would have nothing left in another five years. There wasn't enough! She needed the money to last at least until Kelsey and Sophie were both adults and, at the moment, they were still only eight and ten.

She reflected on her decision five years ago to rent a property and use the money from the divorce settlement to provide for her daughters as best she could. It had seemed like a good idea at the time but now she wasn't so sure.

There was nothing else for it, she would just have to cut back. The prospect of it disturbed her. She hated to deny the girls anything. They'd been through enough as it was, having to cope with their father walking out of the family home when they were only young.

Her mind drifted to thoughts of her ex. Bloody Roy! It had been such a shock when he'd told her he'd fallen for another woman and then left her struggling with two children. But she wasn't the type to beg him to stay. Silly vain man going off with a younger woman. It was such a bloody cliché. To hell with him! She'd managed well enough up to now.

Sue stopped herself before she got carried away. Although they'd coped without him, it can't have been easy for her girls seeing him with his new family. She wondered how they would be getting along now at Roy's house.

It had been over a month since their last visit and Sue was aware that he was seeing less and less of his girls as time went on. He rarely bought them anything either, protesting that the maintenance he paid should provide for them. But even with maintenance Sue's income wasn't enough to buy her girls everything they needed.

Despite her opinion of Roy, thoughts of her girls cheered her up. They'd be home in a couple of hours, so she'd best crack on with the housework.

Sophie and Kelsey were sitting in their dad's living room feeling bored. They were two attractive young girls with mid-brown hair and dark eyes that sparkled with vitality, but Sophie was the tomboy of the two and in her opinion, Kelsey was far prettier.

They'd finished the polite chit-chat with their father in the car so by the time they were seated inside the house drinking the lemonades he had just brought them, there was nothing left to talk about.

'I've got a spelling test on Monday,' said Kelsey, and

Sophie could tell it was just for the sake of having something to say.

It would have been easy to chat amongst themselves, but they were too polite and well-brought-up to exclude their father from the conversation.

'Are you good at spelling?' Roy asked Kelsey, and Sophie stifled the urge to tut. As their father he should have known the answer to that question.

'Not bad,' said Kelsey. 'But I haven't spent enough time learning these.'

'Well, you'll just have to put the hours in, won't you?' he said, attempting to sound jovial but missing the mark.

After a few more uncomfortable seconds had passed, Sophie turned her attention to her four-year-old half-sister, Grace, who was pulling one of her moody faces. Sophie and Kelsey laughed as they did whenever Grace pulled a face as it reminded them of their nickname for her, Grace the Face. They would also refer to her eighteen-month-old brother as Brett the Brat.

As Sophie watched Grace, she also noticed the sound of slamming doors indicating that Roy's second wife, Leah, was approaching the living room. Their laughing stopped.

'I want Mummy,' announced Grace, getting up and stomping across to the living room door then pulling down hard on the handle.

'Do you want some help with that?' asked Roy on his way over to her.

'No, I can do it all by myself.'

Leah burst through the door with Brett in one arm. Grace quickly grabbed her free hand and clung tightly to her side. There was a self-satisfied look on Grace's face.

'Oh, are you two still here?' asked Leah, looking down her nose at the two girls.

'They've not been here five minutes,' said Roy, following up with a chuckle to lessen the impact of his words.

Leah looked down her nose again. 'Well, you might bloody help me with these two, Roy. I can't move here.'

He rushed over to her and tried to take Grace by the other hand, but she pulled against him. 'No, want Mummy,' she squealed, so he took his son from Leah instead.

'Who's a good boy, then?' he asked. 'Have you had a nice sleep?'

The child responded by blowing raspberries, and Roy gave another exaggerated chuckle. Then he noticed what his son was wearing: a pink babygrow.

'What the bloody hell's he wearing, Leah? Pink! You're not trying to turn him gay, are you?' Then he laughed. 'Eh, I'm having no son of mine turning gay.'

'Oh, shut up. It's only for in the house. It's an old one of Grace's. His others are in the wash.

'D'you know, it took me bloody ages to get him off after you'd gone. He wouldn't settle. I don't know what's wrong with him lately. Anyway, it's your turn to have him now. You can take him off my hands while I start the tea.' Then she addressed the girls. 'I suppose you two will be wanting to get back home soon, won't you?'

'Give over, Leah,' Roy complained. 'It's only just gone half three.'

'Yeah, but you'll have to run them home then get back here for your tea, won't you? So, you can't leave it too late to take them back, unless *she* picks them up.'

Sophie was affronted by the hostility in Leah's tone when referring to her mother, and she quickly jumped in. 'Mum doesn't have a car anymore.'

'Why not?' demanded Leah.

'She couldn't afford to pay for the repairs,' said Roy.

'I don't see why not. You pay her enough in bloody maintenance.'

Roy didn't respond. Instead, he turned his attention to Brett and started playing 'This Little Piggy' on his fingers. Straightaway, Grace rushed over, demanding that he play it with her too.

Once free of her demanding daughter, Leah stormed into the kitchen, slamming the door behind her. Sophie and Kelsey could hear Leah banging things and cursing, and the girls could tell it was because they weren't wanted.

After a while, Kelsey asked, 'Do you want to go to the park, Dad?'

'Yeah, come on, let's go,' he said.

He got the children's coats from the hall and passed Grace's to Sophie who went over to help the child put it on. 'No!' yelled Grace. 'I want Daddy to help me.'

'Come on, Grace, let your sister help you with your coat.'

Grace screeched. 'No! I don't like her. *Not* my sister!'

Sophie retaliated. 'Well, I don't like you either. You're a spoilt little horror!'

'Don't you dare call her that!' yelled Roy. 'Come here and help Brett instead while I help Grace.'

Sophie noticed his failure to chastise his youngest daughter but she did as he said, eager to get out of the stifling atmosphere inside the house. Unfortunately, the time spent in the park was more of the same with Grace throwing tantrums and demanding attention till she got her own way.

'Can't we go home now?' asked Sophie, becoming irritable. 'I'm sick to death of Grace acting like a brat.'

'Hey, don't you talk about your sister like that,' warned Roy, going red in the face, but Sophie ignored him and stormed off to the car with Kelsey.

It was silent on the journey home, apart from Brett sobbing. Grace had fallen asleep almost as soon as the car started. Once they arrived, Sophie couldn't wait to escape but as she grasped the door handle of the car her father finally spoke to her.

'Hang on a minute. You haven't heard the last of this, lady,' he said. 'I'll be speaking to your mother about your attitude.'

'Yeah, whatever,' said Sophie, getting out of the car and stomping across the pavement to her garden gate.

Kelsey followed her and slammed the car door. Neither of them said goodbye to their father.

2

Sue was in the living room when she saw Roy's car pull up. It was apparent straightaway that there was something wrong. She could tell from the slamming of the car door, and the way Roy sped off without waiting for the girls to get indoors. She met them in the hallway. One look at the expressions on their faces confirmed her suspicions.

'I'm never going there again!' Sophie raged.

'Me neither,' Kelsey chipped in.

'What on earth's the matter?' asked Sue, surprised to see the girls so fired up.

The girls started talking both at once, their mouths spewing a list of complaints from their spoilt half-siblings to their stepmother's hostility and their father's indifference.

'It's obvious they don't want us there,' complained Sophie. 'He's too busy looking after his little brats.'

'Hey, that's a bit harsh,' said Sue.

'Well, it's true.'

Then the girls both tramped up the stairs and Sue was left pondering about the situation. The relationship between her girls and their father was becoming increasingly strained. They never seemed happy when they came home. Most times they said nothing, but their troubled looks did the talking for them. From the bits that they had told her though it was obvious that Roy's second wife didn't want them around. She detested Leah's attitude towards her daughters and had spoken to Roy about it several times, but it didn't seem to make any difference.

Despite all the problems, Sue had worked at building a relationship between her girls and their father. They were unaware of the phone calls she made to him when they were out of the house, pleading with him to see his daughters and trying to counter his various excuses when he put off their visits.

Sue thought again about how angry her daughters had been when they returned home. She'd never seen them that wound up by the situation before and she wondered whether they had finally had enough. There was going to be a lot of bridges to build this time, but she'd let the girls calm down first then try speaking to them.

It was after they had eaten that Sue decided to tackle the girls. Kelsey was just about to leave the table when Sue stopped her.

'Hang on, love, I want a word with you both before you disappear to your room. Don't look at me like that, Sophie. We need to discuss things.'

'About my dad I suppose?'

'Yes, that's right. We need to sort things out before you see him again.'

'We're not seeing him anymore.'

Sue's eyes flitted from Sophie to Kelsey and back again. 'What d'you mean?'

'What I said. We're not seeing him anymore. Are we, Kelsey?'

'No, we're not.'

'You can't do that, girls. He's your father.'

'So?' said Kelsey. 'That doesn't mean we have to see him.'

'Yeah, why should we have to?' asked Sophie. 'He doesn't want to see us.'

'Oh, course he does.' But Sue's words lacked conviction.

'No, he doesn't. All he's interested in is his new family. And that Leah's horrible.'

'Eh, that's enough!'

'Well, she is,' Kelsey chipped in. 'She's always in a mood when we're there. She can't wait for us to go home.'

'I'm sure that's not true. She's probably just busy. It's hard work bringing up two young children, y'know.'

'No, you're wrong, Mum,' said, Sophie, staring directly into Sue's eyes, her tone now calm but firm. 'You know he doesn't want to see us, so why don't you just admit it?'

Sue was flabbergasted. She'd tried so hard to protect them but had underestimated just how grown up they were for their ages. They weren't babies anymore and she couldn't just fob them off. They were becoming wise to it. And it suddenly dawned on her that by putting them through these repeated rejections, she might have been doing harm even though that wasn't her intention.

While she was still struggling for words with which to

defend her ex-husband, Sophie spoke again. 'Anyway, I'm sorry, Mum, but our minds are made up. We're not going round there anymore.'

Then Sophie pushed her chair back and left the room. Sue watched as Kelsey did the same. But she didn't try to stop them. Because, deep down, she knew it was probably for the best.

3

May 2004

It had been more than three years since the girls had decided not to visit their dad, and Sue was currently at home catching up with the housework while her daughters were at school. She smiled thinking about Sophie's reaction that morning when she had asked her to wear the cardigan she had knitted for her. She understood her objections. At nearly fourteen Sophie was developing her own sense of style, which didn't match that of her friends.

Sue supposed it was some form of teenage rebellion and, although she allowed her to wear black eyeliner, she drew the line at letting her dye her hair black or wear piercings, which she'd pestered her about for months. Still, she couldn't complain – her daughters were both good kids.

She yawned as she dragged the hoover from room to room. What she wouldn't give right now for a sit-down, a cup of tea and a dose of daytime TV. But that wouldn't get things done so she had to soldier on even though she was bone-weary.

Nowadays, she was going through the savings even faster since the girls had started secondary school and her outgoings had escalated. There was always something they needed, and her monthly pay never seemed to stretch far enough.

Sue was constantly trying to make it up to the girls for the absence of a father figure. Even though the marriage breakdown wasn't her fault, she still felt guilty that they were missing out. They hadn't seen anything of Roy in the last three years.

There were times when Sue thought she should have put up more of a fight and insisted that they saw him. But it wouldn't have been easy when everyone around her seemed to think it was the right decision. After all, Roy hadn't made much of an effort to stay in touch. Instead, he had seemed relieved when she had rung to tell him their girls' decision and asked him for his take on what had happened.

Still, it wasn't ideal having to take care of everything alone. She was weighed down by all her responsibilities and worried for the future when the money had all gone, and she had to manage on her meagre wage. Even the thought of her busy day ahead made her feel exhausted, but she knew she had to carry on as best she could. She owed it to her lovely daughters to do her best for them.

'Come on, slow coach,' shouted Sophie to her sister who was walking across the playing field of their secondary school in Gorton, a working-class area of Manchester.

Sophie was waiting at the top corner of the school grounds so she and her sister could go home together. She watched as her sister took the shortcut across the field, squeezing through the gap in the railings.

'How come you've not walked home with your mates?' asked Kelsey.

'They were in a rush and I wanted to wait for you.'

'How come?'

'No reason.' Sophie laughed. 'Can't your big sister wait for you without needing a reason? Where have you been anyway?'

'The games teacher wanted to see me. She wants to make me captain of the netball team.'

'That's brilliant. I heard about your goal.'

'Who told you?'

'Everyone. I've heard about nothing else all day; about how you scored the winning goal from miles away and were the hero of the hour. And Mrs Crowcroft bent down and kissed your feet. Then the rest of the team picked you up and ran around the field with you, cheering, while the crowd threw flowers. Then the BBC arrived and said they wanted to film the winning goal so they could show it on *Grandstand* on Saturday.'

Kelsey laughed. 'Ah, shut up.' Then she added, 'It did feel good though.'

Sophie smiled. 'Good. I'm really chuffed for you.'

They walked along Abbey Hey Lane and chatted amicably about their day for a while. To anyone passing by, they presented the perfect picture of two happy, attractive young girls who were blossoming into womanhood.

Then Sophie heard somebody shouting after them. She turned around and saw that it was their mother crossing the street opposite a nearby side road, which she must have stepped out of. Sue dashed towards them, unhampered by the shopping bag she was carrying, in her eagerness to get to her girls.

'Hiya, girls. Have you had a good day?' she asked cheerily.

Sophie noticed that her mother had her hair tied up. She liked it when she wore her hair like that as it showed off her pretty face. Sue had pleasant features with striking eyes and dark hair and, although still only forty-six, she wasn't interested in meeting another man as her girls were her world. Sophie knew she was lucky to have a mum like hers who was so devoted to her daughters.

As soon as they reached home and got inside, Sue put down the shopping bag and plonked herself in an armchair. The girls went up to their room and occupied themselves for a while with their homework. When it got to 5.30pm, Sophie was beginning to feel hungry.

'Should we go down and see if tea's ready?' she asked.

'Yeah, come on.'

Sophie was perturbed to find her mother still asleep in the armchair. 'Aw,' said Kelsey. 'She's fell asleep.'

Sophie turned to her sister. 'She must have been really tired.'

'Yeah, but you know Mum, always on the go. She's worn herself out.'

'Maybe we should have a word with her and tell her to take it easier.'

'We could but I don't think she'd listen. Anyway, we could do the tea if you want.'

Sophie eyed the shopping bag, which was still on the living room floor and she felt a pang of guilt for having left it there when her mother was so shattered. 'Yeah, come on,' she said. 'Let's have a look what she's bought.'

They took the bag into the kitchen and emptied out the contents. 'Pizza, great!' she said. 'At least we know how to make that.'

They busied themselves lighting the oven, taking the plates and cutlery out and setting the table. Between them they threw together a meal then went to wake their mother.

Sophie shook her by the shoulder. 'Mum, tea's ready,' she said.

Sue woke up with a start. 'What? What time is it?' She looked across at the clock. 'Oh my God! It's turned six o'clock. How did that happen?'

'Come on, Mum. We need to eat it before it goes cold.'

She returned to the kitchen and Sue joined them a few seconds later to see the meal all laid out on the placemats with the cutlery arranged around the plates and a fresh brew for each of them standing on the matching coasters.

'Aw, girls, that's lovely!' Sue declared.

'It's only pizza and oven chips, Mum,' said Sophie and, as she spoke, she could see tears in her mother's eyes. 'Sit down and eat it or me and Kelsey will be finished before you've even started. And don't worry about the pots. We'll do them once you've eaten your tea.'

'Thank you. What have I done to deserve such lovely daughters? I'm so proud of you both.'

Sophie smiled at her mother, but she couldn't help noticing that her mother's eyes were still glazed over. She decided not to say anything even though she thought it was a bit strange that her mother should get so emotional just because she and Kelsey had made the tea. There again, it was the first time they had done it and she promised to herself that she'd make sure they did it more often in future.

By the time the girls had finished, their mother was still toying with her food. 'We'll come back and do the pots when you've eaten yours,' said Sophie, heading upstairs. She expected her mother to protest as she usually did but instead, she thanked them again.

When they heard their mother switch the TV on in the living room, Sophie and Kelsey went back into the kitchen. Sophie looked at the abandoned pots lying on the table. Her plate was clear of food, as was Kelsey's, but she was disturbed to see that her mother's plate was still almost full. Maybe it was their cooking, but she didn't think so. An uneasy feeling was beginning to creep up on her. Something about her mother wasn't quite right.

4

July 2004

Sue looked around the crowded waiting room. She had been waiting twenty minutes already and only three people had gone in to see the consultant. She knew she was in for the long haul as most of the other patients had arrived before her.

She tried to focus on the tiny TV screen, which was fixed to a bracket high up on the far wall. Fern Britton and Phillip Schofield were interviewing somebody on *This Morning*. The interviewee seemed passionate about her subject and had Fern and Phillip clinging on avidly to what she was saying. Sue wouldn't have minded finding out what it was about but the sound of crying babies and loud chatter drowned out the woman's voice, and she couldn't concentrate anyway.

Sue was worried. She'd put off going to the doctor's for weeks, telling herself she was just overtired, and the bloating might have been because of a food intolerance. She was prone to IBS anyway, so it was probably just worse than usual.

Then she thought about the expression on her GP's face when she had told him all her symptoms, and the way he had rushed through her hospital appointment. She tried not to read too much into it; doctors had to be cautious. And he *had* told her that it was probably nothing sinister and that he was referring her to hospital to be on the safe side.

Sue's mind drifted back to her own parents who had both died young. The thought filled her with anxiety. What if that should happen to her? How would her girls cope? Maybe she should let them know she was ill, give them a bit of advance warning to prepare them for whatever the outcome might be.

But then she stopped herself before she got too carried away. She hadn't even had the tests yet. No, she'd wait a while longer before she said anything to the girls. She didn't want to worry them unduly, especially as it might turn out to be nothing serious.

Sophie was surprised when her mother was late home. She hadn't warned her she'd be out when they got back from school. It's a good job she had her own key, she thought, otherwise she and Kelsey would have been out on the street waiting.

When Sophie heard her mother come in through the door, she and Kelsey went downstairs, curious as to why she was late.

'Hi, Mum, where have you been?' Sophie asked.

'Work, why?'

'Oh, I didn't know you were at work today. I thought it was your day off.'

'I've been working overtime. Didn't I tell you?'

'No. Why are you wearing your best jacket anyway?'

'Because I felt like it. I like to make the effort once in a while, y'know.'

The girls went back to their bedroom, but Sophie couldn't settle. She had too much on her mind.

'I'm going for a walk,' she said.

'Where to? Do you want me to come with you?' asked Kelsey.

'No, nowhere special. I just need a bit of time on my own.'

Sophie noticed how put out Kelsey looked, and she felt a surge of guilt. She loved her sister to bits and normally they did most things together, but not today.

'I'm going out, Mum,' she called as she was leaving the house.

'Oh, where to?'

'Just to see a mate. I'll be back before tea.'

The reference to a mate was a fabrication; Sophie wasn't going anywhere other than a brisk walk around the streets near her home while she thrashed out all her worries inside her head.

Her first concern was for her mother. Sophie had noticed how tired and ill she was looking. She knew she should have stayed and helped her with the tea, knowing how exhausted she always seemed to be lately but at the moment she had troubles of her own.

That day at school had brought it home to her. It had started out as a throwaway comment from her friend, Kara, about a boy who they had passed in the corridor.

'There's that lad again,' she had whispered.

'What lad?'

'The gay one.'

'How do you know he's gay?' Sophie had asked.

'It's obvious. You can see by the way he walks, and he talks like a girl too.'

Just at that moment a group of boys passed him and one of them tripped him up, sending the poor lad sprawling across the floor. The group laughed and jeered and, to Sophie's consternation, Kara joined in with their laughter. They watched as the lad picked himself up off the ground and wiped his grazed hands on his trousers, his face ablaze with humiliation.

'It's not funny!' snapped Sophie. 'He's not doing anyone any harm.'

'Ew! What's got into you?' mocked Kara but Sophie didn't respond. She didn't want to draw the attention of the crowd to herself.

Once the boys had gone, Kara persisted with the topic of homosexuality. 'Eh, I wonder how you can tell if a girl is gay. Do you think it's because they act and talk like men? I bet that girl in the year below us is gay. Y'know, her with cropped hair who walks really manly? Jade, I think she's called.'

Sophie had shrugged, not really wanting to continue this conversation.

'Mind you,' Kara continued, 'I've heard women can be gay even if they act feminine. Ew, just imagine, one of them could be eyeing us up while we're getting ready for PE and we wouldn't even know.'

'Give it a rest, will you, Kara? I thought you said you had nothing against them.'

'I haven't. God, what's wrong with you? You're usually up for a laugh but you've been dead miserable lately.'

As she replayed the scene in her mind, Sophie felt a flutter of fear. If only she hadn't reacted so vehemently. She hoped she hadn't raised Kara's suspicions. The last thing she needed was for her friends to turn against her if they thought she might be gay.

The problem was Sophie wasn't even sure herself about her sexuality. But she knew she felt different. She had never been into the same things as her friends, never liked pretty clothes or feminine pastimes and hated the way her friends babbled on about the boys they fancied.

Sophie didn't fancy boys at all, but she couldn't risk anybody finding out how she really felt because she didn't want to become another victim of the bullies. And as she was getting older, those feelings were manifesting themselves in other ways too because she was starting to realise that she was attracted to girls, not boys. And, even worse, she had a crush on her best friend Kara.

The thought of Kara finding out terrified her. She had felt bad enough about it before but now she knew Kara's feelings about gays, it made her even more wary. This battle over her feelings was startling and the confusion was beating her up inside.

She knew she'd have to confide in someone sooner or later before it drove her bonkers. The obvious choice was her sister, Kelsey. But she wasn't sure whether even Kelsey would understand. They'd always been close, but Sophie felt that her sexuality set her apart from everyone she knew, and she feared that once Kelsey knew the truth, their relationship might never be the same again.

5

As Sophie walked home from school she could see Kelsey just ahead of her so she rushed to catch up.

'Hey, Kelsey, wait for me,' she shouted.

Kelsey turned around and smiled while Sophie trotted towards her. She waited to regain her breath before she asked, 'Have you noticed how odd Mum seems lately?'

'Oh, you mean her being tired all the time?' asked Kelsey.

'Not just that. She looks rough as well, and I could have sworn I saw her clutching her tummy this morning as though she was in pain.'

'Really, why didn't you say?'

'I dunno, I didn't want to worry you. It might be nothing. But I'm not sure. And why was she wearing her best jacket a couple of weeks ago when she got in from work? Well, she *said* she'd been to work but I don't believe her.'

'Eh, you don't think she's got a man, do you?'

Sophie shrugged. 'I don't know. But that wouldn't explain why she looks so rough and is tired all the time.'

'Wouldn't it?' asked Kelsey, grinning.

'No, it can't be. I mean, we haven't seen her bringing anyone back, have we? Unless she sneaks him in when we're in bed.'

'Maybe we should ask her.'

'Oh, yeah, I can imagine how that would go. Why are you so tired all the time, Mum? Have you got a man who's wearing you out?'

'Ew, shut up!' said Kelsey, laughing. Then the conversation stalled. Neither of them had anything more to add to their speculation. They were still a few minutes from home and Sophie wanted to raise the other matter that had been bothering her before she ran out of time.

'Kelsey, I've got something to tell you,' she began. She could feel her heartbeat speeding up as she nervously anticipated Kelsey's reaction. As soon as her sister flashed her a look of curiosity, Sophie came straight out with it, eager to unburden herself. 'I think I might be gay.'

At first Kelsey laughed, making Sophie regret that she had confided in her. But then she seemed to notice the look of disappointment on Sophie's face, and her laughter faded. 'You're serious, aren't you?'

Sophie nodded.

'Sorry, I shouldn't have laughed. I didn't mean it… Why? What makes you think you're gay?'

The switch in her sister's attitude gave Sophie the confidence to go ahead. She explained everything about the way she felt.

'God, I'm shocked!' said Kelsey. 'But I suppose you've always been a bit different. Y'know, the way you dress and do your makeup. But I thought that was just you. I didn't think it meant you were gay.'

'It doesn't,' Sophie protested. 'I'd still be alternative even if I weren't gay. That's just me.'

Kelsey smiled. 'Well, you're still the best sister in the world and I don't care if you are gay.'

Sophie felt a surge of relief, which brought a tear to her eye. 'Come here,' said Kelsey, flinging her arms round her. 'It doesn't make any difference to me. I wouldn't tell Kara how you feel though if I was you.'

'No! Will I 'eck. She doesn't even *like* gays.'

'Well maybe you've got the wrong mates then. I've never liked that Kara. She's always seemed a bit snobby.'

'You don't know her, Kelsey. She's alright really and a great laugh.'

'OK, it's up to you who you hang about with, but seriously, Sophie, I wouldn't tell anyone else if I were you. I don't wanna see everyone teasing you at school.'

Sophie agreed to take Kelsey's advice, relieved that her sister was OK about her sexuality and surprised at how mature her sister was for a twelve-year-old. It felt good to have her support.

Before they could discuss the matter further, they arrived home. Sophie was the first to put her key in the lock. She expected her mother to be home, knowing it was her day off but, yet again, she wasn't there. The girls looked at each other, curious, then Kelsey shouted for their mother. But there was no response.

'Don't tell me she's doing overtime again and forgot to tell us,' said Sophie. 'Because I won't believe her.'

'Me neither. Come on, let's watch some TV and wait for her to come home.'

They hadn't been home for long before they heard their mother's key in the lock and they both dashed to the front door to find out where she had been. She was panting for breath, and Sophie wondered if she had been rushing to get home before them but hadn't made it. But there was something else too. Their mother was wearing her best jacket again.

6

July 2004

'Don't tell me... you've been working overtime?' said Sophie. Her sarcasm was an attempt to make light of the situation.

'Not exactly, no.' Sue removed her jacket and hung it on a peg in the tiny hallway. She seemed deep in thought for a moment. Finally, she spoke, her tone one of resignation. 'Come on, let's go in there.' She nodded towards the living room. 'There's something I need to talk to you both about.'

Sophie felt her heart thudding, nervous about what her mother was going to reveal. She had a bad feeling as she sat on the sofa with Kelsey, both staring across at their mother who was sitting on the mismatched armchair adjacent to them wearing a pained expression.

'I haven't been to work, and I wasn't there last time I told you I'd worked overtime either. To be honest, it's taking me all my time to work my normal hours, at the moment, never mind overtime.'

Sophie willed her mother to get on with it.

'I've been to the hospital. I had to get the results of some tests they took a couple of weeks ago.'

She paused to take a deep breath before continuing, her voice shaky. The words 'hospital' and 'tests' struck fear into Sophie and her sister echoed her feelings when she said, 'Mum, what is it? You're scaring us.'

'I-It's not good.'

'Oh no! I knew it,' yelled Sophie. 'There's something wrong with you, isn't there?'

Sue nodded and Sophie noticed a tear roll down her face. 'I'm sorry, girls,' she said, her voice breaking on a sob. 'It's cancer.'

Sophie's hand shot to her mouth as Kelsey yelled, 'No!'

They both dashed over to their mother and wrapped their arms around her. Sue was crying openly by now but kept trying to calm herself down so she could carry on speaking.

'It's OK, Mum,' said Sophie, tears now flooding her own eyes. 'Cry if you want to. Anybody would cry if they'd been told they had cancer.'

They remained there for several minutes till they were all calmer. Then Sue spoke again, between sobs. 'Sit down, girls. There's more I need to tell you.'

The girls sat back on the sofa and stared, wide-eyed at their mother, anxious to hear what else she had to say.

Sue carried on speaking, her voice tiny. 'The doctor says it's terminal.'

'What? No!' screamed Kelsey.

Sophie caught hold of her, stroking her back to calm her down while she demanded answers from her mother. 'Why, Mum? Why is it terminal? Surely, they can do something! Can't they remove it? Remember that girl in our school who had a tumour? They operated on it and got rid of it. Can't they do that with you?'

Sophie was firing questions at her mother who was in a distressed state herself. But she couldn't help it. She needed to know her mum was going to be alright.

'I'm sorry, Sophie, but it's at an advanced stage unfortunately.'

Voicing that fact brought fresh tears to Sue's eyes and Sophie was torn as to who to comfort the most, pushing her own sorrow to one side as concern for her mother and sister took over.

'But there must be something they can do?' asked Sophie.

'They're talking about chemo. But to be honest, they don't know how much it will help. The cancer has spread widely so it might be too late for that.'

'Oh no!' yelled Sophie who let go of her sister and rushed to her mother, flinging her arms around her once more and kneeling on the floor with her head buried in her mother's lap. She could hear Kelsey wailing in the background.

After spending several minutes like this, Sophie raised her head and turned to look at her sister. She was shocked at the sight of Kelsey whose sad eyes were red-rimmed, and whose face was blotchy with clumps of hair pasted to the sides of her damp cheeks. Within the space of a few minutes her beautiful features had become tainted by sorrow.

Sophie turned back to her mother. There was a question she needed to ask. She dreaded the answer but, nevertheless, she felt compelled. 'How long have you got?'

'They don't know for sure,' her mother answered bravely. 'Maybe weeks, maybe months. It's hard to tell.'

'What? That soon?'

Her mother nodded and forced a wry smile.

It was a while before Sophie and Kelsey went to bed. None of them had eaten much; they were all too upset for food. During the evening they had asked countless questions and Sophie couldn't help but admire her mother's resilience as she had tried to be frank with her answers despite her obvious distress.

Apparently, it wouldn't be long before she gave up work, partly because she would no longer be well enough and partly because she wanted to spend as much time with them as possible. But she had assured them that nurses or carers would visit the house to provide help and reassurance so the responsibility for her care wouldn't fall solely on the girls.

It was all so much to take in and now, as they got ready for bed, each battling with her own concerns, the girls remained silent. Once Sophie was settled and ready to switch off the bedside lamp, she looked across at her sister. Kelsey was just kicking her slippers off ready to jump in bed when her eyes met Sophie's. The emotional connection between them was so strong that Sophie became weepy again.

Without speaking Kelsey crossed the room and got into bed beside Sophie, snuggling up close so that each of them could draw comfort from the other's embrace. Kelsey stayed there for the rest of the night, locked in her sister's arms, and crying silently.

Despite the comfort provided by her sister, Sophie was unable to sleep as she was consumed with troubling thoughts. For as far back as she could recall, it had been about the three of them. Her mother and Kelsey were the two people closest to her in the world and she couldn't stand the thought of losing either one of them.

But then a thought occurred to her; it was the one question she hadn't thought to ask. When the inevitable happened and their mother passed away, who was going to look after her and Kelsey?

7

August 2004

Sue looked at the clock. Her helper, Marion, wasn't due for another hour and she desperately wanted a cup of tea. She struggled out of the armchair and felt a sharp pain pierce her insides. It took her breath away and she stopped for a moment and inhaled deeply to calm herself.

By the time she had made the tea and struggled back to the living room, she felt as though she had climbed a mountain. Her legs were weak, and she was light-headed. It was a relief to be able to put down her cup, settle back into her armchair and wait for the throbbing to die down.

Pain now dominated her life; it never went away completely no matter what medication she took but at least it eased a bit when she wasn't moving around. Her time with the girls was spent trying to hide the agony from them and when alone she willed herself not to succumb to despair.

Sue could feel herself becoming weaker each day and often wished she had visited the doctor earlier. If only she had done something about her symptoms rather than being forever busy with other things, then she might not be in this state and her girls wouldn't face the prospect of being without a mother.

There were also times when she wanted the end to come as soon as possible because the pain as well as the hopelessness of it all threatened to overwhelm her. But as soon as she thought about the desire for a quick death, she regretted it. It wasn't right to want to leave her girls. This maelstrom of desperate thoughts brought a tear to her eyes as it did most days.

The plight of her girls was always uppermost in her mind. The morning after she had broken the dreaded news, Sophie had asked what would become of them. At that point she couldn't give her an answer. All she could say was that she'd have a word with their father and take it from there.

Because she had been through bereavement herself at such a young age, she knew exactly how her daughters would feel. The sorrow. The emptiness. The sheer devastation that would hamper their lives. And perhaps if she hadn't have felt so alone then she wouldn't have rushed into marrying someone who was so unsuitable.

And that brought her to Roy; that sad, pathetic excuse for a man. Sue looked at the clock. There was still time to ring him before Marion arrived. She picked up the phone from its new place at the side of her chair where it had been placed so that she could call for help if she needed it.

Roy answered on the eighth ring. 'Sue, I haven't got long. I'm at work.'

'Yeah, I know. Don't worry, this won't take long. I just

wanted to know if you'd thought any more about what we discussed.'

She heard him sigh. 'Yeah, I have.'

'And?'

'It's hard, Sue. Leah's not happy about it at all.'

'Never mind, Leah. What about you? You're their father, not Leah.'

There was silence for a while. Then, another sigh, and: 'I can't do it, Sue. I'm too busy with my own family to take on the girls as well.'

The word 'own' rankled, suggesting that Sophie and Kelsey were no longer a part of him. Bastard! If only she had the strength, she'd give him and his trumped-up second wife a piece of her mind. But she *didn't* have the strength, so she just said, 'Right, I'll speak to social services.' Then she cut the call.

Sue had been trying for weeks to persuade Roy to take on his daughters after she was gone. She'd already got social services involved and the lovely social worker, Janice Gibb, had confided to Sue that she'd been shocked at Roy's refusal, even though she had tried to shame him into taking responsibility.

Janice was doing her best to find foster carers who would take on the girls but up to now she hadn't had any joy. Apparently, it was harder to place older children. She'd assured Sue, though, that she would do her best and told her not to worry.

But Sue was worried. She knew how devastated her daughters would be. In fact, she was so anxious about the outcome that she hadn't even told her girls what was happening. She presumed they thought they'd end up with their father, and she didn't have the heart to tell them otherwise. She vowed to herself that she would do so soon; it was only fair that they were forewarned.

But it never seemed to be the right time to tell her girls that, not only were they going to lose their mother, but their father had rejected them too.

8

October 2004

Sophie was waiting for Kelsey again. She had been walking home from school with her a lot lately as their shared sorrow and worry had brought them even closer. It seemed like the best time to talk, when they were free of social workers, nurses, and home helps, unlike at home, which now seemed an alien environment to them.

'You alright?' asked Sophie as they began their walk home.

'Yeah, suppose so. It's been a bit of a shit day really.'

'Why?'

'Dunno, I'm just bored with everything.'

Sophie could identify with that. School seemed insignificant in comparison to what they were going through.

'Wonder what she'll be like tonight,' said Kelsey.

'Probably just the same,' Sophie replied.

It was an automatic response, and she didn't know why she'd said it. It was clear to both her and Kelsey that their mother *wasn't* the same. In fact, she was deteriorating rapidly. The weight loss, sallow complexion and frailty made it seem as though she had aged thirty years in a matter of months.

During the past few weeks there had been another marked change. Their mother was now having difficulty walking unassisted so whenever the nurses and home helps weren't around it was up to the girls to help her get to the bathroom and up to bed. For most of the time she sat in the same chair, often falling asleep but occasionally chatting to them.

Last night's conversation had been particularly heart-rending.

'I'm sorry, girls, but your father says he won't be able to take care of you. I'm hoping he'll change his mind but… well… we'll see,' Sue had said.

Sophie had felt put out. Even though she and Kelsey had agreed that the prospect of living with moody Leah and her spoilt brats wasn't exactly appealing, at least it gave them a degree of certainty. And it would mean they could at least be with one of their parents. It was hurtful to think that their dad could reject them in view of all they were going through, and it made Sophie feel angry and unloved. She was also frightened of a future without their mother.

'What will happen if he doesn't have us?' Sophie had asked.

'Well, Janice is looking for a foster family. Don't worry, Janice is good at what she does, and she'll be pulling out all the stops. You never know, once you get used to it, you might even enjoy it.'

Then Kelsey had become emotional. 'How can you even say that, Mum? It won't be the same.'

She stormed out of the room, but Sophie stayed with her mother. It was clear to her that her mum was only trying to make them feel better and Sophie thought again about how brave she was for trying to gee them up despite what she was going through.

'Don't worry, she's just upset about you, Mum. I'll have a word with her later.'

Her mother had held out a fragile hand and touched Sophie's arm. As she felt the lightness of her mother's touch, Sophie bit down on her inside cheek to stop herself from crying. It was painful to see her mother so weak.

'I need to tell you something, but it can wait till Kelsey's calmed down. I'll tell you both together. But, apart from that, there's something I want to ask you, Sophie. I need to ask Kelsey too, but I'll catch her again when she's a bit calmer.'

'Yes?'

'I want you to promise me that, whatever happens, you and Kelsey will always look after each other.'

Again, Sophie had to fight back the tears as her eyes misted over. 'Don't, Mum, it could be months yet.'

But, despite her brave words, she knew her mother no longer had months. She was losing strength each day and it tore a gaping wound inside Sophie's heart every time she walked into the house to see a feeble old lady instead of the vibrant young woman her mother used to be.

'Penny for them?' asked Kelsey, bringing Sophie back to the present.

'Oh, sorry. I was just, y'know, thinking about the usual and wondering what's going to happen to us.'

'I know,' said Kelsey but she didn't add anything.

There was nothing more to add. They'd already discussed the situation indefatigably and they both knew that no matter what they said, it wouldn't make any difference. The day of their mother's death was rapidly approaching and, despite the reassuring words of their mother and the social worker, Janice, neither of the girls knew what to expect in the future.

The conversation switched to school friends and gossip, both of them opting for safer ground. Anybody watching them would never have guessed the tragedy that was playing out in their young lives.

Sophie was the first one through the door when they reached home. Repeating the routine that they had adopted over the past few months, she raced through to the living room to check on their mother. But she was alarmed to find that Sue wasn't sitting in her armchair as usual. She exchanged worried looks with her sister.

'One of the nurses might have put her to bed,' said Kelsey and she began shouting to her mother while climbing the stairs.

Sophie followed behind, despite feeling that they were unlikely to find her upstairs. If her mother was that ill that she needed putting to bed in the daytime, then the nurse would probably not have left her on her own.

As she suspected, the bedroom was empty. The girls quickly scoured the house, but it soon became apparent that their mother wasn't home. There was no point trying the garden; it was too cold for Sue to be sitting outside in her state of health.

Lost as to what else to do, they made their way back to the living room and plonked down on the sofa. 'What the hell?' asked Kelsey, and Sophie noticed the puzzled frown on her forehead.

She looked away, lost in her own concerns once more. And it was as she gazed across at the mantelpiece that she saw the envelope. She walked over and picked it up. Her name and Kelsey's were scrawled across it in weak, spidery print. She opened the envelope and pulled out a letter, which was written in the same scrawl. Sophie checked the signature at the bottom then looked up at her sister.

'It's from Mum.'

As Sophie quickly scanned the contents, Kelsey stood at the side of her, trying to peep over her shoulder so that she could read it too. When she reached the end of the letter, Sophie looked up at her sister, her face ashen and her hand covering her chest.

'Shit!'

'What is it?' asked Kelsey.

Sophie fought to stay calm as she replied. 'She's been taken to hospital.'

'Oh my God! What are we gonna do?'

Sophie glanced across at the clock. 'We need to see her. I wanna make sure she's alright.'

9

October 2004

Sue sat up in bed and grabbed the magazine, which her Macmillan nurse, Linda, had left her. She had been allocated a side ward after spending hours in A & E where she had been assessed. Linda had been a godsend and had waited with her all those hours, only just having gone home.

She had felt weaker than usual that day, and the pain was becoming unbearable. When Linda had arrived, after asking Sue how she was, she'd carried out various checks and then declared, 'I'm sorry, Sue, but I think it's time we got you to hospital.'

That had been almost five hours ago, and now Sue was finally alone, thankfully not in as much pain due to the stronger medication supplied by the hospital. But the emotional pain was troubling her now.

She glanced at the cover of the magazine and read the headings but none of them registered with her. She couldn't even focus on the words as her mind was on her girls. Sue knew she was nearing the end of her life and there was nobody else to look after them. The worry had been with her ever since her diagnosis but now that her time was getting nearer, she found it difficult to think about anything else.

She needed to speak to them about the financial side of things too. She had intended to do so last night until Kelsey had become upset and stormed off to her room. But maybe tonight would be the wrong time to do so. The girls would still be reeling from the shock of finding out she had been taken to hospital.

Sue knew that social services would know about her deterioration by now. While the doctors and nurses had been examining her, Linda had slipped away to make some calls. She wondered whether Janice Gibb had contacted the girls yet. Sue hoped not, in a way, because it would be good to spend some time alone with them before social services took over.

As she thought about the prospect of a last few hours alone with her daughters, Sue felt the urge to weep. It was all so bloody hopeless!

Sophie arrived at the hospital clutching her mother's letter with Kelsey by her side.

'We need to find A & E so we can ask them where they've sent her,' she said to Kelsey.

They scanned the hospital signs and followed the one directing them to A & E and, after waiting for the receptionist to find out where their mother had been taken, they looked for signs for that ward.

By the time they arrived at the ward both girls were out

of breath, having dashed along the lengthy corridors of the Manchester Royal Infirmary. A nurse stopped them.

'Can I help you?' she asked.

'Yeah, we're here to see Susan Tailor.'

'OK, you'd better go in. We've put her in a side ward, third door on the left.'

Sophie thanked the nurse but, at the same time, she felt her heart racing at the thought of what they might find. When they walked into the side ward, the sterile smell of disinfectant hit Sophie straightaway. She was relieved to find their mother sat up in bed and as she and Kelsey looked at her, Sue beamed at them. The girls dashed over, one on either side of the bed, and clung to her.

'Oh, Mum, you had us so worried,' said Sophie, her voice shaky.

Kelsey didn't add anything but a quick glance at her told Sophie that she was upset. The sight of her sister like that got to Sophie and she too could feel the sting of tears.

'Eh now, come on, you two,' said Sue. 'I'm still here, aren't I?'

'But... but... what happened?' asked Sophie.

'Nothing. I just woke up in a bit more pain than usual and when Linda arrived, she decided it was time to get me to the hospital.'

'Does that mean you won't be coming home?' asked Kelsey.

'I don't know yet. But don't worry. Everything will be taken care of.' Then Sue sighed in mock exasperation. 'We've talked about this, haven't we? Janice has got everything in hand, and she's promised me she'll make sure you stay together too.'

'But it won't be the same without you,' Kelsey sobbed.

'I know, but there's nothing I can do about that, love. Why don't we make the most of the time we've got together, eh? At least I'm not in so much pain now. The tablets they've given me here are smashing. By the way, there's a vending machine down the corridor. Why don't I treat you to some coffee and biscuits? My handbag's in the locker. Fish my purse out and I'll find some change.'

Once again Sophie admired her mother's resilience in the face of what was happening. While they went to the vending machine, Sophie voiced her thoughts to Kelsey and they agreed that they would make it as easy for their mother as possible because, as Sophie said, 'If we're finding it hard then just imagine how Mum must be feeling.' The fact that she didn't show it didn't fool Sophie. She must have been going through hell.

When the girls got back to their mother, they all carried on as though it was like any other day, talking about school and any other topics they could think of. Then the staff came with Sue's tea and, after picking at it for about ten minutes, she pushed the plate to one side.

'That's about all I can manage but I bet you two are hungry by now, aren't you?'

'A bit,' said Sophie.

'Well, it's probably about time you were going, isn't it?'

'But, Mum,' Kelsey protested. 'I don't mind having my tea later.'

'Me neither,' said Sophie.

'No, I think it's best if you go now otherwise it'll be late by the time you get home, and I don't like you wandering about on your own.'

The thought of leaving her there brought fresh tears to Sophie's eyes, and she could see that Kelsey was crying too.

'Eh, now don't go getting upset again. I'll still be here tomorrow. Janice will be getting in touch with you anyway. In fact, I'm surprised we haven't heard from her by now. Go and wait at home for her to contact you then have a chat with her. She'll probably let you stay off school so you can come and spend some more time with me.'

'OK, we'll see you tomorrow,' said Sophie, leaning over to hug her mother and planting a kiss on her cheek.

Kelsey followed her lead, and it wasn't until they had left the hospital that Sophie released the emotions that had been bubbling up inside her all the time they had been with their mother. As she sobbed uncontrollably, Kelsey took her in her arms, and they cried together.

Eventually, Sophie broke away from her sister's embrace and wiped her moist cheeks on her sleeves. 'Come on, we'd better go and get the bus,' she said to Kelsey.

It was almost an hour later by the time they reached their neighbourhood. By now Sophie's stomach was rumbling and, despite her distress, her thoughts had turned to what they could put together quickly for their tea.

As they neared their home, Sophie noticed the car that was parked outside, a silver Ford Focus, and she recognised it instantly. She also recognised the slightly rounded form, strawberry blonde hair and kind features of the woman who stepped from the vehicle. It was Janice Gibb, the social worker.

10

October 2004

As the girls approached, Janice attempted a weak smile and followed them into the house and through to the lounge.

'Sit down, girls. I need to talk to you both,' she said.

Sophie felt herself tense, her hunger temporarily forgotten, as she waited to hear what Janice had to say.

'Now that your mother has been admitted to hospital, I'm afraid I will have to make some arrangements for you.'

'But... but... she might come home,' Kelsey responded, desperately. 'Can't we stay here and wait for her?'

'I'm afraid that isn't looking likely with your mother's state of health. And, even if she does come home, I won't be able to leave you here on your own in the meantime.'

'What will happen to us? Are we going to live at Dad's?' asked Kelsey.

'No. I'm sorry but your father has still not agreed to that.'

'I don't want to live with that bitch Leah anyway!' said Sophie. 'Why can't we stay here? We can look after ourselves! I'm fourteen!'

'Sorry but I can't let you. You're below the legal age.'

'But we've stayed on our own before when Mum was at work before she got ill.'

'Well, I'm afraid that's a bit different than being left alone indefinitely and overnight.'

Kelsey began to cry again. 'Does that mean we'll never see Mum again?'

'No no, of course not,' said Janice. 'In fact, I'll get you special permission to miss school so that you can spend as much time with her as possible. How does that sound?'

'Like she's dying,' snapped Sophie.

Janice came to sit beside her on the sofa, an expression of concern on her face. She took hold of Sophie's hands and stared into her eyes. 'Your mother is very ill and I'm afraid I can't do anything about that. But what I can do is make sure that you spend as much time with her as possible and that you're well taken care of should the worst happen.'

Janice's words cut through Sophie, but her anger stopped her from weeping like her sister. Instead, she dragged her hands away from Janice's and got up off the sofa, stomping across the room till she had put some distance between them. She didn't want the social worker to see her glistening tears, feeling as though it was an invasion of her grief.

Janice continued, undeterred. 'Now, as I've already mentioned, I'll make arrangements for you to take time off school and tomorrow either myself or one of my colleagues will take you to the hospital to visit your mother. But my priority is to take you to a place where you can stay for the night.'

'What, you mean like a kids' home?' asked Kelsey.

'It's a children's care home. But it's only temporary. I'm hopeful of placing you with foster parents in the long-term.'

'You're acting as though she's already dead!' Sophie yelled.

'Sorry, I didn't mean to be indiscreet, but I just want to assure you that we've got your best interests at heart and we want to take care of all eventualities.'

Sophie didn't say anything further, but she stood glaring at the social worker as though she was personally responsible for their current circumstances. She needed an outlet for her grief and anger and, unfortunately for Janice, there was nobody else she could direct it at.

'Why don't I make us a brew while you put some things together?' asked Janice with forced cheeriness. 'I suppose you must be hungry too. Have you had anything to eat?' Then, without waiting for their reply, she added, 'I'll go into the kitchen and see what I can rustle up, shall I, while you two pack? Don't worry about taking everything, just another outfit, a few sets of clean underwear and some toiletries will do. We can come back for more later.'

Then she vanished into the kitchen without further discussion.

Later, when Janice turned her car into a street lined with characterful Victorian houses, Sophie was impressed despite herself. She couldn't help but stare out of the window. These houses were huge, and their front gardens were full of mature shrubs, pretty flowers and neat drives with up-to-the-minute family saloons parked on them. It was far different to her street where many of the houses were run down, their gardens untended, and most of the cars old bangers.

'This is the street. It's just a bit further up,' said Janice.

Sophie looked across at Kelsey, but her sister's expression wasn't giving much away.

'Here we are,' said Janice turning into the drive of a house, which was huge like the rest of them in the street.

The gates were open and as they passed through them Sophie noticed the stone pillars at either side of the drive with the name Rushthorpe etched into one of them. Once they were inside the gates, Sophie could see that the garden had been adapted as a car park and a quick glance told her that there were already three vehicles parked up.

'Where are we?' asked Sophie, aware that they were some distance from their home.

'Chorlton,' said Janice. 'But don't worry, you won't have to change schools. We'll arrange transport for you each day.'

Sophie was disconcerted, recognising that this sounded like a long-term arrangement.

When Janice got out of the car the girls followed her up the large stone steps and they waited for somebody to answer the doorbell. Sophie could feel a flutter of nerves as they stood gazing at the large wooden door, which slowly opened revealing a youngish man.

'Hi, Tim,' said Janice. 'This is Sophie and Kelsey.'

Tim held out his hand and shook each of theirs in turn. 'Hi, Sophie. Hi, Kelsey. Welcome to Rushthorpe. Let me show you around.'

While he spoke, Sophie took in his appearance. He looked to be in his thirties and was dressed casually in jeans and a checked flannel shirt, which needed ironing. His hair was shoulder-length and slightly dishevelled. Sophie was familiar with his type. She'd had a couple of teachers like him, eternally young and desperately trying to be 'down with the kids'.

Janice stood back so the girls could enter first and Sophie stepped into a large hallway, which was covered in mosaic tiles that had become faded and discoloured with time. Although the walls were painted cream, the rest of the hallway hinted at former grandeur with an intricately carved ceiling rose and cornices, and an impressive archway further down the hall, which led on to the next part of the house. She and Kelsey couldn't help but stare about them, amazed by its vastness.

Tim seemed to pick up on their wonderment. 'Huge, isn't it?' Then he sniggered. 'That's nothing. Wait till you see the rest of the house.'

He led them along the hallway, on to a door marked 'Office' through which Sophie could see two other members of staff seated at office desks.

'Hazel, Sandra. Meet Sophie and Kelsey, our two new girls.'

The two women got up to say hello to the girls and then shook their hands as Tim had done. 'Welcome,' said Hazel. 'We'll leave Tim to show you round.'

'Come on then, let's go,' said Tim, leading them further down the hallway. 'By the way, the office is strictly for staff but if you need anything and the door is shut, just give it a knock and one of us will tend to you.' He turned and smiled as he said the last couple of words, then added, 'Here we go. The recreation room.'

He stood back and put out his hand in a flourish, inviting the girls to step forward, which they did while Tim and Janice hung back in the corridor. Sophie became aware straightaway of several pairs of eyes staring at her and Kelsey, and she felt uncomfortable.

Her eyes took in the room which, like the hall, was enormous with plain, painted walls and original but jaded features. Unlike the hall though, this room had a carpet, but it was the utilitarian type rather than a soft one that you could sink your feet into. There was a TV in the corner and board games dotted about the room as well as a few shelves along one wall, which were lined with books.

'Go on, girls, go inside,' urged Tim. 'They won't bite.'

Sophie and Kelsey did as he suggested, and Tim introduced them to the other children, giving them a quick rundown of all the children's names and ages. There were six other children there, which was too many for Sophie to take in straightaway, but one boy stood out. He was called Lloyd and was slightly older than her, which made him the nearest to Sophie's age of all the children in the home.

Lloyd was small for his age and had one of those faces that made him appear aggressive with his mouth forming a snarl and eyes that narrowed into slits. He seemed to stare more blatantly at Sophie and her sister than any of the other children in the room. As he stared, a smug grin played across his lips. Sophie took an instant dislike to him.

'Don't worry. We don't expect you to remember them all straight off. You'll soon get to know who everyone is,' said Tim.

The tour of the house continued with Tim showing them the kitchen. This room was just as enormous as the last and doubled up as a dining room with a long, scrubbed pine table running down the centre of it. The table appeared battered yet characterful, the history of the home and its various inhabitants etched into the woodwork.

Then he showed them the staff quarters downstairs, where the team slept, before taking them to the upstairs bedrooms. Each of the rooms was decorated similarly to downstairs with bare painted walls and functional carpets. They finally reached the upstairs room that had been allocated to the girls.

'Your bedroom,' said Tim. 'I'll leave you to settle in and then perhaps you could come and join the other children in the recreation room. See you later.'

Again, there was that mock cheeriness as he left them and Janice in the room. 'Be with you in a minute, Tim,' called Janice. Then she turned to the girls. 'Everything OK? Is there anything you want to ask before I leave you to it?'

'No,' said Kelsey while Sophie shrugged.

'OK. Well, I'll see you tomorrow then and take you to the hospital to see your mum. Tim will tell you what time to expect me. I'll let him know once I've sorted things out.'

Once she was gone, Sophie felt inexplicably sad and frightened.

'Should we go down and see the other kids?' asked Kelsey.

'No, I'm staying here and unpacking. You go if you want to.'

'No, I'm not going without you.'

The girls chose to stay there for the rest of the evening, needing to chat to one another about the house, its other inhabitants and speculation over what was going to happen to them. Amid all this change and worry about the future, Sophie drew some comfort in at least having her sister to confide in about how she was feeling.

11

October 2004

The next morning, Tim took Sophie and Kelsey down to breakfast. Seated at the table were Lloyd and a girl who was a bit younger than Kelsey, called Emily. Kelsey tried to make conversation with her, but she replied to Kelsey's questions as briefly as possible.

'She's shy,' said Lloyd. Then he looked at Emily and raised his voice: 'Aren't you, Emily?'

He chuckled as Emily blushed and tried to lower her head even further, and Sophie's dislike of him intensified.

'Where are you two from anyway?' he demanded.

'Gorton,' said Kelsey.

Lloyd laughed. 'Ooh, nice area. Not.'

Sophie rushed to defend her hometown. 'It's not that bad.'

Lloyd laughed again, this time more extremely. 'Not if you like being mugged or robbed.'

'Be nice, Lloyd,' said one of the staff who was buttering toast.

'I am. I'm just saying.'

'Well don't, please.'

Lloyd turned his attention back to Sophie and Kelsey. 'What are you here for anyway?'

'None of your business,' snapped Sophie just as Kelsey was about to speak.

'Ooh be like that then,' said Lloyd, finally getting up and leaving the room.

He was gone, for now, but Sophie sensed he was going to be a problem.

Later that morning, Sophie heard a knock on the bedroom door and, before she or Kelsey had a chance to respond, Tim stuck his head inside.

'Hi, girls, Janice will be here in about an hour to take you to the hospital.'

They both thanked him, but he seemed to linger for a minute before leaving them. 'Are you settling in OK?' he asked. 'I see you experienced some of the Lloyd charm over breakfast. Don't worry about him – it's just his way. You give him as good as he gives you and he'll soon get tired of it.'

While he spoke to them, Sophie noticed his eyes taking in the whole room. They seemed to flit from her to Kelsey to their knick-knacks dotted about the place and back to them again. He didn't say anything further but something about him unnerved Sophie. She didn't trust him; nobody could be that nice all the time.

When they arrived at the hospital with Janice, Sophie and Kelsey raced through the corridors so fast that they left

Janice a few steps behind. They were delighted to find their mother in the same side ward, and Sophie was relieved that, again, she didn't look as ill as she had done when she was at home. She dared to hope that maybe her mother would be cured and would eventually return home with them.

For a while they talked about the children's home and how things were for Sue in the hospital. While they did so, Janice hovered in the background. It was disconcerting for Sophie who felt as though they were already losing a part of their mother; that comfortable intimacy families share and which nobody else should invade.

The rest of the week carried on in a similar vein with a social worker collecting them each day and taking them to the hospital. To Sophie the routine had become boring, although she felt guilty admitting it even to herself. There was nothing to talk about other than the children's home where nothing exciting happened, and Sophie didn't want to worry her mother by discussing her uneasy feelings concerning Lloyd and Tim. Besides, it would have been difficult with a social worker listening in.

Sophie tried to ask her mother for more details about her health, but Sue's answers were vague. All she would say was that the staff were keeping her comfortable and doing their best. Finally, fed up with getting nowhere, Sophie came straight out with it, 'Mum, will you be getting better, and will you be coming home again?'

Janice rushed over. 'Sophie, I think your mum needs to rest now. We've been here a while. I think it's time we were getting back to Rushthorpe.'

'But I need to know,' Sophie protested, looking over at her

mother. She noticed that her mother was looking exhausted, and she felt a pang of guilt.

'Do as Janice asks, please, love. We can talk tomorrow,' said Sue before turning her head into the pillow.

The following day, it was late afternoon before Janice arrived at the home. 'We're ready,' said Sophie.

Janice sat down on the bed next to her. 'Kelsey, would you like to come over?' she asked. 'There's something I need to say to you both.'

Sophie saw the serious expression on Janice's face, and felt herself tense. *No, please no,* she kept repeating in her mind.

'I'm afraid we won't be going to the hospital today,' said Janice. Sophie knew what was coming next and a feeling of nausea washed over her.

'Is she OK?' she demanded. 'Is my mum OK?'

'I'm afraid not,' said Janice, and Sophie noticed a tear in her eye.

'Please don't say she's dead,' begged Sophie, feeling desperate, and Kelsey burst out crying.

'I'm afraid so.' Janice took a packet of tissues out of her handbag and passed one to each of the girls. 'She passed away this morning, at...' Then her voice broke before she could get the rest of her words out.

Janice went to put her arms around the two girls, but Sophie wanted her sister. She pushed the social worker away then stepped round her, kneeling in front of Kelsey, and grabbing hold of her. They cried together, something they were doing a lot of recently. As they hugged each other, they became oblivious to the presence of the social worker who slipped quietly from the room and left them to their grief.

12

October 2004

Ten minutes after Janice had left, Tim peeped round the door without knocking. Sophie broke away from her sister's embrace and looked up when she heard the door open.

'Sorry, girls. I heard the news and wondered if I can do anything for you. Get you a drink perhaps?'

His usual upbeat tone of voice seemed insensitive under the circumstances and Sophie reacted angrily. 'No!' she snapped. All she wanted was for she and her sister to be left to share their grief in private. 'Go away!'

'Oops, sorry,' said Tim, his tone odiously cheerful again. 'I can see you need some time to yourselves. I'll come back later.'

He shut the door softly. 'Prat!' muttered Sophie and Kelsey laughed, despite her sadness.

Sophie pulled away from her sister and stared at her. She was surprised to hear Kelsey laugh considering what they were going through. But Kelsey's laughter didn't stop. In fact, it became more unruly, and Sophie could tell she was becoming hysterical.

'Stop it, Kelsey. Stop it!' she yelled, grabbing her sister by the shoulders, and shaking her.

Kelsey's laughter dissolved into sorrow once more and Sophie felt an immense sadness knowing that her sister was finding this just as difficult as she was. But she was the eldest and felt responsible for Kelsey. She stayed with her for a while longer, offering her comfort. Then she decided that perhaps a hot drink would help after all.

Despite her attempts to be brave, her voice trembled as she spoke. 'You stay here, Kelsey. I'll fetch us both a cup of tea.'

Kelsey nodded, and Sophie left the bedroom, determined to get back to her sister as quickly as possible. Unfortunately, she bumped into Lloyd in the hallway, who had just walked in from school. He was the last person she wanted to see when it was obvious just from looking at her that she had been crying.

'Ha-ha, what's wrong with you?' he taunted. 'Can't you hack it in the home now you're not with Mummy and Daddy?'

At the mention of her mother, Sophie exploded. 'Don't you fuckin' dare mention my mum!' she yelled. 'You sly little prick.'

Lloyd was just about to retaliate when Tim ran out of the office. 'What's going on here?' he asked, and Sophie was relieved that at least his voice had now taken on a more serious tone.

'Nothing. It's her. All I did was ask her what was wrong, and she went off her head.'

'Go to your room, Lloyd,' said Tim.

'But I was gonna get a drink.'

'Go to your room!' Tim's voice was firmer this time. 'I'll bring you a drink later.'

Lloyd slouched off upstairs, murmuring to himself. 'She was the one shouting, not me.'

Tim ignored him. Instead, he put his arm around Sophie's shoulders. 'You OK, Soph?' he asked.

Apart from feeling annoyed at Lloyd, Sophie didn't like Tim putting his arm around her or using the shortened version of her name. From someone she hardly knew, it felt inappropriate. She shrugged him off and walked towards the kitchen.

'Yeah, I'm fine. I just want to get a drink for me and Kelsey, that's all.'

'It's OK, I'll bring some drinks up to your room. You can go back to your sister.'

'I want to do it myself,' said Sophie. 'Just because my mum's died, it doesn't make me useless!'

Tim stared at her, a look of alarm on his face, and for a moment he hesitated as if wondering what to say next. Then he turned away. 'OK, I'll leave you to it. You take care and I'll come up later to see how you and your sister are doing.'

Sophie felt like telling him not to bother. She was glad there was no one else in the kitchen and she quickly flicked the switch on the kettle and took two cups from the cupboard, conscious all the time that she had left Kelsey upset and alone. Damn Lloyd! She could have had the drinks made by now and be on her way back upstairs if it weren't for him.

Next, she found the container where the teabags were kept, and she tried to prise off the lid. But it was stuck fast. She ran her fingers around it, trying it from all sides but the lid still wouldn't budge. For a fleeting second, she thought about asking one of the staff to help but then she dismissed the notion. She didn't want to see smarmy Tim again.

Feeling frustrated, she continued trying unsuccessfully to loosen the lid. 'Damn!' she yelled, banging it on the worktop in the hope that that would loosen it. But the lid remained tightly fastened, and the barely suppressed fury that Sophie had felt since she heard the news of her mother's death was now building within her. In a fit of rage, she slung the container at the wall. Needing an outlet for her anger and grief, she picked it back up and threw it again. And again.

By now, the lid had loosened, and the teabags had spilt out. But Sophie was heedless; she just needed to vent. Feeling hyped up with anger, her hands shaking and her heart pounding, she tugged open a cupboard door and reached inside for the plates, dragging out a stack of them. Then she hurled them across the kitchen floor. The plates shattered and fragments of pottery littered the ground.

Still furious, she grabbed another stack and smashed them one by one onto the floor, chipping the tiles as well as smashing the plates. When the plates were gone, she went on to the cups then the dishes.

The cupboard was soon empty and, pausing for breath, she gazed at the work surface, which was full of kitchen utensils to which somebody had added a couple of dirty plates and glasses. Sophie ran her arm swiftly along its surface, dragging everything with her. Then she levered her arm, so the contents crashed to the floor.

She felt the sting of heat on her wrist then realised the kettle was amongst the items. Sophie jumped back, shocked by her own rash behaviour, as the kettle tumbled onto the floor, forcing the lid off. A spray of scalding water rose up like a fierce fountain just as Tim walked through the door to see what all the commotion was about.

He caught the tail end of the spray on his legs and yelled in alarm. 'Jesus Christ! What have you done, Sophie?'

She watched, dumbstruck, as he tore off his jeans and ran to the sink, calling out for one of the other helpers. While Tim drenched his legs in cold water, Hazel and Sandra dashed into the room and raced over to Sophie.

Seeing the scald mark on Sophie's wrist, Hazel grabbed hold of her other arm and led her from the room, assisted by Sandra. 'You've scalded yourself, Sophie. We need to get it under water.'

They rushed her to the nearest bathroom and bathed her arm, making her stay there for ages. Sophie was already feeling remorseful, and being with them felt awkward. She yearned to break away so she could cry out her grief and shame without other people watching.

It was later that day when Tim popped his head around the bedroom door without knocking again.

'Kelsey, would you like to go downstairs for a while please? I need to speak to Sophie.'

Both girls recognised that it was more of an order than a request and Kelsey headed for the door, flashing Sophie a look of concern. Sophie felt beset with nerves and swamped with shame at what she had done.

'Right, Sophie,' said Tim, walking over to her but not sitting down. 'I need to point out that your behaviour earlier was completely unacceptable and won't be tolerated in this house. Do you understand?'

His unusually strident tone of voice wasn't lost on Sophie and she nodded solemnly. Her eyes clouded over, threatening tears once again but she fought to contain them.

'That sort of behaviour doesn't go unpunished, I'm afraid. Do you realise you've actually committed criminal damage and we could have you prosecuted?'

Sophie panicked, worried that it would mean she'd be separated from Kelsey. 'No, please don't!' she begged.

Tim carried on as though she hadn't spoken. 'And that's not to mention the scalding on my legs.'

'I'm so sorry,' Sophie mumbled, feeling her lips quiver.

Tim sighed. 'Look, Sophie, I realise that you're going through a lot at the moment so I'm willing to make an exception. That means you won't face prosecution, but you'll still be punished. We've decided to stop you going on the trip to Chester Zoo at the weekend. Kelsey will still be going, of course, but you'll be staying here. Hazel will be looking after you while the rest of us are on the trip.'

'OK,' Sophie muttered. Then she lowered her head, refusing to meet his eyes.

'Look at me when I'm speaking to you, Sophie.' Once he had gained her full attention, Tim continued. 'If you ever attempt anything like that again during your stay here then you will be in serious trouble. Luckily for you, my injuries were only superficial, but we can't risk the sort of behaviour that puts the staff or the other children at risk. Do you understand?'

Sophie nodded then lowered her head again. Once Tim was gone, she released the emotions that had been building up. Becoming overwhelmed with sorrow, bitterness, and shame, she continued to sob intermittently for the rest of the evening and well into the night.

13

November 2004

It was a few days later and Sophie and Kelsey were still reeling from the death of their mother. Only that morning they had had a good chat about things.

'I still can't believe it's happened,' Kelsey had said. 'I mean, we knew she was ill. But I didn't think it would be that soon.'

'Me neither,' Sophie replied. Lost for any other words with which to soothe her sister, she had taken her in her arms instead and stroked her hair while Kelsey cried for the umpteenth time.

Sophie was finding it hard to be the strong one and her sorrow often took the form of anger. The children's home was so impersonal, and she missed the natural bond they had shared with their mother who always seemed to instinctively know how she was feeling.

Since their mother had passed away the staff were pussyfooting around them. The younger children didn't know what to say in their presence either, so they tended to clam up whenever Sophie and Kelsey were around. This made Sophie feel alien. And as for Lloyd, he was as obnoxious as ever.

As she was sitting on her bed with all these thoughts going through her mind, she heard Tim call them downstairs. It was a Sunday, and the staff were preparing dinner. As they walked out onto the landing Sophie could smell the tantalising aroma of roast beef and roast potatoes and they rushed downstairs.

To her consternation, Lloyd was already sitting at the large dining table when they walked into the kitchen. Sophie plonked herself down on an empty seat as far away from Lloyd as possible while the cook served up their dinner. Between Sophie and Lloyd, Tim was seated with Sandra and Hazel nearer to the door. Lloyd looked across at her and grinned slyly.

'You missed a brilliant day out yesterday, Sophie!' he announced at the top of his voice. 'You should have been there... Oh no, you weren't allowed, were you? Was that because you smashed the kitchen up?'

'That's enough, Lloyd!' warned Tim.

'Why? I'm only saying what a brilliant day it was. Thanks, Tim. Thanks, Sandra.'

'That's alright,' said Sandra while Tim carried on watching Lloyd.

But Lloyd wasn't finished yet. 'Kelsey enjoyed the trip, didn't you, Kelsey? Her and Emily were getting on really well. In fact, Emily wasn't so shy yesterday. You'll have to come on the next trip, Sophie. Well, that's if you're allowed.'

'I said that's enough, Lloyd!' Tim admonished.

'I'm just saying. Why should we all have to watch what

we say just because their mum's died? I didn't smash no kitchen up when my mum died.'

Before Tim had a chance to say anything further, Sophie was up out of her seat and rushing towards Lloyd with her fists clenched.

'Don't you fuckin' say anything about my mum!' she yelled.

As Lloyd grinned smugly, knowing that he had ignited the flame of Sophie's anger, Tim jumped out of his seat to stop Sophie from reaching him. But Sophie's temper was boiling over. All she could think of was hitting back at Lloyd for some of the hurt she was going through.

Sophie went to side-step Tim, but he barred her way. Undeterred, she tried to push him aside and, when that didn't work, she reached around him, swinging her fists wildly, determined to land one on Lloyd. Behind her someone was pulling her back; Kelsey was yelling for her to stop and one of the younger children was screaming. But Sophie was oblivious to it all.

She viciously dragged her arms away from whoever was holding them back and continued to push against Tim, desperate by now to reach Lloyd. Her anger and frustration erupted in bitter tears and howls, which transcended the rest of the clamour in the room.

In the background she could hear Lloyd laughing, mocking her, which made her even more furious. Regardless of who she was hurting now, she carried on fighting, feeling gratified when her fists connected with flesh. In her blind rage she had lost sight of who was on the receiving end of her blows. It was all as one now; the people in that room were a manifestation of her hurt and sorrow and she wanted to get back at them any way she could.

It was the feel of Tim's fingers pressing hard into her flesh, which brought her to her senses. Her arms were pinned to her sides now; two heavy hands holding them tight from in front and two softer ones holding them from behind. For a moment she continued to struggle until she realised it was futile and Tim's voice penetrated her awareness.

'Sophie! Sophie! Calm yourself down for heaven's sake!'

The haze was beginning to clear now, and she looked up into his face, her eyes filled with remorse. Then she spotted the blood spurting from his nose and realised she was the culprit.

'Oh my God!' she muttered, taking in the irate expression on Tim's face.

'You might well say that!' raged Tim. 'Now get to your room. I'll have words with you later.'

Defeated, Sophie slumped out of the kitchen with an empty stomach and a heavy heart, the sound of Lloyd's laughter ringing in her ears.

14

November 2004

Sophie and Kelsey soon learnt how things worked in the home. Although Tim was their keyworker, if they wanted to discuss something of an intimate nature then they would speak to Hazel or Sandra.

The washing all got taken care of by a lady called Sheila who came in to help with the cleaning. Sophie was fine with that, but she preferred to wash her underwear by hand at the bathroom sink and hang it on the radiator in her room to dry.

One day when they returned from school, they found Tim in their room examining a pair of knickers, which he had taken off the radiator.

'What are you doing?' demanded Sophie, feeling herself blush.

Tim quickly put the knickers back down. He looked awkward, but he soon recovered. 'I might well ask you the same thing. You can't be putting wet garments on the radiators. They've been dripping all over the carpet.'

'But, but, I don't want to put my underwear in the wash,' said Sophie.

Tim sighed dramatically, 'Sophie, everybody puts their underwear in the wash. It's no big deal. It's all the same to Sheila; she's seen it all before. Now please do as I ask and make sure you put them in the laundry basket next time.'

Then he was gone, and Sophie was relieved. She didn't want to discuss it any further; she felt too uncomfortable.

'That was weird,' said Kelsey after he had gone.

'I know. Why did he need to pick them up? He could have just told me about it without touching them.'

'Yeah, or better still, he could have got one of the women to tell you and then you wouldn't have been so embarrassed.'

'He gives me the creeps,' said Sophie.

'I know, me too.'

It was only a few days later when they returned from school to find Tim in their room again. This time he was standing by the chest of drawers wearing a guilty expression. Although the drawers were closed, the top one wasn't quite flush, and Sophie wondered whether he had been looking inside it or whether she or Kelsey had perhaps forgotten to shut it properly that morning.

As they walked into the room, he began making his way towards the door. 'Hi, girls, had a nice day?' he asked. 'I'm just checking everything's in order. Glad to see you're no longer putting wet clothing on the radiator.'

Once he had left them, Sophie stared at her sister whose freaked-out expression mirrored her own. Instinctively, she rushed to the chest of drawers and pulled open the drawer that wasn't quite shut. She could tell straightaway that her underwear had been disturbed.

Sophie turned to Kelsey. 'He's been going through my underwear.'

'Ew, no! What a perve.'

'I'm gonna tell him,' raged Sophie, stepping towards the door.

'No, don't!' warned Kelsey. 'You'll only end up in trouble again. And he'll probably deny it.'

'What can I do then, Kelsey?'

'Nothing. It's his word against ours. You'll just have to put up with it, Sophie. Even if we tell Hazel or Sandra, they probably won't believe us.'

Sophie plonked herself down on the bed. She was raging but then she began to think about the wider implications. If Tim was into examining their underwear, then what else was he into? It might be a waste of time reporting him, but she needed to take some sort of action to protect herself and her sister.

Eventually Sophie spoke. 'Right, Kelsey, we need to make sure that none of us is ever in this bedroom alone in case Tim comes in, so we need to stay together all the time.'

'What if we're having a shower?'

'We'll have to go in together. Don't worry, I'll keep my back to you, and you can do the same.'

'Sophie, you're scaring me. You don't think he's going to do something to us, do you?'

'Probably not,' said Sophie, trying to reassure Kelsey who she could see was becoming worked up. 'But, just in case, let's not take any chances. We also need to make sure we're never alone with him anywhere in the house, so we'll have to go everywhere together.'

Sophie got up from the bed and walked over to Kelsey then put her arm around her. 'Don't worry, everything will be fine as long as we stay together.'

15

November 2004

Janice arrived at the meeting flustered and five minutes late. That day had been a demanding one and the last thing she needed was this. She had come straight from visiting a family where there was suspected abuse, having grabbed a quick sandwich in the car in place of her evening meal. Then she'd had the added stress of finding a parking space in the centre of Manchester.

She apologised as half a dozen pairs of eyes looked up at her. As they stared, she quickly took in the people who were present. At the head of the table was her boss, Roger, a portly middle-aged man who oozed authority.

Next to him was the only vacant seat at this end of the large meeting table so she sat on it and nodded at the keyworker, Tim, who was seated at the other side of her. Across the table were two teachers from Sophie and Kelsey's school with an education welfare officer further on from them, and to the other side of Tim was the girls' GP.

'So, to recap,' said Roger, his tone even sterner than his expression. 'Tim was just telling us about a couple of incidents involving Sophie.'

Janice was already aware of the two incidents. Despite her knowledge of the events, she waited patiently while Tim outlined what had happened.

'Without paying any regard for the safety of either herself or any of the other staff or children, she launched the kettle across the kitchen floor as well as various items of crockery. The kettle was full of hot water at the time and when I went to find out what all the commotion was about, I was scalded.'

Surprised at hearing such emotive language, Janice felt she had to butt in. 'Hang on, Tim, I thought you said it was only a tiny splash that hit you.'

'Well, yes,' he responded, puffing out his chest. 'But the point is, it could have been much worse, and it could have been anybody walking into the kitchen. Imagine the distress she could have caused to a small child if they were injured.'

Roger looked across at Janice. 'I think Tim does have a fair point.'

Janice nodded and was then forced to carry on listening to Tim. Feeling validated by Roger, Tim had now launched into a vivid description of how Sophie had gone on to viciously attack him in the kitchen a few days after the first incident. He ended by saying, 'The girl actually drew blood. She was like a banshee, totally out of control.'

When he had finished speaking, Roger turned to Janice. 'Well?' he asked. 'Do you have anything to add before I ask the girls' teachers for a report of their behaviour at school?'

'Yes, I do,' said Janice. 'Whilst I acknowledge that Sophie's behaviour was unacceptable on these two occasions, I think we need to bear in mind that this young lady is going through a period of grief having just lost her mother and, furthermore, having been rejected by her own father.'

'But her sister isn't reacting in this way,' said Tim.

'The girls have different personalities, and everyone reacts to grief in different ways,' Janice bit back. 'It's very early days and I think we need to give her time to adjust.'

'But we can't afford to condone such behaviour in the meantime,' Roger countered.

'I wasn't suggesting that—' Janice began before she was cut off by Roger speaking again.

'I think we should get a report from Sophie's schoolteacher before we can decide on an appropriate course of action.' He nodded across at the young woman sitting two seats down on his left-hand side. 'Miss Roberts, please.'

Miss Roberts cleared her throat before she began to speak. 'Sophie has been a bit quieter than usual lately, but I suppose that's understandable under the circumstances.'

She paused, so Roger prompted her to elaborate. 'What about her schoolwork?'

'Well, I must admit she's fallen behind a bit recently.'

'Since her mother died?' asked Roger.

'Well, no, before that really. But then, her mother was ill for a period, so I think her work started to slide around the time that she found out about her mother's illness.'

Tim butted in. 'In view of Sophie's behaviour as well as the deterioration in her schoolwork, I think she isn't ready to be placed in foster care yet.'

'Maybe not quite yet,' said Janice. 'Like I said, I think she just needs a bit of time to adapt. I feel sure that the tight bond with her sister as well as any additional support we can provide will help her to get through this. And bear in mind, Tim, that all this is recent. She is still in the early stages of grieving.'

Roger addressed Tim. 'You mentioned the sister – Kelsey. How is she coping in the home?'

'Good. She seems to have settled in well.'

'Great. Perhaps we could hear from her teacher too,' said Roger.

Janice took a deep breath and tried to remain calm. She had a bad feeling about where this was heading.

Sophie and Kelsey were in the recreation room playing draughts. It was just over a week since Sophie's meltdown at Sunday dinner and she was desperately trying to fit in. Her experience at the children's home hadn't been a positive one up to now. She'd made an enemy in Lloyd, wrecked the kitchen, and even attacked her keyworker, and now she just wanted her time there to pass as peacefully as possible.

She and her sister were still hurting over their mother's death. Many of the adults had told them things would start getting better once the funeral was over, but they'd attended it two days ago and Sophie didn't feel any different. Sometimes she thought she would never get over her mother's death but at least she could help herself by making her time here pass as easily as possible.

As Kelsey took another one of her pieces, Sophie found her mind drifting to the talk she had had with Tim following her meltdown. He had informed her that her future at the home was in jeopardy if she carried on misbehaving and she might even end up in full-time residential care. He'd also told her that Lloyd had been given a stern warning about his behaviour, and since then Sophie and Lloyd had made an unofficial truce.

The idea of a residential home had terrified Sophie who had pleaded to be given another chance. Sophie couldn't bear the prospect of being removed from the home, her sister, and all that she was familiar with. It was bad enough that she had lost her mother.

'Come on,' said Kelsey. 'It's your go.'

'What? Oh, sorry,' said Sophie, staring vacantly at the draughts board, her mind still on other matters.

Sophie's eyes drifted across the room to where Lloyd was sat watching *The Simpsons* on TV and laughing far too loudly. As she caught his eye, he smiled at her, but the smile seemed forced. Sophie still didn't trust him and felt that it was only a matter of time before he returned to his sly ways.

She looked at the clock on the wall: 7pm. It was still early enough to go out. 'I've had enough of board games, Kelsey. Should we go for a walk instead?'

Kelsey smiled. 'I have too. I just didn't want to spoil it for you.'

Sophie smiled back, thankful for such a caring sister. 'Come on then. Let's go. There's a top I want to show you in a shop window. I've been saving up for it out of my pocket money.'

Five minutes later, the girls were on their way into the town centre. As they walked up the street arm in arm, they had no idea that their future was currently being decided by a team of professionals who had called a meeting specifically for that purpose.

16

The girls had now been living in the children's home for three months and were getting used to it. Sophie had reached the stage where she no longer cried every night, but she knew Kelsey still did because she often heard her sobbing into her pillow and had climbed into bed with her a few times to offer comfort.

Sophie might not cry so much now, but she still felt an overwhelming rage at times, particularly when Lloyd was around. He was gradually returning to his old ways and she was getting fed up with his sly looks, fake laughter, and little digs. But, at Kelsey's insistence, she was trying her best not to rise to it. She didn't want to end up in trouble again.

Since they had lived in the children's home, the girls' bond had grown tighter. Because of their shared grief it had seemed natural for the girls to turn to each other for emotional support in a house full of strangers. Their family unit had shrunk from three to two, and they now lived further away from their school friends, so they relied on each other for a social outlet too.

It was the weekend and they had just come back from the shops. As they passed the office, Sophie noticed that the door was open. She glanced curiously as she passed by and noticed Tim sitting at his desk. He stirred and she heard him call after her sister.

'Oh, Kelsey, can I have a word please?'

Kelsey looked at Sophie, shrugged and turned back to the office. Sophie was curious; it wasn't usual for Kelsey to be called in to the office especially as she didn't generally misbehave. It was a few minutes later when Kelsey joined her in the bedroom and Sophie could tell straightaway that she wasn't happy.

'What is it? What did he want?'

'I'm not allowed to say. He wants to see you.'

'It's summat bad, isn't it?'

Kelsey's eyes welled up. 'I can't tell you, Sophie. He told me he was going to tell you himself.'

Sophie walked down to the office, her heart thundering in her chest. To her it felt like the day of her mother's funeral when she had had to wait for the moment when the curtains closed, and her mother's coffin was shunted away to be cremated. Now, just like then, she knew something bad was about to happen and the feeling of trepidation churned her up inside.

She was soon outside the office door where she could see Tim still seated at his desk. None of the other staff were there. 'Come in, Sophie, and close the door behind you.'

Tim's tone was serious. That was the first bad sign; the other bad sign was that he had asked her to close the door behind her. This was obviously a private meeting, and one that had upset her sister.

'Sit down,' he said, attempting a smile, and she did as he asked. On the desk was a stray paper clip and Sophie picked it up and began to fiddle with it nervously. 'Now then, Sophie, I've just spoken to your sister so I thought it would be best to explain the situation to you too.' He paused and took a deep breath before continuing. 'We've found Kelsey a foster place but I'm afraid she'll be going alone.'

Tim's words hit her like a thunderbolt and Sophie's eyes immediately clouded over. 'What? But Janice said...'

'I know, I know what Janice said,' Tim pre-empted. 'And if we could have kept you together, we would have done, but I'm afraid it's just not possible.'

'But...' Sophie wanted to say something, but she wasn't sure what. The shock had clouded her mind.

'We've been trying for the past few weeks to find places for you both but I'm afraid places for two children together are more difficult to find. Added to that, most foster parents prefer younger children, which is why you and Lloyd have been with us longer than most.'

Sophie finally found her voice. 'No! No, you can't do that. She's my sister. We've got to stay together! Can't she stay here till you've found us a place together?'

Tim let out a puff of air. 'I'm afraid that would take some time, Sophie. You see, we don't actually think you're ready to be placed into foster care yet.'

'What? What do you mean?'

'Your behaviour, Sophie. We can't have you going around smashing people's homes up or attacking them.'

So, he'd lied when he said they'd been looking for foster parents for them both. Despite the betrayal, Sophie didn't lose her temper. There was too much at stake. 'I'm sorry. I didn't mean it. I was just upset over my mum. I've been good lately. Please don't take Kelsey away from me. I promise, I'll do anything. Please keep her here.'

'Now come on, Sophie, surely you don't think that's fair to your sister. She's being offered a good opportunity in a nice home. You wouldn't deny her the chance to be with a loving family, would you? Besides, you'll still see her every day at school. And we could arrange for you to see each other at weekends too.'

At the mention of a loving family, Sophie's mind flashed back to their time at home when it had been just the three of them; her, Kelsey, and their mum. In her head, she pictured herself and her mother transposed by two other people, a new set of parents for Kelsey, and it tore at her heart.

But she also felt a tug of guilt. Tim was right. How could she deny Kelsey this chance, knowing it might be a way for her to eventually find happiness again?

When Sophie returned to her room, she found Kelsey sitting on her bed looking solemn. Her sister raced over to Sophie and flung her arms around her.

'I'm not going without you, Sophie. They can't make me.'

Sophie pulled away from her and stared into her sister's eyes, fighting back her distress. 'You've got to go, Kelsey. It's a brilliant opportunity for you. The family sound really nice from what Tim's told me.'

'But what about you? What will you do?'

Sophie raised a false chuckle. 'Me? What do you think I'll do? I'll stay here till they find me a place.'

'But Janice said they'd find us a place together.'

'She said she'd try but they haven't been able to. If we wait for that then we could both be stuck here forever... with Lloyd... and Tim. You wouldn't want that, would you?'

'But that means you'll be stuck here on your own with them.'

'Yeah, but not for long. It's easier to find a foster home if there's just one of you. It shouldn't take too long. Anyway, I'll still see you at school.'

Kelsey looked glum. 'Are you sure this is what you want?'

'Yeah, course it is, Kelsey. Don't worry about me, I'll be fine. I'm getting used to this place now. Anyway, I asked Tim what will happen to your bed and he said they'll probably put a new girl in with me. So, there you go. I'll have a new mate.'

The look of disappointment on Kelsey's face cut right through Sophie. It was going to be difficult to keep up this pretence when the thought of losing her sister broke her heart and she knew that whoever they put in with her, they could never replace Kelsey. But she had to do it; she had no choice. Sophie knew she couldn't hold her sister back when she had the chance of a better life.

Then she picked up a book and sat reading, making sure it covered her face. It was her way of telling Kelsey that the conversation was over. But it was just a guise to stop Kelsey from seeing the tears that misted her eyes.

17

January 2005

Janice hated days like today. It was bad enough working on a Saturday without the terrible sadness of the occasion. Most kids were glad to see the back of the place but not when they were about to be parted from their sibling. And not when that sibling was the only person they had left who was close to them.

Tim answered the door to Rushthorpe with a cheery smile as though she was a visiting relative. She could have throttled him. Didn't the man have any feelings?

'The girls are in the rec room,' he said. 'Can I have a quick word before you go through?'

That annoyed her as well. Strictly speaking, she shouldn't even have been here on a Saturday and yet Tim expected her to carry on as though it was any other working day. But she went into the office anyway; at least it was a way of delaying the inevitable. She could hear children's voices coming from the rec room and her feeling of sadness intensified.

★

The day of Kelsey's departure had come around too soon. Sophie had been aware of it all week, but she'd tried to shun its ominous arrival as though by doing so she could somehow prevent it. Kelsey hadn't mentioned it either until that morning.

'What time did Tim say Janice is coming?'

Sophie shrugged. 'You're already packed anyway.'

'I know but I just wanted to check.'

Sophie was determined to make the most of their time together before Janice arrived. 'Come on, we'll go for a walk,' she had said.

But Tim had stopped them before they got out of the door. 'I think it's best if you stay here, Kelsey. Janice could be here any time.'

Sophie tutted, the pressure of their situation getting to her. 'Come on, we'll go in the rec room instead.'

'You don't have to, Soph. You can go for a walk round the shops if you want.'

'Are you joking?' she asked, more loudly than she meant. 'I want to be here to say goodbye, don't I?'

The word 'goodbye' struck her, giving her a powerful jolt of emotion and she struggled to hold back the tears she had been suppressing all week.

Two hours later and they were still sitting in the rec room playing a boring game of snakes and ladders when they heard the doorbell ring followed by the sound of Janice's voice along with Tim's and then the sound of the front door shutting. Their voices faded and when Sophie heard a second door being shut, she assumed they'd gone into the office. The two girls looked across the table at each other.

'I'd better get my case,' said Kelsey, her voice shaking.

Now that the time was almost here, Sophie didn't want Kelsey out of her sight any longer than necessary. 'I'll come with you.'

They trundled up the stairs and Sophie watched while Kelsey grabbed her suitcase. Sophie couldn't trust herself to speak, she was so choked up with sorrow, so she stayed silent as she slowly followed Kelsey back down the stairs.

Janice was waiting at the bottom. 'Aah, you've got your case. Good. Do you want to say goodbye to the other children before I take you to your new foster family?' As she spoke her eyes flitted between Kelsey and Sophie.

Sophie followed Kelsey into the rec room while she said goodbye to the other children. When it came to Emily's turn, the girl sprang up off her seat and flung her arms around Kelsey. 'I'm going to miss you,' she said.

'Me too,' Kelsey replied, and Sophie could see the beginning of tears.

'I'll come to the car with you,' said Sophie, and they both followed Janice down the hallway and out of the front door.

Tim had also joined the small party and had taken Kelsey's case. He was walking alongside Janice with the girls behind, firstly Kelsey and then Sophie. Because her sister was in front of her, Sophie couldn't see her face, but she could hear her crying and see her shoulders shudder.

Sophie rushed to catch up with her and managed to grab her just before they reached Janice's car. 'Come here,' she said, her voice trembling, and she turned Kelsey around and held her tightly.

The sight of Kelsey sobbing was too much. Sophie finally lost control. All the emotions that she had been holding in now erupted. 'It's OK,' she said, her voice shaking. 'It's OK. I'll still see you at school and Tim said we can see each other at weekends too.'

She sensed Tim and Janice hovering in the background and heard him speak. 'That's right. You'll still be able to see each other. So, come on now, Kelsey. Let's get you into the car. Janice is waiting.'

Sophie felt Kelsey's hold on her strengthen. Her sister's tears were now gushing down her face and Sophie felt the force of her body clinging to her as she sobbed violently. Despite Tim beckoning Kelsey to get into the car, she didn't loosen her grip and Sophie didn't try to part her sister from her either.

Like Kelsey, Sophie was grasping these few moments together. She realised that Kelsey's departure from the home represented a significant change in their lives and that thought was unbearable.

'Come on, girls, it's time for Kelsey to go,' Tim beckoned again.

Sophie heard Janice say softly, 'Just give them a minute.'

That minute only seemed to last seconds before Tim was encouraging Kelsey to get inside the car again. This time, Janice joined in with him. But the girls gripped even more tightly to each other till Sophie could see Janice trying to prise Kelsey away and could feel Tim's hands pulling at her from behind.

The girls became hysterical and fought to hold on to each

other. Sophie could feel her hold weakening as Tim pulled hard. As she tried to hang on to Kelsey, she blocked her mind to everything that was going on around her: Tim's shouting. Janice's coaxing. And Kelsey's distressed wailing. The only thing that mattered to Sophie was holding on to her sister for as long as she could.

As Tim tugged at Sophie, she felt her grip loosen. The girls' bodies parted, and Sophie quickly reached out and grabbed Kelsey's hands. 'No! Please don't take my sister,' she yelled.

But Tim was relentless until even Kelsey's hands started to slip away. The last thing Sophie felt was the touch of her sister's fingers against her own. Then even they were gone, and Janice quickly led Kelsey to her car.

Sophie dropped to the ground, howling after her sister, and calling out her name till she saw the car disappear out of the gates of Rushthorpe. She had never in her life felt so alone.

PART TWO

ABANDONED
(2005–2006)

18

January 2005

Sophie had wanted to ring her sister at the foster home all weekend, but Tim had refused to give her the phone number, telling her that Kelsey needed time to settle in with her new family. His insensitive choice of words had made Sophie seethe with anger.

For the rest of that weekend Sophie had felt not only upset and lonely but helpless too. She didn't trust Tim. The only way she was able to sleep in the children's home was after she had filled her suitcase with the heaviest items she could find and dragged it behind her bedroom door so that she would be disturbed if anybody tried to get inside. It became her night-time routine.

Sophie was glad when Monday arrived. At last, she would be able to see Kelsey. She looked out for her all morning at school but didn't manage to have a word with her until the lunch break when she spotted her in the corridor with some friends. Sophie rushed up to her and the girls flung their arms around each other.

'I've really missed you,' said Sophie. 'How are you? What's the foster home like?' she gushed.

'I'm fine, Sophie, don't worry about me. The foster home is great, honestly. They're a nice couple and they've got a daughter my age called Leanne. We get on really well. What about you? What's it been like since I left?'

'Same, really,' said Sophie, feeling a bit put out that Kelsey seemed so happy in her new environment. She had hoped that her sister might have missed her as much as Sophie had missed Kelsey. 'Tim's just as horrible as ever but at least Lloyd's kept out of my way.'

'Oh, that's good then,' said Kelsey. 'Have they said anything about who's going to share your room with you?'

'Not yet, no. Do *you* have to share a bedroom?'

'Yeah, with Leanne, but she's really nice.'

'Yeah, you said.' Then, noticing the look on her sister's face, Sophie realised that she was being a bit peevish, and she quickly backtracked. 'I'm glad you like it there, Kelsey. I hope you'll be alright.'

'Aw thanks, Sophie. I hope you'll be alright too.'

Then one of Kelsey's friends caught her attention. 'I've got to go,' said Kelsey, 'but I'll see you later.'

Sophie felt dejected once her sister had walked away. She was still the same old Kelsey, but Sophie sensed that she was already beginning to drift away from her.

Later that week, Sophie was delighted when Tim told her that a visit with Kelsey had been arranged for the coming Saturday. All week she could hardly contain her excitement and when she'd had snatched conversations with her sister in school, Kelsey had seemed just as excited.

By the time Saturday arrived, Sophie couldn't settle, rushing out into the hallway every time she heard a car outside, expecting her sister to come walking through the door any second. When Kelsey finally did arrive, she was accompanied by Janice who agreed to leave her for a few hours and return later to pick her up.

'Thanks, Janice,' said Sophie, over Kelsey's shoulder as she clung on fast to her sister once more.

They dashed up to Sophie's bedroom, where they chatted for the next half hour, catching up on everything that had happened in the week. They no longer walked home from school together as Kelsey lived in a different area now, and Sophie had missed their catch-ups about their school day.

Eventually they decided to go to the shops together. Sophie felt reassured by the familiar routine they had shared in the home, but her upbeat frame of mind soon changed when Kelsey started telling her about her new life.

When Kelsey mentioned Leanne's name for the umpteenth time, Sophie snapped. 'For God's sake, Kelsey, can't you think of anything else to talk about?'

'What?' asked Kelsey.

'Well, it's Leanne this and Leanne that. I'm sick of hearing her name.'

'What do you expect me to talk about? I do live with her, y'know. And she's really nice.'

'Yeah, you said, loads of times. Don't you want to know me now you've got your new sister?'

'Don't be daft,' said Kelsey, looking hurt. 'Course I still want to know you. And she's not my sister, you are.'

Sophie nodded, feeling a pang of guilt for being so touchy. For a few moments, the atmosphere between them was strained as Kelsey tried to talk about other things and Sophie tried to reciprocate. She knew their time together was limited and she didn't want to spend it arguing.

It was soon time to go back to the house and they both waited in the recreation room until Janice came to pick Kelsey up. Sophie didn't want another emotional departure, so she did her best to contain her emotions till Kelsey had gone. Then she rushed upstairs, anxious to get inside her own room before anybody noticed how upset she was.

But she was shocked when she opened the door and peered inside through bleary eyes. There was a strange girl inside the room. Sophie immediately felt embarrassed that the girl had witnessed her anguish and she couldn't help but feel annoyed when the girl stared at her with a smirk on her face. And, if that wasn't bad enough, she was also sitting on Kelsey's bed.

19

January 2005

Despite the way Sophie had assured Kelsey that she would have a new mate once the staff put somebody else in her bed, the truth was that she didn't want anybody trying to replace her sister. And the way she was feeling now, she just wanted to be left alone.

Sophie surveyed the girl sitting across from her. She had poker-straight red hair that came to her shoulders and a fair complexion with an abundance of freckles. At a guess Sophie would have said she was a bit older than her, so perhaps around fifteen. Her face looked friendly enough and moderately attractive but there was an air of mischief about her.

She was quick to introduce herself. 'Hi, are you Sophie? I'm Shannon. I'm gonna be sharing with you.'

Before Sophie had a chance to reply, Shannon had taken something from the bag that she had placed at the side of Kelsey's bed and walked over to the window. She opened it a fraction then, to Sophie's astonishment, lit a cigarette and began blowing smoke outside.

'You're not allowed to do that,' said Sophie, choking back her emotions.

'So? They won't know, will they? If someone opens the door, I'll put it out, stuff it in my pocket and pretend I'm looking out of the window.'

'But what if they catch you? You'll get in trouble.'

'Why? What they gonna do? Chuck me out? I doubt it. They're not gonna send me somewhere else just for having a cig. And even if they do, it's no big deal. This place is a shithole anyway. I have been caught before, y'know. All Tim did was give me a warning.'

'What? You mean you've stayed here before?'

'A couple of times, yeah.'

'How come?' asked Sophie, curious.

'Mum's an alcy. They've took us off her a few times. But every time they hand us back, she starts on the drink again. Well, I don't think she ever gives it up really; she just pretends to them that she has so she'll get us back.'

'So, you've got other brothers and sisters?'

'Yeah, one of each but they're both younger than me, and they've gone into foster care.'

'Don't you miss them?'

Shannon shrugged. 'I'm used to it. It's no biggie. What about you?'

'My mum died.' Sophie could feel her lip tremble as she spoke.

'Ah, so that's why you were crying?'

'Not only that.' Sophie took a deep breath trying to steady herself before she mentioned Kelsey.

'Do you wanna drag of this cig?' Shannon cut in.

Sophie shook her head, automatically thinking how her mother would disapprove.

'Why not? It'll make you feel better, honest. Or are you scared of trying it?'

'I'm not scared,' said Sophie, feeling a touch of irritation.

'Well do it then. Like I said, they're not gonna do owt. Tim'll just tell you off, that's all.'

Sophie thought about Tim, his insensitivity, the way he pried into her personal belongings and the way he seemed to speak down to her. She also thought about the way her sister had been snatched from her. Suddenly, she felt a familiar sense of anger, which made her want to kick back.

'Go on then, just one drag,' she said, looking over her shoulder to check the door was shut as she walked over to the window.

Sophie didn't really enjoy her first drag of a cigarette; it felt raw on her throat and she wanted to cough. But in a way the sense of rebellion made her feel grown up and more in charge of her life and her own decisions. After a couple of drags, she felt more relaxed and ready to tell Shannon about Kelsey.

'Sounds like she doesn't want to know you now she's got this new mate, if you ask me,' said Shannon after Sophie had filled her in on what had been happening.

'No, it isn't like that.'

'What is it like then?' asked Shannon but Sophie couldn't think of what to say. 'Fuck her!'

Sophie was shocked. 'But she's my sister.'

'So? Do you think she's thinking about you when she's

palling around with this new mate, nice and cushy in her fuckin' posh foster home?'

Sophie didn't necessarily agree with Shannon's opinion, but the girl was forceful, and she found it difficult to put up an argument. She'd never met anyone quite like Shannon before. Out of her friendship group, Sophie had the most dominant personality, and she was used to people accepting her opinion for the main part.

After spending some time with Shannon, Sophie was realising just how different she was. Shannon was loud and overbearing but she was also mischievous and had a great sense of fun and, the way Sophie was currently feeling, Shannon was just the tonic she needed.

Within the space of an hour, Sophie had told Shannon all about her circumstances. Her take on matters had surprised Sophie. Having spent most of her childhood in the care system, Shannon had a resilience about her. She seemed to accept her circumstances readily and had a way of seeing the funny side of things. She made Sophie laugh so much that for the first time in days she was managing to take her mind off how much she was missing her sister.

20

March 2005

Sophie stormed into the bedroom and plonked herself down onto the bed where she lay fully outstretched sobbing into her pillow. On the way into the room, she passed Lloyd who had been hovering at the doorway.

'Go on, little boy. You're not wanted here anymore,' said Shannon, waving her little finger at him, in a parody of his manhood.

'Bitch!' yelled Lloyd, before stomping away up the landing.

Shannon giggled then changed her expression when she noticed how troubled Sophie was. After leaving her for a few minutes, Shannon sighed heavily and asked, 'What is it this time? The usual?'

Sophie had just returned from the rec room where she had spent some time with her sister. It was the first visit in two weeks and only the fourth visit in the seven weeks since Kelsey had left the children's home. Sophie was sick of the excuses she was offered when she couldn't see her sister at weekends. She looked up at Shannon, her face tear-stained. 'She doesn't want to know me anymore.'

'Why? What's she said?'

'Oh, all about her weekend away last week and what a good time her and that Leanne had, and how wonderful Leanne's parents are and all that crap!'

'So? Did you have a go back like I told you?' asked Shannon. She had been living in the children's home for six weeks now and had already become Sophie's confidante and closest ally.

'What's the point? She knows how bad it is in here, no matter how much I try to make it sound cool.'

'Yeah, but we have a good laugh, don't we? I bet she doesn't with this Leanne. I bet she's a right snobby little cow. Anyway, you don't have to put up with that shit if you don't want, y'know,' Shannon continued.

'What d'you mean?'

'Well, if you stopped seeing her you wouldn't be pissed off every time, would you?'

'But I couldn't do that.'

'Why not? You stopped seeing your dad when he treated you like shit, didn't you?'

'Yeah, but that was different.'

'Why? From what you've told me she winds you up even more than your dad and his wife.'

Sophie didn't respond. She'd never thought of it like that before and for a moment she was confused. She didn't want to stop seeing her sister; she wanted to get back on track with her. But maybe Shannon had a point. Whenever she saw Kelsey lately, it always seemed to make her upset.

After a few moments she dismissed the thought; no

matter what happened she knew she could never stop seeing Kelsey. She was her sister and Sophie still had dreams that one day they would be together, and things could go back to the way they were.

Shannon seemed to sense it was the end of the conversation because she suddenly announced: 'Anyway, Sophie, I've been waiting for you to get back so I can have a shower without worrying about the knicker sniffer peeping in. I haven't had one yet today.'

As Sophie and Shannon had got to know each other, they had adopted the same system Sophie and Kelsey had shared by going in the bathroom together to protect themselves from Tim as there was no lock on the door.

Sophie dried her eyes and walked over the hallway with Shannon, and into the bathroom. Then she turned her back to her while Shannon took off her clothes and stepped into the shower. Sophie stayed next to the door, smiling to herself when Shannon began singing Dido's 'White Flag' badly.

Then the singing stopped. 'Shit,' said Shannon. 'The shampoo's run out. Is there any more in the cabinet?'

'Hang on, I'll have a look,' said Sophie, stepping to the bathroom cabinet and pulling open the door. 'Yeah, there's some here.'

'Pass it to me.'

Sophie crossed the bathroom and held out the shampoo, nervous about opening the shower curtain. 'Here.'

'Where? I can't bloody see it.'

Before Sophie could stretch her hand round to the inside of the curtain, Shannon had pulled the curtain back and stood naked, facing her. Sophie couldn't help but stare. She'd never seen a naked woman before, but she'd always admired the female form and now, seeing her friend unclothed, she felt the first stirrings of desire.

'Well?' Shannon repeated. 'Don't just stand there with yer gob wide open. Give it to me.'

She reached out and grabbed the shampoo then she seemed to pick up on something and stood there grinning for a moment. Sophie felt Shannon's eyes on her and blushed. She quickly turned around again and walked back to the door, feeling embarrassed. Shannon might not have said anything but the way she had grinned told Sophie that she knew.

21

March 2005

'It's becoming a problem, Tim,' said Janice. 'It's really unsettling for Sophie every time she's told she can't see her sister and, to be frank, it's not fair. Apparently, the Harrises think Sophie is a bad influence – ever since Kelsey let slip that she smokes. How long has that been going on anyway?'

'What? Sophie smoking? I had no idea.'

Janice was sitting across from Tim in the office of the children's home. 'Well apparently she is. To be honest, Tim, I don't think this new girl, Shannon, is a good influence on Sophie. Can't anything be done about it? Is there no room for her elsewhere?'

'I'm afraid not, Janice. You know how the system works. There are no other rooms available here and your team have already told me there's nowhere else to put her at the moment.'

Janice shrugged. 'Well, I'm concerned about Sophie. Things have been getting to her recently. It seems that she thinks Kelsey doesn't want to know her now she's happily settled with her new foster family.'

'I thought they saw each other at school,' said Tim.

'They do but, according to Sophie, it's not the same as it used to be. They no longer walk home together, and Kelsey is always in a rush to get back to her friends whenever Sophie stops to talk to her. I think the conversation is limited too as their lives are different from each other now. I think they could do with more one-on-one time to enable them to stay connected. What's Sophie been like here? Have you noticed any changes?'

'Not good, I'm afraid. She seems to be rebelling lately, staying out late, backchatting, that sort of thing.'

'OK. And I don't suppose she's doing all that alone, is she? I take it Shannon's involved too.'

'Well, yes. I mean, the two of them do hang around together.'

Janice couldn't resist tutting, knowing that she was faced with a situation she could do nothing about. She'd seen it all before, unfortunately, where troubled children entered the system and were led astray by those who had already become hardened to the way of life. But perhaps she could do something about the visits with Kelsey.

'Alright, thanks for your input. I'll have a word with Kelsey's foster parents, see if I can persuade them to let Sophie see more of her sister. After all, it's in Kelsey's best interests as well as Sophie's to carry on seeing each other.'

Sophie was in the bedroom she shared with Shannon, watching her shave one side of her hair with an electric razor.

'I love that hairstyle,' she said.

'D'you want me to do it on you after I've finished?'

Sophie hesitated at first, knowing the staff wouldn't be happy but then she thought, *Why shouldn't I?* 'Yeah, go on then.'

Sophie was really pleased with the results and she stood admiring herself in the bedroom mirror. 'Thanks, Shannon. I've always loved this hairstyle. It looks good with dark eye makeup too, but I've run out of eyeliner.'

'I've got some. Do you want me to do your makeup for you?'

'Would you?' asked Sophie, warming to the idea.

She sat while Shannon applied a pale foundation then lashings of mascara and some dark kohl under her eyes. Then she went over to the mirror once more. Sophie was thrilled. 'I love it. I look all edgy and a bit like a goth.'

Shannon smiled. 'Yeah, it looks cool.'

Sophie was so pleased with her new look that she was no longer concerned about how the staff would react. So many aspects of her life were now out of her control and it felt good to at least be in charge of her own image.

'By the way, how did you go on with your social worker?' asked Shannon.

'I told her everything,' said Sophie. 'About how fed up I am that I can't see Kelsey every weekend and about how she is with me.'

As she spoke Sophie could feel her lip tremble. The thought of Kelsey's rejection always upset her. Shannon crossed the room and sat next to her on the bed. 'I've told you, Soph, you don't need to put up with that shit. If she doesn't want to know you, then fuck her. Tell your social worker you don't want to see her anymore.'

But the thought of breaking ties with Kelsey upset Sophie.

'Come here, you soft cow,' said Shannon, taking her head in her arms.

Sophie snuggled into Shannon, becoming lost in her embrace. For a second, she was transported back to how it was with her mother, always there to comfort her whenever she was troubled, and Sophie let the tears fall. She returned to reality when Shannon pulled away and Sophie stared at her, embarrassed to have become so carried away.

'I'm sorry,' she said, sniffing back the mucus that threatened to dribble from her nose and wiping her eyes on the sleeve of her top.

'It's OK,' said Shannon, smiling and, as Sophie stared back at her, she noticed the gleam in her eye.

For a short while they continued to stare at each other. Sophie recalled Shannon's reaction when she had seen her naked in the bathroom, and she felt something stir within her. As Shannon held her gaze, she could sense there was something in her too, a force that was pulling them together.

When Shannon leant in for a kiss, Sophie found herself reciprocating. She could feel Shannon's hands exploring her body, gently stroking her breasts, and she shivered. Then Shannon ran her hands up her top and popped open her bra, her hands now caressing Sophie's bare flesh.

Sophie sighed with pleasure and mirrored Shannon's movements. The two of them became immersed in the thrill of it but the moment was lost when Sophie became aware of footsteps inside their room. She pulled away from Shannon, dreading Tim's reaction. In the heat of passion, she had forgotten to block the bedroom door. Sophie soon realised that it wasn't Tim at the door, but Lloyd. When he let out a roar of laughter, she realised that him spotting them was just as bad.

'Ha-ha! You're a pair of dirty fuckin' lesbos.'

The girls moved away from each other. Sophie was stunned into silence but not Shannon. She picked up a shoe and launched it at Lloyd.

'Fuck off! You shouldn't even be in our room, watching us, you fuckin' perve,' she yelled.

Lloyd grabbed his arm where the shoe had hit him and rubbed it furiously. 'Bitches!' he yelled. 'You won't fuckin' get away with this.'

Sophie sat with her mouth open, in a state of shock, not just because of Lloyd but because of her own actions. She had felt an attraction to girls for a long time but had never acted on it until now. But it didn't feel good. The way Lloyd had reacted made her feel ashamed.

Knowing how sly Lloyd was, a feeling of intense unease settled on Sophie. Her mind was in turmoil. Not only was she troubled about her sister, but she was also coming to terms with her own sexuality. And now she had another problem.

For the past few weeks Lloyd had been fighting a losing battle. He was no match against Shannon's forceful personality and Sophie had sensed his resentment at his ineptitude against the girls. But now he had found his weapon and Sophie felt certain that he would take full advantage of it.

22

March 2005

For days Sophie had been struggling with her emotions. Everything was going round in her head in a mishmash of thoughts: her fancying girls, the threat from Lloyd and her feelings about her sister.

With all these concerns, Sophie had decided she needed to speak to Janice who was due to arrive any minute. Sophie was on edge as she waited for her to get there, and the slightest thing was setting her off, including Shannon's out-of-tune singing.

'For God's sake, Shannon!' she snapped. 'Will you shut the fuck up? You sound like a cat that's being strangled.'

'Alright, keep your hair on!' Shannon yelled back. 'You don't normally say owt about me singing.'

But Sophie knew she wouldn't take offence. Shannon was thick-skinned and in the few weeks she had known her Sophie had learnt to reciprocate Shannon's manner of speech. It seemed to be the only language she understood.

'Is this about Janice coming?' asked Shannon.

Sophie shrugged, not wanting to discuss it now. She preferred to just get it out of the way.

'It'll be OK, y'know.'

Sophie shrugged again, hoping Shannon would take the hint and stop pressing her to talk. She was relieved when Shannon announced that she was going out and she flounced out of the room.

A few moments later, Sophie heard footsteps on the stairs, and hoped it was Janice. Her hopes were answered when Janice walked into the bedroom, shutting the door behind her, and sitting across from Sophie on Shannon's bed.

'Well, Sophie, judging by the look on your face I'm guessing this isn't going to be good,' she said.

Sophie dropped her gaze and for a moment she thought she was going to lose her nerve. But then she pulled herself together. Janice was here now so it was best that she just got it over with.

She had become so anxious that her words came out in a rush. 'I don't want to see Kelsey anymore.'

Janice didn't respond straightaway. Instead, she stared back at Sophie wearing a confused expression. Finally, she spoke. 'You what? Are you sure about this, Sophie?'

Sophie nodded then spoke clearly. 'Yes. I am.' She was trying to appear resolute but already her composure was slipping.

'What's brought this on?'

'She doesn't want to know me anymore, so I don't see the point.'

'But of course she does. She's your sister and anybody can see how close you two are.'

'Not anymore,' said Sophie, her voice now trembling

despite her attempts to stay strong. 'I'm sick of hearing about her new family.'

She didn't say anything further as she was too upset. Janice got up off the bed and approached her then sat down next to her on Sophie's bed. 'You're her family, nobody else. And nothing can change that, Sophie.'

Sophie shook her head, fighting the tears that threatened to spill. 'She doesn't think so,' she complained. 'The way she goes on about Leanne, anybody would think she was her sister.'

Janice was leaning over towards Sophie now, trying to hold her gaze, but Sophie had closed herself off, staring straight ahead with her hands clenched tightly together on her lap. 'Sophie, look at me.' She waited till Sophie had turned her head to face her before continuing. 'You will regret this decision. Kelsey doesn't mean to hurt you when she talks about her foster family. She's perhaps just getting carried away by her new situation.'

'Yeah, with her new posh family while I'm stuck in this fuckin' dump with creepy Tim and a load of fuckin' kids who no one wants!' As she spoke, Sophie got up and paced across the room, creating distance between herself and Janice, her back turned to her so she couldn't see how upset she was.

'Eh, now I'm sure you don't mean that,' said Janice. 'Just because you're in here doesn't mean nobody wants you. It's just a bit harder to place older children, that's all.'

Sophie didn't voice the thoughts that were racing around inside her mind. She hadn't meant herself. She had been referring to the situation in general. But the fact that Janice thought she had been talking about her personally only reinforced her feelings of rejection.

After waiting a while for her response, and receiving none, Janice spoke again, her voice full of resignation. 'OK, I'm going to leave you alone now. But before I go, I want to check with you that you're sure about this decision.'

'Yes, I am!' Sophie snapped.

'Right, well I won't announce it to anybody for a few days in case you change your mind. I want you to have a good think about this, Sophie. I understand you feeling upset, but you need to think about how you would feel if you were never to see your sister again.'

Sophie let out an unwelcome sob then tried to swallow it down. 'I'll still see her at school if she can be bothered to talk to me.'

As she remained standing with her back to Janice, she heard her stand up and take the few steps across the room till she was standing just behind her. Then she felt Janice pat her on the back. 'You've got my number, Sophie. Have a good think about things and if you change your mind, call me.'

Once she was gone Sophie stormed across the room, slammed the door shut then threw herself onto her bed and sobbed into her pillow. She knew she wouldn't change her mind; she was convinced that it was the best course of action for both her and Kelsey.

The longer she kept up the visits with Kelsey, the more it would hurt every time she heard her talking about her foster family. And she couldn't take it anymore. At school she would avoid her sister as much as possible so she wouldn't be drawn into another conversation she didn't want to hear. She was convinced that Kelsey had thrown her over in favour of her new family, and the sooner she pulled away and left her to get on with her happy life, the better.

It was almost an hour later. Sophie was still in her room, but she had managed to calm herself down when she heard a knock on the door. 'Who is it?' she called, wary of pulling the overstuffed suitcase away from the door in case it was Tim.

'It's Lloyd.'

A feeling of dread descended on Sophie. 'I don't want to talk to you.'

'Right, do you want me to talk about it out here then? Maybe the staff will be interested in what you've been up to.'

Her dread intensified. She had hoped that Lloyd's threat might have been an idle one but now she realised that he had probably just been biding his time till he could get her alone. She stomped across the room, heaved at the suitcase, and dragged the door open.

'What do you want?' she demanded, opening the door to allow Lloyd to come into the room.

He stood looking at her for a while with a smirk on his face. Sophie glared back at him, tempted to slap him till the smirk disappeared but she resisted. He lowered his eyes, and she followed his line of vision, shocked to notice that her top had slipped down while she had been lying on the bed, revealing the tops of her breasts. She quickly covered herself up.

He laughed. 'Nice tits.'

'You shouldn't have been looking.'

'Ha! Is only Shannon allowed to do that?'

Sophie tutted. 'What do you want, Lloyd?' she repeated.

His grin widened as he contemplated his reply. 'A taste of what Shannon's having. Only better. I want you to go down on me.'

'No!' Sophie yelled. Then she raced to the door and heaved it open. 'Get out!'

Lloyd strolled to the door, locking eyes with her on his way out. When he bent his head towards hers, Sophie flinched, expecting him to attempt an uninvited kiss. But instead, he put his mouth to her ear and whispered menacingly.

'Right, suit yourself. I'll just have to tell Tim what you've been up to.' He gave her another smug grin as he walked away.

'Bastard!' Sophie cursed but as he skulked away towards the stairs, panic seized her. 'Wait!'

Lloyd turned around, a look of unconcealed glee planted across his smarmy face as he headed back to Sophie's room and stepped inside.

'OK, I'll do it.' He began unzipping his flies. 'Not now! I was supposed to meet Shannon at the shops ten minutes ago. She'll be wondering where I am.'

Lloyd made a show of pulling his zip back up. 'You'd better not be fuckin' lying!'

'No, I'm not. I promise. Look, I've got to go. I'll see you later and we can sort it out then.'

Without waiting for his reply, Sophie dashed past him and down the stairs. Then she fled from the house and didn't stop till she came across Shannon who was on her way back to the home.

'Where the hell have you been?' Shannon demanded. 'I've been waiting ages. And what the fuck's wrong with you?'

Sophie leant forward, clutching her chest and panting. She could feel the burn of her breath as it cut a trail down her throat and seared into her lungs. For a moment she fought to steady it before she could speak.

'It's Lloyd. I told you he'd do summat, didn't I?'

'Phut! Lloyd's a little wimp. You've no need to be scared of him.'

Sophie grabbed hold of Shannon's forearm, demanding her attention. 'It's not him I'm scared of, Shannon. He's going to tell Tim. He's threatened me. Just now. I told you he would.'

'Why? What did he say?'

Sophie repeated her earlier conversation with Lloyd.

'The little twat! I'll fuckin' have him.'

'No! Don't, Shannon. Please! If you go saying anything to him then he'll definitely tell on us.'

'What you gonna do then? You're not gonna give in to him, are you?'

Sophie felt her voice crack as she cried. 'I don't know.'

23

April 2005

Sophie had been doing a lot of thinking about the threat that Lloyd presented. In fact, she'd found it difficult to think about anything else and was constantly on edge about the risk of being outed.

She recalled her father's homophobic views and couldn't help worrying whether her mother had shared them. It was something they had never discussed before her death. What if her mother had felt the same? There was a chance she might have done. After all, she had married a homophobe. The thought that she might have been a disappointment to her mother filled Sophie with angst.

Then there was the staff to worry about. What if they were to find out and banish her from the home? If they sent her somewhere miles away, then she might never get to see Kelsey.

She had managed to avoid Lloyd for a few days, taking care not to be in her room alone and accompanying Shannon everywhere she went. But this day Sophie was out of luck.

Lloyd must have got wise to her evasion tactics and he was waiting on the upstairs landing for her when she got there.

'Thought you'd escaped me, didn't you?' he said, sidling up to her and grasping her buttock.

Sophie slapped his hand away. 'Get lost, Lloyd!'

'No chance. Tonight, that's when you'll do it. My room after tea otherwise I'll go straight to Tim and tell him about you and that other lesbo you share a room with.'

Once he'd said what he had to say, Lloyd sidled off leaving Sophie trembling in the hallway. She dashed into her room, relieved to find Shannon lounging on her bed reading a copy of *Smash Hits*. She moved up in the bed and gazed over the top of her magazine.

'Jesus! What's wrong with you? You look as if you've just seen a ghost.'

'Lloyd was in the hallway waiting for me.'

'Really? What did the dickhead say?'

'He wants me to go to his room tonight after tea.'

'You're not gonna do it are you?'

'I dunno. If I don't, he said he's gonna go straight to Tim to tell him about us.'

'So? Let him fuckin' tell him. We'll just deny it anyway.'

'But what if Tim splits us up? He might even send us to one of those really bad homes that are miles away.'

'Will he fuck! Not for summat like that.'

But Sophie was troubled. If she were honest with herself, she might have broken ties with Kelsey, but she still couldn't help looking out for her at school each day, and if she were sent to a residential home, she wouldn't be able to do that. It hurt to think how much she and her sister had drifted apart but, despite everything, it comforted her in a way to see her sister relatively happy.

Then there was Shannon. She might have been brash at times and a bit overbearing, but she was the person Sophie confided in. Without her she'd find things difficult.

Teatime came round too quickly, and Sophie felt tense as she descended the stairs on her way to the kitchen. Lloyd was already there when she arrived, sitting at the end of the table with his usual smug grin plastered all over his face.

While she was eating Lloyd called out to Tim, 'Can I come and see you after tea, please?'

'Of course,' said Tim. 'You don't need to make an appointment, Lloyd.'

'OK. I thought I'd check because I need to tell you something.'

Sophie inhaled sharply and choked on a bit of her mashed potato, causing her to cough.

Lloyd laughed. 'Looks like Sophie's had a taste of something that she doesn't like.'

Only the two girls understood his hidden meaning and Shannon scowled at him while Sophie tried to compose herself. Once they had finished eating, Sophie and Shannon headed to their room but again Lloyd was waiting on the upstairs landing.

'Come on then, Sophie. Let's go,' he said.

'Fuck off, Lloyd,' yelled Shannon. 'She's not doing it.'

Lloyd made as if to walk down the stairs. 'I suppose I'd best go and have that meeting with Tim then.'

Sophie panicked. 'No, wait! I'll come with you.'

'You're a fuckin' mug, Sophie!' said Shannon who then walked away, scowling.

Sophie followed Lloyd to his room and shut the door behind them. Like all the children's rooms at the home it didn't have a lock, so Sophie searched around desperately for something with which to block the door.

'Use the chair,' said Lloyd.

Once Sophie had hooked the chair under the door handle, Lloyd strode over to the bed, plonked himself down and began undoing his flies.

'I-I don't want to do that,' said Sophie, besieged by nerves.

'What the fuck are you here for then?'

'I'll do it with my hand instead.'

Lloyd flashed one of his self-satisfied grins. 'OK, come on then.'

She tiptoed across the room and sat down tentatively on the bed. Then, turning away she held out her hand, feeling her way to his trousers. Tutting, Lloyd grabbed her hand and shoved it onto his erect penis. She shuddered, her fingers resting tentatively on his flesh, and continued looking away, trying to disengage herself from what she was about to do.

'Well, get hold of it then, for fuck's sake!'

Sophie did as he said, complying with his instructions while he criticised her performance. Not hard enough. Not fast enough. Rubbish! Pinching his skin. After a while, her wrist began to ache.

'How long do I have to keep doing this?' she asked.

'Shut up! Go faster,' ordered Lloyd who then let out a groan.

Sophie felt his penis go limp in her hand then something moist and sticky covered her fingers. Feeling repulsed she turned around to examine her hand. 'Ew!' she yelled, wiping her fingers on the bedding. Then she fled from the room, dragging the chair away from the door so forcefully that it toppled over.

Lloyd chuckled then shouted after her. 'Can't wait for next time now you know what to do.'

When Sophie arrived back in her room, Shannon asked, 'Was it horrible?' Sophie didn't reply, so she added, 'Oh well, at least you've got it over and done with now. You won't have to do it again.'

Sophie nodded despondently. 'I will. He's going to make me do it again. Only, next time, he might make me do something even worse.'

24

April 2005

For the next week Sophie managed to escape Lloyd's clutches by making sure she always had Shannon with her. This particular day, the children were all seated around the dining table while Tim was at the kitchen counter helping the cook dish out the food.

Lloyd made a point of staring at Sophie then lifting his hand and pointing first at her then at himself and nodding.

'Ignore him, he's a dick,' said Shannon, careful not to let the staff hear her.

Sophie took her advice and looked away. But Lloyd was determined to maintain her attention. 'Er, Tim,' he called over, until both girls looked up at him again, curious.

'What?'

Making sure Sophie was listening, Lloyd said to Tim, 'There's something I need to talk to you about.'

'Can't it wait? I'm in the middle of serving dinner.'

'Yeah, course it can. It's not urgent. In fact, it's something that's been going on for a while. But I think it's something you should know.'

Sophie felt her heart thumping. This was it! He was finally going to tell Tim her secret and all the staff would know.

'Ignore him,' Shannon whispered. 'He's only winding you up. If he goes to see Tim, he'll make up some crappy story. He just wants you to think it's about us when it isn't.'

'I don't know,' said Sophie who was really worried by now and was becoming red in the face at the thought of being exposed.

'You dare go and see him again, Sophie!' warned Shannon. 'You can't let the little shit get to you.'

Their conversation was halted when Tim and the cook served up the meal. But Sophie couldn't eat much, and she was glad when it was all over, and she could escape to her room with Shannon. Lloyd had already left the kitchen and she pictured him sitting in his room waiting for her to intercept his meeting with Tim.

For a few minutes she sat on her bed, restless and troubled by frightening thoughts. What if Lloyd got fed up of waiting and carried out his threat to tell Tim?

'You're not thinking of going, are you?' demanded Shannon.

'Dunno. I don't want to but what if he tells on us, Shannon?'

'I've told you, he won't. He's just bullshitting.'

Sophie stuck it out, gradually calming when a few more minutes passed and nothing had happened. But then she heard someone outside. Whoever it was pushed the door open and she looked across to see Lloyd standing there, his expression gleeful.

'Tim wants to see you in his office, Sophie, straightaway,' he said before looking at Shannon and laughing. 'It'll be your turn later.'

He disappeared, and Sophie flashed Shannon a look of alarm before she left the bedroom and prepared herself to face the staff.

When Sophie walked into the office, she found not only Tim but Hazel and Sandra too. Tim pointed to a vacant seat, his expression serious.

'Sit down, Sophie. We've got something important to discuss with you.'

Sophie's heart was beating so frantically by now that she felt as though it was going to burst through her chest. She tried to calm herself as she sat down. Then Tim spoke.

'I'm pleased to tell you we've found a foster family for you.'

Sophie's jaw dropped. 'What? You mean...?'

'Yes. Sophie?'

'Nothing. I mean. Good.'

'Right, glad to hear it. Well, you'll be wanting to find out more about them so here goes. They're a couple actually. There aren't any other children staying with them at the moment, but they are experienced foster parents and have helped a lot of children over the years. Their names are Kenneth and Cynthia. Now, because it's difficult to place older children, I'm afraid they're from out of the area, which means you'll have a very lengthy journey to and from school.'

Sophie was so relieved that, at first, she didn't take in everything Tim said until he mentioned that it was out of the area. 'How far?' she asked.

'Rochdale.'

'Where's that?'

'Well, allowing for rush hour traffic, it's probably an hour away from your school.'

'Oh, so that means an hour there and an hour back every day?'

'I'm afraid so, Sophie. But, like I say, they're a really nice couple and we...' He looked at Hazel and Sandra to garner their support before continuing, 'We all think it's a very good opportunity for you.'

Sophie was dumbfounded. She'd had no idea that this was what Tim had in mind when he asked to see her. It had come as a complete surprise and she was finding it difficult to take it all in.

'Is it the long journey you're bothered about?' asked Hazel after Sophie hadn't spoken for a while.

'A bit, yeah.'

'Well,' said Tim. 'I'm afraid there's no other alternative unless you want to change schools and I don't think that would be a good idea. It would mean you wouldn't see your sister at all and...'

By this time Sophie had thought about the need to get away from Lloyd and his threat to expose her. Tim was right; it was a good opportunity. It would provide her with a means of escape. 'Yeah, I'll do it,' she said.

'What, you mean, you'll take up the foster place or you'll change schools?'

'The foster place,' said Sophie thinking that she wouldn't miss this place.

The only person here that she would miss was Shannon, but she could easily arrange to meet up with her at the weekends assuming that there was a train or bus that would take her from Rochdale into Manchester.

'Now I want you to think about things very carefully,' said Tim. 'You don't have to decide straightaway. You won't be leaving until a week on Saturday so give it some careful consideration. I'll mention it to Janice too.'

'OK, thanks,' said Sophie.

When Tim dismissed her, she trundled back to her room with mixed feelings. Yet again her life was going to change. But then she thought of all the unhappiness she had endured since she came into the children's home. Being split from her sister and seeing her drift away. The sterile environment. The lack of emotional support from the staff. And Lloyd's blackmail.

Maybe having her own foster family would make all the difference. After all, Kelsey seemed a lot happier now she was with Leanne and her family so hopefully she would be too.

She concluded that the change would be for the best because, surely, it couldn't get any worse.

25

April 2005

Janice couldn't sleep. The thought of what was going to happen tomorrow was playing on her mind. She knew she shouldn't get too attached to the children but sometimes she couldn't help it. Janice had a particular soft spot for Sophie and Kelsey Tailor. What had happened in their young lives should never happen to girls of their age.

But out of the two girls it was the older sister she worried about the most: Sophie. Kelsey seemed to have settled into her life with her new foster family relatively smoothly but with Sophie it was another matter. Janice had never been comfortable about leaving her in the children's home without her sister and it seemed she had been right.

She wished that Sophie were joining a ready-made family like her sister had done. But she wasn't: she was going to live with Kenneth and Cynthia Rowbotham. They were nice enough people and competent at looking after troubled children even though they were a bit strange. And Janice couldn't help but wonder if she had made the right decision. Would Sophie get along alright with them?

The day of Sophie's departure came round quickly. While Sophie had been waiting for the day to arrive, she had asked the staff to keep it quiet from the other children on the pretence that she would find it difficult to deal with all the fuss over her leaving. But the real reason was because she didn't want Lloyd to know.

Since the news of her foster place, Sophie had managed to keep Lloyd at bay, but he was putting her under increasing pressure. Knowing she wouldn't be able to put him off for much longer, she had finally arranged to visit his room that morning.

Sophie was pleased to see Janice arrive a little before eleven. It was exciting to be escaping the home and moving in with her own foster family but, at the same time, she was a bit nervous, hoping that her new foster parents would be just as nice as Kelsey's. Tim had assured her that they were a nice couple though, so she hoped he was right.

Janice's timing was also perfect in terms of what Sophie had planned for her departure. 'Can I have a few minutes to say goodbye to the kids in the rec room?' she asked.

'Certainly. I'll just be in the office. I need to have a word with Sandra anyway. Give me a shout as soon as you're ready.'

Shannon helped Sophie downstairs with her suitcase and some of her personal possessions and accompanied her to the rec room. Sophie was pleased to find that all the children were there except for Lloyd. She said her goodbyes and did her best to hold it together while the younger children made a fuss.

Then she turned to Shannon. 'Right, it's time. But don't forget what I said about meeting me in town next Saturday.'

'No, course I won't,' said Shannon. 'We'll have a good laugh.'

Sophie called in at the office and said her goodbyes to the staff then Janice got up to leave with her. They made their way to the door with the younger children and staff members following behind. Sophie gave Shannon a last hug then, while the children and staff stood on the steps of Rushthorpe children's home, Sophie made her way to Janice's car.

When Janice put her suitcase in the boot, Sophie turned around and gave a last wave to everyone. She noticed Lloyd standing at the back of the small group, his body language advertising his anger. It amused Sophie, knowing that he would have been roused from his room by curiosity, having heard the commotion downstairs. And when Lloyd discovered she was leaving he would have felt completely floored as she and Shannon had deliberately kept him in the dark.

But what amused her most of all was that Lloyd would have been full of smug satisfaction anticipating Sophie's arrival at his bedroom. In fact, Sophie may have arranged to visit him again, but she'd had no intentions of going through with it, which was why she had arranged to see him ten minutes after Janice was due to arrive.

Sophie got inside the car then glanced again at everybody. Lloyd had now forced his way to the front of the group and was gesticulating angrily at Sophie. She gave him a special wave and flashed him one of his own smug grins while Shannon cheered and fist-pumped behind him.

As Janice drove away, she turned to Sophie. 'Are you OK?'

'Yeah.'

For a few seconds they didn't speak. Sophie was still revelling in the thought that she'd managed to foil Lloyd when Janice asked, 'Are you sure you're alright?'

'Yeah, why?'

'Nothing, it's just, I didn't expect to see you so happy to leave your friends at the home.'

Janice's words brought Sophie back to her senses and her smile slipped. Her joy at escaping from the threat of Lloyd's exposure was short-lived. Now she had the future to think about and suddenly, she felt some trepidation about what might lie in store for her in her new foster home.

26

April 2005

'Sophie, meet your new foster parents: Cynthia and Kenneth,' said Janice.

Sophie stared at the couple, taking in their dated hairstyles, old-fashioned clothing, and joyful faces. Kenneth was wearing a pair of trousers that hung loosely on his skinny frame. His shirt had tiny checks and a collar that was shiny round the edges from many years of ironing. On top of the shirt, he wore a bottle-green tank top and Sophie almost recoiled at the sight of him. *Who still wears tank tops, for God's sake?* she thought.

His wife was slightly plump and she too looked old-fashioned with a pleated skirt and a crew-necked pullover that clung around her stomach. Sophie guessed that it must have fitted her years ago. Her hair was peppered with grey and in a nondescript style. They were possibly in their forties although their out-of-date dress sense made them appear much older.

Sophie had been so eager to escape the home that she

hadn't known quite what to expect. Ever since she had been placed into care, finding foster parents had been presented to her like the grand solution and her sister's successful placement had reinforced that idea. On encountering the reality of Cynthia and Kenneth, though, she was secretly disappointed. But she was far too polite to let them know that.

Cynthia stepped forward, eager to shake hands with her. 'Hello, Sophie. Welcome to our humble abode,' she said and they both chuckled falsely at what Sophie guessed was a well-worn phrase.

'Yes, welcome,' said Kenneth, also stepping forward.

Sophie allowed the woman to shake her hand, then forced a weak smile, but she didn't speak. To fill the void left by Sophie's lack of communication, Cynthia carried on speaking. 'Come inside, dear.' She beckoned Sophie inside the hallway and Janice followed, then Cynthia continued waffling. 'I'm afraid you're the only child with us at the moment. Well, young lady, I should say.'

'Erm, would you like me to take your case?' asked Kenneth. 'And then perhaps we could show you to your room?'

'Well, Sophie?' prompted Janice when Sophie still didn't speak. Then, turning to the couple, she added, 'I'm afraid Sophie's just a bit overawed.'

'Oh, that's OK,' said Cynthia. 'We understand. It can all seem a bit strange at first but, don't worry, you'll soon settle in.'

'Thank you, Cynthia,' said the social worker. Then she made a show of looking at her watch. 'Well, I'll leave Sophie in your capable hands. I'll be in contact soon for an update.'

Her last comment was addressed to Sophie as well as the couple before she said, 'Goodbye, Sophie,' and allowed Kenneth to lead her out of the door.

Cynthia took Sophie through to the lounge. 'Once Kenneth comes back, he'll show you your room while I finish the tea,' she said. 'Unless you'd like to help me.'

'No, it's OK,' said Sophie, eager to see where she would be sleeping.

'Oh, there you are,' said Cynthia as soon as Kenneth popped his head round the door. 'Would you mind taking Sophie up to her room, and her case as well?'

'Not at all, my dear.'

He bustled over to them, picked up Sophie's case and swung it enthusiastically as he pranced back across the lounge and into the hallway then up the stairs. 'Come on, Sophie,' he called as she trudged after him.

'It's not a bad size actually for a second bedroom,' he said, putting the case down next to the bed. 'The bathroom's across the landing, there's a desk there to do your studies and of course the wardrobe and chest of drawers that you'll need.'

Sophie couldn't understand his need to point everything out to her. It felt as though he was seeking her approval and when he turned and smiled ingratiatingly, she was obliged to utter, 'Thank you,' convinced that she wouldn't get rid of him otherwise.

'Very well, I'll leave you to unpack your belongings. We'll give you a shout when dinner's ready, but I don't think it will be long. Cynthia does a lovely shepherd's pie; I think you'll like it.'

Then he was gone, and Sophie was relieved. This couple

were weird! She hoped they would be OK to live with but she wasn't sure. It was too late now though; she'd made her decision, so she'd just have to live with it.

Her eyes took in her surroundings. The chest of drawers and wardrobe were very old-fashioned, but they looked sturdy and good quality. She swung open the wardrobe door and was greeted by the smell of mothballs. Next, she examined the chest of drawers, which had fragranced drawer liners, and the sweet sickly smell reminded her of old women's perfume.

The bed and curtains were in a matching floral material and when she lay on the bed to try it out, she found that it also smelt flowery. But something else she noticed was that it was the most comfortable bed she had ever lain on, even more comfortable than her old bed at home. She felt sorry for thinking badly of the couple who were obviously trying their best to make her welcome.

Thinking about her bed at home led to thoughts of her mother and Kelsey, and she wondered what her sister was doing now. They were never far from her mind even though it was now several months since her mother had passed away. Memories of her family filled her with sadness, but she pushed it aside and turned to her unpacking instead.

Kenneth stepped into the kitchen, shutting the door behind him then looking over his shoulder just to make sure Sophie hadn't followed him downstairs.

'Sophie's going to unpack,' he said. Then whispered, 'I think we're going to have a few problems with this one, Cynthia. She strikes me as the rebellious type.'

Cynthia paused from pulling plates out of the cupboard and turned to look at him. 'What makes you say that?'

'Well, look at her hair for one thing and all that heavy makeup. I never was a fan of too much makeup, as you know.'

'Nonsense, Kenneth. She's just expressing herself, that's all. A lot of the youngsters have shaven hair these days. It's the fashion.'

'I'm not sure, Cynthia. She's not very communicative, is she?'

'Give her a chance. She's only just got here. She might be nervous in a new environment. Just because she has a bold image, doesn't necessarily mean she's bold in character, Kenneth. She might be just as doubtful of us as we are of her.'

Kenneth shrugged.

'From what we've been told,' Cynthia continued, 'she has been through a lot, after all. Don't worry, we'll soon win her round. We have had worse to deal with when all's said and done. Remember that God is on our side, Kenneth. Now, if you don't mind, dinner is almost ready. Can you call Sophie down please? Tell her she can finish her unpacking later if necessary as it's important that we all eat together.'

Sophie was surprised to see Kenneth again so soon after he had left her. 'Dinner's ready!' he announced. She looked at the clothes still in her case and was about to speak but he pre-empted her. 'It's fine. You can finish unpacking after we've eaten. Best to get it while it's hot.' A cheery smile accompanied his last few words.

Sophie followed Kenneth back down the stairs and through to the dining room. She hadn't been in here yet and the first thing that hit her was the smell again, but this time it was the cloying aroma of air freshener. The table was laid out with lacy placemats and a matching runner. On each of the placemats was a plate full of steaming shepherd's pie and vegetables.

Cynthia was already sitting at one end of the table, and Kenneth took his seat at the other end. He pointed to a place setting midway along the table. 'This one's for you,' he said to Sophie, and Cynthia smiled and nodded.

Sophie obliged the couple by pulling out her chair and sitting down then picking up her knife and fork. She was just about to tuck into the meal when Cynthia stopped her.

'Oh no, not yet, my dear. Good grief, no!'

Then she put her hands together and Kenneth did the same. 'We don't eat till we've thanked the good Lord for the food that he puts on our table,' she said. 'Now then, Sophie and Kenneth, let us pray.'

27

It was nearly three months later, and Sophie was feeling down. She was lonely in the foster home where she had spare time to think, and she was desperately missing her mum and Kelsey. In the children's home, she had been too busy surviving to dwell on things. And now it surprised her that, despite the problems with Tim and Lloyd, she missed the children's home too, especially Shannon who always managed to lift her spirits.

Sophie had only seen Shannon once since she had left the children's home. They'd met in Manchester and had a good day out. Apart from shopping, Sophie had had her lip pierced and was pleased with the results. It fitted in nicely with the image she was trying to create along with her dark heavy makeup and partly shaved hair, which she had also started dying jet black.

Despite arranging to meet in the city centre again, Shannon hadn't turned up on that second occasion. Sophie's sister had been a disappointment too, and it bothered her.

After Janice had spoken to her, Kelsey had made the effort to speak to Sophie at school, but her renewed effort hadn't lasted long and now it was just a quick hello in the corridor and a forced smile.

Most of all Sophie was missing her mother and as she thought about her, Kelsey, and the things she was missing about the children's home, she allowed the tears to fall. She had never settled into the foster home with the couple who still seemed strange to her. Saying prayers before meals was bad enough but they had even asked her to go to church on Sundays and had seemed really put out when she had refused.

Aside from that, their false bonhomie was starting to grate on her. Not only did it remind her of how Tim had been at first, but she also felt suffocated by their kindness.

While all this was going on in her mind, Kenneth knocked on the bedroom door then let himself in. Sophie had been lying down on the bed, crying into her pillow, and she quickly sat up when Kenneth entered the room. She felt invaded as she didn't like people seeing her upset.

'Oops, sorry, Sophie,' he said, appearing awkward when he noticed her distress. 'I just called to see if you would like a cup of tea.'

'No,' she snapped.

'You sure?'

'Yes, if I want one, I'll go and get one myself.'

He looked disappointed. 'Oh, OK,' he said but then, instead of going, he hovered next to the door. 'If you don't mind me saying, you look as though you could do with a cuppa.'

'For God's sake! Why don't you just fuck off and leave me alone?' Sophie yelled.

To her surprise, rather than reprimanding her for her bad language, he shut the door and went back downstairs.

'Whatever's the matter?' asked Cynthia when Kenneth came back into the kitchen.

'I think we've got a problem, dear.'

'What do you mean?'

'Well, I think we may have bitten off more than we can chew with this one. She just swore at me, not mild swearing either. The F word. I think she's getting away with too much. We should have said something about the piercing really on top of the crazy hairstyle and makeup.'

'No, no, no, Kenneth, that would have been the wrong reaction. I've told you before, it's best not to show them you're bothered. The more you do so, the more they'll rebel.'

Kenneth shifted uncomfortably from foot to foot. 'Alright. To be honest, she seemed as though she might have been crying.'

Cynthia who had been preparing that evening's meal, stopped what she was doing and put a reassuring hand on Kenneth's forearm before saying, 'Be patient, Kenneth, and put your trust in our good Lord. He will help us to find a way.'

The following day Cynthia went up to Sophie's room. She knocked on the door and waited for Sophie to answer it before stepping inside.

'Sit down, Sophie,' she said, indicating the bed. 'And I hope you won't mind if I join you.'

She sat down on the bed taking care to keep a distance between her and Sophie, then she turned towards her. 'We've noticed that you've been quite unhappy since you've arrived here, and I wondered if there was anything I could do to make things easier for you?'

Sophie looked surprised at her forthright approach, but she just shrugged in response.

'I know it can't be easy for you,' Cynthia continued. 'You have been through a lot recently when all's said and done.'

'You don't know anything about me!' snapped Sophie.

'Oh, I think I do. I know that you're hurting, and I know that you're having trouble settling in with a couple of old odd bods like us. And I know that Kenneth gets on your nerves from time to time.' She detected the faintest hint of a smile, so she continued, hopeful that she was getting through to Sophie. 'It's just his way, dear. He's only trying to help. But, if you want, I'll ask him to give you a bit more space.'

'Why should he care?'

'Because he knows a little of how you feel.'

'What do you mean?' How would *he* know how I feel?'

'Well, because we lost somebody close to us too.'

Sophie didn't say anything, but her face bore an inquisitive expression, so Cynthia continued, surprising herself when her voice cracked a little.

'We had a daughter – Lindsay. She wasn't much older than you. Only seventeen at the time. She'd gone out with some friends and, unknown to us, they were getting up to mischief drinking in the park. She must have had a fair bit by the time she walked home. She didn't notice the car that was heading towards her when she crossed the road. According to the driver, she was completely oblivious.'

Cynthia paused for a moment, trying to keep a grip on her feelings before she continued.

'She was killed outright. It was very difficult for some time after that. She was our only child, and it came completely out of the blue. We had to get used to a life without Lindsay. Our religion helped us to get through and later we decided to look after other children and offer them our guidance.'

Cynthia stopped speaking then, worried she may have caused Sophie more upset by making her reflect on her own grief. But then Sophie raised her head and spoke.

'I'm sorry that happened to you. I know what it feels like. And I'm sorry for being a pain.'

Cynthia made one of her reassuring gestures, patting Sophie on the forearm. 'Don't worry, it's perfectly understandable.' Then she stood up. 'I'm going to leave you alone now till teatime but if you ever want to talk, I'm always here.'

By the time Cynthia left Sophie's room, her eyes were clouding over. It had been difficult reliving what had happened to Lindsay, but it had been worth it in a way because she knew she had just made a huge breakthrough in gaining Sophie's trust.

28

January 2006

Janice was feeling optimistic as she parked her car outside the home of Kenneth and Cynthia Rowbotham and walked up the driveway. Sophie had been living with them for nine months now and she seemed a lot happier in herself. The report from her schoolteacher was good as well. Janice had been so glad to get her away from the influence of Shannon and she felt that with Kenneth and Cynthia's guidance she might even begin to flourish.

Kenneth gave her a cheery hello when she entered the hallway of the Rowbothams' home. The couple had been expecting her visit, but they didn't yet know what it was about.

'Come through to the lounge,' said Kenneth. 'We've told the children we're in a meeting, so they know not to disturb us.'

Janice smiled knowing that the Rowbothams were also now looking after an eleven-year-old boy called Toby. From what they had told her, Sophie had formed a good relationship with the young lad, acting like a big sister to him.

'Hello,' Cynthia greeted. 'I'll just fetch us some drinks and then we can get started.'

Janice thanked her and sat down on the armchair offered by Kenneth.

'Now then,' she began, once Cynthia was back in the room. 'The reason I've called this meeting today is not only for a progress report on Sophie but also because I want to discuss her relationship with her sister.'

'Well, she's doing wonderfully,' said Cynthia. 'She's like a different girl from the one who came to stay with us nine months ago.'

'That's great to hear,' said Janice before coming to the reason for her visit. 'I've been concerned for some time that Sophie hardly sees Kelsey. Unfortunately, their relationship has now been reduced to a brief hello and a smile in the school corridors.

'Although Sophie seems more settled in herself, I'm sure it must trouble her and Kelsey, and I think that we need to try to rebuild their relationship with each other. I also think that now is a good time as both girls are a lot more settled.'

'I totally agree,' said Cynthia while Kenneth nodded his head.

'Well, Cynthia. I was wondering… as you have such a good rapport with Sophie, how would you feel about broaching the subject with her?'

'Certainly, I'll give it a try,' she said.

'Brilliant. Well, I'll sort out matters at the other end and see if I can get Kelsey's agreement too. I'm sure it won't be a problem. Last time I spoke to her, she seemed to regret that they had drifted, and now she finds it awkward trying to get things back on track.'

It was later that day when Cynthia went up to Sophie's room for a chat. Nowadays Sophie was always happy to see Cynthia. She was so easy to talk to and Sophie had drawn comfort in being able to confide in her whenever anything was troubling her.

'Hi, come in,' she said, smiling when Cynthia hovered by the door.

Cynthia parked herself next to Sophie on her bed. 'You already know about the visit from Janice earlier. Well, she mentioned that she would like us to try and rebuild the relationship between you and Kelsey. How do you feel about that?'

Sophie's smile slipped as thoughts of her sister's rejection immediately put her on her guard. 'I don't think she wants to know me since she got her new family.'

'I don't think that's the case, Sophie, not from what Janice has told me anyway.'

But the prospect of listening to Kelsey wittering on about her new family still got to Sophie. And the idea of a reunion filled her with trepidation.

Cynthia seemed to pick up on her unease as she placed her hand on Sophie's arm. 'I know from what you told me previously that you felt excluded by Kelsey when she went to live with her foster family.'

'Yeah, that's right. She's got a new sister now; she doesn't need me anymore.'

'That's where you're wrong, Sophie. Everybody needs

family, real family, and nobody else can take their place.' Sophie thought she detected a tremble in Cynthia's tone, but she quickly calmed herself and continued. 'Look, Janice is aware of the circumstances that led to the problems between you and Kelsey. I'm sure Kelsey now regrets it too. She was probably so excited at the time about getting away from the children's home and going to live with this well-to-do family that she didn't think about your feelings. Or maybe she did, and she just wanted to share her excitement with you.'

Sophie shrugged. 'Well, take it from me, Sophie, Janice will have a word with her to make sure the same thing doesn't happen again. Now, what do you say? Do you want to give it a try?'

'Suppose so,' said Sophie but, despite her apparent nonchalance, she had dreamed for a long time of the moment when she and Kelsey were reunited. She only wished it could be like it was before their mother died. But maybe, just maybe, if Kelsey stopped gushing about her new family and focused on them instead, then things might turn out alright.

29

January 2006

It was another week before Sophie heard anything further regarding the proposed meeting with her sister. Janice sent a message via Cynthia that the meeting would go ahead at the end of the month as Kelsey's foster parents were too busy to schedule it in before then.

Sophie was filled with excitement at the thought of seeing her sister properly for the first time in ages. But she had some doubts too. What would they talk about and would they get along like they used to? She hoped so.

When Cynthia broke the news, Sophie couldn't help but show her eagerness, but Cynthia warned her not to get too carried away. She would need to work at rebuilding the relationship with Kelsey, but Cynthia was confident that it was possible. Sophie knew that Cynthia was right; she was always on hand to offer good advice.

After Sophie had been having a good think overnight, she decided to have a chat with Cynthia the following day about another aspect of her life that she was still struggling with. She arranged to see her in her room after their evening meal but suddenly found herself nervous.

'Come on, Sophie, out with it,' said Cynthia, sitting on Sophie's bed where she had turned to face her. 'I'm sure it can't be that bad. Most things are fixable if you have faith in our good Lord.'

Her kind words gave Sophie the confidence to go ahead. She rushed her words, wanting to get it out of the way as quickly as possible. 'I-I think I might be gay.'

Cynthia pulled her head and shoulders back, her expression one of shock. 'I beg your pardon?'

Unsettled by her reaction, Sophie lowered her voice. 'I said, I think I might be gay.'

'No, surely not!'

'I think so. I mean, I've never fancied boys, but I do fancy girls. In fact, I had a girlfriend, sort of…'

'No, no, no!' Cynthia interrupted. 'I'm sure you've got it wrong, Sophie. You're confused. It's probably because of what you've been through. Who was this so-called girlfriend? Somebody you met in the children's home?'

Sophie lowered her head as she replied, 'Yes.'

'Well, thank heavens we got you out of there when we did.' She took a deep breath, stared pointedly at Sophie and said, 'I want you to put all impure thoughts out of your head, Sophie. That sort of behaviour is not acceptable in the eyes of our good Lord. Now let that be the last of it.'

Then she stood up and walked out of the bedroom.

Sophie was flabbergasted and, although Cynthia had said that was the last of it, she somehow knew that it wouldn't be. Curious, she decided to listen to what Cynthia had to say to her husband. She crept down the stairs and up to the living room door, which was shut. Then she put her ear to the door and listened to the conversation that was taking place.

The first voice she heard was Kenneth's and he didn't sound so happy. 'Surely we can't allow the child to remain under our roof. What if another young girl came to stay with us? It could place her at risk. In fact, if she's been engaging in sexual practices, then Toby could be in danger as we speak. She might have already done something to him for all we know.'

Then Sophie heard Cynthia butt in. 'Now then, let's not get carried away. We don't know that she's done anything to him, do we?'

'Well, what *has* she done? What about this girl she mentioned? Did she say what they had got up to?'

'I didn't ask, Kenneth. I don't want to hear of such practices, thank you very much. Anyway, she *is* only fifteen. As far as I can make out, I think she has acted under the influence of some wicked girl in the children's home, which by the way, I'll make sure I bring to Janice's attention.'

'I should think so too.'

There was a moment's silence. Sophie could feel her own heart pounding, expecting the door to open any minute. But then she heard Cynthia speak again and she pictured her going over to Kenneth and giving him one of her reassuring pats.

'Fear not, Kenneth, this situation is salvageable. God has put his trust in us, don't forget, and I'm sure he will give us guidance on how to cure Sophie of her wicked ways.'

The word 'wicked' cut through Sophie like a sharp knife slicing through her heart. She couldn't stand to listen anymore, so she turned and fled up the stairs and back to her room. Sophie couldn't believe how a few words had changed everything. She had put her trust in Cynthia and like everyone else in her life, she had let her down.

Sophie didn't want to be 'cured'. What the hell did 'cured' mean anyway? How did you cure someone of who they were? She was gay. That was the way she was and why the hell should she deny any of it? If Kenneth and Cynthia wanted to send her away, then let them.

But then she thought about the children's home and dreaded having to return. She also thought about her lovely sister, Kelsey. If she went back to the children's home, would she still get the chance to see her? Sophie was so confused and wasn't sure about anything anymore, except for one thing. She cast her mind back to her life with Kelsey and the day when she had confessed to her about her sexuality. Kelsey had advised her to keep it to herself. She had been right.

30

January 2006

Later that day, Cynthia and Kenneth decided to have a word with Sophie. Cynthia opened the conversation.

'Sophie, I have been speaking to Kenneth about what you told me today. Obviously, as I explained, that sort of behaviour is not acceptable in the eyes of the Lord.'

Kenneth interrupted. 'It's an abomination!'

'Yes, Kenneth's quite right. It *is* an abomination as stated quite rightly in the Bible. Now, in view of what you have told me, we must think about the protection of other children we look after. If we were to have a young girl staying with us, for example, then it could present a problem.'

'No, it wouldn't!' complained Sophie. 'What do you think I am? A rapist or something? I wouldn't do anything to the other children.'

'But you did things in the children's home, didn't you?' Kenneth chipped in again.

Sophie didn't know what to say in her defence, so she sat

in silence while Cynthia carried on. 'We're prepared to let you stay here but only on the condition that you agree to become cured.'

This time Sophie refused to keep quiet. 'Cured? What do you mean cured?'

'Cured of your wicked ways,' said Kenneth. 'We need to make sure that we're not putting the other children at risk.'

'But you wouldn't be,' said Sophie. 'And you can't cure someone of being gay – that's stupid!' she hollered.

'Now then, don't go getting upset, dear,' said Cynthia. 'I think it would be better if we explained what's required of you. We would like to enlighten you with the teachings of the Bible regarding such sexual practices. We will get started straightaway, and every evening until you acknowledge that you understand what behaviour is appropriate and acceptable.'

She turned to her husband who had a Bible in front of him. Kenneth turned the pages till he found the one he was looking for. Then he cleared his throat. 'The following passage is from Romans, chapter one, verses twenty-six to thirty-two.'

'For this cause God gave them up unto vile affections: for even their women did change the natural use into that which is against nature:
'And likewise also the men, leaving the natural use of the woman, burned in their lust one toward another; men with men working that which is unseemly, and receiving in themselves that recompense of their error which was meet.

On and on it went and Sophie found herself switching off until Kenneth read the final verse:

'*Who knowing the judgement of God, that they which commit such things are worthy of death, not only do the same, but have pleasure in them that do them.*'

He closed the Bible and put it to one side, then looked across at Sophie with a self-satisfied expression on his face.

'Do you understand what the words of the Bible are telling us, Sophie?'

When Sophie shrugged in response, Cynthia turned to Kenneth again. 'Would you mind repeating the last verse please, Kenneth.'

He grabbed his Bible, flicking to the relevant page, and read the final verse again, stopping at the word 'death', and emphasising it.

'Do you really want to risk the wrath of God?' Cynthia asked Sophie.

Sophie shrugged again. 'Dunno, doesn't really matter to me. I don't believe in it anyway.'

Cynthia's mouth dropped open wide, and she inhaled sharply.

'Then she'll have to go!' said Kenneth, addressing Cynthia as though Sophie didn't exist.

'Is that what you want, Sophie?' asked Cynthia.

'No, course I don't. I like it here.'

'Then you must agree to adhere to the words of the Bible and put a stop to all unnatural acts. Are you prepared to do that?'

Sophie thought about the situation at the home. Not

only was she at risk of Lloyd telling the staff about her but it would mean more people would find out that she was gay and now it was bad enough that Cynthia and Kenneth knew. What if she never got another foster place because of it?

With all this going around in her head, she conceded to Cynthia and Kenneth's wishes. What harm could it do? All she had to do was listen to a few crappy lines from the Bible then pretend to her foster parents that she wasn't gay anymore.

The Bible readings continued each night after their evening meal, with Cynthia then interpreting the text and explaining to Sophie what was required of her. It was boring and offensive, but Sophie considered it a small sacrifice if it meant she could stay in the foster home. Apart from these activities, life inside the foster home went on as before and Cynthia was more approachable towards her when Kenneth wasn't around.

But one evening, Cynthia asked her to stay seated because they had something else they wanted to discuss with her. 'It's about your forthcoming meeting with your sister,' said Cynthia. 'I think that under the circumstances it would be best if we cancelled it. We could always reschedule when we're satisfied that we have cured you of your wicked ways.'

This news took Sophie completely by surprise. She couldn't believe that Cynthia and Kenneth could be so cruel in the name of religion.

'But you can't do that!' she protested. 'You know how much I've been looking forward to seeing her.'

'It won't be forever,' said Cynthia. 'Only until we think you've made sufficient reparation for your sins.'

'But how long will that take?' Sophie cried.

'Several months I should think,' said Kenneth.

'No! You can't do that. You can't fuckin' do that!'

Cynthia held her hand up, trying to placate Sophie. 'Now then, dear, don't go getting upset. You know that sort of language is unacceptable.'

But Sophie was beyond pacifying by now. 'I don't give a shit what you think is acceptable, and I don't give a shit about your fuckin' religion either. It's all a load of bollocks.'

Then she kicked out her chair, slamming it back into the table before she fled from the room in a rage, to the sound of Kenneth shouting after her. 'Come back here at once. We'll be speaking to your social worker about this behaviour.'

Once she was back inside her bedroom, it took an age for Sophie to calm down. She'd been looking forward to seeing Kelsey for so long and now, when there was only a couple of days to go, they'd stopped her visit. The pain of it was unbearable, and she was sick to death of having religion rammed down her throat because of what she was.

It was only when she became calmer that she began thinking about the implications of what had happened. She doubted whether they'd let her continue staying here. They were going to report her outburst to Janice. And when they did that, she would be taken somewhere else.

She recalled Shannon telling her about the residential homes. Where you had to stay locked in and where the kids were rough and went around beating up other kids while the staff turned a blind eye. She was terrified of ending up somewhere like that and, if that happened, she would never get a chance to see Kelsey.

She had to do something before Kenneth reported her to Janice, otherwise it would be too late. For the rest of the evening Sophie racked her brains thinking about a way around the problem. But after fretting over it for hours, there was only one alternative she could come up with.

She would do a runner. It was the only way. And once she was free of this place she'd see if there was a way of contacting Kelsey and getting her back into her life.

PART THREE

HOMELESS (2006–2007)

31

January 2006

It was the early hours of the morning. Sophie had spent the rest of the evening putting together her most treasured possessions. She had some savings, which should be enough to stay in a B & B for a few nights. Her hope was that she'd find a job so that she could provide for herself and stay in the B & B for a bit longer or maybe even find a place to rent.

Sophie took as much as she could fit inside her suitcase and left the rest in the foster home. She felt the weight of the case and couldn't help but wish she had one with wheels instead of the battered old case her mother had kept for years.

Once she was certain that Kenneth, Cynthia and Toby would be fast asleep, she crept down the stairs and undid the lock on the front door. The door creaked as she opened it, sounding noisy in the still of the night, and Sophie tensed. Taking care to open it as gently as possible, she stopped once it was ajar and slid through the gap and out into the unknown.

After waiting for almost an hour for a bus to arrive, Sophie realised that at this time in the morning they probably weren't running, and she set off on a walk to the nearest town of Rochdale. It took her almost half an hour and when she arrived, shattered from lugging the heavy suitcase all that way, she headed straight for the train station, intending to catch a train to Manchester.

Sophie was disappointed to find that the earliest train was at almost six o'clock in the morning. She checked the time. Ten to three. That meant she had over three hours to pass before the train arrived. There was nowhere open, and Sophie began to panic over what to do. But then she pulled herself together, remembering there was a park in Rochdale that she'd been to with Cynthia. She'd just have to spend the rest of the night there on a bench.

By the time she reached the park, which was about half a mile away, her arms were aching. She was exhausted and just wanted somewhere she could lie down for a couple of hours.

She sneaked inside the park, feeling more nervous now she was away from the streets. Once she was out of view of the entranceway, she found a bench and lay down with her suitcase propped up next to her. But sleep evaded her. The bench was uncomfortable, and she had become aware of strange sounds coming from the trees that ran alongside the pathway.

Sophie tried to calm down, telling herself it was just animals but then a loud screech made her jump. She sat up and looked around, feeling threatened by the ominous night-time gloom, but there was nobody there.

Eventually she dropped off, waking up with a start at what seemed like only a few minutes later. Something had disturbed her; a sound but she wasn't sure what had caused it. She shot up and looked around her, the adrenalin pumping fiercely around her body. There was nothing there. Maybe it was animal noises again.

Sophie checked her watch and was shocked to discover it was only twenty-five minutes till her train was due. Despite carrying excess baggage, Sophie rushed to the station and made it with five minutes to spare. By the time she had bought her ticket and raced to the platform, the train was already waiting to set off. She jumped aboard, found herself a seat and heaved a sigh of relief.

Sophie had hoped for a temporary reprieve from her problems once she arrived in Manchester. At least here she would be able to get a bed for a few nights until she could sort out a way of earning some money. But she was perturbed to find no cheap B & Bs in the city centre. It was full of hotels, and they were expensive.

Desperate, Sophie asked a passer-by where she could find a cheap hotel and she was directed to the Northern Quarter and told that renting a room above a pub would be the cheapest option. She knew that it would be a few hours till the pubs were open so, tired again from dragging the suitcase around, she took up a bench in Piccadilly Gardens and spent the time watching people go about their business.

She was bored, cold, and fed up by the time she arrived at an old-style pub and asked at the bar whether they had any rooms available. The barmaid looked her up and down and Sophie was glad she had topped up her makeup in the public toilets so that she looked older than her fifteen years.

The barmaid shouted through to someone in the back called Brian, and he led her up the stairs and to a vacant single room. Sophie looked around. It wasn't exactly luxurious, but it would suffice as long as it wasn't too expensive.

'How much?'

'Thirty pounds a night, and you get your breakfast thrown in for that.'

'Can I book it for three nights?' asked Sophie, doing a quick calculation in her head.

Sophie was relieved that at least she had found a room and somewhere to sleep for the next three nights. That would give her a little time to see if she could find work. What she would do if she didn't manage to find any work, she didn't know.

As soon as Janice arrived at the Rowbothams' home that Saturday morning, she instinctively knew there was something wrong. Not only did Cynthia's tense body language spell trouble but there was also the fact that Kenneth was hovering uncertainly behind her.

'Is she ready?' asked Janice.

'Not exactly, no,' said Cynthia, a look of contrition pasted on her face. 'I think you'd better come through to the lounge. Would you like a drink?' she asked.

'No thanks,' said Janice.

Cynthia pointed Janice to an armchair and when she perched on the edge of the sofa, Kenneth joined her as though the couple drew strength from their proximity.

'I'm afraid it's about Sophie,' Cynthia began. 'She, erm, she's no longer with us.'

'What do you mean?'

'She's left us.'

'Left you? Why? Where's she gone?'

Cynthia flashed a worried look at Kenneth who picked up the story. 'We don't know. We just got up and she was no longer here.'

'When was this?'

'The night before last. Well, it was yesterday morning when we discovered she was missing.'

'Then why on earth didn't you report it?'

'We-we hoped she'd come back, and then when she didn't return by late last night, we knew we would be seeing you today anyway, so we felt it was best to take it up with you once you arrived.'

Janice tried to stem her annoyance. Instinct as well as their continuing awkward body language told her that there must be a reason why they had chosen to wait. She was about to ask when Kenneth pre-empted her.

'We thought she'd return once she'd calmed down.'

Aah, now she was getting to the crux of it. 'Calmed down? Why would she need to calm down? Was she angry about something?'

Cynthia looked across at her husband again but this time she seemed irritated. 'She was a little upset yes. Kenneth told her we might have to delay the meeting with her sister.'

Then she quickly added, 'We were going to speak with you about it first of course.'

Janice sighed. 'What's this about?'

Then she listened while the couple told her all about Sophie's revelation, their feelings about it and the fact that they had been teaching her the ways of the Bible to correct her unruly behaviour. Cynthia emphasised that Sophie had been willing to change but it was the prospect of not being able to see her sister that had troubled her.'

'For God's sake!' said Janice, unable to hide her anger any longer. 'Do you realise what courage it must have taken for her to open up to you about her sexuality? The poor girl must be so confused.'

'Nevertheless, it's wrong according to the Bible,' said Kenneth smugly.

Janice wanted to say that she didn't give a flying fuck about their religion but she resisted. She was more concerned about the fact that their pious ways had driven a young girl out of the safety of their home.

Janice knew she'd have to speak to her supervisor about the Rowbothams' part in this before deciding on the next course of action. It wouldn't be wise to make any hasty decisions. The couple had been excellent foster parents over the years. Although she was aware of their religion, it had never before presented a problem. But, then again, they had never looked after a child who had openly admitted to being gay.

Her biggest worry was for Sophie, and her heart went out to the poor girl. Janice knew Sophie's history and she also knew that she had nowhere else to go. She hoped there might be somebody unknown to her who might have taken

Sophie in because the alternative was too dire to think about.

As soon as she was back at work and had managed to calm down a bit, Janice called the police. She preferred to report Sophie's disappearance herself rather than rely on the couple who had already let Sophie down, in Janice's opinion.

It was frustrating having to spend almost half an hour on the phone giving them all Sophie's details, knowing she was running late for her next meeting. But Janice hoped that by doing so the police would have a chance of finding her. Finally, once she had finished the call, she took a moment to compose herself.

She hoped to God that the police would find Sophie soon because she didn't like to think of the dangers lurking out there. She was just a young girl, feeling rejected and confused. And the thought that she might be forced to face the dangers of life on the streets filled Janice with horror.

32

February 2006

Sophie's money had now run out and she'd had nothing to eat since breakfast that morning prior to checking out of the pub. Before going she had asked the proprietor if there were any jobs available but had been told there was nothing. She hadn't had any luck elsewhere either. Everywhere she'd tried had wanted references or proof of her age.

It was now night-time, and she had been wandering the streets intermittently for hours, stopping to rest in Piccadilly Gardens when her case became too heavy. It had given her a lot of time to dwell on her predicament, but she hadn't come up with any answers. Sophie knew she daren't return to the foster home.

As she took up her place on a bench for the fourth time that day, tears of desperation rolled down her face. Manchester city centre was a vastly different place at night, and she was frightened, her senses alert to everything that was going on around her. There were all sorts of dubious people hanging around and, as a girl on her own, she felt vulnerable.

On the other side of Piccadilly Gardens, she could see a group of noisy youths heading in her direction. She was tempted to get up and walk but she was tired, and it wasn't practical to do that every time she saw a group of males. At some point, she knew she would have to settle somewhere and get some sleep. Where she wasn't sure, but she would have to figure something out.

The group had stopped a few metres away from her and the sound of their voices carried. They seemed to be joking around together. But then the atmosphere between them turned ugly; Sophie could hear shouting and bad language. She gazed surreptitiously at them and noticed one of them hurling abuse at another, his hands bunched into fists. Then he charged towards him.

Before long, the two lads were engaged in a brutal fight while their friends stood around watching. Scared she might get dragged into it, Sophie got up from the bench and walked away, dragging the heavy suitcase with her once more. She looked over her shoulder to check they hadn't followed her and when she was sure they hadn't she slowed down but carried on walking.

After wandering around for a while longer, Sophie passed the back alleyway to a row of shops in the Northern Quarter. She was tempted to settle down there, but fear inhibited her. She carried on for a few paces, but her arms were aching, and her fingers were burning where they clung on tightly to the suitcase. In the end, defeated by tiredness, she went back. It was dark and forbidding but at least it was out of the view of passers-by.

Before plonking herself down for the night, Sophie looked back at the mouth of the alleyway, making sure nobody had followed her. Then she propped her case against the wall and lay down in the back doorway of one of the shops, trying to ignore the putrid smell of rotten food coming from the industrial waste bins that were dotted about.

Sophie couldn't sleep at first; her eyes were closed but her mind was still open to frightening thoughts and the ground was hard and uncomfortable. It was only when exhaustion overwhelmed her that she finally drifted off.

She woke up with a start shivering from the cold, her teeth chattering uncontrollably. But something else had alerted her; it sounded like squeaking and chattering coming from the huge waste bin that was only about a metre away. She looked up then jumped back in alarm at the sight of three big rats busying themselves rooting through the rubbish. One of them was the size of a cat and Sophie let out a frightened yell.

The dark was oppressive by now, but Sophie was still tired, so she moved on to another doorway away from the rats and settled down to sleep again. The next time she awoke, it was movement that disturbed her. The door against which she had been lying was being pulled open and Sophie felt herself hit the floor with a thump.

Standing over her was a large man carrying a handful of waste. 'Wakey wakey!' he mocked. 'Some of us have got work to do.'

Feeling ashamed, Sophie curled up tight against the wall while the man barged past her and put the waste in the bin. 'Time to go, love,' he said. 'I don't want you staying here. It's bad for business.'

'Yeah, sure,' said Sophie, gathering her stuff together, her face crimson with shame.

She dashed out of the alleyway, and turned into the street, surprised to find another girl leaning against the wall. She was a few years older than Sophie and was wearing a leather studded jacket draped over an abundance of woollens, and she had fingerless gloves on her hands. Her boots were scuffed but looked sturdy and practical and she had a long flowing skirt hanging over them.

As she spoke, Sophie took in her weather-worn features and her tattered hair. 'Did he move you on?' she asked, smirking.

Sophie could feel her cheeks burn with embarrassment. 'Yeah,' she said, turning her head downwards.

'Don't worry about it. Happens all the time. Is this your first night on the streets?'

Despite her embarrassment, Sophie was curious. She looked up again. 'Yeah, how did you know?'

'I saw you last night, lugging that suitcase around. It's a dead giveaway. I'm Lacey by the way.'

'Are you homeless too?' asked Sophie.

'Yeah, shit innit?'

Sophie nodded before asking, 'How long have you been homeless?'

'Only about three months but some of 'em have been on the streets for years. What happened?'

'What, oh, er…'

'It's OK, you don't have to tell me. Let me guess – yer mum and dad kicked you out or you ran away from a kids' home.'

'Kind of,' admitted Sophie.

'My boyfriend kicked me out after a row. Bastard!'

'Why didn't you go back home?'

'I'd already fell out with my mum and dad when I took up with him. They told me he was no fuckin' good and that if I went off with him then not to bother coming back again. It looks like they were right.'

'Oh.'

Lacey grinned. 'Finding it tough, aren't you?'

'A bit yeah.'

'Well, here's some tips from me. But don't think everyone on the street's got your back. Some of 'em would take yer fuckin' eyeballs out and come back for the sockets, especially the druggies. They'll do anything to get a fix.

'The first thing you need to do is ditch the case. When you're on the streets you learn to travel as lightly as possible. You don't want people thinking you've got stuff in there worth nicking either. It should fetch a bit at a second-hand shop, and you'd be best flogging anything else you don't need too.'

'Do you know where there is one?' asked Sophie and she listened as Lacey outlined the route.

'The other thing you'll need to know about is the shelters. There are a few of 'em but you need to get there early, especially for the free ones. They have a queuing system and it's first come first served.'

She told Sophie the names and addresses of a few and Sophie tried to take it in, but she was having trouble remembering all the information. 'How much do the others charge?' she asked.

'Not much. Usually, a fiver a night at the most. Flogging your stuff should help you pay for the first couple of nights.

After that you'll have to manage as best you can, like we all do. Anyway, I need to go now. I've got to speak to someone about my benefits. See yer.'

Before Sophie had a chance to ask her anything else, she was gone. She looked around her, wondering where to go next. Then she thought about Lacey's advice to sell her case and belongings. She was reluctant to do so but at least it would pay for some time in a shelter. Sophie only wished she had known about the shelters before she had spent up on the room above the pub.

She'd taken a mental note of the name of the second-hand shop and knew that it was somewhere on Shudehill, but she'd already forgotten most of the details of the shelters. Sophie didn't know where Shudehill was either, but she asked a woman who pointed her in the right direction. Before she set off Sophie opened her suitcase out on the pavement and transferred the items she really needed into carrier bags, leaving the others inside the case.

The owner of the shop struck a hard bargain and refused to let her have more than twenty-five pounds for her case and most of her clothing. He must have sensed how desperate she was for cash. Despite his stinginess, she walked away from the shop feeling lighter both because she no longer had to drag the heavy case around but also because she had a bit of money for shelter and something to eat.

The only problems remaining for the moment were what to do with herself for the rest of the day and how to find the shelters from the limited details she could remember.

★

It was four days since Janice had reported Sophie missing to the police. Since then, she'd had a call from them asking for further details but, other than that, she'd heard nothing. She'd asked her admin assistant to chase them up the previous day but from what she had told Janice, she hadn't got very far. Growing increasingly concerned for Sophie's safety, Janice decided to ring the police herself to check whether they had any further news.

The person who took the call wasn't the most forthcoming. 'We're doing everything we can,' was the stock answer she received when she asked how things were progressing.

But Janice refused to be put off. 'And what exactly does that entail?' she asked.

She heard the officer take a deep breath and could tell he was feeling put out by her probing questions. Then she heard him tap a few keys on the computer. 'Well, we've spoken to the Rowbothams, but they couldn't tell us anything further. Oh, and we've also contacted the local hospitals and spoken to the staff at the children's care home where she was living.' He sighed, 'But no, I'm afraid no one's been able to shed any light on where she might be.'

'What about her sister? Have you spoken to her?' Janice asked.

'Not yet, no. But, from what we're told, the sister had no recent contact with her apart from the odd glimpse at school. We understand they weren't speaking much lately so it's unlikely that the sister would be able to provide any more information.'

'But she might know somebody; a friend perhaps or a distant relative who Sophie might have gone to.'

The man sighed again. 'Yes, I suppose there is that possibility. I'll make a note to pursue that line of inquiry.'

'And how long is that likely to take?' asked Janice. 'And what about notifying the public to see if anybody might know about a missing girl?'

'I'm afraid we just don't have the resources for that,' the officer snapped. 'If we went to those lengths for every teenager who ran away from home, then we'd need a lot more resources than we have.'

'But she's vulnerable,' pleaded Janice.

This time she didn't receive a response and when the line remained silent for several seconds, she knew she was wasting her time. Janice let out an angry puff of air and cut the call. 'For God's sake!' she muttered, wondering yet again what might have become of poor Sophie.

33

February 2006

Sophie was walking along Market Street in Manchester when she noticed a commotion taking place outside one of the shops. It was only as she drew nearer that she realised her new friend, Lacey, was at the centre of the commotion. She was being confronted by a rough-looking youth with a ragged, pockmarked complexion.

He was squaring up to Lacey and yelling at her, but she was having a go back. Sophie couldn't tell what was being said from where she was but then a man walked up to the youth and grabbed the top of his hoody, his stance aggressive as he muttered something to him. He then shoved him as if to send him on his way.

Once the youth had distanced himself, the crowd began to depart. The man had a word with Lacey who nodded her head and then retreated into a shop doorway where she sat down on the floor. Sophie rushed to have a word with Lacey and check she was alright.

She noticed that Lacey was sitting on top of a folded-up

sleeping bag with an oversized scarf wrapped around her and a dish next to her containing a few coppers. Sophie was shocked to see her begging.

At first, she stood there with her mouth wide open. Lacey looked back. 'You OK? What's wrong? Didn't you expect to see me begging?' Then she chuckled. 'How else d'you think you make money on the streets?'

Sophie felt a pang of guilt. 'Sorry, I didn't mean to stare. It's just, I was a bit shocked, that's all.'

Lacey shook her head slowly from side to side. 'You've got a lot to learn about life on the streets.'

Sophie felt foolish and naïve, and she quickly switched the conversation. 'Are you alright? Only, I saw that guy with you, and he didn't look very friendly.'

'You don't want to know. He's bad news.'

Again, Sophie felt foolish. This conversation was becoming awkward. 'Erm, I'm glad I've seen you actually. I found that second-hand shop and flogged my stuff, thanks.'

'Did he give you much?'

'Not really, no. Twenty-five quid.'

'He's a stingy old bastard. You should have tried to get a bit more out of him. Still, it's a start innit? You going in a shelter tonight then?'

'That's what I wanted to ask you about. I've forgotten some of the names and addresses you gave me.'

Sophie had found a pad and paper, which she had decided to keep in case they came in handy. She fished them out and wrote down the details Lacey gave her.

Feeling obliged to stay a while after Lacey had helped her so much, she hung around making small talk. But then Lacey surprised her by saying, 'Do you mind going now?'

'What?'

Lacey flashed a smile to soften her abruptness. 'Well, I'm not gonna make much money with you hanging around, am I? You're spoiling my lonely and helpless image.'

Realisation dawned on Sophie and she smiled. 'Oh, OK. I'm going.'

'No worries, kidda see you around.' Before Sophie was out of hearing range, Lacey quickly added, 'Make sure you don't leave anything lying around in the shelter or you'll have nowt left in the morning.'

Sophie thanked her and carried on up Market Street.

Despite Sophie arriving early at the shelter, there was still a long queue outside the door. She took up her place and waited for the doors to open. The shelter was a church building a couple of miles outside the city centre in Salford, and Sophie's feet were aching from all the walking by the time she arrived. At least she had got rid of a lot of her stuff, she thought as she glanced at the two carrier bags in her hands that contained her remaining belongings.

She couldn't help but gaze around at the other people in the queue who were a motley crowd. Most of them were young but there were also a couple of older people, one of whom was directly ahead of Sophie in the line. She was what Sophie thought of as a typical bag lady with her tattered clothes hanging in voluminous layers around her scrawny body.

There was a lot of activity in the queue with people chatting and a couple of youths taking swigs from a bottle of cider. But the two most noticeable people were a young couple who were becoming argumentative. Both had coarse complexions and their body language was jumpy as though they had taken some form of drug. This was confirmed when Sophie heard the girl yelling at the youth for using the last of their coke.

Sophie could feel her heart pounding. The couple were making her nervous and she was careful not to make eye contact. Everybody else seemed oblivious to the couple's behaviour though and when the force of a swipe from the youth sent his girlfriend reeling backwards, the old woman stood aside to give her space then cackled when the girl hit the floor.

'Shut your fuckin' gob!' yelled the girl once she had got back onto her feet, and the old woman turned away.

Sophie was relieved when the doors opened, and she hoped that the sight of someone in authority might bring some calm. There was a shift in the queue. The two youths dumped the cider next to the church wall and the girl stormed off down the street, yelling at her boyfriend to fuck off.

The head of the queue had reached the church foyer and Sophie could see four members of staff on the other side of a table taking down details of the guests. When the youth who had struck his girlfriend reached the head of the queue, things came to a standstill. Sophie could see a heated discussion taking place between him and the staff.

Then she jumped in alarm when she saw him hammer his fist on the table before slamming the table back into the staff and then barging his way past the queue of people as he fled the building. The old woman turned back to Sophie and sniffed in disdain. 'I knew they wouldn't let him in. He was as high as a kite. Serves him right.'

Sophie just smiled at the old woman and didn't speak. She was glad to see that the queue had speeded up now and it wasn't long before she reached the table.

The staff took her details, and Sophie was pointed to a side room where food was being served. She hadn't expected that, and she ate every bit, unsure when she would get her next meal. Once they had finished eating, she followed the old woman into the hall where they were to sleep.

The room had that musty smell of old buildings. It was filled with metal-framed camp beds in three rows, placed only a metre apart, and Sophie felt alarmed that they had to share the space with the men. 'There's a bathroom over there,' said the old woman. 'But no one changes for bed here.' Then she cackled again.

Sophie, feeling uncertain, followed the lead of the other guests, taking her belongings with her when she went to visit the bathroom before settling in for the night. Remembering Lacey's words as well as those of the old woman, she kept all her clothes on including her shoes. As she looked around, she noticed the other guests doing the same.

But she was unsure how to keep her bags safe till she noticed the old woman lift the bed and tuck the handles of her carrier bags under the metal frame. Again, she did the same. She wasn't sure how much protection that would provide though. The beds were lightweight, the cheapest kind of camp beds with painfully thin mattresses. Likewise, the bedding was meagre but serviceable with thin duvets and plain covers in the same colour throughout the hall.

Ten minutes later, one of the members of staff announced that it was time for lights out and she flicked the set of switches near the hall doorway. With darkness, Sophie's fear intensified. Many of the guests were still awake and she could hear laughter and frenzied conversations. A man shouted at someone to 'shut the fuck up' and all went quiet for a while.

Then Sophie saw the shadow of a person moving on the other side of the hall. Its movement stopped at one of the beds and was followed by whispered conversation and giggling. From what she could make out, it seemed that someone was getting into someone else's bed.

Sophie lay wide awake for a long time, disturbed by the movement across the hall, and the suppressed groaning. She felt just as ill at ease as she had been in the back alleyway. Even though it was preferable to sleeping on the street, Sophie couldn't shake the knowledge that she was in a room of unpredictable strangers, and she was dreading the moment when she shut her eyes and drifted off to sleep.

34

February 2006

Jake Carter was a cunning youth of eighteen. Tall and slim, he was good-looking with an easy charm, which belied his calculating and, at times, ruthless nature. He had been living on the streets and on his wits for almost two years now and, like many of his friends and acquaintances, he was a drug addict. Despite the ravages of his drug addiction, he had not lost any of his attraction. In fact, the lack of flesh gave his face a chiselled appearance.

He had spotted Sophie when she walked into the dining hall. Her image was the first thing he noticed; attractive in a modern, edgy way with her jet-black hair shaved at one side, her dark eye makeup, and her piercings. She gave off a streetwise vibe, but her body language told him otherwise.

Sophie approached the serving hatch with an air of uncertainty, her appearance shrunken as though she was trying to hide from herself. And even as she ate her food, her eyes darted around the room, alert to every raised voice or sign of a scuffle, her features suffused with fear.

He suspected that her heavy makeup was hiding her real age. At a guess he put her at around fifteen or sixteen, and he deduced that she hadn't been on the streets long. She was probably a runaway like many youngsters who ended up homeless.

He made sure he found a bed on the next row, close to hers, and his friend, Wes, took up the bed next to him. Before lights out he had a quick chat with Wes, making sure nobody else could overhear, especially the new girl.

'See the newbie there?' he asked. 'Don't make it obvious. She's the punky-looking one with the black shaved hair and piercings.'

Wes glanced casually across to Sophie then averted his gaze. 'Yeah, I know the one you mean.'

'Right, well once she's asleep I want you to do me a favour. See them bags she's put under the legs of her bed... I want you to grab one.'

'Why? If you want to nick her stuff, why don't you do it yourself?'

'Don't worry, Wes. I'll see you right. You know I always do, don't you?'

'Yeah, but I don't get it. Why do you want *me* to do it for you?'

Jake put his arm around Wes's shoulders in a show of camaraderie. 'Because, mate, I'm about to become her knight in shining fuckin' armour.'

It was the second night that Sophie had been awoken by a sudden movement. But this time it was the feel of her bed being slowly raised from the bottom end. She sat up, startled, and saw a youth trying to get at her bags. But before she could do anything, another youth had grabbed hold of him and pulled him away, hissing at him, 'Pack it in, you cheeky fucker!'

Once the thief had slithered back to his own bed, the youth who had stopped him, stepped closer to Sophie until she could pick out his features in the dim light of the moon that streamed in through the cheap, flimsy curtains. 'Shush, don't say a word to the staff. I'll deal with the thieving bastard,' he whispered.

Sophie gazed at him inquisitively. 'But why?'

'It'll land him in deep shit. He's not bad really, just needs to learn not to steal from his own. But he's desperate for cash. Don't worry, I'll sort him out in the morning. You get back to sleep. I'll make sure he doesn't try owt again.'

Sophie drifted back off eventually but as soon as she awoke in the morning, the first thing on her mind was the two youths who had disturbed her in the night. She looked across and saw that they were already awake and gathering their things together.

She caught the eye of one of them who sauntered over. 'Thanks for not saying owt about Wes. Like I say, I'll sort him. You alright?' he asked.

Sophie noticed his good looks straight away. That didn't really interest her, but he had a charm and affability that drew her in. She hadn't expected to meet someone so friendly in such a threatening environment. Maybe it was like a community where everyone looked out for each other with the odd exception. First there was Lacey yesterday and now him, and his friendly face together with the way he had come to her rescue in the middle of the night helped her to feel more at ease.

'I'm Jake by the way,' he said. 'And that knobhead over there is Wes. Don't worry, he's alright once you get to know him but he's always looking for an opportunity, and he swoops in on the newbies.'

'Newbies?'

'Yeah, those that haven't been on the streets long. I presume you haven't; I ain't seen you around before.'

'No, I haven't. That was only my second night.'

'Scary innit?' He smiled disarmingly. 'Don't worry, you'll soon learn the ropes. You staying here tonight?'

'Yeah, for a couple of nights but after that, I dunno.'

'Where did you stay last night?'

Sophie blushed, embarrassed to admit it. 'In an alleyway in the Northern Quarter. It was shit.'

'Eh, don't be embarrassed. You do what you have to do. We've all been there. But I can show you better places than that to stay. I ain't got any cash to stay here tonight but I usually hang about in Exchange Square a lot, especially in the evenings. There's a whole crowd of us. We have a bit of a laugh. Why don't you come and find us tonight?'

'I don't know where it is.'

'You doing owt now?' Sophie shook her head. 'Come on, I'll take you.'

Sophie thought she might as well. He seemed friendly enough. It felt comforting to have an ally and after Lacey had been eager to get rid of her yesterday, she figured she might as well latch on to Jake.

By the time they reached Exchange Square they had found

out a lot about each other. Jake had told her all about how he had fled home at sixteen to get away from his abusive stepfather who used to beat him up. He was so easy to talk to that Sophie soon found herself telling him a bit about her life and what had caused her to be homeless.

She confided that her foster parents had been religious maniacs who gave her hell if she didn't fit in with their religious preaching, but she stopped short about confiding in him that she was gay. After the way Lloyd had tried to blackmail her and the extreme reactions from her foster parents, she felt even more uncomfortable about her sexuality and had decided to keep it to herself for now.

'Right, we're here,' said Jake. 'I've got to go now but do you wanna meet back here again tonight? About nine?'

'Yeah, sure,' said Sophie.

She walked away, feeling a lot easier in herself than she had been for some time.

35

February 2006

It was two days later and having spent most of her money on the shelter and food, Sophie had arranged to meet Jake at Exchange Square again that morning. He was already there when she arrived.

'Jesus, you look stressed,' he said.

'I am. I'm out of money and I don't wanna spend tonight in that fuckin' alleyway again. It was bad enough last time but now I've got rid of most of my gear and I'll be freezing.'

'You not got a sleeping bag?'

'No.'

'Right, for a kick-off I'll take you to one of the charities. They give out sleeping bags and other stuff sometimes. You can even get a hot drink there.'

Sophie smiled. She was so glad to have hooked up with Jake.

On the way there she asked, 'What do you do all day anyway?'

'What d'you think? I beg like most of us.'

Sophie didn't say anything, but her face must have conveyed her distaste.

'Eh, don't knock it. You can make a lot of money.'

'Enough for a shelter and food?'

'Oh yeah, and other stuff. Like cigs, and anything else you might be into. I'll take you to my spot on Piccadilly when we've finished here. You can stand back and watch me operate.'

He grinned and Sophie returned his smile.

After they had collected the sleeping bag, Jake asked, 'You got a hiding place?'

'What do you mean?'

'For your sleeping bag and any other stuff. You don't wanna go dragging everything about with you all day unless it's freezing and you wanna use it while you're sat begging. You'll be knackered if you carry on like that.'

Sophie remembered seeing a recess in the wall along the alleyway where she had spent the night. It looked like an old doorway that had been boarded up and she thought that might be a good place to store some things. But she clung on to them for now while she walked to Piccadilly with Jake.

'Right, this one's my spot,' said Jake, stopping outside a shop. 'Go and stand over the other side of the pavement as though you're waiting for a bus and you can watch me in action.'

Sophie did as he asked. Even though the thought of begging didn't appeal to her, the way Jake had spoken about it made it seem like an easy way to earn the money she desperately needed. She couldn't help but feel amused as she watched him shaking a tin and trying to make eye contact with the women who walked by. And it was working, especially with the older ones. He seemed to bring out their maternal instincts.

After half an hour she walked back over to him, laughing. 'You're good, I'll give you that,' she said. 'I think half these women want to take you back home with them.'

Jake flashed one of his smiles. 'I told you it was a good earner. Why don't you give it a try? Not here though. We'll earn more if we separate. That looks a good spot over there just down from that newsagent's.'

Sophie shrugged, unsure. 'Suit yourself, but you'll fuckin' wish you had when you see me going to the shelter tonight and you're sat shivering in that shitty back alleyway.'

In the end, Sophie conceded. She was glad she had kept hold of the sleeping bag as it gave her a comfy place to sit once she had folded it over. But she hated having to beg. Most people looked away and walked by or stared at her with contempt before carrying on ahead. Some people dropped a few coins her way, but she wasn't as successful as Jake.

Sophie felt an overwhelming sense of shame that she had reached this low. What would her mother have thought if she'd have known – and Kelsey? Sophie hoped to God that her sister never found her like this.

As much as Sophie detested asking strangers for money, it seemed like it was the thing to do if you were going to have any chance on the streets. And she grudgingly admitted to herself that as the tin Jake had lent her started to fill up with coppers and silver, she felt a sense of relief. At least she would be able to eat today.

She was finally growing confident in this new role and when a middle-aged man stopped and looked at her, she held out her tin and gave him a smile. But her smile wasn't returned. Instead, he adopted a sneer.

'You must be fuckin' joking! Why don't you go and get a job like the rest of us? You fuckin' dosser!' Then he swiped at the tin, sending the money rolling down the pavement, and he walked briskly away.

'Bastard!' Sophie yelled after him, chasing her coins along the pavement and putting them back into the tin. Nobody stopped to help, and she felt her cheeks burn with humiliation as she negotiated her way around the passers-by on this busy stretch of road while she bent to pick up the coins and put them back into her tin.

Seeing the ruckus, Jake ran over to her. 'You alright?' he asked as he searched through the crowd for the man.

'Yeah, it's alright. He's gone,' said Sophie. 'I can't believe he did that!'

'Better get used to it, Sophie. You'll have to put up with a lot worse while you're living on the streets. Right, I'll leave you to it.'

Once Jake had gone, Sophie felt unsettled. She was no longer able to force a smile at the passers-by, so it was a while before anybody dropped any money into the tin. Any confidence she had felt was now gone and she was back to feeling ashamed, inadequate and scared of what the future held.

She checked the time. It wasn't yet two-thirty and there was no way she wanted to sit about here till the end of the day. As she sat there trying to avoid the hostile gaze of some of the passers-by, an idea came to her. School was due to finish in an hour's time. What was to stop her jumping on a bus and going to meet Kelsey outside the school gates?

Sophie had thought about doing it since she went on the run, but she had been too preoccupied with getting by in the few days since she'd been homeless. Now, though, it seemed like an ideal opportunity. She didn't think Jake would approve of her idea and she felt as though she didn't quite know him well enough to share her thoughts yet. So, she waited till he wasn't looking and took off to the bus stop.

Almost an hour later Sophie was over the road from Moreford Grange High School. She had been careful not to stand too close to the gates in case one of the staff spotted her, so she waited a bit further up the road, taking shelter in the doorway of a derelict shop.

She still had another ten minutes till the bell went so she waited patiently until she saw a few stragglers coming out of the gates and starting to make their way home. The few stragglers soon turned into groups of children, chatting excitedly about their day as they shuffled along the main road outside the school. As the crowd of animated schoolkids grew denser, Sophie suddenly became nervous about seeing Kelsey and she could feel her heart thudding inside her chest.

For a few long minutes, she searched through the sea of faces, anxious to catch a glimpse of Kelsey. When the hordes slowed to a trickle Sophie began to despair of ever seeing her sister. She racked her brains, trying to think whether Kelsey had an after-school club on a Wednesday. But no, she didn't think she did unless she had joined one recently.

Then Sophie spotted them, Kelsey's group of friends. She grew excited, her heartbeat thudding even louder as her eyes took in the girls and she looked amongst them for Kelsey. But she couldn't see her.

In her desperation, Sophie almost rushed to join them. But then she stopped herself, remembering that she mustn't risk being caught. She waited until the girls had walked a few metres then she followed them, keeping her head low and her hoody pulled over so that nobody would recognise her.

When she felt sure they were a safe distance away, Sophie approached the girls and tapped one of them on the shoulder. The girl swung back, a look of alarm on her face.

'I'm looking for Kelsey,' said Sophie. 'Any idea where she is?'

'She doesn't go to this school anymore. She's left. I thought you'd have known.'

Sophie felt put out that Kelsey hadn't told her. But maybe she had planned to at the meeting that never happened. 'No, I didn't. Do you know where she went?'

'I can't remember. But it sounded like some posh school her foster parents wanted her to go to. It's the same school as Leanne.'

Sophie thought of the girl Kelsey now lived with, Leanne, and she couldn't help a stab of envy when she remembered how much her sister used to talk about her. It was only when one of the girls spoke that she became aware of herself, standing silent with her jaw slack.

'We've got to go now. Sorry.'

The girls looked uncomfortable as they took in Sophie's shabby appearance for the last time before walking away. Sophie stared after them. A feeling of dread had settled in the pit of her stomach. She had hoped so much to still be able to get in touch with her sister and now that that possibility had gone, she didn't know how she would cope.

36

February 2006

Despite Jake telling her that they would have money for a shelter that night, it didn't work out that way. By the time it reached five o'clock, Sophie was back at the doorway begging again and it wasn't long before Jake walked over. She noticed that he seemed to be getting jittery.

'Where've you been?' he asked. 'I was looking for you.'

Sophie was still upset from finding out her sister had moved schools and she was worried that if she confided in Jake, she wouldn't be able to hide it. She didn't want him to think of her as a wuss, so she said, 'There was just summat I needed to sort out, that's all.'

Jake seemed to accept her response, eager to be on his way. 'You ready to go for summat to eat?' he asked.

'Yeah.'

'OK, but I've gotta see a mate of mine first.'

'Oh right. Can't we go for summat to eat first? I'm starving!'

'No, I need to see him straightaway,' Jake snapped, and Sophie could see how on edge he was.

She sighed. 'OK. Where are you meeting him?'

'In the Northern Quarter. It won't take long.'

'What do you need to see him for?'

'Fuck's sake, Sophie! You're getting a bit fuckin' clingy, aren't you, considering I've only just met you?'

Sophie snapped back. 'Alright! I didn't mean anything by it.'

'Well, you don't have to come with me if you don't want to.'

'Right then, I won't,' she said.

She walked off and left him in the middle of Piccadilly, furious that he had spoken to her like that. She went into the nearest burger bar and filled up on burgers, chips, and a frothy, milky shake. Knowing she'd still have enough money left for the shelter that night, she also treated herself to a packet of cigarettes then went to the hiding place she had found in the Northern Quarter and hid her belongings.

There was still a couple of hours to pass before the night shelter opened and Sophie was wondering what to do to pass the time. By now she was regretting leaving Jake even though he had annoyed her. She couldn't understand the change in his mood but when she thought about everything he'd done for her, his moodiness didn't seem that bad in comparison.

The other reason she regretted leaving Jake was because he made her feel safe. The streets were already beginning to crowd with evening revellers – amongst them groups of lads acting cocky and aggressive. Then there were the alcoholics and drug addicts to worry about. They could be so unpredictable, and she always felt herself tense when she walked past someone who was acting strange.

Being with Jake also eased some of the boredom. Hanging out with him would be preferable to wandering the streets, which she was now doing, feeling that she would be safer if she kept moving, and puffing on a cigarette to calm her nerves. In the end she decided to swallow her pride and see if she could spot Jake on Exchange Square where he hung out. She might even spot Lacey, the homeless girl who she had met.

When she met Jake, he was like a completely different person from the one she had left in Piccadilly just over an hour ago. As soon as he saw Sophie, he stepped away from the crowd he was standing with and came over to her. As he walked, his movements were animated as though he was pumped up with excitement for some reason. She made the mistake of thinking it was because of her.

'Hi, Sophie, you alright?' he asked, putting his arm around her shoulders in a friendly gesture then lowering his voice. 'Sorry I was a bit snappy before. I was desperate for a fix.'

Sophie was shocked. 'A fix?'

'Yeah, my mate let me have some speed. Don't look so shocked – we all use it. We couldn't fuckin' manage on the streets without it. Anyway, come and join the gang. We're having a good laugh.'

Despite her unease at discovering Jake used drugs, she joined his friends. Wes was amongst them. Sophie didn't like being in his company after he had tried to steal her bag, but she felt assured that Jake would put a stop to him if he tried anything. She presumed he must have taken some speed too as, like Jake, he seemed hyper, but she decided that there was no way she was taking anything no matter what Jake said. She'd heard too many bad stories about drugs and the damage they could do.

Sophie didn't feel as though she fitted in with the crowd. She liked a laugh as much as anyone, but their humour seemed different somehow. They had their own in-jokes and used words and phrases that she didn't understand. Jake had to explain to her what the street slang meant. A lot of it was references to drugs, which made her feel out of place in their company as well as a bit young and naïve.

Sophie checked the time on her old watch as she had been doing every few minutes since she arrived in the square. She turned to Jake and asked, 'Should we go to the shelter now before it gets too late?'

'You'll have to go without me. I'm out of cash; spent it all.'

'What, on drugs?'

'Yeah, not just for me though. I got a mate some too. I owed him a favour. Anyway, it's OK, I've got a place to go. You can come with me if you like.'

'Where is it?'

'Up Deansgate.'

'How much is it?'

'Nowt.'

Sophie saw that some of the crowd were watching her, and Wes was smirking. Suddenly feeling self-conscious, she stopped asking Jake questions. The thought of going to the shelter on her own didn't appeal. She recalled her experience there the first time and some of the dubious characters.

'OK, I'll come with you,' she whispered to Jake.

Jake smiled and patted her on the back. 'Nice one.'

It was a long time before they left the group. Sophie was growing impatient, but she didn't want to draw attention to herself again, so she didn't complain as she waited for Jake. She tried to fit in, but it wasn't easy. When she refused one of the small pills that were being passed around, there was a loud groan of disappointment from everyone.

At last Jake announced that he was going, high-fiving everyone before leaving his friends, with Sophie following behind him. 'Where are we going?' she asked.

'It's a surprise. Just follow me – you'll soon find out.'

As they walked, Sophie remembered something. 'Do you know a homeless girl called Lacey?'

She described to Jake the girl she had met on her first night on the streets and then told him about the incident that had taken place in Market Street. 'Yeah, I know her,' said Jake.

'Have you seen her lately?'

'Not for ages. Why?'

'Well, it's just that I haven't seen her for two days and I was a bit worried in case the guy who was hassling her has done something to her.'

'She's probably OD'd,' Jake quipped.

Sophie was astounded by his casual attitude. 'What? How can you fuckin' joke about summat like that?'

'I wasn't joking. I was fuckin' serious. Anyway, I hardly even knew her.'

'Well, I did! She was really nice to me the first night I was on the streets.'

Sophie was embarrassed when she felt her lip tremble. She had always been so strong but these past few months she seemed to feel the constant need to cry. It was probably because of her mum dying and then losing Kelsey too, she decided, but as she thought about them, the need to cry intensified.

Jake looked across at her. 'For fuck's sake, Sophie. I can't believe you're crying over someone you've only just met. You seriously need to toughen up if you're gonna survive on the streets.'

'I wasn't crying!' Sophie protested, choking back the tears.

Then he seemed to relent, reaching over to her, and putting his arm around her shoulders. 'Come here, you daft cow. You'll be alright with me. Don't worry.'

Sophie didn't speak for the rest of their walk until Jake stopped in the middle of Deansgate just outside the entranceway to a shop. It was wide and had a deep recess that led to the shop door. Jake pointed to it. 'Just wait here in case anyone tries to take that space. I'll be five minutes.'

Sophie eyed up the shop doorway and realisation dawned on her. Surely, he wasn't expecting them to spend the night here! She called after him but he either didn't hear her or he chose not to.

Jake was soon back, carrying with him a sleeping bag and some blankets. 'My hiding place is just behind this row but don't tell anyone,' he said, laughing.

'You didn't tell me we'd be sleeping rough,' complained Sophie.

'What did you expect? A fuckin' five-star hotel?'

Sophie didn't reply but she looked disconcertingly at the clubgoers who were still thronging the streets. 'Don't worry about them. You'll get used to 'em. Anyway, they won't be able to see us much once we're in the sleeping bag. And if they try owt they'll have me to fuckin' deal with.'

She didn't know what to do. It was too late now to go to the shelter, so the only alternative was to pound the streets all night or go back to that alleyway and spend the night alone. Even if she chose to stay with Jake, she'd have to go back there as she'd need her sleeping bag.

'Will you come with me while I get my stuff?' she asked.

'What? Nah, we'll lose this spot by the time we get back. Everyone'll be bunking down for the night soon. You can get in with me. This sleeping bag's massive and we'll keep warmer if we get in together.'

Again, Sophie was doubtful but somewhere in the back of her mind she had already accepted that if she wanted to receive Jake's protection then she would have to do whatever came with it. What choice did she have? She knew she'd have to keep her sexuality a secret; she couldn't risk any further backlash. And the best way to do that would be to have a relationship with a man.

In the end she accepted his offer and snuggled up next to him in the sleeping bag with blankets draped over them and another forming a pillow for their heads. At least it felt cosier than the back alleyway, but she still couldn't settle. Jake took out some pills and offered her one.

'What are they?'

'Vallies. They'll help you sleep.'

'What? Like sleeping tablets?'

'Yeah, that's right. They're harmless. Doctors prescribe them so they can't be bad for you, can they?'

Sophie was hesitant. 'Are you sure?'

He nodded. 'Course I'm sure.'

Sophie needed a good night's sleep, something she hadn't had since she'd become homeless. She was tempted to take one of the pills, but she'd wait first and make sure it didn't harm Jake.

'How do you feel?' she asked after ten minutes.

'Brilliant. Really chilled. In fact, I was just nodding off then.'

That ten minutes waiting for his reaction had seemed to last forever and Sophie hated the prospect of lying awake for hours aware of passers-by looking down on them. She just wanted to close her eyes and be transported away from all this.

She looked intently at Jake. 'OK,' she said. 'Give me one,' and Jake smiled as he popped the pill inside her mouth.

37

February 2006

Janice was sitting in the living room of the Harrises' home while Mr Harris was at the bottom of the stairs shouting at Kelsey to come and join them. Mrs Harris smiled endearingly at Janice and, as she made polite small talk, Janice glanced casually around the room. There was no doubt that it was a lovely home and Kelsey's foster parents seemed good people.

Although Janice had been perturbed when they had discouraged meetings between the sisters, she could understand it in a way. They had wanted the best for Kelsey and to them that meant encouraging her to fit into the new life they had built for her. Part of that process was to manoeuvre her away from her old life and any bad influences. Unfortunately, in their minds, that also entailed separating her from Sophie.

When Kelsey and her foster father joined them in the living room, it was evident from the young girl's relaxed manner towards the Harrises that she got along well with them. But Janice couldn't help but spot her tense reaction when she caught sight of her. Kelsey's taut features spoke of her unease and Janice guessed it was because Sophie still wasn't far from her mind.

'Sit down, Kelsey. Janice would like to speak to us all together,' said Mrs Harris and the girl nestled up close to her foster mother on the sofa as though seeking her comfort.

'I'm afraid I've got some bad news for you,' said Janice, establishing eye contact with Kelsey. 'It's about Sophie.'

Kelsey's face blanched and her foster mother placed a reassuring hand on her arm.

Janice continued, 'She's disappeared from her foster home.' Her words hung in the air and Janice quickly elaborated, wanting to break the tense silence. 'We were hoping she might have returned by now but unfortunately she hasn't.'

Kelsey's hand shot to her mouth and Mrs Harris put her arm around the girl's shoulder and drew her closer till she relaxed her hand. 'It's my fault, isn't it?' she asked.

'Of course it isn't,' said Mrs Harris.

'It is. It's because we're not as close as we were. I tried to be, but she didn't like me talking about me and Leanne, and I could tell she was in a mood whenever we met. That's why I didn't talk to her much in school. I didn't want her being funny with me. Is that why the meeting was cancelled – because she didn't want to see me?'

'No, of course not,' said Janice.

While Mrs Harris tried to reassure Kelsey, Mr Harris addressed Janice. 'Hang on, when exactly did Sophie disappear? Don't tell me she had already gone missing when the meeting was cancelled.'

'Yes, she had. But at that point we still had hopes that she would turn up again.'

'But that's almost three weeks ago. Why are we only just being informed of this?'

This was the reaction Janice had been dreading. 'Like I say, we had hoped Sophie would turn up again. It occasionally happens with children in care. Usually, once they are away from the…' Janice hesitated over the next word. She had been about to say 'safety' but realised that it would have caused more alarm. 'Away from the comfort,' she quickly added, 'of their home, they soon return.'

'But not in this case,' said Mr Harris. 'And where do you think she might be?'

'At this point we're not exactly sure.'

Kelsey began weeping despite Janice's attempt to soften her response to Mr Harris's questions, and her foster mother wrapped her arms more firmly around her and drew her head into her bosom. 'It's OK, Kelsey. She'll be alright. She's probably found someone to stay with.'

'Have you checked?' Mr Harris demanded of Janice.

'Yes, we've been in touch with all known contacts, but nobody has seen her.' Janice then gave her assurances that they were doing everything they could to find Sophie and that the police had been informed.

She thought about the efforts she had gone to personally, ringing the police several times to make sure they had explored every avenue but finding out that none of Sophie's contacts knew anything. She'd even resorted to touring the streets of Manchester herself in the hope of finding Sophie and therefore avoiding this painful meeting.

But, despite showing Sophie's photo to members of the public and calling at several shelters in the city, she had got nowhere. The shelters had refused to tell her anything due to privacy issues and nobody recognised Sophie from the photo.

But she didn't disclose any of this to the Harrises. She knew that the action she had taken was over and above her job requirements, and she didn't want to upset Kelsey any further by highlighting her own concerns for Sophie.

So, instead of elucidating, she asked, 'Is there anywhere you can think of, Kelsey, where your sister might have gone?'

Kelsey shook her head and her crying intensified. For what seemed like an age they sat uncomfortably with Kelsey's sobs the only sounds punctuating the oppressive silence. After politely waiting for a few minutes, Janice made her excuses and was about to leave when Mr Harris stopped her.

'Actually, there's something else we need to discuss.' He turned to Kelsey. 'Would you be OK going to your room for a bit? I promise we'll be up to see if you're alright when the meeting is over.'

Once Kelsey had disappeared upstairs, Mr Harris came straight to the point.

'I think you should know that we would like to adopt Kelsey. She's settled in very well, she and Leanne get on like a house on fire, and I think she would have a good future here with us. We've already discussed it with Kelsey and she's happy with the situation.'

Janice was floored, her mind focusing on how this would affect Sophie if she were ever to find out. 'Oh, I... well, yes... that's excellent. I'm sure Kelsey will be happy here... And, of course, you have my backing.'

Janice felt dreadful as she drove away from the Harrises' home. She had been putting off telling them about Sophie for almost three weeks, which made her even worse than the Rowbothams who she had criticised for their delay in reporting Sophie missing. If only Sophie had turned up, then she could have spared Kelsey's feelings.

But Sophie hadn't turned up and, apparently, Kelsey had been asking questions as to why the meeting with Sophie hadn't gone ahead. Janice had therefore had no choice other than to confront them with the devastating news.

She hoped Kelsey would be alright. But, thinking about how caring her foster parents were and their intentions to adopt her, Janice felt confident that she would have all the emotional support she needed. Although Mr Harris had been brusque with her, Janice understood his reaction. He was only looking out for Kelsey's best interests, after all.

But it was Sophie that Janice was most concerned about. She must have been very troubled to have fled from the Rowbothams' home like that. And the fact that there was nobody she could have gone to made her disappearance all the worse. There was only one place Sophie could be and that was on the streets.

Janice thought of the perils that would face a vulnerable and homeless young girl and her heart cried out to Sophie. She wondered where she had fled to and what she would be doing right now. Wherever she was and whatever situation she had got herself into, Janice prayed that she would be safe.

38

February 2006

'Right, promise me,' said Sophie. 'That if I manage to pull this off, we can spend the night in the shelter.'

Jake shrugged. 'I don't know what's wrong with where we've been sleeping for the past two weeks. If we stay there we can save our money for other things.'

Sophie knew exactly what the other things would be: drugs. But she couldn't really use that argument on him, not when she had been relying on diazepam every night to help her sleep. And then, a few nights ago, she had given in to the temptation and taken some speed. It had seemed like a good idea at the time; all of Jake's crowd had been pressurising her to join in with them and she was sick of being the outsider.

So, she'd done it. And not only had she taken speed, but she'd enjoyed the feeling it gave her; excited and as though she wanted to chat all night about anything and everything. People who previously seemed intimidating, no longer did. She could relate to them and finally felt like she belonged in their group.

That had been the first night she'd had sex with Jake in the shop doorway. It was late when they got there, and she was still high. When Jake had made advances towards her, assuring her that nobody could see what they were doing in the sleeping bag, she hadn't protested. And although she hadn't enjoyed it, she'd been glad to get it out of the way.

Sophie had known for some time that it was inevitable. Jake had been talking as though they were in a relationship together and, although she didn't fancy him despite his good looks, she wanted to stay with him. By now she was realising that being on the streets was all about survival and she had a much better chance if she was with Jake than if she tried to go it alone.

'But if I pull this off, we'll have more money anyway. And I'm sick of being cold. It would be nice just to be warm for a change.'

'Alright, stop whinging. Let's see how much you get and then we'll decide.'

For a while they followed the crowds down Market Street until Jake spotted a potential target. 'There,' he whispered.

Sophie followed his gaze till she saw a man in a bomber jacket with a bulge in the back pocket of his jeans. It was obviously a wallet and Sophie was amazed to think that someone would take such a risk. She snuck up on the man with Jake walking by her side.

Deftly she reached into the man's pocket, feeling the leather under her fingers. Then she grasped it quick and passed it straight to Jake who disappeared in the crowd.

Feeling her touch, the man swung around and faced her. Sophie carried on walking, adopting a casual stride as though she was unaware that there was anything wrong.

'Eh, you! Come back here,' yelled the man, patting his empty back pocket.

Sophie had passed the man by now and she turned back, 'Are you talking to me?'

'Yeah you. You've just swiped my wallet.'

'No, I haven't!' protested Sophie.

Hearing his complaints, a crowd started to gather. As the man accused her, and Sophie continued to protest, a woman in the crowd yelled to Sophie. 'Prove it! Empty your pockets.'

'Sure,' said Sophie, turning out each of her pockets in turn to prove there was nothing in them. 'There, I told you I hadn't taken it,' she said.

The man gazed at her, incredulous, 'But, but...'

'I think what you're trying to say is sorry.'

'Yeah, I think you should apologise to her,' said the woman.

The man flushed. 'I-I'm sorry but you were behind me when I turned around. I thought it was you.'

'Yeah, usual story,' said Sophie. 'Just because I shave my hair and wear piercings, doesn't mean I'm a thief.'

'I'm sorry,' the man repeated. 'I wasn't implying...'

'Save it,' said Sophie. Then she shook her head back as though offended and walked away in search of Jake.

He was just where she thought he'd be, in Exchange Square, and he was wearing a huge smile when she approached him. 'How much?'

'Fifty,' he said, pulling a wad of notes from his pocket. 'I've already dumped the wallet.' He peeled off a few fivers and handed them to her. 'Here's your share. Well done.'

Sophie smiled back but as she gazed at the money in her hand, she felt an attack of conscience. She pictured the man's face when he had realised his wallet was missing. As well as anger she had detected a note of distress in his sad eyes and that was what she could picture now.

She tried to hide her sentiment knowing Jake would see it as weakness. After all, he had been the one who had persuaded her to pickpocket as a quick and easy way to make the money they needed. But the thought of losing your hard-earned money to a thief played on her mind and when she spoke, she failed to hide the tremor in her voice. 'I take it we're in the shelter tonight then?'

Jake grinned but then picked up on her glum expression despite her attempts to disguise it. 'What's wrong?'

'Nothing. I just feel a bit bad about taking that bloke's money, that's all.'

'Well don't,' said Jake, putting his arm around her. 'Don't forget, if he's carrying that much around with him, he's probably got a good job and he can soon earn it back. We ain't got a job, have we? And we've got no chance of getting one either. Who wants to employ people like us who've been living on the streets?'

The reality of what she was hit Sophie hard. Jake was right. This was her life now and there was little prospect of changing it. But the guilt wouldn't go away so, even though she accepted the cash, she vowed to herself that it was the last time she would pickpocket.

The sound of Jake's voice again broke her away from her thoughts. 'You bet we're going in the fuckin' shelter tonight.'

When Jake had arrived at Exchange Square there had been no one around. It was still a bit early for his crowd to appear, but he'd had to wait till Sophie got back from pickpocketing. Now that she was here, he was eager to get away.

'I'm going to see a mate. You can wait here if you want. Some of the crowd might be here in a bit.'

'I'll come with you if you like.'

'No, it's best if you don't.'

'Why not?'

'It just is.'

Without waiting to hear any further argument from her, Jake walked away. Sophie could be clingy and at times he just wanted his own space. Besides, he had a wad of cash in his pocket and he was eager to spend it. She could make do with the speed for now but he was off to score some coke.

Despite his eagerness to take a break from her for a while, he was feeling upbeat. Things were working out fine with Sophie and he could deal with the fact that she was clingy because that meant she was already reliant on him.

He realised that it was only the start. If everything went according to plan, she would become even more reliant on him. He couldn't help but grin at the prospect because once he had Sophie totally dependent, he'd be able to get her to do anything he wanted.

39

April 2006

Sophie had now been homeless for three months and she was getting used to the life. Most of her nights were spent with Jake in the shop doorway because that was his preference.

She knew the reason Jake wouldn't go in the shelter so much. It was because it curtailed his freedom to take as many drugs as he could afford. If the staff spotted that he was high, then they would turn him away at the door and there was no way he'd be able to top up during the night as he sometimes did when they were in the shop doorway.

As well as getting used to the life, Sophie was also becoming more reliant on Jake. At night she was regularly taking diazepam. She was also in the habit of taking speed and cannabis and sometimes snorting cocaine. The drugs helped to numb her to that life making the perpetual cold, fear and uncertainty easier to handle, and she was now enjoying the camaraderie with the group of homeless youngsters. In essence, she was now one of them.

Currently she was in one of Manchester's main stores looking for a good opportunity to pocket something she could later sell on to a dodgy dealer Jake knew in Cheetham Hill. She'd given up the pickpocketing. Even with the drugs inside her and Jake's persuasion she couldn't bring herself to do it again. It was too personal whereas she figured that the big stores could well afford to lose a few items.

Sophie was familiar with the layout in the jewellery department. She had already passed the jewellery counters several times on a recce. One day she had even pretended to consider buying a necklace so she could see how the assistants operated and how the display cabinets worked.

Today she had deliberately chosen a quiet time when there wouldn't be many customers around and, as she walked through the store, she couldn't believe her luck. The girl behind one of the counters had decided to leave her post, shouting to her colleague on the next counter that she would be back soon.

Her colleague looked across, acknowledged her departure then returned to what she had been doing before; stocking up the cabinet that faced away from her colleague's display. Seizing her chance, Sophie quickly ducked behind the counter, kneeling on the floor so no one could see. With her heart pounding, she examined the back of the displays and felt a surge of excitement when she spotted that the silly cow had left the key dangling from one of the locks.

Keeping her head below the counter, Sophie lifted her hand and turned the key. Then she grasped the handle and pulled. The drawer opened easily, and Sophie reached inside, grabbing as much jewellery as she could and stuffing it in her pockets.

With her pockets full, Sophie peeked over the cabinet. Spotting that no one was around, and the other assistant still had her back to her, Sophie stood up, walked round to the display side of the cabinet then strode briskly towards the exit. As she passed the security guard her heart was thundering, expecting him to stop her at any moment. But he didn't and Sophie was soon outside and dashing along Market Street, trying to put as much distance as possible between her and the store.

Her thoughts were now on Jake and how impressed he would be when he saw her haul. He'd previously made out she was soft when she refused to pickpocket. She didn't like that and although she had been determined not to give in to his persuasion by stealing from passers-by, she was still eager to please him.

Sophie was so overjoyed at having pulled off a successful shoplifting trip that she didn't think about the poor shop assistant who would find herself in a heap of trouble when the theft came to light. In her naivety, Sophie hadn't realised that somebody apart from the tycoon store owner would pay for her theft. Instead, Sophie's thoughts were on Jake and what they could buy with the money that the jewellery would fetch. She might even be able to persuade him to spend a few nights in the shelter with her. It would be so good to feel warm again.

When Sophie reached Exchange Square, Jake wasn't there but some of her new friends were. Still a bit wary of them, she decided not to tell them about her haul. She figured that's what Jake would have advised anyway. Despite her mistrust, while she waited for Jake, she passed the time chatting and furtively smoking weed with them.

She liked the feeling weed gave her. It made her feel chilled and helped her escape from her problems.

Jake was feeling pleased with himself by the time he reached Exchange Square and judging by the look on Sophie's face, it seemed he wasn't the only one. He guessed she must have taken something again. As he drew near to the group, she pulled away from them and rushed towards him.

'Jake, I've got some brilliant news!' she panted.

Her vibrancy made him smile. 'I bet it's not as good as mine.'

'What's that?' she asked.

'I've only gone and got us a fuckin' squat.'

'What, you mean…?'

'Yeah, somewhere to stay that's nice and warm and dry, and you won't have to put up with dickheads giving us grief as they walk past.' She went to hug him, but he held her off then lowered his voice. 'Eh, keep it from that fuckin' lot for now. I want us to have first dibs.'

The way he referred to his friends as 'that fuckin' lot' went unnoticed by Sophie who focused instead on the fact that he was taking care of the two of them. 'That's brilliant!' she said. 'Where is it? How did you find it?'

'It's an old office block not too far from here. A mate of mine put me onto it. It's been empty for a few weeks and the rumour is that it won't be redeveloped for fuckin' ages so we should be OK there for a while.'

'Brilliant!' Sophie repeated, thrilled that she had found somewhere to stay at last even if it was only in a squat with an uncertain future. She was so excited that she had almost forgotten to share her own good news until he prompted her.

'I got a load of stuff from the shops. Proper nice jewellery. Wait till you fuckin' see it.'

'OK, keep it hidden for now. I'm gonna say a quick hello then I wanna suss out the squat while it's still a goer.'

It was half an hour later when they arrived at the squat. Jake took Sophie round the back as his friend had instructed. There was a yard there formerly used for service vehicles and a broken window that was boarded up. The board came away easily as his friend had said it would and they crawled through the hole where the glass should have been and went straight up to the second floor as the first floor was full of debris.

Jake was pleased to see that there weren't too many people in there yet, which meant they could get a good spot. A tall guy, in his thirties and looking like a new age hippy with messy dreads, facial piercings and a shabby overcoat, came forward to greet them. 'Hi, I'm Quinn. I presume Travis sent you,' he said.

'Yeah, that's right,' said Jake. 'He's a good mate of mine. I'm Jake by the way and this is Sophie.'

The man shook their hands and said, 'Pick your spot,' freeing his hand and waving it around the room to indicate all the empty space.

'Cheers,' said Jake who had already noticed some dividing screens left over from whichever company occupied the building last. 'Do those belong to anyone?' he asked.

'No, take your pick before they're all gone.'

'What about the mattresses? How do you get them in?'

'That's easy. Once you've got in through the window, you can open the back door. The lock's knackered so you just have to undo the metal bars that secure it. We like to keep it locked when we're not using it though.'

'Sure,' said Jake who had already asked Trav about helping him to bring a mattress from a second-hand shop on Cheetham Hill.

He turned to Sophie. 'Right, we're having that corner over there. Help me take some screens over then you can wait there while I go and get our stuff.'

'But-but, can't I come with you?' she asked.

'No fuckin' chance. That corner and those screens won't keep for long and someone's gotta mind them.'

'Well, I'll go for our stuff then while you stay here.'

'No, it's best if I go. Trav said he can help me fetch a mattress, so I'll sort that too while I'm at it.' He looked at the terrified expression on Sophie's face. 'Eh, you're not fuckin' scared, are you?' She denied it but he'd noticed her looking suspiciously at the people who were already there. 'You'll be alright, y'know. You saw how friendly that guy was.'

Then he remembered something. 'Eh, once we've dragged those screens over, you can show me what you got. Keep it out of view though.' She smiled and he realised he'd managed to switch her attention.

After they'd put the screens in position, affording them a private square area in which they could fit a mattress and a few more items, she removed her haul from her pockets and showed it to him.

'Fuckin' hell! You did do well, didn't you? I tell you what, while I'm out, I'll cash that lot in. It should fetch a fair few quid. I think you and me will be fuckin' partying tonight.'

She still looked a little troubled, so he gave her a spliff. 'Here, have this while I'm gone. That should chill you out a bit till I can get summat stronger.'

Jake grinned as she passed the jewellery over. Everything was coming together nicely. Sophie had proved even easier to manipulate than he'd thought. But then, she was just a naïve kid who was new to the streets. She wasn't doing badly at earning some cash either, although there was room for improvement.

Now they'd got a place to stay, it wouldn't be long till he shifted things up a gear. He'd have to keep working on her, but he was feeling confident. He'd soon have her earning so much that he'd never have to worry about money again.

40

April 2006

Sophie felt nervous in the squat at first. It was full of strange characters and she didn't recognise any of them from the streets. Most of them were male and she had noticed the looks she'd attracted when she walked into the room, which made her feel even more ill at ease.

Taking Jake's advice, she lit the spliff to calm her down, hoping if she smoked it behind the screens, she wouldn't be noticed. But either the smoke or the smell must have given her away because it wasn't long before a rough-looking youth prised apart the gap between the two screens until he was inside the area Jake had designated for them and standing in front of her.

'Give us a spliff,' he demanded.

'It's the only one I've got. My boyfriend gave it me before he went. He'll be back in a minute.'

Sophie was waffling, hoping that the mention of a boyfriend might afford her some protection. But as soon as he knew he wasn't going to get a joint from her, the youth left her alone. She figured it would be safer to stand the other side of the screens in full view of everyone, so she stepped out.

Straightaway, Sophie caught the eye of a skinny youth who came over. He wasn't aggressive-looking like the other youth so although she was still wary, she wasn't quite as nervous. She took in his features: the too-large nose and pasty complexion with sunken cheeks, which were offset by his piercing blue eyes.

He smiled. 'Hi, I'm Skinner. I saw you walk in. Was that your boyfriend?'

Quinn shouted over. 'Eh, I'd watch him if I were you, Sophie. Don't leave anything lying around. He's a bit light-fingered is Skinner.'

'Eh, you're just jealous 'cos I'm a better lifter than you,' Skinner shouted back.

Realising that they were bantering, Sophie joined in their laughter. There was something about Skinner that made her feel at ease even if he was a renowned thief.

'Where were you before?' he asked.

'Here and there,' said Sophie.

'On the streets, you mean?' Sophie nodded. 'I know, it's shit, isn't it? I've been here a few days. It's alright. They're not a bad crowd. That one who came over before, he's harmless really. He's just always on the cadge. Was that your boyfriend you were with?' he asked again.

'Yeah, he's gone to get our stuff and see if he can get hold of a mattress.'

'I'm here on my jack. Well, look at me.' He laughed, his

arms opened wide and fingers splayed so Sophie could take in his skinny appearance. 'The birds aren't gonna want me for my muscular physique, are they?'

Sophie took to Skinner straightaway. He was full of nervous energy and didn't stop talking but that was OK. It was a change to meet someone on the streets who was so open, and she liked his self-deprecating style of humour. They chatted for almost two hours about anything and everything, and it felt good to share certain aspects of her past. Jake hadn't been that interested; it was only the present and immediate future that bothered him.

The time flew by in Skinner's company, and it didn't seem long till Jake walked into the room, hauling a mattress with another man Sophie hadn't seen before. The man, who she assumed was Trav, left him at the door, and Jake called her over. 'Sophie, get hold of the other end of this will yer?'

Smiling at Skinner, she rushed over and helped Jake to drag the mattress across the floor and into the space behind the screens. Then Jake asked her to go downstairs with him where he had left Trav guarding their things. After only a cursory introduction, he said goodbye to Trav then instructed her to help him take their stuff up the stairs.

Once they'd finished arranging everything, Sophie stood back, satisfied at seeing all their belongings together. Compared to how she'd been living for the past three months, it felt homely, and she couldn't resist a smile. 'Thanks, Jake. You've done well.'

'So have you,' he said, pulling a wad of cash from his pocket.

It was then that she noticed he was already high, but she tried not to let it bother her as he counted out the money and gave her half of it. After all, if it weren't for Jake, she wouldn't be here now, and it was much better than sleeping outside in the cold. He might take extra drugs when he was away from her but that didn't stop him providing for her too so she couldn't really complain.

'I've got some other stuff as well,' he said. 'But I'm saving it for later. Once it's dark we'll be able to have it for ourselves without any fucker else trying to nab it.'

Thinking about the guy who'd asked her for a spliff, she knew exactly what he meant. By now she had no qualms about taking drugs. As Jake had said, they made life on the streets much easier than it would have otherwise been.

Sophie gazed around at their little dwelling again and smiled once more, feeling happier and more secure than she had since she'd left the foster home. She had Jake to protect her, a home of sorts and a new friend. Yes, things were definitely on the up for her.

The following day Sophie was at Manchester Central Library with her new friend, Skinner. After telling him what had happened between her and Kelsey and the fact that her sister had left their old school, Skinner had suggested they get in touch with social services. They walked into the reference section of the library and spoke to a helpful assistant who gave them the relevant phone number.

'Come on, we'll do it outside,' said Sophie.

They went down the walkway between the library and the town hall where they knew it would be quieter and more private. Sophie took out her mobile phone and made the call with shaking hands.

'Hello, can I speak to Janice Gibb please?' asked Sophie.

'What's it in connection with?' asked the woman on the other end of the phone.

'Kelsey Tailor.'

'And who should I say is calling?'

'Oh, erm, I'm her cousin. I'm trying to get in touch with her,' said Sophie who had prepared her story for Janice but hadn't expected the person answering the phone to be so inquisitive.

At Skinner's suggestion she was going to pretend there had been an emergency in the family and that she needed to find out how to contact Kelsey. If the social worker wouldn't put her in touch with Kelsey, then she was going to leave her mobile number for Kelsey to phone her. She knew it was risky, but she hoped it might work.

'If you can hold the line, I'll go and see if I can find her.'

Sophie looked at Skinner and let out a breath. 'She's going to fetch her,' she whispered, becoming aware of her racing heart.

After a busy morning, Janice had taken advantage of an eventual lull and had nipped out for coffee. As soon as she walked back through the door into the office, one of the admin support staff, Lynn, came charging over to her.

'There's a call for you,' she said.

Lynn was a busybody who most people had little time for. Judging by her body language and the gleeful look on her face, something had got Lynn excited, and Janice wondered what it might be.

'OK, I'm coming over,' she said, crossing the office and putting her coffee down on her desk. 'Any idea who it is?'

Lynn closed in on her and muttered conspiratorially, 'She says she's Kelsey Tailor's cousin. Eh, what if it's the sister?'

Being the busybody that she was, Lynn knew the stories of most of the children they looked after, and it seemed at times that she revelled in their misfortunes as a chance for a bit of office gossip. Janice tutted at the volume of Lynn's voice, which would have been clearly heard on the other end of the phone. Then she picked up the receiver.

'Hello, Janice Gibb speaking.' But to her consternation the line was dead. 'Hello,' she repeated even though she knew the caller had gone.

She cut the call and glared at Lynn who asked, 'Well, what happened?'

'I'll tell you what happened. She overheard you and decided not to go through with the call. In future, will you learn to be more discreet? There's a young girl out there who desperately needs our help, and, thanks to you, we've probably lost any chance we had of finding her.'

Lynn had the good grace to make herself scarce following her faux pas, but Janice couldn't stop thinking about Sophie for the rest of the day. One of the most satisfying aspects of her job was in making a difference to the lives of the young people she worked with. But with cases like that of Sophie, she couldn't help but feel that she had failed.

If only she had known what had been happening between Sophie and the Rowbothams, there was so much she could have done. But now all she could do was wonder what had become of her and pray that she was safe wherever she was.

41

August 2006

Sophie watched Skinner walking across the old office building and heading towards her. It always amused her how he strode in that particular way of his; trying to mask his self-consciousness with a cocky strut, which he didn't quite manage to pull off. He was full of smiles but that didn't surprise her as he often was, and he nearly always managed to cheer her up. It was the first time she'd seen him that day as he was out by the time she woke up.

'Alright?' he asked. 'Happy birthday to my number-one babe.'

'Cheers but it's not exactly the best way to spend your sixteenth birthday, is it?'

'Could be worse. Anyway, what's the boyf getting you? A diamond necklace, a new merc, a weekend in London?'

Sophie chuckled. 'Yeah, he's probably sorting it out at this very minute.'

'Has he not given you anything yet then?'

'Nah, but he did wish me happy birthday this morning and told me we'd be celebrating tonight.'

Skinner shrugged but didn't say anything. He didn't have to. In the four months since Sophie had been living in the squat, Skinner had got to know her and Jake as a couple and she knew that he didn't think much of her choice of boyfriend. He was also wary of him.

Sophie knew Jake wasn't perfect. Skinner was the one she went to if she wanted cheering up or just someone to confide in. Since she'd met Skinner, she had regained the sense of humour and mischievous streak that had been lacking since she'd become homeless, and she had become more like her old self.

The relationship with Skinner was different to what she had with Jake. He was a friend and would never be anything else. She wasn't attracted to him for one thing, not that she was attracted to Jake but being with a good-looking guy helped her to keep up the pretence that she wasn't gay.

But Jake fulfilled his role of boyfriend in the way she needed. He was her protector, and the one who had taken her under his wing and looked after her when she was new to the streets. He was also her provider. When it came to making money for food, drugs, and anything else they needed, Jake was much better at it than her. He was an adept pickpocket and also gained money by other means that remained a mystery.

Sophie's main concern with Jake was that his drug addiction was spiralling out of control. Virtually everyone she knew took drugs in this new world in which she existed. But, even at her age, Sophie could recognise the difference between Jake and other drug users. With Jake there was a need for more and more drugs and that need never seemed to be fulfilled. She had confided in Skinner about her concerns but, like her, he didn't know what he could do to change the situation.

'By the way,' said Skinner, pulling a spliff from his pocket and handing it to her. 'Here's a little birthday pres.' When she smiled, he added, 'See, I told you to get with me. Here's a guy who really knows how to treat a girl.' Then he stepped up to her and planted a kiss on her cheek. 'Happy birthday, babe.'

Sophie mockingly pushed him away, laughing. 'Fuck off, Skinner, you lech.'

When they'd stopped clowning around, Skinner asked, 'Do you fancy coming shopping?'

Sophie laughed again. She knew that was Skinner's witty way of asking her to go shoplifting with him. 'Yeah, why not? I might get myself a few treats for my birthday.'

It was at that moment that Jake walked in and came straight over to her. Skinner made himself scarce, but Sophie could see that he was waiting on the other side of the room for her.

'You got money?' asked Jake, and Sophie could tell he had already taken something.

'No, why – have you?' Jake shook his head. 'Well, me and Skinner are just about to go lifting. Maybe we'll get something that'll fetch a bit of cash.'

'Ha-ha, I doubt it. You've not exactly been lucky with that, have you?'

'Eh, what about the jewellery?'

'That was fuckin' months ago. What've you lifted lately? A fuckin' scarf that we couldn't even give away, and some makeup that fetched next to nowt.'

Sophie felt wounded by his attack, but she couldn't argue her case, knowing he was right. So, she kept quiet. 'Don't go getting all touchy,' he said.

'I'm not,' Sophie replied but as she spoke, she could hear the hurt in her shaky voice.

'Look, I might have a better idea. Wait here, I just wanna have a word with someone.'

Sophie watched him walk over to Quinn, but she didn't stay put. Instead, she went to join Skinner. 'Sorry but I can't come lifting with you,' she said.

'Why not?'

'Oh, Jake's got other plans.'

'Ooh, maybe it's that big birthday surprise you've been waiting for.'

Sophie feigned amusement but she knew he was being sarcastic. He knew as well as she did that the only gift she'd get for her birthday would be drugs and maybe a few drinks as well to acknowledge the day.

'Sorry,' she repeated. 'We'll do it another day.'

Then she walked back to the corner of the room that she and Jake shared and waited for him to come back.

'Right, it's sorted,' said Jake after he had spoken to Quinn.

'What is?'

'A better way to earn some cash. Don't worry, I'll tell you later but, before that, we're gonna go and do a bit of begging to get some cash so we can sort summat out for your birthday.'

'But I could have gone shoplifting with Skinner.'

'It isn't ready cash,' he snapped. 'And we don't even know if you'll get anything worth flogging. This way at least we'll get the dosh straightaway.'

Jake did have a point. Since he had introduced her to crack a few weeks ago she found herself constantly thinking of ways that she could access more of the drug. And if she went too long without, she felt an intense hunger in her gut that only the drug could feed. So, even though she wasn't pleased at being told she couldn't go out with Skinner, Sophie did as Jake said and followed him out of the building and into the Manchester streets.

Jake was feeling jittery. Even though he'd had a fair bit of coke that morning, he was already craving it again. But his supplier was refusing to let him have any more unless he had ready cash, which was why he was resorting to begging. It would be a while until he'd earnt enough for a fix but, in the meantime, he'd just have to have some diazepam or weed to calm him down a bit.

He was feeling irritated with Sophie. Sometimes she didn't have a fuckin' clue, clowning around with that dickhead Skinner, like the pair of kids they were. But he was the one who earnt all the money to keep them in the drugs she enjoyed so much. It wouldn't do to get snappy with her though, especially today of all days. He needed her co-operation.

But even as the negative thoughts circulated his brain, Jake knew there was a reason he provided for Sophie. It wasn't because he was in love with her or even that he particularly cared about her. She was a nice kid and attractive in her own way. But Jake knew he was a good-looking guy who could soon find himself a replacement.

It was her vulnerability that had attracted him. Jake was smart enough to know a target when he saw one and Sophie had had 'target' written all over her. But he was through with being the breadwinner. He'd always known that it wouldn't last forever. The real reason he'd done it was because Sophie was his investment.

He thought about the conversation he'd had with Quinn and knew that it was time. He'd spent months working on Sophie, building up her trust and making her dependent on him, and it was working. She was now a willing party to any drugs he cared to throw at her. And if she wanted to carry on taking them then it was about time he cashed in on his investment.

42

August 2006

Sophie was back at the squat after spending a few hours begging with Jake. She'd returned alone as Jake had gone to get some supplies, taking with him most of the money she'd collected. He had insisted it would be worth her while as he was going to make sure they celebrated her birthday in style.

When he returned, Sophie was lying down on the mattress waiting. She sat up as she saw him peep round the screen. 'Hi, babe, you alright?' he asked.

Sophie could see that he was in a much better mood than earlier, an obvious sign that yet again he'd already taken some drugs. But she wasn't fazed; she preferred him like this than when he was snappy and picking fault.

'Wait till you see what I've got,' he said, emptying his pockets out and placing an array of drugs onto the mattress.

'Wow! Fuckin' hell, you have got a lot.'

'Shush!' he interrupted. 'Don't let that lot know. I've got

a few cans hidden downstairs. I'll share those around later but this fuckin' lot is for us.'

'How the hell did you afford all that?' asked Sophie. 'We didn't make that much, and you were skint before.'

Jake tapped the side of his nose. 'Never you mind. Nothing for you to worry about. Just enjoy it. Oh, by the way, I got you this too.'

Jake pulled a bracelet out of his pocket. It was plastic and beaded, the type you could pick up from the market for a couple of quid, that is if he had paid for it at all. But at least he had got her something, which showed he cared. 'You might have wrapped it,' she mocked, grabbing the bracelet, and thanking him.

'Oh yeah, 'cos I just happen to have wrapping paper and Sellotape handy.'

Sophie felt a stab of conscience. It was easy to forget sometimes the sort of environment she now inhabited, and her brain could easily drift back to a time of carefully wrapped and tagged presents given with love and kindness.

She thought of her sister who should have been spending this special day with her, but she quickly swallowed down the painful notion. Now wasn't a good time to dwell. It was bad enough having to spend her sixteenth birthday in a squat. But at least she was no longer alone.

She forced a smile, thinking of the celebration they were going to have for her birthday. Jake might have his faults, but he always found a way to come through for her. And later, she would push all recollections of the past to one side; it was her birthday, and she was going to enjoy it in the best way she could.

*

It was a few hours later. Sophie and Jake were seated in an area in the centre of the office floor on old beer crates. Most of the other inhabitants had joined them and were sitting around on a variety of makeshift seats sharing the beer that Jake had brought earlier, and smoking weed.

Sophie and Jake had already taken a few lines of coke before the party started. Then Jake had hidden his drug supplies under the mattress he and Sophie shared, and they went back to it at intervals to top up. They even indulged in some crack, which Jake had brought especially for the occasion.

She felt great, higher than she'd ever felt before. Skinner was amongst the group of friends and they were all having a laugh at some of the things he said and lots of other random stuff that wouldn't have much meaning ordinarily, but which Sophie found hilarious under the influence of a cocktail of drugs.

At some point in the night, Jake went to talk to Quinn who was sitting at the edge of the group, making it difficult to overhear what they were talking about. But Sophie was oblivious anyway; she was too busy carrying on the party with Skinner and some of the others. Somebody was playing music and when one of the few other girls got up to dance, Sophie joined in.

While she was dancing around, enjoying herself, Sophie happened to glance in Jake's direction. He was sitting in a chair across from Quinn now and she could tell from their body language that things were getting heated. Curious, she went over to find out what was going on.

As soon as she approached them, they brought the conversation to a close, but she caught a few words before they finished talking. 'Tomorrow, I promise,' said Jake before spotting Sophie then getting up and walking away.

'It better fuckin' had be,' said Quinn.

Jake didn't reply. He carried on walking back to his area at the corner of the room. Sophie followed him and saw how agitated he seemed as he grabbed a bag of multicoloured pills and popped one in his mouth before offering the bag to Sophie.

Refusing to be distracted, Sophie asked, 'What the hell's going on with you and Quinn?'

'It's nothing. Leave it.'

'But he was really annoyed.'

'I said leave it!'

The fierce tone of his voice took Sophie by surprise and she noticed how he was clenching his jaw with his fists bunched tightly by his sides. Although he often got snappy when he was craving drugs, she had never seen him quite so aggressive, and he wasn't even craving them now.

'Come on, let's get back to the party. It is your birthday after all,' said Jake, pushing past her as he went to join the rest of the group.

Sophie stared at his back, baffled as to what had caused this swift change of mood. But it was obvious she wasn't going to find out anything from him now. And she was still too high to let it bother her that much. She looked across at the rest of the group, most of whom were now up dancing, and decided to go and join them. She wasn't going to let her birthday be spoilt over some disagreement between Jake and Quinn. It was probably nothing to do with her anyway.

The next day Sophie woke up with a throbbing head and shaking hands. She decided she needed something to calm her racing heart but wasn't sure what Jake had left. His supply was tucked away under the mattress and she knew she'd have to disturb him to get at it.

She shook him. 'Jake, wake up!'

'What the fuck?' he asked, yawning, and stretching his arms.

'Wake up sleepyhead,' she said. 'Time to get up.'

She waited till he was fully awake before saying anything further. 'I feel like shit. You got anything?'

'In a bit.'

'Aw no, Jake, now! I feel rough.'

'For fuck's sake! I said in a bit.'

His aggressive manner reminded her of how he had been last night and, determined to get to the bottom of it, she asked, 'What were you and Quinn talking about last night?'

Jake sat up, reaching for his haul, and popping a pill in his mouth. Sophie held out her hand. 'No, not yet.'

'Jake? What the fuck's got into you?'

He sniggered. 'I wish my life was as fuckin' easy as yours… that I could just hold out my hand whenever I wanted summat.'

'But I helped to pay for them. I gave you the money I made yesterday.'

'And who the fuck d'you think pays for most of what we have?'

'Alright, alright, I told you I was gonna do some lifting, but you stopped me.'

'Yeah, because you're fuckin' useless at it.'

'Jake, what the fuck has got into you?' she repeated. 'Is this summat to do with your row with Quinn last night? If so, then I wish you'd stop taking it out on me.'

Jake stared pointedly at her. 'Yeah, it has actually. You're right, you did help to pay for that lot last night but not in the way you think. I wanted to give you a good time for your birthday and I knew we couldn't afford that on what we'd make begging. So, I sold the only fuckin' thing we've got worth selling.'

'Jake, Jake, you're scaring me now. What are you talking about?'

'I'm talking about you, Sophie. I sold you.'

'What d'you mean?' Sophie asked even though she had guessed what he was talking about.

'Do I have to spell it out? Quinn wanted you last night. I said we should leave you to enjoy your birthday first. But I persuaded him to pay up front so I could get the supplies in. So now we've got a debt to settle.'

A pang of fear shot through her. 'No, I won't do it!'

'You've got no fuckin' choice! Like I said, he's already paid, and I promised him he could have you today.'

'But you'd no right to do that. If I'd have known, I never would have agreed to it. I'd rather not have had the party.'

'Oh, you'd have had the party alright, but you'd have expected me to provide everything like you always do. What do you think I have to do to get us all this gear Sophie? I put myself at risk every fuckin' day to keep us supplied. I've done a lot for you. If it weren't for me, you'd still be shitting yourself sleeping next to a fuckin' dustbin. And you just sit there with your hand out expecting it all for nowt. Well now it's about fuckin' time you started earning. It's only a one-off anyway and it's no different to what you do with me, so what's the problem?'

'No, fuck off! I'm not doing it.'

'OK, suit yourself,' said Jake, tucking the bag back under the bed. 'You refuse this, and you'll be back out on your arse, me too. Do you honestly fuckin' think Quinn will let us stay if we don't give him what he paid for? And if that happens, Sophie, you're on your own. Your days of sponging off me are over.'

Sophie could feel the sting of tears, but she fought to hold them back. She didn't want to look like the pathetic little girl he obviously thought she was. She was so angry at what he had done and the way he had backed her into a corner.

If she didn't do as he asked, she would be forced to sleep outdoors again and would need to find a way of getting hold of the drugs he kept her readily supplied with.

'You fuckin' sly bastard!' she yelled, before storming off and leaving him sitting alone on the bed.

As soon as she was on the other side of the screen, she spotted Quinn across the room. Flashing him a look of contempt, she strode straight out of the office and down the stairs. But she hadn't even reached the bottom of the two flights before she regretted her rash action. After her excesses of the previous night, she was desperate for a fix. Her jitteriness of earlier was spiralling into anxiety. Apart from her shaky hands and throbbing head, her heart was racing, and she was taking shallow gasps of air.

At the bottom of the stairs, Sophie stopped while she tried

to take deep calming breaths and think about her options. She had little money for either drugs or food, and nowhere to sleep other than on the streets. What bit of money Jake had handed back to her wouldn't stretch far. She didn't even know any drug dealers outside of the squat, and knew it was risky buying drugs from a stranger.

Sophie was tempted to ring Janice but that meant she'd probably end up back in the children's home where she'd have to do the very thing with Lloyd that she was now trying to avoid. In the end she decided that if she went through with Jake's wishes, at least she'd get a fix.

Back on the second floor she walked over to Quinn and swallowed back the hostile retort that was threatening to erupt. She knew she was beaten so, instead, trying to control the shaking in her voice, she looked directly at him and said, 'Come on then, where do you want me?'

43

February 2007

It was a few months later and life for Sophie was beginning to take on a regular pattern. She was fully addicted to drugs by now and knew as well as Jake did that one of the easiest ways for them to earn money to pay for both their habits was for her to sleep with other men in the squat in return for payment either in cash or in drugs.

Jake earnt his share too, she reasoned to herself, by begging and in any other way he could think of. But she knew that he couldn't make enough on his own to feed both their habits.

Last night had been different. Unlike other nights when she had had sex with one or two men, things had shifted up a gear. Her memory was a bit hazy because she'd been so high, but she had a vague recollection of being passed around the group like a cheap kid's present on Christmas Day. The throbbing between her thighs bore witness to that.

Jake was already out when she woke up, so she went over to see Skinner. 'Fancy doing a bit of lifting?' she asked.

Her hope was that if she earnt enough, she could avoid having to give any more sexual favours tonight. In the sober light of day, the thought of what she had done repulsed her. She now felt dirty and used and vowed to stop doing it. But her resolve was no different than what she told herself every day. The problem was that once the cravings started, the need to make easy money was too strong.

It wasn't long before she and Skinner were on their way to the shops. She could tell he had something on his mind as he wasn't his usual witty self. 'What's wrong, Skinner?' she asked.

He looked awkward as he answered with his own question. 'Do you remember much about last night?'

She flushed. 'A bit.'

'So, you know what you were doing then?'

'Fuck off, Skinner! Who are you to judge?'

'I'm not judging you, Soph. I can see what's happening. It's Jake who's putting you up to it just so he can get more money for drugs. He even offered you to *me*.'

Sophie looked at him, astonished. 'Really?' Then she tried to make light of it to cover up her shock. 'What, and you turned me down?'

But Skinner didn't find it funny. Instead, his face took on a serious expression. 'I wouldn't do that to you, Sophie. You deserve better. What Jake's doing is wrong.'

Unsure how to cover her shame, Sophie was still on the attack. 'Well, we can't all be as fuckin' good at thieving as you, Skinner so we have to find other ways to make money. Anyway, I owe him. He's looked after me ever since I became homeless. I don't know what I would have done without him.'

'Yeah, I bet he doesn't know what he would have done without you either.'

'Look, Skinner, I do what I have to do like all of us. Anyway, it's only the same as what I do with Jake, so what's the big deal?'

'No, it isn't, Sophie. You're in a relationship with Jake. You love him. Well, I take it you do, don't you?' Sophie shrugged. 'Well, you must at least fancy him otherwise why are you with him?'

Sophie couldn't hide how she felt. What Skinner said had hit home, making her realise just what she had done, and she suddenly felt a need to unburden herself. 'It wasn't like that. He was just... just there. And he helped me when I was feeling really scared. And it seemed like if I was gonna be with him then I had to do that. It's what all couples do, isn't it?'

'So, what you're saying is that you went into a relationship with him for what? For protection?'

'Yeah, that's right.'

'So, you don't even fancy him?'

'No, I don't.'

'Fuck, Sophie, I'm confused. Jake's a good-looking guy. I thought you must at least have fancied him. Why not?'

'Because I'm gay, Skinner.'

'Oh, fuck! You're joking.' Then he seemed to realise how extreme his reaction had been. 'Sorry I didn't mean... well, what I mean is, that makes it even worse... what you're doing.'

'Don't you think I fuckin' know that?' she bawled. 'But I don't have a choice, do I?'

Skinner reached over and put his arm around her shoulders and pulled her into him.

'Please, don't tell anyone, Skinner. 'Cos if you do, that'll knacker things up with Jake altogether, and then what will I do?'

'It's no biggie to me, Sophie. You should be who you want to be. But OK, if you don't want anyone to know then I won't tell them.'

She smiled and tried to compose herself. Then she turned to her friend and said, 'Anyway, if we get enough stuff to sell today, I won't have to do it tonight, will I?'

'Right,' said Skinner. 'I tell you what, I'll make fuckin' sure we do.'

Before long they were in the same department store where Sophie had stolen the jewellery almost a year previously. 'It was this counter,' whispered Sophie as they passed it. 'But I could never do it again. I've watched the staff. They always take the fuckin' keys with them if they leave the counter now, and the other staff watch it like a hawk while they're gone.'

'I bet I could pull it off,' said Skinner.

'What? No! Even you couldn't do it Skinner.'

'I bet I fuckin' could. You watch, I'll show you how.'

'No, it's not worth the risk of getting caught,' said Sophie.

'Who said anything about getting caught? I tell you what, if you're worried, keep your distance – then you're not taking any risk. If owt goes down, get the fuck out.'

'You sure, Skinner?' she asked.

'Yeah, course I am. But I might not do that counter. It depends which one's the easiest. I'll have to see.'

'Alright, as long as you're sure,' said Sophie who could

feel her heart begin to race at the prospect of what Skinner was about to do.

They walked back through the jewellery department with Sophie staying a step behind Skinner. As she walked, she found herself eyeing the jewellery counters wondering which one Skinner would hit and when. Ahead of her was an L-shaped counter, and the assistant was at the other side handing a watch over to a customer so she could try it on.

Sophie hardly had a chance to think about the opportunity before Skinner had shot behind the opposite end of the counter and was pulling open the drawer. She carried on walking, keeping her distance as Skinner had advised. But she couldn't help but speed up, her eyes darting around the store. Behind her she heard someone yell, 'Thief!' Then she spotted a security guard racing across to where Skinner was.

She kept a brisk pace. Tiny shivers of fear ran down her spine as she anticipated someone stopping her. But they didn't. A feeling of relief hit her as soon as she walked through the exit. Too afraid to turn back, Sophie took to her heels. She didn't stop running till she was a few streets away.

When Sophie arrived back at the squat, she was still breathless, and her heart was pounding. She dashed up the stairs and found Jake in conversation with two of the other squatters.

'What the fuck's wrong with you?' he asked when he spotted how out of breath she was and then saw her flushed face covered in a sheen of sweat.

'It's Skinner, I think he's been fuckin' nabbed!'

'What? Shoplifting?'

'Yeah.'

She quickly related what had happened to Jake who asked, 'What? You mean you did a fuckin' runner and left him to it?'

'Only because he told me to. He said there was no point in both of us getting caught. I knew it was risky. I told him so. I shouldn't have fuckin' let him do it! Shit, I feel so bad now.'

Jake laughed and Sophie felt a stab of irritation on realising he was already off his face. 'Calm the fuck down. You don't need to feel bad. You don't even know if they've caught him yet. He'll probably be alright.' Then he seemed to notice the worried expression on Sophie's face. 'Here, have this,' he said, pulling a spliff from his pocket and handing it to her. It was Jake's answer to everything.

Sophie took it, but she didn't stay around Jake. His attitude was irritating her. He didn't seem bothered about Skinner. But she was. If Jake were so sure that Skinner would be alright, then why the fuck wasn't he back yet?

44

February 2007

Sophie had never been so pleased to see Skinner who had been gone for three hours. She heard him before she saw him, shouting cheerily to the other squatters who rushed to ask him what had happened. Sophie peeped from behind the screen and caught his eye. He strutted cockily towards her, bouncing even more than usual, a big grin all over his face.

'Don't tell me you got away?' she asked as soon as he reached her.

'Did I fuck! Didn't you see that fuckin' big security guard running over to me. The bastard got me in a bear hug then marched me to the office.'

'Aw, Skinner, I'm so sorry for doing a runner,' Sophie gushed.

'Don't be fuckin' daft. I told you to. There was no point in us both getting caught, was there? Anyway, it was no biggie. They let me off with a warning. Believe it or not, it's the first time I've ever been caught. That bastard security guard shit me up though. I thought he was gonna smack me one.'

'How come you've been gone so long?' asked Sophie. 'Did they keep you in the office all that time?'

'Nah, did they fuck! I just didn't wanna come back empty-handed so I did some lifting in another shop and flogged the gear then had a little spending spree.'

Sophie couldn't help but laugh. 'Shit, Skinner! Here's me, worried out of my fuckin' brain while you're off having a shopping trip.'

'Well, I had to get summat out of it, didn't I? Anyway, I've got you something,' he said, putting his hand into his pocket and pulling out some pills.

'Cheers, Skinner,' said Sophie. 'But I haven't got owt to pay you with.'

'Don't worry about it. You have 'em. Just don't tell Jake. Those are for you.'

'Don't worry, I won't. He's already off his face.'

'I know,' said Skinner. 'Anyway, what do you wanna do for the rest of the day? There's still time to do some more lifting if you wanna make some money.'

Sophie laughed. 'Nah, I think I've had enough for one day. I'm gonna stay here and chill.'

Just then Jake walked over, putting an end to their conversation. But Skinner added a few last words before walking away. 'The offer's still on to come with me if you want, Sophie.'

'No, it's alright. But thanks anyway, Skinner.'

Sophie had spotted the look on Skinner's face when Jake came over. It was a look of contempt. And she knew the reason he had made the offer again for her to go shoplifting with him. It was because if she didn't earn cash that way then Jake would make sure he found another way for her to make enough to keep them in drugs for the rest of the night.

Jake didn't waste any time in coming to the point. 'We're out of coke. Quinn has asked for you. He'll pay me in advance, so I'll go and get us some while you're busy. I've found a new supplier too. He's cheaper so we should be able to get plenty with what Quinn pays us.'

Sophie didn't want to go with Quinn any more than she did any other night but after the day she'd had, she needed something too. Having been taking drugs for a year now, she regularly got cravings and knew the pills Skinner had given her wouldn't be enough.

'OK, I'll do it, but that's the only one tonight. I'm still fuckin' sore from last night.'

Jake didn't say anything but at least he looked a bit guilty. She didn't want to get into a discussion with him about last night; she still felt overwhelmed with shame, so she left their little corner and went in search of Quinn who didn't even wait till she had reached him before he got up off the beer crate that he'd been sitting on.

Sophie changed direction and went towards the storage room that was used as a private area. As she turned, she noticed to her dismay that Jake was already on his way out of the door.

The room wasn't very big and was lined with shelves on either side, which were now empty. On the floor was an old single mattress and it just about fitted into the area. Once the door was shut the room became dark inside, which heightened her feeling of dread.

It was difficult to manoeuvre yourself around the mattress without risking losing your footing. Sophie had accidentally banged herself on the shelves a few times. But, despite all that, Sophie insisted on keeping the door shut. It was bad enough having to do this without doing it to an audience too.

She sat down on the mattress and began removing her clothes. She could only see a vague outline of Quinn who seemed to be doing likewise. Once she was fully undressed, she lay down on the bed and waited but Quinn didn't join her.

'No, not like that,' he said. 'On your knees.'

Sophie turned over and did as he said. It wasn't long until she felt his slimy flesh make contact with her from behind and only moments later before he entered her. She gritted her teeth, as she felt him rub against her tender flesh. Then he began plunging inside her, slowly at first but then faster and more intense. She stifled the urge to squeal as he tore at her insides, knowing that it would soon be all over.

Once he had finished, Sophie put her clothes back on. She could see from Quinn's vague outline that he was getting dressed too. Then he left the room without saying another word apart from cursing as he banged his head on the shelves. Sophie felt the urge to giggle; at least he had got some comeuppance for what he had just done.

In the main office area, Sophie noticed that Jake was already back, and he was sitting chatting to two guys. She walked over. Straightaway she felt annoyed. If he was arranging for her to sleep with even more of them then she was determined to refuse. She was so sore that the thought of having sex with anyone else tonight was abhorrent.

'You got anything for me?' she whispered to him, making sure he knew she expected something in return for what she had just done.

Jake stood up but he seemed unsteady on his feet. 'Yeah,' he said, looking around him as though confused.

He walked across the office to the corner he shared with Sophie and she followed him. From behind he looked as though he was trying to rush but couldn't quite manage it. She could see that he was well drugged up.

When they reached the corner, Jake plunged his hand into his pocket and withdrew a container of white powder, his hands shaking. 'Fuckin' good stuff this.'

'Yeah, I can tell.'

'Fuckin' hell! I well need some more,' he said, struggling to get the lid off the container.

Sophie could see he was becoming agitated, and she went to grab it. 'Give it here.'

She got the lid off and dipped her finger in, holding it to her nose then sniffing it up. While she waited for the rush, Jake also snorted some. 'I can't fuckin' feel it,' he said, pacing the small area around the mattress. 'It's taking fuckin' ages.'

'Give it chance,' said Sophie, noticing how edgy he was. Apart from pacing, his limbs were twitchy.

Jake stopped pacing but his body was still full of movement, his head jerking from side to side and his hands shaky. He managed to put his hand inside his pocket again and he pulled out a little plastic bag containing small lumps of something that looked like rock salt or misshapen sugar cubes.

'Is that what I think it is?' asked Sophie.

'Yeah, crack. We need to heat it up!' He tried to take one of the lumps out of the bag, but it dropped out of his unsteady hands and down to the ground. 'Shit!' he cried, so distressed that he dropped the entire bag and Sophie watched as most of the pieces spilt out and scattered across the floor.

Jake also dropped to the ground, searching frantically for the shattered pieces then desperately trying to collect them and put them back in the bag. But his fingers were clumsy and as the pieces kept dropping back out of his hands, he yelled, 'Fuckin' help me, will you?'

Alarmed at his tone of voice, Sophie quickly dropped to the ground and helped him scoop the crystals back up.

Once they had collected them Jake repeated, 'We need to heat it, but I haven't got a lighter!'

'I can't find mine either.'

'Get someone to help!'

Sophie was glad of an excuse to get away from him. By now the rush of cocaine powder had hit her but she was still aware of what was happening. Jake's behaviour was more extreme than usual, and she wasn't sure about letting him have any crack. She searched for Skinner but was told he'd gone out so, reluctantly, she confided in Quinn.

'Jake's got some crack. He wants to heat it up but I'm not sure he should.'

'Why?'

'I think he's had enough. He's all over the place and getting really worked up. Come and have a look, tell me what you think.'

She dashed back to the corner of the room and pulled back one of the screens to see Jake lying on the mattress and rolling around on his back. His lips had a bluish tint, and he was struggling to get his breath. This was causing him to panic, and he was panting heavily.

Then his movements became more frantic, his body jerking convulsively and out of control. 'Jake, Jake!' shrieked Sophie but, despite his movements, Jake seemed oblivious to the sound of her voice.

Sophie felt someone grab her shoulder and pull her back. She looked up to see Quinn, his expression anxious. 'Get back. He's having a fuckin' seizure,' he said.

Quinn rushed over to Jake and rolled him onto his side. He grabbed hold of a pullover that was lying around, folded it up and gently lifted Jake's head before placing the pullover underneath. Then he loosened Jake's shirt buttons.

Sophie watched in alarm as Jake continued moving fitfully. 'It's OK. It'll be over in a few minutes,' Quinn reassured her.

By this time a few of the others had heard the commotion and were peeping around the screen to see what was happening. One or two of them stepped inside. 'Stand back! Give him some fuckin' space till he comes out of it,' ordered Quinn.

To Sophie it seemed to last forever, and she could feel her heart beating frantically at the sight of Jake. Then it was over, and she felt herself let out a large puff of air. Jake looked up at them, bewildered. 'What happened?'

'It's OK, you just had a seizure,' said Quinn. 'I'd ease up on the fuckin' charlie if I were you though, mate.'

Sophie was just about to say something when Jake had another seizure. By this time, the other squatters had left them to it and she and Quinn were the only two people still there. 'Fuck's sake!' yelled Quinn. 'He's having another one. Call a fuckin' ambulance!'

Gone was his reassuring tone of earlier and Sophie realised that this was serious. She ran out into the office and, noticing that Skinner had now returned, she dashed straight over to him. 'We need to call an ambulance! Jake's having seizures. Quinn thinks it's because he's had too much coke.'

'Fuck!' said Skinner.

One of the other squatters pulled out a mobile phone and quickly keyed in 999. Sophie waited by the phone with him so she could give details to the operator. As soon as the call was over and an ambulance was on its way, she raced back to see if Jake was alright, accompanied by Skinner.

This time when she peered behind the screen, Jake was no longer moving. Instead, he was lying on the bed, still. Quinn was sitting beside him, feeling for a pulse.

'No!' shrieked Sophie.

'Shush,' said Quinn. 'Let me fuckin' concentrate, will yer?'

She waited, and waited, noticing Quinn's features becoming more strained as he felt desperately for a pulse, first on Jake's wrist, then his throat. Leaning over him, he put his ear to Jake's chest, listening for a heartbeat. Then he looked up, his tear-filled eyes meeting Sophie's.

'I'm sorry. He's gone.'

'No!' she screamed, rushing over to Jake while Quinn and Skinner pulled her back.

'Leave him, there's nowt you can do,' ordered Quinn. 'We've got to leave it to the paramedics now.'

'I want a few minutes with him before they get here.'

Skinner looked at Quinn as though seeking approval. 'Alright,' he said. 'Come on, Skinner. We'll wait out there – let her have a few minutes.'

Sophie sat on the bed looking at Jake's inert form. He looked so pale and still. It was hard to believe how full of life he had been not so long ago. But then she remembered how he had been topping up the drugs all day long, how agitated he had been, even more so than usual, and how his drugs problem had been getting more and more out of control.

She realised in that moment that his death had been inevitable. But it was her first experience of death since her mother and it had shocked her. She wept, wiping the streaming mucus on the sleeve of her pullover. It seemed like Quinn and Skinner had only just left them alone when the paramedics arrived, pushing her to one side so they could tend to Jake.

Skinner took her in his arms and led her into the outer office. 'Quinn needs a word with you,' he whispered gently, and Sophie looked over to where Quinn was standing looking troubled.

She walked over. 'Sophie, when they take him, you're not to go with them.'

'What? Why? Why not?'

'Because he's OD'd. Those guys will be on to the cops straightaway. We need to get the fuck out of here.'

Even though she wasn't in love with Jake, Sophie cared about him and to her the thought of leaving him alone was callous. 'No, I need to stay with him,' she said.

'Suit yourself,' he said, 'but I'm off.'

After Quinn had gone, Skinner held Sophie for a few seconds, but she could sense his unease. He pulled away from her. 'You're after going too, aren't you?'

'Yeah, and so should you, Sophie. We're gonna be well in the shit when the cops arrive so you need to get out of here.'

'But all my stuff's over there,' she pleaded.

'It's best to leave it. Come on, I'll help you out till we get settled somewhere else.'

It took Skinner a few minutes to persuade her but eventually he succeeded. Sophie could see all the other squatters getting out of there one by one and she didn't want to be left alone to face the police so she helped Skinner to scoop together as many of his belongings as they could carry. Her things would have to remain where they were as she was afraid of the reaction from the paramedics.

She was bereft. Jake's death had shaken her badly and, now that he was gone, she didn't know what she would do. Her mind was so overwhelmed that she followed Skinner in a zombified state not knowing where they would go or how they would manage.

45

February 2007

Skinner wedged the crowbar under the hardboard that was covering the back window. He and Sophie were back at the office block that had previously been their squat. He heaved till the hardboard gave. Three nails shot out and landed on the floor. Skinner put the crowbar down on the ground and took hold of the hardboard in his hands, tugging at it to prise it fully away from the window.

'Give us a fuckin' hand, Soph,' he said.

Sophie had been standing watching him, her mind on other things. She hadn't wanted to come back to their old squat, but Skinner had persuaded her. In the end it made sense because she had left all her stuff there and was struggling without it. Skinner had helped her out, lending her one of his blankets. But that wasn't enough to protect her against the chill of night.

For the past few nights, they had struggled, having to sleep outside in shop doorways, back alleyways, under the railway arches or anywhere else they could find. Money was tight but they had managed to spend one night in a shelter, which had enabled them to take a shower.

Sophie had taken to begging again but it didn't always provide enough to feed her drugs habit and she found herself with constant cravings. Thank God she had Skinner who sometimes helped her out with the money he had gained through shoplifting. Skinner often found ways of getting hold of stuff, including the crowbar that he had brought with him today.

The sound of Skinner shouting again made her snap to and she rushed to help him drag the hardboard away from the window. Once they had managed to remove it, Skinner took the crowbar again and, checking first that there was no one around, he smashed the window. Together they removed the bits of fragmented glass still clinging to the frame.

'Right,' said Skinner, checking around him once more. 'You ready for this?'

Sophie nodded and when he climbed through the window, she followed him. They sped up the back steps and made their way to the second floor. Their intention wasn't to hang around. As Skinner had said, there was always a risk of the police returning to check on the building so their plan was to grab as many of Sophie's belongings as they could carry and get back out of there as soon as possible.

They made their way to the corner where Sophie used to sleep, and Skinner pulled back one of the screens. Sophie's breath caught in her throat as she stared at the mattress where she and Jake had bedded down. She could picture him, his lips blue, and his skin pallid and the realisation of what had happened hit her again.

For the past few days, she had been plagued by thoughts of Jake's death. It could just as easily have been her or any of the other friends she had lived with in the squat. Knowing she was an addict too made it more disturbing. But she also felt culpable because she had earned the money to supply the drugs that had killed Jake.

'C'mon, Soph, we need to be quick,' said Skinner, rummaging through hers and Jake's belongings and pocketing what he could.

His blasé attitude niggled at her, but she tried to ignore it as she joined him in collecting the items. She couldn't help but notice the way he grabbed at Jake's belongings, though, pushing those he didn't want to one side in his haste to get at the good stuff.

'C'mon,' she said, once she had taken what she could. She was anxious to get out of there. It had stirred up so much emotion in her and she couldn't wait to get away. Then she thought of Jake's words when he had said she had to toughen up if she was going to live on the streets and she fought to stay composed.

Sophie was on her way out of the office door when she noticed Skinner wasn't behind her. She looked back to see him rifling through some other items that had been left behind.

'Skinner, let's go!' she shouted, failing to hide her irritation this time. After what had happened to Jake, she would have expected Skinner to at least show a bit of compassion but all he could think about was what he could get his hands on.

He dashed towards her and spoke, his words edged with excitement. 'Look at this,' he said, showing her an expensive-looking lighter. 'I bet Quinn didn't expect to leave this behind. I always fancied it for myself but could never get near it. Ah well, it's mine now.' He put it inside his pocket.

'You can give it to Quinn next time we bump into him,' said Sophie.

'No chance, what's the point? He won't even know I've got it.'

'The point is, Skinner, it's not yours. It might be a present someone's bought him in the past. He's probably gutted that he's lost it.'

Skinner didn't reply but she knew what he was thinking. There was no way he was going to give the lighter back. That was the only thing she disliked about Skinner; when it came to getting his hands on other people's property, he didn't have much of a conscience.

Sophie decided not to comment. After all, he'd been helping her out for the last few days with the proceeds of his thieving so she could hardly complain. Maybe she was feeling oversensitive because the visit to the squat had affected her more than she thought it would.

When night-time came, they were hanging out with some friends on Exchange Square, passing time till they could bed down somewhere. But Sophie wasn't feeling the camaraderie tonight. She was becoming aware of the fact that she was putting on Skinner and she didn't like having to take handouts from him.

Sophie had thought of a way to earn some money. She'd toyed with the idea for the past day or so, but it wasn't really appealing. Despite her qualms, though, she knew it would be a good earner. Once she had taken some coke and drunk a few cans of beer, she was feeling more confident. Her idea made sense and she now decided to go for it.

'Skinner, there's somewhere I've got to go,' she said. 'Where will you be when I get back?'

'Why, what's happening?'

'Nothing, it's just something I've got to do.'

Skinner looked put out that she wasn't sharing it with him but now that she had become determined to see it through, she didn't want Skinner talking her out of it.

Sophie made her way through the back streets till she arrived at the red-light area, her heart pounding in her chest at the thought of what she was about to do. Along the road she could see scantily dressed girls lining the pavements and looking out for potential customers.

She approached one girl but just as she was about to speak to her a car pulled up and the girl got inside. Sophie made her way to the next girl along the road but as she drew near the girl gave her a sly look and Sophie lost her nerve. She became annoyed with herself and vowed that she would speak to the next girl along.

Her choice was a woman who had dyed blonde hair with the dark roots showing. She was skinny and frail-looking and appeared to be in her mid-thirties. Her feeble state gave Sophie the confidence to speak to her.

'How do I get started?' she asked.

The woman stood back and eyed her warily. Then she laughed. 'I've never heard that one before.'

Sophie felt awkward. 'I mean, y'know, do I have to OK it

with the other girls? I've heard they don't like it if you take their spot.'

'Real newbie you, aren't you, love? I'd go and see her up there if I were you.'

'Who?' asked Sophie.

The woman nodded her head to the next girl along. 'Her with the red hair. Crystal, she's called. She was with that pimp called Gilly till he was put inside.'

'Thanks,' said Sophie, walking away, and the woman laughed again.

'Hi,' she said when she reached Crystal, an older girl with fake breasts and an abundance of makeup.

Crystal smiled at her. 'You alright?'

'Yeah. I... erm... I ... That woman up there told me to come and see you to ask if there's a spot where I can work.'

Crystal's smile grew wider, and Sophie noticed how wild her hair was. It was a punky style and, to Sophie, there was something individual about her. Sophie knew a kindred spirit when she saw one and she took to her instantly.

'It's a pity Gilly isn't around,' said Crystal. 'He would have liked to have you as one of his girls. You're a bit different with your piercings and alternative hairstyle, and sometimes the clients go for different.'

'Who's Gilly?'

'The bloke I was with. He used to look after us girls.'

'Oh, does that mean I can't work here then?'

'No, does it heck. If that's what you want to do then I won't stop you. Is it your first time?'

'Kind of, yeah. But I need the cash.'

'What's your name?'

'Sophie.'

'OK, Sophie. You seem a nice kid so, I tell you what, I'm gonna take you under my wing. Rule number one, never let the clients know your name. Sapphire would be better. Gilly used to give us all jewel names, so he'd like that. In fact, he'll probably take you on when he gets out. Rule number two, don't nick anyone else's pitch.'

'OK, where can I go then?'

Just then a car pulled up and Crystal walked across the pavement towards the driver while she continued to talk to Sophie. 'Walk up the road to where you see the last girl then stand a few metres away from her. You won't get as many clients as the rest of us but you've gotta start somewhere.'

'OK, thanks,' said Sophie.

By this time Crystal had pulled open the car door but she stopped to say one last thing before she sped away. 'If you want to meet some of the other girls, come in the Rose and Crown tomorrow night before work. That's if you last that long.'

Then she was gone, and Sophie carried on to the end of the row of girls as instructed. Now she had taken that first step, she resigned herself to the fact that she was going to do this. She'd slept with plenty of the guys in the squat, so how different could this be?

PART FOUR

CHANGES (2010–2012)

46

April 2010

It was a chilly evening and Sapphire had just come back from the shops. She was glad to get indoors even though it wasn't much warmer inside the squat as the central heating wasn't working.

She was living in an abandoned house on a council estate just outside the city centre. It had been left in a mess after the previous occupants had flitted and Sapphire was now sharing it with Skinner and a few others. The council had boarded it up ready to do some repairs and redecoration before the next tenants moved in, but the squatters had got there first.

As there were only a few of them there, Sapphire had managed to bag one of the smallest bedrooms all to herself. It had taken a while to clean it up and get rid of the smell of cat urine and faeces but with hard work and plenty of disinfectant she'd eventually succeeded. She had even had a lock fitted to the bedroom door so that nobody could disturb her things while she was out.

Sapphire was aware that she was only there temporarily and that eventually she would have to leave the squat as she had done with many others over the years. For this reason, she took care to live minimally so that she wouldn't have too many things to transport onto the streets when the day of her eviction arrived.

Nevertheless, she had a mattress on the floor together with her sleeping bag. Her toiletries and a few clothes were in carrier bags in the corner of the room and the only item remotely resembling a piece of furniture was an old wooden crate she had found lying in the kitchen. She had cleaned it up and upended it so that she could place personal items on the top.

Today the crate would come in handy because it was a special day, and one that Sapphire intended to celebrate. She opened the carrier bag she had brought back from the shops and took out a cake and some candles. She stood the candles on top of the cake then carefully put it down onto the crate. Then she placed a bottle of fizzy plonk next to it together with a plastic cup.

Next, she brought out a card and a pen. Sapphire had spent ages selecting the card as she wanted the words to be just right. She opened it up and read the verse over again, her eyes steamy:

Happy 18th!
For a sister who is thought of all year round
You deserve the very best in life
May you have everything you wish for
And may all your dreams come true
No matter how far we may drift

Our love will always bind us
And distance will never tear us apart
Thank you deeply for all that you are
And for all that we've shared
Have fun celebrating your special day

Underneath the verse she added some words of her own, 'To Kelsey, All my love, now and always, Sophie.' A fat tear dropped onto the card. She tried to brush it away, but it smudged her writing and she grimaced in frustration. Trying to ignore the smear, she stood the card up on the crate, taking care not to place it too near to the candles.

She thought about what Kelsey might be doing to celebrate her eighteenth birthday. Would she be going out with Leanne and other friends? Perhaps her foster parents had arranged a slap-up meal for her or maybe even a lavish birthday party with all their relatives and friends.

But the thought of Kelsey celebrating without her was too painful. She took several deep breaths to calm herself and fought back the tears. She wouldn't let upsetting thoughts stop her from celebrating Kelsey's birthday in her own way. But she'd do it alone knowing that none of the others in the house would understand.

She lit the candles and sang happy birthday to her sister. Then she blew them out and popped the cork on the fizzy plonk. Pouring some into the cup, she held it high. 'To Kelsey,' she said before draining the glass in one huge gulp then refilling it.

'Are you alright?' she heard Skinner shout from outside her bedroom.

'Yeah, fine,' she shouted back, quickly taking the candles off the cake and tucking them out of the way.

'Was that you singing?'

Sapphire picked up the cake and booze and came to the bedroom door. She opened it and smiled. 'Yeah, I'm getting pissed. Fancy joining me downstairs?'

'Sure,' said Skinner. 'What's the cake for?'

'I just fancied it. Come on, we'll take it downstairs and have some of that too.'

All the other occupants were out so Sapphire and Skinner drank the booze between them.

An hour later Sapphire was ready to go out. But she didn't want anyone cramping her style and it had taken a while to persuade Skinner that she wanted to be alone. She headed for Manchester's Gay Village knowing exactly what she was going to do to celebrate Kelsey's birthday, and content that Kelsey would have approved.

She met Lexie in a trendy bar on Canal Street. It was the third time she'd seen her, but they had shared no more than a kiss when they'd previously met. She was a bit older than Sapphire at twenty-one, petite and attractive with her blonde hair in a trendy asymmetrical bob and her clothing smart but understated.

Sapphire had been drawn to Lexie straightaway. She knew that tonight she wanted to take things further. And Sapphire couldn't think of anyone she would prefer to spend her sister's birthday with apart from Kelsey herself, but that wasn't possible.

Thinking of her sister gave Sapphire the courage to be herself and to go for it. So, when they reached the early hours, Sapphire suggested they spend the night together. She knew Lexie lived with her parents, but she hadn't told her about her own situation.

'We can go back to mine,' she said. 'But it's a squat. I hope you don't mind.'

Lexie, a university student, was drunk by this time and she found the prospect of spending the night in a squat more of an adventure than a threat. 'Yeah, let's go for it. I've never been in a squat before. What's it like?'

Sapphire forced a smile. 'You'll find out when we get there.'

When they got out of the taxi Lexie seemed excited. 'How do you get in?' she asked, eyeing the boarded-up windows and doors.

'Round the back, some of the boards are loose.'

She followed Sapphire, jumping through the gap in the open window where the hardboard was loose and following her up the stairs. Taking in the small room where Sapphire chose to sleep, Lexie seemed unperturbed by the lack of home furnishings. Kissing Sapphire passionately, and clasping her buttocks, she was more intent on the reason for her visit.

It wasn't long before they had shed their clothes and were in bed pleasuring each other. Sapphire was burning with desire. Men could never make her feel the way she felt when she was having sex with a woman. And, as the saying went, only another woman truly understands what a woman wants in the bedroom. Eventually, satiated, she drifted off to sleep.

In the morning she was woken by movement and she sat up when she saw Lexie holding Kelsey's card and reading it.

'I didn't know you had a sister,' she said. Sapphire nodded. 'Where is she then?'

'She doesn't live here,' answered Sapphire. 'She was adopted.'

'Aah, right. Did she not want the card when you gave it her? Have you fallen out?'

'I didn't take it to her,' said Sapphire feeling a sense of disquiet.

'Aah, right. So how come you've stood it up here?'

Sapphire sighed, uncomfortable with Lexie's probing questions. She had forgotten about the card when she'd brought her back last night and wished now that she had hidden it. 'It's just to remember her,' snapped Sapphire. 'You wouldn't understand.'

'Aah, right,' said Lexie.

She didn't say anything further but seemed to have become aware that it was a sore subject. Her eyes then began roaming around the room and her expression told Sapphire that she wasn't impressed with what she saw now that she was sober.

'I've got to get back home,' she said, reaching for her clothes.

Sapphire picked up on Lexie's eagerness to escape from the squat. 'OK, I'll show you how to get out,' she said, resignedly, reaching for her own clothes.

Bitter disappointment niggled away at her. She would have liked to carry on what they had started but knew it would be the last time she saw Lexie. It was always the same for Sapphire; the more her partners learnt about her, the less they were inclined to stick around.

And Sapphire realised the sad reality of her situation: it was difficult to maintain a relationship when you were a homeless druggie who sold her body to make ends meet.

47

April 2010

Sapphire smiled as she watched Crystal's hurried entrance into the Rose and Crown. As was often the case, Crystal's hair was sticking up haphazardly and it was obvious she had got ready quickly.

'You wanna drink?' she shouted over to Sapphire as she made her way to the bar.

'No, I'm fine, thanks. I've just got one.'

Crystal rushed back from the bar and plonked herself next to Sapphire. 'Thank Christ I've got time for a quick one before work. It's been a mad rush trying to get Candice ready and drop her at my mum and dad's.'

'You alright?' asked Sapphire.

'Yeah. How are you anyway? Are you still in that same squat?'

'Yeah.'

Crystal gave Sapphire a pitying look. 'I wish you didn't have to, y'know. I'd let you stay at mine but it's bad enough me being on the beat and my parents not knowing. Then there's Candice to consider. And Gilly. He might not like it if there's another girl ...'

'Shush, it's fine,' interrupted Sapphire.

Although she'd never met Crystal's partner, Gilly, she had heard enough about him to know that he could be a problem. He was currently serving time for giving Crystal a savage beating. Knowing the strong character that Crystal was, it was beyond Sapphire as to why she stayed with him. But then, love could do strange things to people, she supposed.

'I wouldn't expect you to put me up,' she continued, steering the conversation away from Gilly. 'I probably wouldn't let another street girl live with me if I had a kid. Anyway, I'm OK where I am. I've got my own room.'

'Yeah, but for how long?'

Sapphire shrugged. 'Dunno, but I'm making the most of it while I'm there. Skinner always looks out for me anyway.'

'OK, no worries. How's your love life anyway? Did you hook up with that girl you were telling me about?'

'Lexie? Yeah, but I don't think I'll be seeing her again.'

'Why not? Wasn't she keen on you working the streets? Is that it?'

'I didn't even get as far as telling her that. I think my living arrangements were bad enough.'

'Oh, stuff her then. If she's gonna judge you like that then she's not worth knowing. You'll meet someone special one day, trust me.'

'Yeah, as long as she's OK about me sleeping rough and working the streets.'

'Eh, you never know, your luck might change. Look at

Ruby. She was once like me and you and now she's got her own massage parlour and a lovely partner.'

Sapphire smiled. She wished she had Crystal's confidence but, as things stood, she couldn't see a way out of the lifestyle she had got herself into. Still, it was good to know that Crystal cared.

When Crystal left the pub, Sapphire watched her walk away and smiled to herself. She had been a godsend since Sapphire had first met her over three years ago and was always on hand with advice if she had any problems. In fact, Sapphire didn't know what she'd have done without her.

48

September 2011

As Sapphire had predicted, she was eventually turfed out of the council house where she had had her own bedroom, and a year and a half later here she was sleeping in the back doorway of a nightclub. She had spent the past few nights there ever since she and Skinner had been kicked out of their latest squat. This day, she woke up to the sound of activity and presumed that the nearby shops and businesses were now open.

As homeless spots went, it was one of the best. Because the door was recessed into the wall, it provided shelter. The building also gave off heat until the early hours, which would be handy in the winter although she didn't intend to be there that long. The sound of the music could be a pain and it meant that even on the nights when she wasn't working, she didn't get to sleep till the early hours.

Ever since Jake's death four and a half years ago, she had worked the beat to fund her drugs habit and keep her supplied with anything else she might need. It wasn't a job she enjoyed, and she had found that, unlike in her first squat where everybody knew her and Jake, some of the clients on the streets could be aggressive and unpredictable. The money was better though so she put up with it because she didn't know of any other way to earn as much.

Sapphire had spent most of the time since Jake died going from one squat to another with Skinner but there were periods like now where she was in between squats and had to make do with sleeping on the streets. She would have preferred to spend her nights in a shelter, but Skinner wouldn't go with her and she couldn't hack staying in those places alone.

She and Skinner had remained friends but she sometimes preferred to do her own thing. That was why she had chosen to spend the last few nights separate from him. Even so, it felt good to at least have someone on the streets who she was close to.

A quick look around told her that, as she suspected, things had started to open up. She decided to go and have a wash before finding Skinner and seeing if he wanted to go for a coffee. It wasn't long before she was on the way to Piccadilly station, taking with her just the items she needed and leaving the rest tucked into a corner of the recess.

In the station she headed for the ladies' and opened the bag she had taken with her, reaching for the cheap facial wash that was packed inside. She wet her face under the tap, cleaned it then rinsed off the facial wash before wiping her face dry with a paper towel. Next, she fished for her baby wipes and ran her hand inside her top so she could clean her underarms.

As she was spraying some anti-perspirant, Sapphire

became aware of someone watching her. She glanced to the side and noticed the look of contempt on the face of a woman nearby. Sapphire shrugged it off. She'd become used to people's attitudes over the years, and she no longer let them bother her. It would have been more private to wash herself inside a cubicle, but the space was so restricted that she only used them to clean her most intimate places.

Later, she was glad to see Skinner waiting for her inside one of the station's coffee shops and tucking into a bacon sandwich. 'Alright?' he asked. 'Have a good night?'

'Oh yeah, 'cos I love trying to fall asleep to the sound of the Black Eyed Peas telling me to Rock that Body or better still the Glee cast and a load of pisshead morons yelling Don't Stop Believin'.'

Skinner laughed. 'Bit noisy then, was it?'

'Yeah, I'm fuckin' knackered now.'

'Could have been worse. You could have had a fuckin' pigeon shitting on you.'

As he spoke, Skinner pointed to the white patch on his jeans, and Sapphire couldn't help but giggle. 'They reckon it's good luck.'

'I fuckin' hope so. I'm gonna have a chat with a few mates later, see if they know of any squats. Let's hope that fuckin' pigeon helps us get fixed up.'

While they talked and laughed Sapphire downed her coffee then went with Skinner to pick up the rest of her things from the back door of the nightclub. They were approaching the nightclub when they saw a dustbin van. The refuse collectors were emptying the bins that lined the back alleyway and Sapphire saw one of them approaching the doorway where she had slept.

'Oh no!' she cried, running to catch up with the man and eager to make sure he didn't collect her belongings. As she watched him picking them up, she yelled, 'Stop! That's my stuff.'

Skinner rang alongside her and shouted at the man who either didn't hear them or chose not to listen. By the time Sapphire and Skinner reached the man he had already thrown her things into the back of the dustbin van.

'That's my stuff you've just thrown,' said Sapphire.

The man turned to look at her. 'Just doing my job,' he remarked casually, walking away.

Sapphire followed him. 'Don't you realise, I've got no sleeping bag or anything for tonight now?' she protested but he ignored her and carried on walking.

Feeling angry by now, Sapphire stormed back to the van, aiming to drag her stuff out of it. This caught the man's attention, and he ran over to her. 'Get out of the bloody thing!' he shouted. 'You could get caught up in the mechanism, you silly cow.'

'But my gear's in there. Stop the machine so I can get it.'

'No chance, it's a load of bloody crap anyway. You lot should get a fuckin' job and get yourselves off the streets instead of dossing around taking drugs and making a nuisance of yourselves.'

When the man turned his back on her and walked away again, Sapphire followed, remonstrating with him until Skinner grabbed hold of her arm and pulled her back. 'It's a waste of time, Sophie. The bastard doesn't give a shit so don't bother wasting your breath. It won't get you anywhere.'

Sapphire stopped and blew out an angry breath of air. 'You're right, Skinner.' Then she yelled after the man, 'He's a fuckin' bastard who doesn't give a shit!'

Once she was satisfied that her words had got through to him, she turned to Skinner with despair etched into her features and asked, 'What the hell do I do now?'

49

'So, what did you do?' asked Crystal.

It was early evening and Sapphire and Crystal were having a few drinks in the Rose and Crown before going to work.

'I went with Skinner to a charity. They were brilliant and got me fixed up with a new sleeping bag and some other stuff – toiletries and that.'

'Aw, that's good.'

Crystal was always good to talk to and they'd built up a solid friendship ever since Sapphire's first night on the beat four and a half years ago. Recently, Crystal's sometime partner, Gilly, had been released from prison and he now took a share of Sapphire's earnings along with some of the other girls who worked for him including Crystal. Sapphire didn't mind too much as it meant she was protected and besides, even if she did mind, she wouldn't be foolish enough to cross Gilly who had a reputation for being nasty at times.

Crystal seemed lost in thought for a moment but then she said, 'Why not ask the charity if they can get you housed somewhere? I believe they have contacts with the council so they should be able to help. In fact, I can't understand why you haven't asked before.'

'I'm not sure,' Sapphire replied. 'I don't really want to leave Skinner to go it alone and I don't think I could have him living with me permanently.' She laughed, making light of her next words: 'None of my bloody stuff would be safe with Skinner around.'

'Sod him then. If he's such a thieving little bastard, then he doesn't deserve your loyalty.'

'But Skinner's stuck by me ever since Jake died.'

'What, and there was nothing in it for him? Are you sure, Sapphire?'

Sapphire thought back to the early days following Jake's death. Yes, Skinner had provided for her initially but ever since she'd been on the beat, she seemed to be the one doing most of the providing. If he wasn't cadging money from her, he was pilfering her gear. She'd had it out with him once or twice, but she could never get him to admit he had taken anything.

She had never fallen out with him though. On the streets she found that most people had their faults. It wasn't that they were all bad people; it was more a case of addiction and desperation driving them to do things they wouldn't otherwise. And, overall, she preferred to be with Skinner than without him. They had the same sense of humour and he always managed to cheer her up. He was also usually the one who found a squat for them.

'No, Crystal, I can't do that to him,' she said. 'But thanks anyway.'

It was later that night and Sapphire had picked up a client. He was younger than most and larger than average but other than that he wasn't much different from any other client; ordinary and plain-looking. Sapphire found that they all blended into one after a while and very few of them were memorable unless they were particularly nasty or distasteful.

She was currently sitting next to him inside his car while he drove to a secluded area round the back of some old mills. It wasn't long before they arrived, and he stopped the car. They'd already agreed straight sex up front, and Sapphire fished in her pocket and pulled out a condom.

'Er, I don't think so,' he said. 'It'll be like eating a fuckin' sweet with the wrapper on, and I ain't paying for that.'

'Well, I won't do it without.'

'Well, I won't fuckin' do it with.'

'In that case you can drive me back to where you picked me up.'

'You must be fuckin' joking!' As he spoke, he lifted his arm to his right.

Sapphire's heart pounded as she heard the mechanism of the central locking. Then he fished for the lever to make the seat recline and, before she knew it, she was lying back with the client on top of her.

Sapphire fought to push him off, but her movements were restricted by the force of his weight. She felt his large clumsy hands clawing at her zipper then dragging down her jeans, his hefty legs forcing hers apart and his vile tongue slobbering all over her face.

She shut her eyes and willed it to be over, praying the man wasn't diseased and that there would be no lasting physical damage. The emotional damage was a given and one that she no longer considered. That was what the drugs were for, so that she could switch her mind off from ordeals such as this and enter a world where it no longer preyed on her mind.

When it was over, he threw the money at her then opened the car door and made her get out. 'Bastard!' she shouted as he drove away. She lit a spliff to calm her shaking hands, took her mobile out and punched in Crystal's number, ready to confide in her friend about her ordeal.

50

November 2011

Sapphire was in the nightclub doorway. It was the early hours of the morning and she had spent the last few hours flitting in and out of sleep. She was used to being woken up by sounds: pigeons cooing, the nightclub music and clubgoers chatting and laughing as they made their way through the city-centre streets. But this time she was awoken by movement.

As she came to, she realised that it was more than just movement. She felt something pressing against her repeatedly from behind and opened her eyes to see a group of young men watching her and howling with laughter. Alarmed, she turned around where she saw one of them lying down, spooning against the outline of her body through the sleeping bag. Sapphire pulled away. Her movements were restricted by the sleeping bag, but she was reluctant to emerge from its relative safety.

'Fuck off!' she yelled at the man who got up off the ground and ran to his mates, sniggering.

To Sapphire's relief they walked away once they had had their bit of fun but, once her relief had worn off, she was furious, and she yelled at them till she could no longer be heard.

'Bastards! You need to fuckin' grow up. Come and fuckin' lie here if you want. I'll swap you for your nice cosy house.'

For the next few hours, she slept fitfully, constantly checking the time on her phone and willing the night to be over. In the end she got up early and went to have a wash before going for some breakfast with Skinner.

Once they were fed, they wandered around for an hour, but Sapphire was shattered so she went back to the nightclub doorway to snatch a few more hours of sleep. She didn't normally sleep in the day as it made her more conspicuous but today was an exception and she gave in to her exhaustion.

Sapphire was glad to see Crystal later in the Rose and Crown. She had been sitting inside the pub nursing a cup of tea when Crystal had walked in and come straight over to her. 'What the fuck's that?' she asked pointing to the cup that gave off a waft of steam. 'You not having a drink?'

'No, I've been feeling a bit sick. I think I've got a bug or summat.'

Crystal raised her eyes. 'You sure it's not summat else?'

Sapphire replied instinctively. 'No! Is it 'eck?' But then a recollection hit her with as much force as a slap across the face. 'Shit! I didn't think of that.'

'What? What is it?'

'That client a few weeks ago who wouldn't wear a condom, the one I told you about. The bastard who forced himself on me even though I told him no.'

'Shit! You could be then.'

'No, no chance. Not after one time.'

'I dunno, Sapphire. It depends on the timing.'

'Fuck no! That's all I need.'

'When did you have your last period?'

Sapphire tried to think back. 'I'm not sure. But now I come to think about it, it was a while ago. Shit, what if I am?'

'Well, there's only one way to find out,' said Crystal. 'You need to get a test.'

It only took a moment's thought for Sapphire. Now that Crystal had put the idea inside her head, she knew it was a distinct possibility. She also knew that she wouldn't settle until she found out one way or the other.

By the time Sapphire went on the beat that evening, she put all thoughts of a possible pregnancy out of her head. She'd deal with that tomorrow. Tonight, she'd focus on getting some business while trying to avoid any dangers, same as she did every night.

She had been standing in her spot in the red-light district when she noticed a car cruising past. She felt sure it had already passed her once and guessed that it was a new client trying to size up the girls before he decided what to do. Or perhaps he was nervous and trying to pluck up the courage to stop.

Two minutes later and the car was approaching again. This time it slowed to a crawl, so she stepped out towards the edge of the pavement to give the driver some encouragement. It passed the preceding girl and came to a stop just next to Sapphire.

As the driver wound down the window and leant across the passenger seat, Sapphire moved nearer then bent forward so she could speak to him through the opened passenger window.

'Want some business?' she asked before she caught sight of the driver and the words got stuck in her throat.

He didn't seem to realise there was a problem. But for Sapphire there was. She recognised him instantly, but it was obvious that he didn't recognise her. 'Yes, how much for straight sex?' he asked.

The sound of his voice in that setting was so wrong and she stared at him in horror, her face ablaze with fury. 'You dirty rotten low-down stinking bastard!' she yelled. 'How could you?'

51

November 2011

It wasn't surprising that he didn't recognise her straightaway. She had changed a lot in the past few years. No longer a girl, she was now a woman of twenty-one with her own distinctive sense of style.

A short skirt showed off her long shapely legs, which would have suited heels, but she had opted for utilitarian boots instead. Likewise, her sexy low-cut top was part-covered with a leather bomber jacket. Sapphire's carefully applied makeup, heavy on the eyes, emphasised her good looks but the addition of facial piercings underlined her individuality. Her hair had changed too. Naturally dark-haired, she now regularly dyed it to a jet-black shade and kept it shaved on one side.

He was much easier to recognise. Although he had aged since she had last seen him, he was still good-looking albeit now bald. His cheeks had filled out a bit, the skin less supple and his eyes were hooded and lined with crow's feet. She did a quick mental calculation and realised that he must have been in his early fifties by now.

Whether it was the sound of her voice or the sight of her angry eyes staring back at him, she didn't know, but suddenly recognition dawned.

'Sophie!' he gasped.

By now he was just as shocked as she was, but Sapphire was in no mood for a loving reunion with her long-lost father. They had parted on bad terms more than ten years ago because he didn't have time for her and her sister Kelsey, just like he had had no time for their mother when he had traded her in for a younger model. And the current circumstances were doing nothing to endear her towards him.

'Fuck off, you dirty old bastard!' she stormed, shifting away from the car.

Sapphire stomped up the street, rage propelling her onwards and as far away from him as possible. Behind her she could hear him shouting, 'Sophie! Come back. I can explain. Sophie! What the hell happened to you?'

'Go away! I hate you!' she screamed as she sped up.

Then she heard the engine start and glanced across to see the car pass by, her father gesticulating at her. She turned away and slid into a side road where she leant back against a grimy wall and waited for her racing heart to steady, glad to have escaped her neglectful father but shaken by the experience.

The first thing Sapphire did the following day when she woke up was to ring Crystal. 'Hi, I'm going for that test later. I thought I might do it in the toilets at the Rose and Crown. Do you want to be there? I could do with it if I'm honest.'

'Yeah, sure but, Sapphire, don't worry about it. Even if you are pregnant, it's not the end of the world. There are things you can do, y'know.'

'I don't want to think about that right now,' said Sapphire, a little sharper than she had intended. Maybe it was the sight of her father last night that had brought back memories of family ties, and she needed to confide in someone. 'Eh, you'll never guess who I bumped into last night.'

'Go on.'

'Only my bastard of a father.'

'I take it you weren't happy to see him then.'

'No way! The twat was only trying to do a bit of business with me would you believe?'

'What? With his own daughter? The sick fuck!'

'Oh, he didn't know it was me at first. I haven't seen him for over ten years. But still…'

'I hope you told him where to go.'

'Dead right! I didn't need him when I was a kid, and I don't fuckin' need him now.'

'Good for you,' said Crystal who had already heard the story of Sapphire's childhood.

Sapphire eventually cut the call and, when she was ready, she made her way to Market Street and called at Boots for a pregnancy testing kit. She arrived at the Rose and Crown late afternoon. She had deliberately arranged to meet Crystal earlier than usual to ensure that none of the other girls were in the pub. This was information she wasn't yet ready to share with everybody.

Crystal didn't arrive on time and Sapphire grew impatient, eager to get the test over and done with. By the time Crystal was half an hour late, Sapphire was toying with the idea of doing the test alone. She decided to finish her drink of water first and then do it. When she had almost drained the glass, Crystal arrived looking frazzled and a bit out of breath.

'Sorry, Sapphire. I had to drop Candice at my mum's, and she was that busy gabbing that I couldn't get away.'

Sapphire forced a smile. 'Do you mind if we do it straightaway?'

'Come on then,' said Crystal, leading the way to the ladies' toilets.

Once inside, Sapphire dashed into a cubicle and carried out the test. She emerged and stared at Crystal who looked as apprehensive as she felt. They waited for the test to take effect, Sapphire willing the time to pass, knowing that the longer she waited the less chance there would be of the blue line appearing.

But she was out of luck. When the blue line appeared, she tried to tell herself that she was imagining it but as time elapsed the line became clearer until there was no doubt in her mind. She was pregnant!

'Shit no!' she yelled.

'Oh my God! I was right,' said Crystal. 'What are you gonna do?'

But Sapphire hadn't even got her head round the fact that she was pregnant yet. She was surprised to hear her voice crack when she replied, 'I don't know, Crystal. I just don't fuckin' know!'

52

November 2011

Janice knocked on the door of the three-bedroomed semi and waited for an answer. It wasn't long before Roy Tailor appeared at the door. She hadn't seen him for around ten years and had never liked the man, knowing he had abandoned his daughters in favour of his new family.

He had aged since she'd last seen him, but he still retained his charming manner, beaming a smile as he led her through to the lounge. Janice wasn't taken in by it though; she knew exactly what the man was. In her job she'd come across his type many times before.

She hadn't wanted to come here but he had rung her several times insisting that he needed to tell her something. And, according to him, it was too important to discuss over the phone. So, reluctantly she'd finally made the visit. Strictly speaking, she wasn't obliged to call. His older daughters were no longer children, assuming that's what he wanted to discuss. But Janice had always wondered what had become of Sophie and Kelsey Tailor and, in the end, curiosity had got the better of her.

'Sit down. I'll get you a cuppa. What would you like?'

Before Janice even had a chance to turn down his offer of a drink he had gone through to the kitchen. She sat down on the plush leather sofa and cast her eye around the room. It was modern and full of the latest high-tech gadgets but was nevertheless untidy.

On the sofa, to one side of her, was a hoody, which she assumed belonged to one of the children. There was a pair of trainers on the floor at the other side of the room, their positioning suggesting that they had been carelessly slung. Magazines littered the coffee table along with several dirty cups and various items had been left lying around on top of the furniture: letters on school-headed paper, a pair of gloves and a bunch of keys amongst other things.

As she sat there, a boy of about twelve marched into the living room and looked at her scornfully before heading for the kitchen. 'Dad, where's Mum?' he shouted, without bothering to say hello to Janice.

'At the shops with your sister,' came the reply.

'Aw, not again. I want her.'

'What for?'

'I need her to sew my PE kit.'

'Well, you'll have to bloody wait till she gets back.'

Janice heard a loud tut as the boy stomped back into the lounge, muttering something about his sister being spoilt as he crossed the room then slamming the door on his way out. Janice was relieved that at least the haughty wife wasn't in but then she presumed that, whatever he wanted her here for, he had deliberately chosen a time when she wouldn't be in.

Roy entered the room with two steaming cups in his hands. 'Ignore him. He's at that age.' He cleared a space on the coffee table and placed one of the cups in front of Janice. 'Coffee, isn't it? I remembered from when you used to come here before. I couldn't remember if you take sugar though.'

'No, that's OK,' said Janice, willing him to get straight to the point so she could get this visit over with as soon as possible.

He took a seat across from her and then shuffled awkwardly before he started to speak. 'It's about Sophie,' he began. 'Well, I haven't seen her for years, but I came across her in town recently.'

He paused, an expression of discomfort passing across his face before he carried on. 'I was on my way to meet a mate. I drove through the red-light district, only 'cos it's a short cut like. All these tarts were stood on the pavements waiting for cars to stop and I noticed this one. Well, she came right out into the road so I couldn't miss her really. I nearly died of shock when I realised it was our Sophie, skirt up her arse and face full of makeup.

'I drove past at first. I was so shocked I didn't know what to do but then I realised I couldn't just leave it, so I drove back and pulled over. I couldn't get much sense out of her to be honest. She did a runner before I had a chance to talk to her properly. Must have been ashamed I suppose.'

Janice felt irritated as she listened to his spiel, noticing how he failed to make eye contact. *What a load of old claptrap,* she thought. It was bloody apparent what he had been doing in the red-light district, and it didn't surprise her; he was the type. But it was important to maintain a professional front rather than being judgemental so, instead of saying what was on her mind, she responded with: 'Are you saying you think Sophie is a sex worker?'

'Dead right. It was obvious what she was up to, I mean, from the way she was dressed, and the way she came out into the road as I passed her in my car. What I want to know though is, what can you do about it?'

'Did you speak to her at all?' asked Janice.

'No, like I said, she did a runner. I shouted at her to come back but she just ignored me. But she's my kid at the end of the day, and I hate to think of her out there going with all sorts of deadbeats.'

'Well, I'm afraid it's out of my hands now,' said Janice.

'What? You mean there's nowt you can do?'

'I'm afraid not.'

'But surely you can get her off the streets and on benefits or summat! Anything's better than what she's doing now.'

'She's well above the legal age now so, like I say, I'm afraid it's out of my hands.'

'But she was still one of your kids. I thought you would have wanted to help her. I thought that was what your job was about.'

No, she's not my child, she's yours, Janice thought. *And your lack of support is probably what led to her being in this situation in the first place.* But, again, she refrained from saying what she really felt. 'Mr Tailor, there just aren't the resources to pursue every single case through to adulthood.'

'Yeah, that's all she is to you, a bloody case, isn't she? Well, she's my daughter and I want you to do summat about it.'

Janice stood up, leaving the almost full cup of coffee where it stood. 'Yes, she is your daughter, Mr Tailor, and it's a pity you didn't think of that ten years ago when you refused to provide a home for her and Kelsey.'

She made her way towards the door, reluctant to get into a full-blown argument with him in case she risked saying something she might regret.

'I didn't have any bloody choice. There's no room for 'em here, and we couldn't afford a bigger house. Broke my bloody heart when I had to hand 'em over to your lot. But I would have at least expected you'd have given 'em a good start in life. I got a right shock when I found out our Sophie was a common tart.'

Janice refused to listen to any more of this nonsense. She dashed out of the living room, into the hall and out into the garden. As she sped down the path on the way to her car, she could hear Roy Tailor shouting after her. 'Eh, come back. I haven't finished with you yet. Fuckin' useless the lot of you!'

By the time Janice reached her car her hands were trembling not only because of Roy Tailor's aggressive attitude but also because of the revelation about his daughter. She hated to think of the poor girl out on the streets turning tricks. During the past few years, she had often wondered what had become of her. And now she knew.

Janice felt sick to her stomach. On a good day, her job could be rewarding. But too often things happened that were beyond her control. It seemed that girls like Sophie were destined to have a hard life due to misfortunes that weren't of their own making. Janice had tried her best for the sisters all those years ago but sometimes it felt like her best wasn't good enough.

And it always left her wondering if there was any other way in which she could have helped. But it was too late now; the damage was already done.

53

November 2011

Sapphire was feeling tired, irritable and had hunger pangs that persisted despite the huge amount of food she had consumed that day. She knew all these symptoms were down to her cravings for coke, but she was desperately trying to cut down now that she was pregnant.

'This must be it,' said Crystal.

Sapphire stopped and looked up at the building, checking the number she had written down. 'Yes, it is.'

She eyed the exterior. It was a modern building, possibly only a few years old, and she wondered if it was purpose-built. They knocked on the door and waited, Sapphire unaware that she had been holding her breath until she heard somebody approaching and let out a gasp of air.

Sapphire had been doing a lot of thinking since discovering she was pregnant a couple of weeks previously. Once she had got over the initial shock, Sapphire wondered what to do about the situation. She was tempted to have an abortion, knowing that the child would be fatherless. Not only that, but she hated the idea of bringing up a child that had been forced onto her.

Struggling with her dilemma, on top of bumping into her father, brought back recollections of her own childhood and the way in which he had let her down. But then she thought about her wonderful mother who had been like two parents to Sapphire and her sister Kelsey.

The more she thought about her loving upbringing, the more Sapphire knew that she couldn't abort this child. It felt wrong. In the end she decided that she would bring the child up herself. She knew it would be challenging, but she'd do her best to give it as good a start in life as possible.

Crystal had insisted that Sapphire should reconsider approaching the charity to help her find housing. The more Sapphire thought about it, the more she knew Crystal was right. There was no way she could spend another winter on the streets of Manchester, not when she was carrying a child. Besides, she had promised herself that she would do the best for her child, which meant she would need somewhere to live.

So now, here they were, standing outside the hostel for homeless women. It wasn't long before somebody came to the door. The woman was aged around late thirties to early forties. She was dressed casually and had a welcoming smile. 'You must be Sophie.'

When Sapphire nodded, she opened the door wider. 'I'm Christine. Come in. I'll show you around.'

Sapphire and Crystal followed Christine as she led them down a hall with cream walls and laminate flooring. They passed a woman who looked startled and pulled her young child closer to her. 'Hi, Helenka, how are you today?' asked Christine.

'Not good,' said the woman who spoke with an Eastern European accent. 'I need to get food for my boy.' While she spoke, she eyed them all suspiciously.

'OK, I'll come and have a chat with you later.'

As they walked into a lounge set up with a TV, two sofas and a coffee table, Christine remarked casually, 'Poor woman, she's frightened to death of going out in case she comes across her husband.' Then she tutted before adding, 'It's terrible what she's had to put up with.'

Although curious, Sapphire didn't like to ask what exactly that might be, feeling that it was the woman's own business.

'This is the lounge as you can see,' Christine stated. 'Not many of the women use it. Most of them prefer to stay in their own rooms but we do have a couple who come in here with their children from time to time.' She lowered her voice. 'It can get a bit noisy I'm afraid.'

As though on cue, just at that moment they heard a commotion coming from one of the other rooms. Christine forced a giggle. 'It sounds like they might be in the kitchen now. Come on, I need to show you that next anyway.'

Again, Sapphire and Crystal followed her through the building till they came to the kitchen where they found a young woman trying to separate two small boys who were intent on inflicting damage on each other. Sapphire couldn't help but notice how poorly dressed she was with a tear in her ill-fitting top. The two boys were also unkempt and looked in need of a wash. The woman seemed relieved to see Christine.

'Eh, look who's here. You'd better behave now, or you'll be in trouble.'

The boys didn't take much notice and continued to pummel at each other while the woman tried to separate them.

'Well,' said Christine, addressing the boys. 'This is a fine way to greet me. And to think, I was going to treat you two later as well.'

The two boys stopped what they were doing and peered eagerly at her. 'What have you got for us?' one of them demanded.

'What have I told you about yer manners?' the mother complained in a thick Mancunian accent.

Christine seemed unfazed by it all and continued to address the boys. 'You'll have to wait and see what it is but only if you behave. If your mother tells me you've behaved for the rest of the day, then I might have a little something for you after tea. But *only* if you behave.'

This seemed to do the trick. The boys quietened down, and the stressed-out mother gave Christine a relieved smile before urging the boys out of the kitchen and back to her room. As they passed, Sapphire noticed the stench of body odour emanating from the woman.

Christine carried on speaking to Sapphire as though nothing had happened. 'There's everything you need in here: fridge-freezer, cooker, microwave and washing machine.'

Sapphire looked around the room. Again, it had plain walls and laminate flooring. The cupboards were basic but serviceable and she noticed that, overall, it seemed clean.

The final room they came to was her bedroom. Like the other rooms, it was plain but clean with a bed, wardrobe, and chest of drawers. The room was only small though and she wondered how she would fit a cot in here once her baby arrived. But the housing department had assured her they would try to get her housed as soon as possible because she was expecting, so maybe that wouldn't be a problem.

It wasn't the best place in the world she could have chosen to live. Sapphire suspected that noise would be the least of her worries. If you put a bunch of overstressed, troubled women in a house together, there were bound to be problems. The kitchen would be a challenge when everybody descended on it wanting to cook at the same time, and she wasn't sure she'd even bother with the lounge.

But it was a start and definitely a big improvement on where she had been sleeping for the past few years. With a bit of luck, it would lead to better things and she could forge a decent life for her unborn child.

54

Skinner didn't see Sophie as much as he used to in the days when she was new to the streets. He'd missed her company at first; Sophie was a great girl, and they had a good laugh together. But he understood that their lives had gradually moved in different directions since she'd gone on the beat and met Crystal.

Even though he knew his friendship with Sophie would never amount to anything more than that, he had still enjoyed having her as his special friend. But Skinner had eventually accepted the situation and adapted. He was a resourceful youth who had plenty of other friends and contacts and could always think of new ways to make money.

Currently he was sitting inside a pub watching a couple getting hammered while having a few drinks himself. It had amused him to see how the night had progressed. At first the couple were all loving, having a laugh and competing to see who could down the most shots. Skinner had had the impression they were celebrating something, perhaps an early Christmas drink.

Then, for some reason, their night turned ugly. Skinner wasn't close enough to hear what was being said but their body language said it all. Reminiscent of Kirsty and Shane in *Fairytale of New York* but without the music, they were snapping and snarling at each other, their features strained and their muscles taut, until the boyfriend seemed to have had enough. He stood up angrily, finished his drink, slammed the empty glass down then shoved the table. His girlfriend's drink toppled over, leaving her saturated.

'Bastard!' she yelled after him as he stomped out of the pub.

Skinner knew it was his opportunity. Adopting an expression of concern, he walked over to the girl who had stood up and was ineffectually trying to wipe the spillage from her jeans using a tissue. 'You alright?' he asked.

The girl looked at him, her face a picture of fury and her bottom lip trembled slightly as she snapped, 'Yeah, I'm fine!'

'Well, you don't look fine.' Skinner looked across at a barman collecting glasses. 'Can you fetch us a cloth, mate?' he shouted. Then, while he waited for the barman to bring a cloth, he used a beer mat to scoop some of the liquid off the table and swish it on to the floor.

'I think you need a mop too,' he said to the barman when he fetched the cloth. 'Floor's soaked.' While the barman went off in search of a mop, Skinner said to the girl, 'Waste of bloody good booze if you ask me. What were you drinking anyway?'

'Vodka and lemonade.'

'Wait there.'

Skinner dashed to the bar, ordered a vodka and lemonade and a pint for himself then returned to the table where he had left the girl. He held the drink out for her. 'Here you go.'

'You didn't have to do that,' she slurred.

Skinner adopted his widest smile. 'Just helping a damsel in distress. Eh, I saw what happened. You didn't deserve that. Why did he do that anyway? He seemed alright one minute and the next he'd gone berserk.'

'Fuck knows. You never fuckin' know with him.'

She put the cloth down on the table and Skinner asked, 'You alright now?'

'Suppose so. He'll be all apologies when I get home.'

'Well make him grovel. Have you had your eye on owt in the shops?'

'What do you mean?'

'You know. A nice top, handbag, jewellery.'

Skinner was rewarded with a smile. He was playing for time, knowing that it was a busy pub and if he kept away from his table long enough, it would be taken by some of the groups that were standing around waiting for seats.

'Well, now you come to mention it,' said the girl.

'There you go then. Now's your chance. Take the bastard for every penny.'

She giggled and Skinner could sense that he was reeling her in. He might not have been the best-looking guy around, but he knew how to cheer a girl up and make her laugh. He made as if to go. 'Anyway, you take care of yourself.' Turning around, he was pleased to see his table had been taken. 'Shit! It looks like we're both having an unlucky night. Some bugger's taken my table.'

Skinner made a show of looking around the pub as though searching for somewhere to sit. Fortunately, she fell for it. 'It's OK, you don't have to go. Sit down here.'

'You sure?'

'Yeah, after you've helped me and bought me a drink, it's the least I can do.'

'Cheers,' said Skinner, putting his drink down then pulling out a chair. Then he looked down at his feet. 'Oh, excuse me, my bloody lace has come undone.'

He bent under the table as if to tie his shoelace, reaching into the girl's bag as he did so and grabbing her purse then slipping it underneath the sole of his shoe. Silly cow leaving her bag undone. Skinner had already spotted it when the couple had been arguing. She had been so flustered that she'd slipped the purse into her bag quickly when she'd come back from the bar and hadn't bothered fastening it.

For a while they chatted, Skinner pretending to listen while the girl waffled on drunkenly about her boyfriend. Eventually she decided she needed to visit the ladies'. When she bent to retrieve her handbag, Skinner held his breath, waiting to see if she would notice her missing purse. He had it covered though; he would pretend to find it on the floor where it must have fallen out of her handbag.

But she didn't notice. Chances were that she wouldn't spot it till later. Skinner knew this was his chance. As soon as she was out of view, he bent and retrieved the purse then, checking no one was looking, slipped it into his pocket and left the pub, eager to count his spoils.

Skinner wasn't worried about how she'd get home. In fact, he didn't even think about it. His mind was too focused on making easy money to fund his next fix. It wasn't that he deliberately set out to hurt people; it was more a case of doing what he needed to do without considering the consequences, and his drug addiction was a strong driving force.

When Sapphire arrived in the Rose and Crown that evening, she was surprised to find Crystal with some of the old crowd: Ruby, Amber and another girl who Sapphire wasn't familiar with. It was unusual to see them all in the pub these days as most of them had moved on. Sapphire was eager to share her news with them but, before she had a chance, Ruby spoke to her.

'Hi, girl, how's it going in the hostel?'

'Not bad. There are a couple of nutcases there, sad cases too and sometimes it kicks off but it's nothing I can't handle after so many years on the streets. And it's a damn sight better than where I was sleeping before.'

'Good,' said Crystal. 'And how are you feeling in yourself?'

As she spoke, she eyed Sapphire's tummy. Sapphire smiled. It was her cue to share her good news, the first part of it anyway. Out of her pocket she pulled the image she had been carrying around with her all day and passed it to Crystal. 'It's my scan,' she announced proudly.

While Crystal and the other girls cooed over the picture, Sapphire pointed out the various parts of her baby. It felt good to share it with her friends, knowing how much they cared about her.

She gave them time to study the scan, popping it back into her pocket when they'd finished before she announced her next exciting piece of news. 'I've spoken to housing today. They say there should be a flat ready for me after Christmas.'

'Bloody hell, that's quick!' said Crystal.

'Yeah, apparently one is coming free, but the previous residents left it in a mess, so they've got to spend a bit of time doing it up before it's ready to live in.'

'Will a flat be any good with a baby?' asked Ruby.

'Well, I could wait forever for a house and I'd rather be settled into my own place before the baby's born.'

'Good for you,' said Crystal. 'New Year, new start.'

Sapphire smiled thinking about the plans she'd already shared with her friends. She'd stopped drinking and was cutting down on the drugs and cigs, determined to kick the habit before the baby was born. She'd even started learning to drive so she'd be able to travel about easily with her new baby.

As if reading her mind, Crystal asked, 'How's it going with ditching the drugs?'

'It's killing me,' admitted Sapphire, thinking again about her constant need to do a few lines. 'I can't stop fuckin' eating and my nerves are shot to fuck. But I'm determined to ditch it eventually. I've got to for my baby.' As she spoke the last few words, she subconsciously rubbed her stomach.

Aside from battling her addictions, she had decided to come off the beat. There was no way she'd have time for it once the baby was born but she'd stick at it for now so she could afford to buy all the items she would need like a pram and cot, and a cheap car.

It would be a struggle having to rely on benefits, but Sapphire was determined it wouldn't be forever. Once her child was old enough, she would look into getting a job or taking up a college course to gain some skills. She was so busy daydreaming that she didn't realise Crystal and Ruby were watching her.

'It's good to see you so happy,' said Crystal.

'I am. Y'know, it was a difficult decision about whether to keep the baby, but it feels right. And I've got you to thank. If it hadn't been for you, Crystal, I wouldn't have been getting my own place.'

'It was nothing.'

'Well thanks anyway. Like you say, New Year, new start.'

Sapphire continued to smile as she went over her plans in her head. To her it felt as though things were finally coming together. But memories of all she had been through were never far from her mind, and she just hoped that this time nothing would go wrong.

55

December 2011

'I've got you some breakfast,' said Skinner when Sapphire joined him in a café situated in the Northern Quarter.

Sapphire looked at the plate containing a full English and the cup of tea and scone. 'Bloody hell, you're a bit flush, aren't you? Where did you get the money for this lot?'

'Some bloody thanks that is,' said Skinner, evading her question. 'I thought you'd appreciate it. I was thinking of you and the baby.'

'Sorry. Yeah, thanks. You know how I love a full English.'

'Well, you're eating for two now, aren't you?'

Sapphire smiled and tucked into the breakfast, washing it down with the tea.

'How's things going anyway?' asked Skinner.

'OK, I took a client back to my old place last night.'

Skinner's face adopted a puzzled frown as he wondered which of the squats she could have been talking about. He also wondered how she had managed to access a property they'd previously had to leave for whatever reason. 'Where?'

Sapphire laughed. 'The back entrance of that nightclub where I used to sleep. I gave him a hand job. Y'know, I've always wanted to work in one of them posh nightclubs. Used to fancy my chances as a cocktail waitress. I suppose that's the nearest I'm gonna get now.'

Skinner joined in her laughter, but he knew she had other ambitions now. She had told him about her plans to come off the beat and eventually build a brighter future for herself and her child, and he wondered how she would cope living on benefits.

'You still gonna come off the game?' he asked.

'Dead right, once I've bought all the stuff I need. Eh, I went for my scan yesterday. I'll show you the picture when I've finished this. Then I've got summat else to tell you.'

Skinner waited, sharing her joy once she showed him the image. Even though babies weren't really his thing, he could understand Sapphire's excitement. Then she made her announcement.

'I'm getting my own flat after Christmas.'

This news made Skinner sit up and take notice. 'What? Council?'

Sapphire nodded. 'Well, Housing Association. Same sort of thing though, innit?'

'Yeah, that's brilliant! How many bedrooms?'

'Two.'

'Great! Looks like you'll be getting a lodger then.'

Skinner saw the change of expression on Sapphire's face and had a bad feeling even before she spoke. 'It's for the baby, Skinner.'

'But I thought you weren't supposed to leave babies on their own.'

'Maybe not at first but I'll want the baby to have its own room eventually.'

'Yeah, but that won't be for ages, will it?'

In his naivety he had assumed that she would be OK about him moving in with her. After all, they had always shared squats, and he had usually been the one who had found them. Now, he was shocked to think that she was turning him down.

'It wouldn't work, Skinner. I can't bring a child up to the life I had before. I want a new life for him or her.'

'Aah, right, and there would be no room in that life for a scally like me. Is that it?' He chuckled self-consciously.

'No, I didn't mean it like that, Skinner. But, think about it, the baby would need all its own stuff. A cot and everything. I'll be filling the second bedroom with all that and I want to decorate it all nice as well. There'd be no room in there for an adult's bed. And I'm sure you wouldn't want to sleep surrounded by teddy bears and packets of nappies.

'You know me, Saph. I'll sleep fuckin' anywhere, especially if it's nice and warm. But it's OK, I get it. Don't worry.'

The atmosphere between them shifted then and he could see Sapphire felt bad. He understood her decision in a way, though he couldn't help but feel hurt.

'Still mates?' she asked.

'Yeah, sure,' said Skinner, smiling.

It was the early hours of the morning and Sapphire had returned to the hostel after working. Despite the late hour, she was having difficulty sleeping. It wasn't the most comfortable bed in the world but usually sleep wasn't a problem as she'd been used to much worse in recent years.

Tonight, thoughts of Skinner kept going round inside her head. Apart from that, she had a few stomach pains, which she put down to the indigestion she had been experiencing since becoming pregnant.

Skinner's reaction when she'd told him she didn't want him living with her hadn't been good and she felt guilty. They had been through a lot together and he always cheered her up when she was down. She realised they weren't as close as they had once been; since she had been on the beat, she'd grown increasingly close to Crystal instead. It wasn't always easy to fit in time with Skinner, which was something else she felt guilty for.

But, at the end of the day, she had to do what was best for her and the baby and Skinner didn't fit in with those plans. Sapphire didn't want any child of hers brought up in a place full of druggies. She wanted to wave goodbye to that part of her life. If Skinner lived with her, they'd probably end up falling out big time, so it was best this way. At least they could hopefully get things back on track once he'd got over his disappointment.

As she lay there trying to nod off, Sapphire felt another twinge in her tummy, this time sharper. She tried to ignore it as Crystal had already reassured her that it was possible to feel some aches and discomfort during pregnancy. But then she felt another pain. This time it was stronger and more of a cramp. Again, she tried to ignore it.

By now her mind was flitting from worries about Skinner to concerns about what she was experiencing physically. 'Fuck!' she muttered. 'Now I'll never get to bloody sleep.'

For a while, her irritation overrode further worry. But then she experienced another pain. This time there was no mistaking its cramp-like nature and Sapphire's concern turned to anxiety. But there was something else too. She felt moist between her legs and wondered if she had wet herself.

Curious, she put her hand down there and felt moisture. She lifted her fingers to look at them and was alarmed to see that they were red with blood. She shot up in bed, intending to examine where the blood was coming from so she could establish how heavily she was bleeding.

Then she saw it; a crimson pool on the bed sheets, and she knew what it meant.

'No!' she yelled. 'Please no.'

56

December 2011

Crystal woke up to the sound of her phone ringing and glanced at the bedside clock: 5am! She groaned and turned over. Next to her Gilly stirred. Any hope that the caller might go away was destroyed when the phone rang again. For a few moments Crystal lay there, still drowsy and debating whether to take the call or whether to switch off her phone's volume.

'For fuck's sake answer the bastard thing!' Gilly complained. 'It's fuckin' obvious they're not gonna give up.'

Crystal sighed and picked up her phone. Sapphire's number showed up on the screen and Crystal became alarmed. What if she was still at work and was having problems with a client?

She pressed the call-receive button. 'Hi! Sapphire?'

It became apparent straightaway that Sapphire was distressed. 'Crystal, Crystal. I don't know what to do.' Then she let out a whimper and Crystal realised that she was in pain.

'What is it, Sapphire? What the fuck's wrong?'

It took a while for Sapphire to get her words out. 'You need to go to hospital straightaway,' said Crystal. 'Have you called an ambulance?' She listened to the reply. 'OK. Do it now. I'll meet you there.'

She cut the call and stared across at Gilly who was now fully awake. 'Who was it?'

'Sapphire.'

'What's wrong?'

'She thinks she's losing the baby.'

'Well, why's she ringing you? She needs to call a fuckin' ambulance.'

'I know. I've told her that. She's ringing one now. I've told her I'll meet her at the hospital.'

'Well, you can't.'

'Why?'

'Have you forgotten? You've got a fuckin' kid to take care of. You can't just leave her here on her own.'

'She won't be on her own. She'll be with you, Gilly.'

'For fuck's sake! You know I don't do kids.'

Crystal ignored him and started getting dressed. She hoped he wouldn't kick up a fuss and was thankful when he didn't. Maybe his conscience had been pricked. Candice was his child when all said and done even if he didn't always acknowledge it. Before leaving home, Crystal went into Candice's bedroom and gave her a gentle shake. Then she explained that she had to go to see a friend who was ill in hospital, but that Gilly would look after her till she got back. She didn't want Candice to become alarmed when she found her mother was missing.

Thirty minutes later she arrived at Manchester Royal

Infirmary, parked her car, and raced to the A & E department. It took a while to find out which ward Sapphire was on and then to find the ward itself. When she did so she was told she would have to wait as the doctor was with Sapphire.

It took ages before Crystal was finally allowed onto the ward. She approached Sapphire's bed, curious as to whether they'd been able to save the baby, but Sapphire's face told her the answer straightaway.

'It's gone, Crystal. The baby's gone.'

'Aw, Sapphire, I'm so sorry,' said Crystal, taking her in her arms and letting her cry out all her sorrow.

It was some time until Sapphire spoke. 'I can't believe it, Crystal. I was so looking forward to having this baby. I was gonna change my life for her or him, give up the drugs and everything.'

'I know you were. I'm sorry, Sapphire.'

'Now I'll lose the fuckin' flat as well.'

'What do you mean?'

'Well,' Sapphire replied between sobs. 'They only put me at the top of the list 'cos I was pregnant. Now I'm not, I'll go right back to the bottom. I might even get kicked out of the hostel.'

Her last words brought fresh tears, but Crystal stopped her before she got too carried away. 'No, you fuckin' won't, Sapphire. Nobody needs to know you're not pregnant anymore. You need to keep schtum till after you've moved in. You'll get over the miscarriage in time, Sapphire, I promise but you can't afford to let this ruin your fuckin' life and all your plans.'

Sapphire managed a weak smile and for a while they chatted, Sapphire going over what had happened.

*

When it was time for Crystal to leave, Sapphire was sorry to see her go but she was grateful for the support she had given her at a time when she'd needed it. And Crystal had been right about the flat. It was bad enough that she had lost her baby. Why should she have to lose her home as well?

Once she was left alone to dwell, the guilt and sorrow set in. Sapphire wondered whether her smoking and drug abuse might have been the reason for her miscarriage. She thought about how things could have been if her mother had still been around. Sapphire knew she would have loved having a grandchild and she would have showered it with as much love and attention as she had done for herself and Kelsey.

In a way it was a good job her mother was no longer around because she would never have forgiven her if her drug use had been responsible for losing the baby. The thought of her mother's possible reaction filled her with shame. But her mother wasn't around anymore. Sapphire was alone again. And now she didn't even have the joy of being able to bring a new child into the world.

Ironically, despite being aware that drugs might have been responsible for her miscarriage, Sapphire was craving them now more than ever. Drugs relaxed her, they made her high and took her mind off her troubles. And the way she was feeling right now, she needed that escape.

57

February 2012

'Aw, thanks, lads,' said Sapphire to Skinner and his mate Jono.

It was early February, and they were standing inside her new flat; the lads had just helped her to move in. For Sapphire it was a bittersweet moment. It was great to be out of the hostel and have her own flat at last, but she knew that she should have been making it a home for her and her baby instead of alone.

'OK, we'll be off now,' said Skinner.

Sapphire gave both the lads some money for helping her move in. She had been glad of their help. Crystal would usually have been the first to offer but she had been having a few problems lately. Gilly had died from a drugs overdose towards the end of December and Crystal hadn't been the same since.

Sapphire was relieved that Skinner had agreed to help when she had asked. After she had refused to let him live with her, she was worried that he might have taken offence but, as with most things, Skinner had taken it in his stride.

She still hadn't told him about the miscarriage though – just in case he thought it would be a good opportunity for him to move in. Although there was no longer a baby on the way, Sapphire still preferred to have her own space. Fortunately, he hadn't asked, and she had managed to disguise the fact that she was no longer pregnant by wearing baggy clothing on the few occasions when she had seen him.

For the last couple of months Sapphire had been collecting items for the flat and keeping them in her room at the hostel. The bigger items Skinner and Jono had brought from a second-hand shop using a van Jono had borrowed.

Once the lads had gone, Sapphire wandered around the flat, gazing with satisfaction at the décor and the way she had added her own finishing touches with the items she had been collecting over the weeks. She was feeling quite pleased with herself till she stepped inside the second bedroom and saw only emptiness where the cot should have been.

Suddenly, the sorrow hit her all over again. Her life shouldn't have been like this. She should have been looking forward to her pregnancy, maybe even sharing it with her mother and sister if things had worked out differently. But they were gone now as well as the baby. She had nothing to share and no one to share it with.

She tried to pull herself out of her sorrowful state by thinking about what she did have: her own home and her friends. Crystal was the best of them by far. Ever since she had met her, Crystal had been there for her, but Sapphire didn't like to pressure her while she was going through so much herself. Skinner was a good mate too but in a different way than Crystal. Where Crystal was strong and motherly, Skinner was like a mischievous child.

Sapphire supposed that, in a way, Crystal and Skinner had been like the mother and sister who were now absent from her life. Crystal was the person she turned to whenever she had problems and Skinner was someone she could have a laugh with and share secrets.

But Sapphire knew that, despite having good friends, her life was still sadly lacking. After losing the baby it hadn't taken her long before she had increased her drug intake again. It had helped to numb the pain of her loss and switched her mind off from the guilt that dogged her, knowing that her lifestyle might have been responsible for her miscarriage.

With the drugs came her return to the beat to finance her addictions. She knew it was going against what she had planned for herself but there no longer seemed any point in changing her life so dramatically. The only concession was that she was still managing to have driving lessons in her more sober moments.

The way Sapphire saw it was that she might have gained a flat and had the chance of buying a car for herself but that was all. They were only material possessions but her hopes and aspirations for a future with her own little family had now vanished and Sapphire was back to surviving day by day.

It had been two weeks since Sapphire had moved into the flat and she was becoming accustomed to the area. As she returned from a night on the beat, the decay wasn't difficult to miss even in the gloom of night. As the taxi carrying her drove through the estate, she took in the graffiti daubed on the gable walls of the rundown houses, which had gates missing and rubble-strewn gardens with trodden-down, patchy lawns full of weeds.

It was a rough neighbourhood and threatening even to someone like Sapphire who was used to working the streets. On the rare occasions when she was home in the late evenings, she had heard the rowing neighbours and motorbikes screeching down the road. And when she had ventured to the shops, she had seen the gangs of youths that congregated outside the off-licence once night fell, and the empty syringes and used condoms that littered the streets.

Sapphire hadn't seen much of either Crystal or Skinner since she had moved in. She understood that Crystal was going through her own grief but in the case of Skinner, they had just drifted. Skinner was still living on the streets and, although he had visited her once or twice, she wasn't often in due to her late-night occupation.

Since she had moved here, Sapphire had become lonelier. It was a hostile place, and the neighbours didn't bother much with her. But at least it was home, she thought, as she arrived at her front door and put her key in the lock. And it was an improvement on having to sleep on the streets.

She was so focused on getting inside and getting warm that she didn't notice anything amiss. Everything seemed normal as she walked into the flat until she came to the living room. Sapphire stopped at the open door, the breath catching in her throat as she took in the devastation. The place had been ransacked and all her lovely things were strewn all over the floor.

Instinctively, she went over to the sideboard where she kept her money. The drawers had been wrenched open and she knew what she would find even before she looked. Nothing. It was all gone.

'The thieving bastards!' she yelled.

Her next thought was for her own safety. Wondering how they had got in, she rushed to the window. It looked as though someone had jemmied the locks with a crowbar. How had she not noticed as she came in? Then she realised that because she didn't have to pass the living room window to get to the front door, she hadn't even bothered looking.

With a pounding heart she peered outside. She shivered, thinking that whoever it was could be watching her right now and taking delight at the way in which they had robbed her.

She didn't bother ringing the police. What was the point in an area like this? Break-ins were commonplace. She'd heard talk of them in the local shops. According to the gossips the police didn't do much other than take down the details and as she wasn't insured, she didn't need to register the crime. Instead, she rang Crystal but was unable to get hold of her. Then she tried Skinner who was there within the half hour.

'Thanks,' she said with tears in her eyes.

'It's OK,' he said as he walked inside. 'That's what mates are for.'

She followed him through to the living room. 'Fuckin' hell! They've made a right mess in here, haven't they?'

'Yeah. Twats!'

He turned round to face her. 'Look, don't worry. I can help you get it sorted. Where did they get in?' She pointed to the window and Skinner took a look. 'It's no biggie. I'll soon fix that. I'll get Jono to fetch some tools tomorrow. But you need to get some sleep first. I don't mind kipping on the sofa. Bastards don't scare me!'

Sapphire nodded, grateful to Skinner. Without him there she knew she wouldn't have slept.

The following day as she and Skinner worked their way through the destruction of her home, trying to assess what had been taken, worries were whirling around in Sapphire's mind. After spending years on the streets, this had seemed like her haven. She had never felt at threat inside her own home before. But now she did. It freaked her out knowing they could have been observing her comings and goings. They might have known that she was out most nights and could have been waiting for their chance.

It was a cruel and horrible introduction to the neighbourhood. Sapphire felt invaded. Threatened. Unsafe. And she couldn't help but think that perhaps this was some form of retribution. She had carried a baby while still taking drugs and now she was being punished for the death of her child.

PART FIVE

ALONE (2016–2017)

58

February 2016

Sapphire was inside the Rose and Crown with Amber and Angie, an older woman who was in a poor state of health. It was a pub used regularly by the girls who worked the beat. Sapphire enjoyed having a few drinks and a gossip with them before work but the only one she had formed a lasting friendship with was Crystal who rarely came into the pub these days since she had come off the beat and built a new life for herself.

She noticed how tense Amber was, which wasn't surprising considering how their last meeting had gone two weeks previously. Sapphire had found out from Skinner that the guy Amber was seeing, Kev Pike, had murdered another prostitute called Cora. It had freaked Sapphire out at the time. They'd all been worried for months that there was a killer targeting working girls. That was bad enough but to find out it was Amber's boyfriend was terrifying.

Although Skinner had made Sapphire promise not to say anything because he was frightened of repercussions, how could she not warn Amber? So, she'd searched for her over two consecutive nights and eventually found her on the beat and put her own safety at risk to warn her. But Amber's reaction hadn't been what Sapphire had expected. Instead of thanking her she'd gone into denial. They'd had a few harsh words, and this was the first time she'd seen her since.

Sapphire would like to have known what had happened in the last two weeks. Was Amber still seeing Kev? Had she said anything to him? Was she still in denial? But it was impossible to have a discussion when Angie was sitting with them. One thing she did notice though was that Amber's phone hadn't stopped pinging and every time Amber looked at the screen to see who the text was from she seemed to grow more tense.

'What the bloody hell's wrong with you?' Angie asked Amber. 'You're like a cat on hot bricks. And your phone's not stopped pinging. Is someone after you or summat?'

Sapphire flashed Amber a warning look, dreading it in case she told her about Kev. But Amber didn't say anything. She just sat there looking preoccupied.

'Switch it off if it's bothering you,' said Angie who then began to cough. Sapphire knew she had COPD and was also suffering with a chest infection, so she waited for her coughing to subside before carrying on the conversation. But Angie's coughing didn't stop. Sapphire could hear it rattling through her lungs and she was wheezing too.

When she started struggling for breath, Sapphire shot up out of her seat and slapped her on the back until she brought up the phlegm that had been blocking her windpipe and her breathing eased. Instead of showing concern, Amber snapped at Angie, telling her she shouldn't have been coming out to work when it was cold.

Sapphire had had enough of the tense atmosphere, so she finished her drink and got up to go. Before she left, she told Angie to take care. Then she looked across at Amber hoping she would get the message Sapphire was trying to convey by the hard stare and the edge to her voice when she said, 'You too.'

It was a month later and Sapphire hadn't seen Amber since their last meeting in the pub. She was growing increasingly worried and had shared her concerns with Skinner. But both knew there was nothing they could do. The police were unlikely to believe anything they said, much less put out a search for a working girl. And they didn't want to risk getting on the wrong side of Kev Pike who had a vicious reputation.

Sapphire was sitting in the Rose and Crown with Skinner and a friend of his called Elena, another working girl. Although Elena was aware of Cora's death, she didn't know that Kev Pike was responsible. Sapphire and Skinner were too nervous of Kev Pike to make it common knowledge and risk him finding out it had come from them.

When Kev Pike walked into the pub, Skinner was the first to notice. 'Shit!' he said.

Sapphire saw the look of terror on the face of Skinner who nearly choked on his drink until Elena slapped him on the back. Sapphire could feel the adrenalin pulsing through her body but, despite her own fear, she warned Skinner to keep his cool.

As soon as he noticed them, Kev Pike came straight over and bombarded Sapphire with questions. *Are you a mate of Amber's? Does she come in here? Any idea where she might be?*

Sapphire's heart pounded but she tried to stay calm as she fielded his questions until he walked away.

Skinner gave a whispered commentary on his actions until he finally left the pub. He seemed to have forgotten about Elena as he muttered, 'Thank fuck for that!'

Unfortunately, he alerted Elena's suspicions and she demanded to know what was happening. When Skinner and Sapphire refused to tell her, she stormed out of the pub. Sapphire was too worried about Amber to bother about Elena's tantrum.

'I need to warn Amber,' she said. 'I'm worried shitless that something might happen to her. We need to find Amber before he does. I've got to get to work now – I need the money – but we should do it tomorrow night.'

The following evening, they met up again.

Sapphire was horrified to hear Skinner's latest news. 'There's another girl been killed, and she's been strangled like Cora. I'm worried it might be your mate, especially after he's been looking for her.'

Panic-stricken, they raced from the pub and searched the red-light area once again, stopping to ask the working girls if they had seen anybody matching Amber's description. While Skinner was questioning girls on the other side of the road, Sapphire struck lucky with a tall peroxide blonde who told her Kev Pike had been looking for Amber too.

Sapphire shared her concerns about the possibility of Amber being the murder victim, but the blonde girl put her mind at ease. 'It's not her,' she said. 'They're saying it's a Romanian girl, Elena I think she's called.'

'Shit!' said Sapphire, relieved that it wasn't Amber but upset at the loss of Elena and afraid of what Skinner's reaction would be when she gave him the terrible news.

59

October 2016

Sapphire didn't hear anything for months after that. She was anxious about what might have become of Amber and dreaded hearing the news of a third killing. Apart from all that, she was constantly on edge in case she bumped into Kev Pike again. And, after the news of Elena's death, Skinner had become morose rather than his usual cheerful self.

Then Crystal turned up in the Rose and Crown one night. Sapphire hadn't seen her for an age, so she was shocked to find her sitting alone at their usual table when she arrived for a pre-work drink.

'Thank Christ you're here! I've been hoping to have a word with you,' said Crystal when Sapphire walked over.

Sapphire smiled knowing the peculiar greeting was typical of Crystal. 'Why, what's wrong?'

'Nothing. Well, it's just that, I feel bad that I've not been in touch. But you won't believe what's been going on. Apart from work, it's been mad but there's something else and I thought you should know ...'

Sapphire's eyes opened wide, and Crystal quickly added, 'It's about Amber.'

'Shit, Crystal, you're worrying me. What is it? You know she's been missing for months since that last girl was murdered, don't you?' asked Sapphire, taking care not to mention her suspicions regarding Kev Pike's involvement.

'Don't worry,' said Crystal. 'I know everything.'

'Everything?'

'Yeah, everything. Me and Candice found Amber one day. I nearly didn't bleedin' recognise her she looked that rough. She was outside a shop begging.'

'You're joking!'

'No. She didn't want to be found by Kev Pike so she was too worried to stay on the game. And, to cut a long story short, in the end she was so skint that she ended up homeless. Anyway, after she told me everything, I knew you'd be worried so I thought I'd come here to find you.

'Poor cow's had a really rough ride. She told me all about her home life, her childhood and everything one night after a few glasses of wine. My bleedin' heart wept for her. Anyway, that's her business. I won't say no more. I just wanted you to know she's OK. She's staying with me but keep that to yourself. I don't want her ex finding out. How are you anyway?'

Sapphire was busy trying to take everything in. It was clear from what Crystal had already told her that she had her hands full running her businesses and now she had come to Amber's rescue too. Although Sapphire's life wasn't ideal, she replied automatically, 'I'm OK, same old, same old really, still seeing Skinner and still on the beat, y'know.'

She didn't bother telling Crystal how despondent Skinner had been since Elena's death, how she hated the shitty neighbourhood where she lived or how she'd give anything to be able to kick her drug habit and not have to work the beat. Sapphire was just glad to see her old mate and flattered that she searched her out specially to tell her what had happened to Amber.

Crystal then switched the conversation back to Amber. 'Eh, you be careful out there because that bleedin' Kev Pike is still on the loose. We're gonna take the bastard to court. We need to get him off the streets. Amber told me about a mate of yours who saw him kill Cora. Do you think we could get him to testify in court?'

'I doubt it. He's shit-scared of any comeback.'

'There won't be any bleedin' comeback once we've finished with him. Amber's going to testify about him attacking her too.'

'Attacking her? I didn't know that.'

'Oh yeah, she's been through the mill, poor cow!'

Crystal didn't stay long, saying she had some business to attend to and leaving the pub once Sapphire had promised that she'd do her best to set up a meeting with Skinner. She just hoped she could persuade him to agree to the meeting.

60

February 2017

Sapphire was sitting inside a pub in the Gay Village looking across to the bar where her new girlfriend Natasha was waiting to be served. Even from behind she looked ravishing with her pert behind and her neatly cropped strawberry blonde hair. Like Sapphire, she was edgy but in a petite way that made you feel as though you wanted to protect her.

Despite her diminutive size and pretty features, Natasha was no pushover. In fact, she was very sure of herself and wasn't one to be trampled on. But Sapphire liked that about her as well as her sense of fun. Since they'd met over the Christmas period, they'd had a few nights out and Sapphire could always be sure she'd have a great time whenever they hit the town.

Natasha was also popular and seemed to know a lot of people in the area of Manchester known as the Gay Village. She'd talk to anybody and could soon get lost in conversation. Even if there was no one else worth talking to, Sapphire and Natasha could spend hours in the pub on their own talking about anything and everything.

Over the years Sapphire had had a few girlfriends. They'd come and gone but none of them had stayed around. With Natasha it was different. They'd hit it off straightaway and Natasha hadn't minded that Sapphire worked the beat although she'd insisted there was no way she wanted to do the same. Apart from being great fun to be with, Natasha had a lot in common with Sapphire: same daft TV shows, same music, even a lot of the same food.

Natasha came back from the bar with a wide grin on her face. 'Fancy some blow?' she asked.

'Yeah, but let's drink these first.'

As they drank Natasha regaled Sapphire with stories of mad nights out she'd had previously in this bar, and soon had her laughing. 'We were dancing on the tables at Christmas last year,' she said.

'Didn't the landlord mind?'

'No, he was only glad we were having a good time. He knew we were gonna stay and buy more drinks, didn't he?'

'Did your mum mind the kids for you?'

'Yeah, she always does. Dotes on 'em, doesn't she? And it's a good job cos *he's* a waste of fuckin' time.'

Sapphire knew that the *he* referred to Natasha's former partner who had left her for another woman and who rarely saw the two young children he had fathered with Natasha. Since then, according to Natasha, she was through with men.

'Come on, you ready?' Natasha asked, turning to the couple on the next table and asking them to mind their seats while they nipped to the loos.

They entered a cubicle together and indulged in some coke. When they had finished, Natasha put down the toilet seat and sat on it so that she was facing Sapphire. She laughed. 'Right, now for some fun,' she said, unfastening Sapphire's trousers and underwear then going down on her.

It took Sapphire by surprise but really it was just like Natasha to do something so shocking. She soon relaxed and got into it. That was part of the thrill with Natasha; you never knew what she was going to do next. But it was always enjoyable.

Sapphire adored her and felt sure that Natasha was the one. She just hoped Natasha felt the same way about her.

61

May 2017

Sapphire was having a good time. In fact, it was the best time she'd had for ages aside from when she was with Natasha. She was inside the Rose and Crown with Crystal, Ruby, Amber and Skinner and they had just come back from court where Amber's ex-boyfriend had been tried for murder.

Although it was a grave occasion, Sapphire loved the fact that most of the old crowd were back together with the addition of Skinner who was keeping the girls entertained with his mischievous sense of humour.

Amber had just returned from the ladies' and was trying to squeeze past Ruby as she made her way to her seat. She accidently bumped the table and Ruby grabbed her drink quick before it spilt. 'Eh, careful. You don't wanna go spilling Ruby's drink. She'll fuckin' savage you! She's one feisty chick,' Skinner teased.

Ruby laughed. 'Cheeky little bastard.'

But she didn't take offence. The girls had got to know Skinner and his cheeky sense of humour over the past few weeks and Sapphire was pleased that they all got along well. Surprisingly, Skinner had become a bit of a hero figure to the girls having acted as a witness in the demanding court case.

As she sat there enjoying the banter Sapphire couldn't help but think about how much life had changed for both Crystal and Amber over the past few years. Crystal had turned her life around after the death of Gilly and now ran a chain of upmarket fashion stores, and Amber had been working for her since Crystal had taken her under her wing.

Sapphire's life was different to theirs. She was still working the beat and living in the same flat although she had made it more secure since the break-in years previously by having robust locks fitted as well as sleeping with a baseball bat underneath her bed. But she was happy in her own way. Although she didn't see much of Crystal and the other girls anymore, she was now seeing a lot of Skinner again. There was also a new person in her life, and she couldn't wait to tell Crystal all about her.

Skinner didn't stay the whole night, saying he had a bit of business to tend to and leaving the four girls. Later, when Sapphire returned from the bar, she found Crystal, Ruby and Amber chatting. Crystal turned to her, leaving the other two to carry on their conversation.

'How are you, Sapphire? We've not chatted for a while.'

Sapphire smiled. It was a beaming smile that made her whole face glow. 'I'm good thanks.'

Crystal laughed. 'If you ask me, you're better than good. Go on, what's her name and where's she from?'

Sapphire joined in her laughter. She might have known Crystal would guess; she had always been perceptive. 'OK, she's called Natasha, she's twenty-nine and gorgeous. Oh, and she lives not far from me actually.'

'Is that where you met her, locally?'

'No, that was just a coincidence. I persuaded Skinner to go into the Gay Village with me one night and I met her there.'

'So, is she not on the beat then?'

'No, she doesn't work. She's got two little kids, but her ex fucked off and left her to it.'

'Aah, right. So, she's bi?'

'Kind of. She's been off men since her ex did the dirty on her.'

'Have you met the kids?'

'No, not yet. Her mum minds them while she stays at mine. I've only been seeing her five months. But I am really into her.'

'Five months. Jesus! Is it that long since we chatted?'

It had been a lot longer than that, Sapphire thought to herself before saying, 'It's been a while.'

'Well, I'm glad you've met someone,' said Crystal. 'I hope she makes you happy.'

Sapphire smiled again. 'Yeah, she does.'

They chatted for a while longer then Crystal checked the time on her Gucci watch. 'Jesus! I didn't realise it was that late. I'd better be going,' she announced.

That caught the attention of the other girls who all agreed that it was time to go. Sapphire was disappointed to say goodbye; she'd really enjoyed the night, despite the circumstances.

But before she went, Crystal gave her a big hug. 'We'll have to make sure we don't leave it so long next time,' she said. 'I promise we'll all get together again soon. And you'll have to bring your girlfriend to meet us too.'

'Ooh, sounds interesting,' said Ruby while Amber smiled.

Once they had gone, Sapphire stayed to finish her drink, reflecting on the night as she sat at the table the girls often used to occupy in the old days. She had missed them all, especially Crystal who had been so good to her over the years. Still, she understood that things moved on.

It would have been easy to envy Amber and the new start Crystal had given her. But Sapphire could understand it. Amber had been at a low, not only because she was homeless and because of what she had been through with her ex-boyfriend but because she had lost her mother too.

Thoughts of Amber's mother made Sapphire think about her own as well as her sister. Although she hadn't admitted it to Crystal, things weren't as good as she made out. She had many regrets including the loss of her child years previously, and she hated living in that poxy flat even though she had managed it for the past five years.

Still, at least she had Skinner's friendship and she might even get things back on track with Crystal. But, best of all, she had Natasha and she was looking forward to developing the relationship further and finally getting to meet her girlfriend's children. Who knew what the future held? They might even end up living as a happy family together.

62

Sapphire was standing at the window of her flat looking out into the street. Across the road was a row of houses. Most of them were rundown with shabby, rubbish-strewn gardens that were nothing more than patches of soil with a few clumps of grass and weeds dotted about.

The house immediately opposite was particularly bad and had an assortment of battered toys scattered amongst car tyres and an old, abandoned washing machine. Taking advantage of the summer's night, two young children played amongst the rubble: a girl of about four and a boy a little older.

They seemed to be getting along fine till an argument broke out. Sapphire wasn't sure why; she had only half been paying attention but as the argument became heated the boy lashed out at the girl who screamed at the top of her voice till their mother came rushing out of the house.

'What the fuck's going on?' she yelled.

'He hit me,' cried the girl.

The mother glared at her son. 'Eh, you! Ger here NOW!'

The boy walked towards his mother, dragging his feet and with his shoulders slumped. As soon as he reached her, the mother whacked him on the back of the head before turning her attention to the girl.

'And you can ger in too and stop fuckin' snivelling!'

The girl screeched even louder and refused to go indoors, knowing that she'd probably receive the same punishment as her brother. Sapphire was wondering what the outcome would be when she saw a welcome visitor arriving at the entranceway to the block of flats. Not very tall, with strawberry blonde hair and pretty in a boyish way; it was her girlfriend, Natasha, who was late.

Sapphire felt a flutter of excitement in her stomach. She turned her attention to the flat and, even though she had already tidied, she dashed around making sure the cushions were plumped up and everything was arranged neatly. Then she remembered that she hadn't rung Crystal. It was something she'd intended to do earlier, and she knew she'd forget if she left it. Knowing the lift to her flat on the ninth floor could take ages, she decided to make a quick call while she was waiting for Natasha to arrive.

She was still talking when she heard the doorbell and she dashed to answer it. Watching Natasha walk in, Sapphire pointed to the phone then held up her forefinger to indicate that she would only be a minute. Natasha's facial expression changed as though she was unhappy at having to wait for Sapphire to finish the call.

Sapphire spoke into her mobile while Natasha stomped through to the lounge and sat down on the sofa, shifting one of Sapphire's carefully arranged cushions. 'OK, no worries. I'll catch up with you again.'

She cut the call and walked over to her girlfriend. 'Sorry about that, Tash. I thought I'd be finished by the time you got upstairs.' She bent over and pecked Natasha on the cheek.

'Who was it?' Natasha demanded.

'Oh, only Crystal. I'm trying to arrange a get-together but she's too busy.'

'She's always fuckin' busy. I don't know why you bother.'

'I bother because she's an old mate, and she's been good to me. Crystal's bound to be busy; she's got businesses to run. Anyway, what's got into you?'

Natasha looked up at Sapphire and smiled. 'Sorry, babe. I didn't mean to sound as though I was having a go. I just don't like to think anybody's taking the piss out of you, that's all.'

'Well, they're not. So, now that you're finally here, instead of picking holes in my friends, why don't we arrange to do summat nice for the evening?'

Natasha hesitated as though unsure whether to retaliate or not. But then she must have thought better of it and realised that she was the one who should have been apologising. 'Sorry, babe. I got held up. But you're right, I'm here now, so let's do summat nice.'

Sapphire tried to put it behind her so she could make the most of her time with Natasha. But her words had stung, maybe because they had an element of truth in them. It was the second time she'd rung Crystal since she had seen her in the Rose and Crown the month before. She'd texted her too.

Natasha's words had made her doubt Crystal's loyalty as a friend. She cast her mind back to a couple of years previously when Crystal had snubbed Amber in the street. Sapphire had been disappointed with her friend's actions at the time but had been glad when Crystal had come through for Amber in the end.

Now it felt like Crystal was doing the same thing to her. But, deep down, Sapphire didn't think Crystal would disown her. Perhaps she genuinely was too busy, and she probably thought Sapphire had her life together because she had the flat and a girlfriend whereas Amber had been in a bad way when Crystal had come to her rescue.

The words Crystal had used on the phone hadn't made Sapphire feel any more at ease though. 'Bloody hell, Sapphire, you're keen, aren't you? Anyone would think you had a thing for me,' she had flippantly remarked. But, when Sapphire hadn't seen the funny side of it, Crystal had apologised, saying that it was a cheap joke in poor taste.

Sapphire realised that Natasha did have a point; she was wasting her time keep ringing Crystal if all she did was put her off. So, she decided not to bother again. If Crystal wanted to get together then it was up to her to make the call.

Skinner knocked on the door of the house in Longsight, which was answered by a six-foot-tall black guy with a shaved head. He was wearing a sports vest that revealed his bulging biceps and a variety of tattoos.

'Is Al in?' asked Skinner.

'You're talking to him. Who are you?'

'I'm Skinner. Jono sent me.'

Al stood to one side, allowing Skinner to enter but he stopped him in the hall before letting him get any further inside. 'What you after?'

'Coke and some speed.'

'How much?'

Skinner gave Al the details. Jono had already told him Al's prices and as Skinner had one hundred pounds, he had worked out how many drugs he could afford based on that.

'Wait here,' said Al.

While Skinner waited in the hall, Al went through to another room. Skinner could hear other male voices and then laughter. When Al came back into the hall, he was carrying the drugs Skinner needed.

'That's a hundred and twenty quid. Cash only,' he said, holding out his hand.

Although Skinner had worked out that it should have come to a hundred pounds, he wasn't going to argue with a guy as big as Al. He pulled a wad of cash from his pocket. Skinner knew it was twenty pounds short but, on impulse he decided to try it on anyway.

He handed the cash over. 'There you go, it's all there.' Then he made a grab for the drugs.

Al snatched them away. 'You can fuckin' wait. I ain't checked it yet.'

Skinner broke out in a sweat as he watched Al carefully counting through the cash before announcing. 'It's fuckin' short!'

'Is it? Soz, I thought it was all there.'

'Well, how come you didn't fuckin' count it in front of me then?'

'I, er, Jono told me your prices. I brought what I thought I needed.'

'Well, you didn't fuckin' bring enough. You owe me another twenty.'

Skinner's heart was thundering by now. 'I-I don't have that much. Can I just take a hundred's worth?'

Al scowled at him. He looked down at the drugs in his hand and split both the coke and the speed into two equal lots, handing one lot to Skinner and pocketing the other. Skinner stood staring at him in shock.

'What you fuckin' waiting for?' demanded Al. 'You've got your drugs so fuck off!'

Skinner deliberated over how far to push his luck but in the end his greed exceeded his common sense. 'Don't I get any change?'

Before he knew what was happening, Al had slammed him up against the wall and had his forearm wedged against his throat. 'No, you fuckin' don't! You need to learn a lesson. Nobody takes the piss by trying to short-change me.'

Then he released his hold. 'If you've got any sense, you'll fuck off now and be glad you got summat out of it after the stunt you've just pulled.'

Skinner didn't wait to be asked twice. He made for the door and, with trembling fingers, he fumbled at the catch, glad when he was on the other side to Al. Skinner was shaken as well as disappointed. He had been relying on the drugs to sell a few on and make a bit of a mark-up.

Margins were low though and he knew that after he'd taken what he needed himself, there wouldn't be much left to sell on. He'd be lucky if he made a tenner out of it. But he had to do something. Skinner owed his usual dealer big time and he had to find a way to pay him back before it was too late. Because, as things stood, he was running out of options.

63

June 2017

Sapphire walked into the pub and spotted Skinner across the room. It was nearly eleven o'clock at night. She'd just been at work and had broken off early because Skinner had sounded desperate to see her. Besides, she needed to see him too; she was running out of coke.

The pub wasn't one she was familiar with. It was an estate pub a bit outside the city centre, and Sapphire wondered why Skinner had wanted her to meet out here. When she walked inside, she could see that it was packed and most of the customers had their eyes fixed on two giant TV screens, which were playing reruns of popular football matches.

It took a while till she spotted Skinner, sitting on a table at the far side of the pub with his glass almost empty. She made her way to the bar and bought herself a drink as well as a pint of Skinner's usual lager then went to join him. As she slid into the seat opposite him in the booth, she noticed that he wasn't full of his usual smiles.

'What the fuck's wrong with you?' she asked. 'You look as though you've lost a fiver and found a penny.'

'Yeah, summat like that,' he grumbled.

'Why, what's happened?'

'Well, I was on a good thing, buying my gear off this guy called Marco. I was well in with him too. So, I figured that because he trusted me, he might let me have 'em in bulk so I could sell 'em on and get a mark-up. Easy money, innit?'

'OK. So, what went wrong?'

'Well, he let me have plenty. We had this deal where he let me have the gear up front and I paid him once I'd sold 'em on. I started off small but, as I'd got to know him, I increased it each time. Then one day I decided to double up. Thought I'd make a killing.'

Sapphire noticed that Skinner was now squirming in his seat and she knew there was more to come. He paused to scratch an area on his thigh then twitched his head from side to side before he carried on speaking.

'I didn't even get as far as the end of the street where Marco lives. There was this gang outside the shops. They were only kids so I didn't think they could do me any harm. I carried on walking towards them. But there were about five of them. And they had fuckin' knives. The bastards mugged me, took every fuckin' bit of the gear.'

'How much are we talking about, Skinner?'

'Five hundred quid's worth. Well, that's how much I paid Marco. I'd have got a fuckin' sight more for it on the street.'

'Jesus Christ! Have you told Marco you were mugged?'

'Have I fuck! Guys like Marco don't wanna listen to shit. They just want their fuckin' payment.'

'How long ago was this?'

'A few days. I was supposed to see him the day before yesterday with the cash.'

'Fuckin' hell, Skinner. You've got yourself in a right load of shit, haven't you? How have you been coping since then?'

Sapphire knew Skinner relied on a regular supply to feed his drugs habit. But she was also concerned for herself. Her own supplies were running short, and she had been hoping to buy some gear from Skinner. She listened while he told her about Al and what had happened when he called to see him.

'Skinner, you dick! Why didn't you come straight with him and tell him you didn't have enough money? He might have let you have less drugs.'

'I did, but it was too late by then. He took half the fuckin' gear off me but all my cash. And now I'm right in the shit.'

'Jesus! What are we gonna do for supplies?'

'You'll be OK. My mate, Jono, will see you right. I'll have a word with him. I can get mine from him too once I get some cash. But I'm fuckin' skint at the moment and I need summat bad.' He took a huge gulp from his pint as if emphasising his dire need for toxic substances. 'I don't suppose...'

He looked ingratiatingly at Sapphire who tutted. 'Don't tell me, you want some cash?'

'Yeah, but I'll pay you back, honest. And, well, I could do with summat now.'

'OK, I can spare a hundred at the most and you can take this for now.'

Sapphire sneaked a couple of pills into his hand. 'Aw, cheers, mate. I really appreciate this but, to be honest, I could do with more cash. If I buy plenty, Jono'll let me have 'em cheaper. That way I can still make a mark-up so I can get some cash together to pay Marco. I need to get him off my back. The guy's a fuckin' lunatic if you cross him.'

He picked up his pint and used it to furtively swill down the pills. 'Skinner, I can't really afford any more,' said Sapphire. 'I need to get some gear myself and I've got bills to pay too.'

'I'll pay you back in the next couple of days, honest. When do you need to pay your bills?'

'By the end of the week.'

'You'll be OK then. I'll get the cash back to you well before then. How much can you spare?'

Sapphire knew she'd backed herself into a corner. She shouldn't have told Skinner she had until the end of the week. But she felt bad refusing him now. He was desperate. And he was a mate after all.

'OK, two hundred but that's all I can spare, and I need it back in the next couple of days.'

'Sure, mate. Cheers.'

'What about Jono? Where can I find him?'

'I'll give you his number,' said Skinner, pulling out his phone and sending Jono's details to Sapphire.

Sapphire heard her phone ping and took it out to check. Once she'd seen Jono's details on the screen, she was about to put the phone back in her pocket and give Skinner his cash when it rang. She checked the screen again and saw that it was Natasha.

'I'll just nip outside to take this call. I can't hear a fuckin' thing in here. Be back in a minute.'

*

Skinner was already feeling a bit more relaxed, partly because of the drugs Sophie had given him and partly because of the money. But although the amphetamine pills had helped, he needed more and soon. He was eager for Sapphire to come back and let him have the cash so he could get on his way.

Thank God she had come through for him. He didn't know what he would have done otherwise. Jono had already turned him down because he owed him money from ages ago that he'd not got round to repaying yet, and nobody else he knew would have lent him that amount. He probably could have made some money pickpocketing or doing a bit of lifting. But he needed the cash now.

He was glad to see his friend come back inside the pub but was surprised to see that she was looking gutted. He hoped he hadn't pushed his luck too far. Maybe she had decided she couldn't afford to lend him the money after all. From what he had seen of Natasha he knew that she wouldn't have approved if she knew about it.

Skinner didn't need to ask what was wrong. Sapphire came out with it straight away with a trembling voice. 'That was Natasha. She's just dumped me.'

64

Sapphire was back on the beat, standing in her regular spot and waiting for her next client. She hadn't been to work the previous night, choosing to spend the whole day and evening moping around the flat.

Being without Natasha was taking some getting used to, and Sapphire was finding it difficult. Although they had only been together a few months, Sapphire had been madly in love. She'd never felt like that before, which was what was making it so hard to handle.

Now Natasha was gone, Sapphire felt an emptiness. She found herself analysing everything about the relationship to see if she had missed any tell-tale signs that things weren't right.

She could have got carried away thinking about the whys and wherefores. But then her natural resilience had taken over. She knew she couldn't afford to miss too much work, especially now she had loaned Skinner £200, so she'd dragged herself out of bed and returned to the beat.

Her sorrow over Natasha was now tinged with anger. The dirty two-timing bitch! Sapphire couldn't believe she'd dumped her for a man. Apparently, it was an old boyfriend who had come back into her life and she had been torn between the two of them for the past few weeks. In the end the boyfriend had won. So much for her not bothering with men anymore!

A car pulled up at the kerb, drawing Sapphire away from her troubled thoughts. She approached the passenger window and, after a few words with the driver, she got in. He was a middle-aged man, below average height, skinny and wearing glasses.

'We're going to a hotel,' he said. 'I wanna book you by the hour rather than a set fee.'

'How long do you want to book for?'

'Oh, I think two hours should do it.'

'OK,' said Sapphire, giving him a price, which he seemed satisfied with.

He headed out of the city.

'Eh, it's a bit out of the way, isn't it?' said Sapphire.

'Don't worry, I'll drive you back to town later.'

'OK, as long as it's not too far. Time is money y'know.'

'Don't worry, we've arrived.'

They were in Rusholme, a mile or two out of the city centre and Sapphire wondered where the hotel could be. The client parked his car, and they walked the short distance to the building. Feeling cautious, Sapphire asked, 'Why aren't we parking at the hotel?'

'It doesn't have a car park. Don't worry, we're there now.'

They arrived at the building and Sapphire noticed that it was more of a guest house. The client put his key in the lock, and they went straight upstairs, not passing anybody as they made their way to one of the upstairs rooms.

Sapphire was feeling a little cautious but no more than usual. She'd encountered this situation before and knew that some clients preferred a small guest house where they wouldn't be spotted walking through a hotel lobby with a woman who was obviously too young to be their wife. Nevertheless, she weighed up the situation. The guy wasn't big, and she felt confident that she could easily fight him off if she needed to.

They walked inside the room and the man took his coat off and placed it on a hanger inside the wardrobe. Then he walked to the window and closed the curtains. Sapphire was starting to undress.

'No, not yet!' he ordered, turning away from the window, and walking towards her. 'Just stand there a minute.'

She thought his request was a bit strange, but she did as he said, anxious to see how this panned out. He passed her then went to the bedside cabinet and pulled something out of the drawer, turning swiftly away from the cabinet and back towards her.

By the time Sapphire noticed the glint of steel, he was up against her and had the knife at her throat. She flinched and tried to pull back, but he thrust the knife upwards till the tip of the blade was jabbing into the delicate flesh under her chin. Sapphire felt a sharp prick and drew in her breath.

'Keep still and don't say a fuckin' word!' he ordered. 'I want you to do exactly as I say, and everything will be alright. Is that clear?'

Sapphire couldn't nod in case the knife jabbed further

into her flesh, so she just stared at him, her eyes wide with fear.

'OK, I think I've got your attention now so I'm going to remove the knife in a minute. When I do, I want you to keep quiet. Any screams or sudden moves and you'll find out just how handy this knife can be.'

His words made her look down at the weapon he was wielding, and she noticed how huge it was. Its sturdy steel blade was wide and curved, the type that tapered into a fine point.

'Get on the bed and lie down,' he said, pulling the knife away.

Sapphire did as he ordered, her heart thundering as she anticipated his next move. Then she felt the sharp prod of cold steel again.

'Keep the fuck still!' he yelled, and Sapphire knew that any chance of escape was lost.

She tried to keep calm while he tied her wrists, her attention on the knife, which he had now placed on the ground.

'Don't even fuckin' think about it,' he ordered. 'I'll get to it before you do.'

His eyes were wide, his stare unwavering and his face contorted in some perverse form of glee. Then he spoke again, and his voice became even more threatening. 'I want you to tell me how you feel.'

'How the fuck do you think I feel?' said Sapphire, tearfully.

'I want you to tell me. Properly. Describe the fear.'

Sapphire gazed quizzically at him. 'Scared.'

The man picked up the knife and jabbed it at her throat.

'How scared?' he demanded. 'Describe it! I want to know what you're feeling. The racing heart. The sweaty hands. The need to urinate. All of it. Tell me!'

Sapphire's fear turned to dread. There was no doubt in her mind by now; she was dealing with a fuckin' madman.

65

For the next half an hour he tormented her, running the knife along her body while he made her describe how she felt, his face coloured with some alternative form of emotion midway between ecstasy and contempt.

When he ran the knife up her legs and circled it around her pelvic area, she could feel her body trembling. It was as though the physical demonstration of her fear was the trigger he had been waiting for and he quickly undid his trousers. Sapphire closed her eyes, hoping for it to be over quickly. She felt him tug at her underwear and when her briefs fell away, she realised he had used the knife to cut them from her.

'Open your fuckin' eyes!' he yelled.

Sapphire did as he ordered, just in time to see him enter her still wearing that strange expression. Again, she hoped for it to soon be over. Eventually it was. But the man didn't let her get dressed and go. Instead, he wielded the knife again. She stared at him in horror as she recalled their arrangement. He had paid for two hours.

Skinner was high on drugs. In fact, in the two days since he'd borrowed the money from Sapphire, he'd been on one massive binge. He had intended to sell most of the drugs on, but his cravings had been so bad by the time he got hold of some gear that he hadn't been able to help himself.

Fortunately, he still had some drugs left so he decided to go and see a few old mates who were hanging out in a derelict warehouse on the outskirts of Salford, to see if he could make some quick cash. Skinner sometimes spent the night there himself but, by and large, he preferred to be in the city centre where the action was.

He walked into the warehouse, still on a high, and went over to three of the guys who were sitting on folded-up sleeping bags and passing around a spliff while one of them was playing music off his mobile phone. Despite his intoxication, Skinner picked up on their ill feeling as he approached them. But it wasn't animosity that he saw in their faces: it was shock mixed with fear.

The most outspoken of the group, a guy called Chris said, 'Skinner, what the fuck are you doing here? You do know Marco's been looking for you, don't you?'

'Oh, it's OK, I owe him some money, but I'll soon get it together. That'll make him sweet.'

'No, it's not OK, Skinner,' said Chris, standing up and

pointing at another one of the group. 'Have you seen the fuckin' state of his face?'

Skinner looked at the other guy and noticed that he had a black eye and an angry bruise on the other side of his face.

'Marco did that,' Chris continued. 'Because he wouldn't fuckin' tell him where you were. He didn't know where you were anyway, but Marco still wouldn't take no for an answer.'

Skinner felt the impact of Chris's words. 'Shit! I didn't think he'd go that far.'

'Well, put it this way, if that's what he's done to him then you can bet you're in for some serious shit when he gets his fuckin' hands on you.'

A feeling of intense fear consumed Skinner. He couldn't think about the guy who had been beaten by Marco; he was too concerned for his own safety. Without saying anything further, he turned and ran to the sound of Chris shouting after him, 'You'd better not fuckin' tell him it was me that warned you!'

Skinner had forgotten all about his intention to sell some of the drugs. He was too bothered about Marco. He'd known of Marco's reputation but foolishly believed he'd be able to pacify him once he'd paid what he owed.

But it seemed he'd underestimated him and suddenly memories of some of the things he had been told about Marco came flooding back to him. The shootings. The shattered kneecaps. The missing fingers.

Marco was so good to get along with when you were

buying drugs from him that it was easy to overlook how cruel he could be. But now the reality had hit home, and Skinner became desperate to get away before Marco found him.

66

Two days later and Sapphire was still trembling every time she thought of her terrifying experience at that guest house. To her amazement the attacker had stopped precisely two hours after the time when he had booked her then insisted on driving her back to the red-light area in Manchester. As soon as he had gone, she had returned home and reported the attack to the police.

Despite her fear, she was already back on the beat. She was telling herself she wouldn't be beaten, but she also needed the money. To add to her troubles, in the four days since she had seen Skinner, she hadn't been able to get hold of him and he still had her two hundred quid.

By the time the police had checked the guest house, the man had fled. They told Sapphire they had no leads as he'd checked in under an alias and paid in cash. It left her feeling frustrated and helpless.

That night when she got home, she fell straight into bed. Through the exhaustion of not having slept properly for two nights, Sapphire quickly fell asleep. Unfortunately, it brought her no comfort. She dreamt of her mother, but it was far different from the dreams she used to have.

She pictured her lying on her deathbed, her body emaciated and her face pale and drawn with dark circles beneath her eyes. Then the dream switched; she was back to her old self with a rosy glow on her face and meat on her bones. But her face also bore an expression of terror.

In her dream Sapphire searched to see what had caused her mother alarm. Then Natasha came into the frame, wielding a knife, her face full of menace. For a moment Sapphire watched speechless as Natasha swished the knife to and fro. Realising the threat to her mother, Sapphire jumped forward to stop her, but Natasha was too quick. Before Sapphire could do anything, Natasha was standing over Sue with the knife held tight to her throat.

Sapphire woke up in a sweat with her heart racing. It was the second nightmare she had had since Natasha had ended their relationship. In both nightmares she had pictured her mother dying but this one was by far the most graphic. It took her a while to calm down. She was relieved that the nightmare was over but hoped she wouldn't have any more. Sapphire thought with bitterness about how dreams of her mother used to bring her comfort even when she was at her lowest ebb and living on the streets. But that was no longer the case.

Skinner arrived at the terraced house in Openshaw. It was very much an old person's house with an antiquated front door in a dull shade of brown and faded net curtains at the windows. He knocked tentatively and waited. Thankfully, it was Jono who came to the door and not his Uncle Harry.

'What the fuck are you doing here?' asked Jono. 'I didn't even know you knew where I lived.'

'I dropped you off once in a taxi. Remember?'

Skinner knew Jono was surprised that he had remembered that from so long ago. They had both been stoned at the time, Jono more so than him, which was evident from the way it had escaped Jono's memory.

'What do you want?' demanded Jono, neglecting to ask Skinner inside.

'That's no way to talk to a mate, is it?'

Jono pulled the door till there was only a narrow gap. Then he lowered his voice. 'Look, I don't want any mither. My Uncle Harry's getting on a bit and he doesn't like company. It was hard enough persuading him to let me live here, and if he knew some of the things I get up to, I'd be out on my arse.'

Skinner felt as though Jono had read his mind. 'I wouldn't be here unless I was desperate, Jono. I need somewhere to stay.'

'No fuckin' way!'

'It's only for a few days till I get some cash together to pay Marco. He's after me. The guys at Salford told me. He beat the shit out of one of them. I'm fuckin' scared, Jono. If he gets his hands on me, I'm a goner. I don't know who else to ask. Please, mate.'

'No, Skinner. Even if I agreed to it, I don't think my uncle would.'

Skinner fished in his pocket and pulled out a watch that he had stolen the day before. He knew it was an expensive one and had been intending to sell it but perhaps he could use it for leverage. 'What if I see him right?' he asked.

'Wow!' said Jono. 'That's a good un.' He took hold of it, examining it closely and checking it was showing the right time. 'He might go for it. But what about me?'

Skinner put his hand inside his pocket again and pulled out another designer watch.

'Fuckin' hell, Skinner! Where did you get this lot from?'

Skinner grinned, despite his predicament. 'Never you mind. Are you gonna let me stay, or what? It'll only be for a few days and I'll see you and your uncle right once I get some cash.'

'Wait here,' said Jono, going inside and shutting the door after him.

Skinner waited outside, gazing around him shiftily. He noticed three children playing in the street and two women gossiping outside one of the neighbouring houses. Eventually Jono came to the door.

'Right, he says you can stay but only till weekend, and that's only 'cos I told him your mum's just died and you've got nowhere else to go. And I swear, Skinner, I don't want any fuckin' trouble. You're not to let anyone know where you're living, right? And don't fuckin' nick owt.'

'Don't worry, mate. I won't even be going into town till I've got things sorted. I'm staying as far away from Marco as possible.'

Skinner followed Jono inside. The house had a dirty, untended smell about it. As he walked into the lounge, he saw an old man sitting on an armchair watching TV with a cat on his knee. Skinner noticed that he was already wearing the watch. He was older than Skinner had expected considering Jono was no more than thirty. Skinner put the man at around seventy and guessed he must have been the much older brother of one of Jono's parents.

'Alright?' he asked.

'So, you're Skinner, are you? Right, lad, like Jono's said, you can stay till the weekend and not a minute longer. I'm sorry to hear about your mother.'

Skinner shrugged and adopted a sad expression. 'Thanks.'

'You can doss down on the floor in my room,' said Jono. 'Come on, I'll show you where it is.'

Skinner followed Jono through the house. The strange smell permeated every room and the place looked sorrowfully neglected with dust on every surface and old-fashioned furniture that was worn and had broken handles and scratches. But, compared to some of the places he'd stayed, it wasn't that bad. And at least it was somewhere he would feel safe. For now.

67

June 2017

Jono stared in horror at the man in front of him. Marco. Although only average height he was stocky and had the stance of someone who knew how to handle himself. But the scariest thing about him was his permanent scowl. Even when he was joking around, his face automatically settled back into a scowl once the joke was over. It was as though he had an uncontained aggression that was threatening to erupt at any minute.

How the hell Marco had tracked him down, Jono didn't know. And the fact that he'd met him outside one of his regular haunts told Jono he'd been looking for him. He recognised him straightaway; he'd seen him around plenty of times although he'd never had any dealings with him.

That could only mean one thing: that he was after him in connection with Skinner. Again, Jono didn't have a clue how he'd come by information that suggested he was linked to Skinner. But, knowing of Marco's reputation, he didn't expect he'd find it difficult to extract information out of people.

As if Marco wasn't terrifying enough on his own, he had two of his thugs with him. They were both bigger than Marco and just as mean-looking. Jono looked tiny even in comparison to Marco, let alone the two thugs. He was tempted to run but that would only confirm that he had something to hide. So, he decided to front it out despite his intense fear.

As soon as he drew level with them, they surrounded him. One of the hired muscle grabbed his arm and wrenched it up his back. Then they marched him to their car, a flash Merc that was parked in the next street. The man who had grabbed him, shoved him into the back then climbed in alongside him while Marco got in the front and the other man took the driver's seat.

Turning to face him, Marco said, 'I wanna word with you, Jono. But not here. We'll go somewhere nice and quiet where we won't be disturbed.'

Jono could feel the adrenalin coursing through his body till his mouth became dry and his stomach growled. It didn't take long to arrive in a deserted car park near the wholesale warehouses in Cheetham Hill. Although busy in the day, at this time in the evening, it was deserted. Jono felt as though he was going to be sick.

'Get out!' Marco ordered.

The driver released the door locks and Jono stepped out of the car. He still felt the urge to vomit but he held it back. Jono was determined not to show his fear. That way they wouldn't think he had anything to hide.

'OK, I expect you know what this is about,' said Marco. Jono shrugged.

'Don't play fuckin' games! I know Skinner's a mate of yours. What I don't know though is where he's fucked off to.'

'I didn't know he had,' said Jono, trying to control the shaking in his voice. 'But I don't see that much of him anyway.'

'Don't tell fuckin' lies! I know exactly how pally you two are. He's probably told you how much he owes me too.'

'What? Skinner owes you money? Nah, I'm clueless, mate. He wouldn't tell me that sort of shit. I told you, we're not that close. It's just that he mixes with the same crowd as me.'

Marco nodded to the thug who had been sitting in the back of the car. He responded by thumping Jono so fiercely in the stomach that it winded him. Jono doubled over, clutching his guts.

Not waiting for him to recover, Marco said, 'Where's your mate? And I want no more of your bullshit or you'll get the same again.'

Jono straightened himself up, panting till he got his breath back. Then he replied, 'Sorry, I don't know.'

Again, Marco nodded at the thug. This time he didn't just thump Jono once. And he didn't restrict his punches to Jono's stomach. The attack came hard and fast, and Jono was sent reeling backwards. The man pursued him, punching him viciously in the stomach till Jono was bent double again. Then he grabbed Jono's hair and yanked his head back so that he was upright. He carried on hitting him in the face, head, shoulders, arms, and upper body. Eventually, Jono collapsed to the ground.

Only then did the attack stop, the thug standing back and waiting for Marco to speak. 'Right, have you had enough yet? Or do we have to give you some more? After all, me and Joe here haven't even had a go at you yet.'

Jono took his time getting up off the ground. Still terrified, he was trying to tough it out, not just because of Skinner but because of his uncle. Although he had done some bad things in his life, Jono had a conscience and he didn't want a gang of hard men turning up at his uncle's house, not at his age. There was no predicting what the shock could do to him. He did well, considering he wasn't known for his bravery, holding out for another round of beatings.

By this time, his face was covered in blood and the pain was so bad that he was sure they had broken his nose and maybe a couple of ribs too. Despite his injuries and the intense fear that still gripped him, he was determined not to lead them to his uncle's house. But then one of the thugs reached into his pocket and pulled out a pair of pliers. And that changed everything.

With a look of defeat, Jono gave them his uncle's address. 'Please leave the old man out of it,' he begged. 'He doesn't know fuck-all about Skinner.'

Marco pushed his head forward till it was inches from Jono's, his ever-present sneer making Jono shiver with fear. Then he spoke, his voice low but nonetheless menacing. 'Neither did you a few fuckin' minutes ago.'

Marco searched Jono's pockets and pulled out his phone. He tossed it to the ground and stamped on it several times, grinning as he did so. 'Just in case you're thinking of ringing your *very* close friend and giving him advance warning,' he cautioned.

Then the three men got back in the car, leaving Jono dripping blood.

Sapphire wasn't having a good day. Last night had been another night of disturbed sleep and the nightmares were making her increasingly distressed.

It had been a week since Natasha had dumped her and five days since her attack. One of those events alone would have been hard enough to deal with. Natasha had left her broken-hearted and the attack had left her petrified. But dealing with both traumas at the same time was proving too much.

Sapphire was taking more drugs to help her cope with her stress. She was drinking and smoking more too. But she couldn't escape her troubled thoughts. All her addictions came at a price too and she was getting behind with her bills, especially since Skinner had disappeared owing her two hundred pounds.

She had searched for him several times but all the people she spoke to hadn't seen anything of him. It was worrying in view of what he had told her and for a moment she was tempted to ring her old friend, Crystal, to confide in her about all her problems. But a little voice inside her head told her that Crystal wouldn't be interested; she was too busy running her businesses to have time for her.

There was one person Sapphire hadn't spoken to: Jono, and she thought that maybe he would be able to tell her where Skinner was hiding out. She tried ringing the number Skinner had given her for him but it went straight to voicemail. Then she thought that he perhaps frequented a lot of the same places as Skinner. Tonight, she needed to get to work though; she needed the money. But she decided that tomorrow she would see if she could find Jono.

It hadn't taken Skinner long to ingratiate himself with Jono's Uncle Harry. He'd been close to his own grandfather at one time and knew exactly how to play old people. With a bit of probing, he had found out that Harry used to be a professional boxer in his younger days. He claimed he had given it up because his girlfriend at the time couldn't cope with him getting hurt, but Jono had secretly told Skinner that it was because he hadn't been good enough to go any further.

That didn't stop him bragging about the fights he'd won, every time he reminisced about 'the good old days'. But Harry omitted to mention those he'd lost, and glossed over the couple that he'd drawn. Picking up on his mention of a girlfriend, Skinner cheekily asked, 'I bet you had all the girls after you back then, didn't you?'

The old man had smiled and gone on to brag about his conquests with the opposite sex. Skinner's flattery had worked so he kept piling it on. He also made him endless cups of tea and tonight he had come back from the off-licence with a few cans of beer for them to share while they watched a film on TV.

Skinner wasn't daft. He knew Jono was bored of his uncle's repeated stories of the old days and that he was only there because he needed somewhere cheap to stay. He also knew that Uncle Harry was desperate for company. Even Jono had said that he seemed a lot happier in himself since Skinner had moved in. If he carried on playing up to the old man, then he'd hopefully agree to let him stay a while longer until Skinner could formulate a plan.

They were enjoying the film when they were disturbed by a knock on the door. 'Go and see who that is, will yer?' said Harry, clearly enjoying having Skinner waiting on him. 'I bet Jono's forgot his bloody key again.'

Skinner was quick to respond. Even though he doubted that anyone would find him hiding out here, he preferred to be on the safe side. He dashed to the window, checking whether he could see who was outside but whoever it was must have been too close to the house for him to spot them.

Quietly he crept to the front door and put his ear to the letter box, listening out for any signs of conversation. He couldn't hear anything. So, he pulled the letter box up and peeked. All he could see was the clothing of whoever was standing there but his movement had alerted them.

'Answer the fuckin' door, Skinner! We know you're in there.'

Marco? Shit! How the hell had he found him?

Filled with dread, Skinner dashed through the house and towards the back door to the sound of Harry shouting, 'What the bloody hell's going on?'

With shaking hands, Skinner slid open the bolt on the back door. But his panic had caused him to be careless. He should have checked the back of the house first. As soon as the door was open, two huge men barged in, one of them grabbing Skinner and frogmarching him through to the lounge while the other rushed to open the front door so that Marco could join them.

Uncle Harry jumped up out of his chair, his hands bunched into fists as he took a boxer's stance. 'Get out of my fuckin' house!' he yelled.

'Sit the fuck down, Grandad,' said Marco.

Ignoring his warning, Uncle Harry rushed at the men. As one of them kept a tight hold of Skinner, the other swung his fist at Harry as if he were swatting a fly, and the old man fell to the ground. Not giving him chance to recover, the thug stamped on Harry's back then kept his foot there, pinning him to the ground while the old man groaned with pain.

'Leave him. He hasn't done anything wrong!' Skinner protested.

Marco fled over to Skinner and grabbed him by the throat. 'No but you have, haven't you? And I think it's about time you paid your fuckin' dues.'

68

It took Sapphire a while to find Jono, but she was determined. So, she persevered because she was worried about what had happened to Skinner.

At an old pub in Ancoats she was told that Jono had just moved on. The same people told her that they hadn't seen Skinner for days. When she reached Jono, he was in a state, his face a mass of cuts and bruises, and he was leaning heavily on the bar. He'd obviously had a shitload to drink too and had probably taken something on top of the booze.

'Fuckin' hell! What's happened to your face? And how much have you drunk?' she asked, feeling a little hypocritical when she thought about the amount of drugs she had already taken that day.

'What do *you* want?' he asked, wincing as he tried to straighten up and turned to face her. 'If you're looking for Skinner, you won't fuckin' find him!'

It was evident from his attitude and his intoxicated state that he was troubled about something. And she couldn't help wondering who had given him a beating. 'What's going on, Jono? Where is he?'

Jono shrugged and winced again. 'Dunno.'

'Come on, Jono, you must know something.'

He ignored her last comment and turned his back to her, his body slumped against the bar again. Sapphire grabbed hold of his arm, refusing to be put off. 'Come and sit down, Jono; you don't look so good.'

He snatched his arm away from her. 'I'm alright!'

'Look, Jono, I'm not stupid. I know something's going on because of what Skinner told me last time I saw him.'

This grabbed Jono's attention and he turned around again. 'What?'

'Do you really want me to tell you here?' she asked, indicating the other customers who were gathered at the bar. She took hold of his arm again. 'Come on, there's a quiet corner table over there.'

Jono looked so alarmed that he readily followed her. As soon as they were seated, Sapphire lowered her voice. 'He told me he owed money to a drug dealer called Marco.' She could see from the look on his face that he was familiar with what had happened. 'I'm worried about him, Jono. He was really scared. And I haven't seen owt of him since. He owes me two hundred quid too and I could really do with the money right now.'

Jono's body slumped again but this time it wasn't because of the booze. Sapphire guessed, when he began to speak, that it was part relief at having someone to confide in, and part resignation. 'I'm fuckin' worried too.' She heard the emotion in his voice when he said, 'I didn't wanna tell them where he was but they fuckin' made me!'

'Is that how you got your injuries?'

Jono nodded.

'For fuck's sake, Jono! When did this happen?'

'Last night. I haven't been home since.'

'What? So, he's staying at your place?' Sapphire was surprised as she thought Jono was homeless.

'Not my place. My uncle's. That's where I've been staying, and I'm worried what they've done to the old man.'

'Jesus, Jono! We can't just leave it. We need to get round there *now* and find out what's happened.'

'But what if they're still there?'

'They won't be, not if they went round last night. Haven't Skinner or your uncle contacted you?'

'No. They smashed my fuckin' phone.'

'Jono, we're going, and that's that! We need to know what's happened.'

It didn't take them long to arrive at Jono's uncle's house in Openshaw. Sapphire was driving the old red Golf that she'd bought years ago after she'd learnt to drive. Despite Jono slurring his words, he managed to direct her there. As they entered the street, they could see a cordon had been placed around Jono's uncle's house and there were police guarding the house and preventing people from entering.

'Shit!' said Jono, and Sapphire felt her stomach churn with worry.

Parking spaces were scarce due to the number of emergency vehicles surrounding the property, so she parked the car several metres away. Jono jumped out and limped towards the house.

'Jono stop!' she yelled, chasing after him.

He stopped and looked at her. 'I need to find out what's happened.'

Once she had caught up with him, Sapphire lowered her voice. 'You've got to be careful, Jono. You don't wanna be quizzed by the police. They might think you're involved. And imagine how Marco would react if he thought you'd been taken in for questioning. He'd be waiting for you as soon as you came out of the station to make sure you kept your mouth shut.'

Jono's face drained of colour. 'Fuck!'

'Wait in the car,' said Sapphire, handing him the keys. 'I'll go over and see what I can find out.'

Sapphire joined the crowd of avid onlookers. 'What's happened?' she asked.

A middle-aged woman looked at her. 'I think summat's happened to Harry,' she said, sadly. 'It was me that told the police.' Sapphire could hear the boastful tone of her voice despite her sorrow. 'I came to see if he wanted summat from the shops. I often do that when I'm going, with him getting on a bit. Anyway, there was no answer. The curtains were still shut, which was unusual, and when I looked through the letter box, I couldn't see owt. I thought it was a bit strange. He's had his nephew staying with him, y'know and another lad who looks a bit shifty.

'Anyway, last night I heard a right commotion. I didn't think much of it at the time. Well, I thought he'd just fell out with one of the lads and you don't get involved with other people's arguments, do you?'

Sapphire was becoming irritable and wished that the stupid gossip would just get to the point. 'I kept shouting but there was no sign of life and I thought, well, it was funny that all three of them were out. And, if they were, why did they leave the curtains shut? So, I rang the police. I thought I might be overreacting at first and I didn't really want to waste police time but ...'

'What did the police say?'

'Not much. They asked me a few questions, so I told them about last night. But they asked if I'd seen anybody else entering or leaving the premises last night, which sounds a bit fishy to me. And then they put the tape up. I'm bloody worried sick about what they might have found in there.'

'Right, thanks,' said Sapphire, moving away from the woman.

She could feel a rush of anxiety as she thought about what may have taken place inside that house. The woman was right, it didn't sound good. Worried that Jono might now have joined her, she cast her gaze around the crowd and further up the road. There was no sign of Jono, but a well-dressed man carrying a briefcase was heading towards the house.

'I think this is the doctor,' declared one of the onlookers and an excited murmur travelled around the group. A policeman stepped forward and headed towards the man. This confirmed Sapphire's suspicions that he must be someone important and she slipped away from the group and crept towards the two men.

Sapphire was just in time to overhear part of what the policeman said: '...old man's in a bad way, the paramedics are with him now, and we'll need you to confirm the death of the younger one.'

His words hit Sapphire with the force of a thunderstorm, and she felt the bile rise to her throat. She forced it down, not wanting to draw attention to herself, but the thoughts were crashing around inside her head. Skinner – dead! And Jono's uncle in a bad way. But she hadn't heard them mentioned by name. Maybe she had got it wrong. Maybe there had been somebody else in the house.

She tried to think what the nosy neighbour had told her, but her thoughts were in a quandary. Deciding she needed to know for sure, Sapphire went back to the woman.

'Excuse me, did you notice if anyone else went into the house last night.'

The woman eyed her warily. Asking what had happened once was one thing but asking for further details warranted suspicion. Thankfully for Sapphire, her desire to be the font of all knowledge won.

'Yes, that's what I was trying to tell you until you walked off. Well, I didn't see anybody walk in other than Harry and that lad that's been staying with them. And I don't think Jono was home because I saw him go out earlier in the day. But I did see three big men coming out of the house. They left by the back door too.

'I couldn't make out much detail because it was dark but there were definitely three of them. It was after all that commotion. And the funny thing is …' she then lowered her voice to a whisper as though her next words were too unbearable to speak out loud '…I didn't hear a dicky bird after that.'

Sapphire was so choked up that she didn't even thank the woman. She turned away and noticed the staring eyes of the crowd taking in her shocked expression. Then she heard further murmuring from them. She felt assaulted by her own senses as her anxiety escalated. Everything was magnified. The prying eyes. The noise of the crowd. The thumping of her heart. And the taste of bile on her tongue.

She needed to get away. And she needed to speak to Jono. But what the hell was she going to say to him that would soften the blow?

69

June 2017

Sapphire and Jono shuffled along the pew in the crematorium and waited for the other mourners to arrive. … And waited … Nobody came. *How sad*, thought Sapphire, *to be all alone in the world*. But at least Skinner had her and Jono mourning his death, which made her glad she came.

She felt sorry for Jono. It was his second funeral this week. Unfortunately, his uncle had died on arrival at hospital due to the amount of blood he'd lost. Apparently, the three men had carved him up something wicked. It sickened her to think that they could do that to an innocent old man.

But she had no doubt that his uncle's funeral would have been a more grandiose affair than this one. From what Jono had told her, the old man had taken out a fancy funeral plan, so it was all paid for in advance. And he was also popular with the neighbours and his drinking buddies in the local pub, so the attendance was good.

In contrast, Skinner's funeral had been paid for by the local authority. It shouldn't have surprised Sapphire that there were no other mourners considering nobody had been concerned enough to arrange the funeral.

It was a basic affair: no flowers, no procession and just the one car carrying Skinner's body in a cheap wooden coffin. The committal ceremony was brief and conducted by a representative from Manchester City Council.

'Should we go and find a pub?' asked Jono once it was over.

'Why not? We can drink to his memory.'

It didn't take them long till they were seated inside a local pub with a pint in front of each of them. 'Bloody sad that, wasn't it?' asked Jono.

'Yeah but at least we were there, Jono.'

'Yeah. Thanks for coming with me. I wouldn't have wanted to do it on my own.'

'Course I was gonna come with you. What did you expect? He was a mate.'

'I know but ...'

Sapphire grew suspicious at the way Jono quickly clamped his mouth shut. 'But what?' she snapped.

'Nowt. Forget it.'

Sapphire didn't want to let it go though. 'What is it, Jono? What's he said about me? Is it because I'm gay? He didn't take the piss behind my back, did he?'

'No! Did he 'eck. It was nothing like that.'

'Well, what was it then?'

'Nothing.'

Then a thought occurred to Sapphire. 'Aah, I know what it was. It was because I wouldn't let him move into the flat with me, wasn't it?'

'Kind of,' said Jono, shuffling uncomfortably.

'Go on. What did he say? Was he really pissed off?'

'You could say that, yeah.'

'Well, he hid it well. I thought he wasn't that bothered. Y'know what Skinner was like, happy-go-lucky, water off a duck's back and all that.'

'Fuck, Sapphire! You didn't know him as well as you thought you did.'

'Why? What's he done?'

Jono grabbed his pint and took a quick gulp. He put it back down on the table and his eyes wandered around the room. When the silence between them became stifling, he took another gulp.

'Look, I've got to get going after this pint, Sapphire.'

'Hang on a minute. We've only just got here. I thought we were having a drink for Skinner. It was your idea.'

'Well, I've just remembered I've got a bit of business to attend to.'

Sapphire was growing angry now. It was maddening to think that she had just attended the funeral for someone she thought of as a mate and, from what she was now being told, it appeared that he wasn't such a mate after all. Why? She didn't know. But she intended to find out.

She grabbed hold of Jono's jacket lapel and wrenched it towards her. 'You're not fuckin' going anywhere till you tell me what Skinner's done! I swear, Jono, if I have to use my fuckin' blade, I will do.'

Jono was only a tiny guy, and his courage was even less abundant than his height. Sapphire was bluffing about the knife, but she had surmised that after the hiding from Marco and his thugs, he wouldn't want a repeat performance. She had guessed right. 'OK, OK, I'll tell you. Let go of my fuckin' jacket, will yer?'

Sapphire released him. 'OK, but you'd better fuckin' tell me, Jono, or I swear I'll kick you so hard in the bollocks that you'll be limping all the way home.'

The colour drained from Jono's face. 'Alright, but you're not gonna like it. And don't fuckin' take it out on me.'

'I won't, I promise.'

'Well, you know when you moved in the flat and had that break-in...'

'No!' yelled Sapphire, guessing at what was coming next. 'Please tell me it wasn't Skinner.'

Jono lowered his head and muttered, 'Yeah, it was.'

'You're fuckin' joking! The slimy, sly little bastard. Do you realise how many nights I couldn't sleep after that? It really put the shits up me. You didn't do it with him did you?'

'Did I fuck! I wouldn't do that to a mate. In fact, I told him not to do it.'

Suddenly the idea of drinking to Skinner's memory felt tainted. She had been betrayed by someone she thought was a friend. Her sorrow at Skinner's death now seemed misplaced but the sorrow at his betrayal was far more potent.

Sapphire stamped angrily on the cockroach that was scuttling across the kitchen floor. The crunching of its shell sent a shiver of repulsion through her body. So, the damn things were back! It had been the same story ever since she'd moved in five years ago; the council kept fumigating her flat but in no time at all the insects returned and she became overrun with them. It made her feel dirty and low.

Tonight, she just wanted to drink herself into oblivion. She was already on her way, having decided to stay in the pub with Jono after all. Although she no longer liked the idea of drinking to Skinner's memory, she had still felt in need of a drink.

Sapphire grabbed a glass from the cupboard then threw herself onto the living room sofa and opened the bottle of vodka she had bought on her way home from the funeral alongside a bottle of lemonade. She removed her jacket, emptied the pockets of all the drugs she had bought from Jono, then slung it across the floor.

But her troubled thoughts kept roaring through her brain like a dozen angry lions that had been unleashed. It was hard to get her head around Skinner's betrayal. How could he treat her like that? After all she had done for him. And, to think, she'd been gullible enough to mourn his death. The dirty fuckin' rat could rot in hell for all she cared!

She took a couple of pills off the coffee table and washed them down with a swig of vodka and lemonade. But her thoughts remained. And the more she drank, the more maudlin she became.

She couldn't believe the things that had happened to her. It was as though she was cursed. And what had her life come to? Living in a poxy, infested council flat, hooked on drugs, in debt and having to sell her body to get by. She'd had enough of this life!

She cast her mind back to her wonderful childhood with her beautiful, caring mother and lovely sister, Kelsey.

Her mother was often in her dreams lately, but it seemed as though the dreams were now trying to sully her lovely memories. They were so full of death, violence, and despair.

Sapphire had even lost her baby and the thought of it cut a gash through her heart. She quickly grabbed some more pills off the coffee table and washed them down with the alcohol. In fact, it seemed to her that she eventually lost everyone she became attached to, even the people who had wronged her such as Jake, Natasha and Skinner.

What a bitch Natasha was! Stringing her along while she had been two-timing her with a man. Despite the hurt she had caused, a tiny part of her still loved Natasha. And she despised herself because of it. Why couldn't her heart just let go?

And what about Skinner? To think, she had felt so sorry at the funeral because he had died all alone in the world. But really, she was no different. She was all alone too. Who would give a damn if she were to live or die?

Perhaps Crystal? No, maybe not. It was evident to Sapphire that Crystal no longer wanted her as part of her life. And that hurt, especially as Crystal had been so willing to help Amber in the past.

Sapphire recalled the words Crystal had previously used, "anyone would think you had a thing for me". Crystal had made her feel needy and pathetic, and that wasn't the person she was. Sapphire had always tried to be strong ever since she was a child. Maybe that's why Crystal had helped Amber – because she wasn't as strong.

But now, Sapphire had had enough. A person can only take so much, she thought bitterly. She couldn't see an end to this destructive cycle. The past ten years had been full of disappointments, and people who had used her, abused her, and made her feel like a nobody.

She took a couple more pills and drained her second glass of drink then poured herself another, the vodka far exceeding the lemonade. The more she drank, the more disjointed her thoughts were. Crystal? Yes, that was who she was thinking about. Crystal. Sapphire had thought she was a mate but maybe she had just used her too.

Now that Crystal no longer had to recruit girls for Gilly, she didn't have any use for her. Well, let Crystal have her fancy life. She wouldn't spoil it for her. She'd get by on her own. Or would she? What was the point in trying any longer? As if to reaffirm her thoughts, she grabbed a handful of the pills and swilled them down with her drink.

The drugs and alcohol reinforced her new belief: that there was no point in trying any longer. It was over and she just wanted out. She downed a few more pills, her limbs heavy and clumsy.

Her brain flipped back to her most recent thoughts again. Crystal. But the details had slipped from her mind already. Amongst the fog some positive memories emerged: Crystal helping her get a flat. Crystal being with her when she found out she was pregnant. Crystal comforting her when she lost the baby. Crystal. Crystal. Must speak to Crystal.

She was becoming sleepy now and her body felt heavy. In a last-minute panic Sapphire realised she was in a bad way. Fear set in. Perhaps she didn't want to die after all. She needed help. *Must get help. Oh my God! I don't want to die.*

She fumbled for her phone. But her arms resembled lead

weights and her fingers were like dead meat. She grasped the phone awkwardly and it tumbled to the ground.

Shit! thought Sapphire reaching out and feeling around for her mobile. She thought she saw it. But her vision was blurred. She searched desperately, but everything seemed to have gone into slow motion. Her leaden fingers brushed against the carpet. But she couldn't feel her mobile. Even though she thought she saw it.

Damn! I need the phone. I've gotta make a call. Please, please, let me reach it. I feel sleepy. I just want to close my eyes and sleep. No! Don't sleep. Mustn't sleep. Get the phone. Got to get the phone. Got to make a call. Please let me get to the phone. Before it's too late!

70

June 2017

Crystal wouldn't have known who it was if Sapphire's number hadn't shown up on the screen of her mobile. Her first thought was: *Oh bloody hell, I never did get round to ringing her back*. Her second thought was: *Oh my God! What the hell is wrong with her?*

She heard Sapphire mumbling. It sounded like she was saying Crystal as well as a whole load of other words that Crystal couldn't make out. 'Sapphire, are you OK?' she asked.

But Sapphire went quiet. She was still on the line although she wasn't speaking. 'Sapphire? Talk to me. What's going on?'

Crystal hung on for a while, trying to get Sapphire to speak. She wondered what was wrong. Maybe she had been attacked. A sick client might have bound and gagged her so she couldn't speak. But then she heard something again. It wasn't a word so much as a jumbled mess before everything went quiet.

She cut the call when it became obvious that Sapphire wasn't going to say anything more. Crystal stared at the phone in her hand, confused. Then it dawned on her what had happened.

'Shit!' she yelled, dialling 999. As soon as the operator asked her which service, Crystal cried, 'Ambulance, as soon as possible please.' The operator transferred her, and Crystal tapped her fingers impatiently as she waited for the ambulance service to pick up the call. Without waiting for the person to speak, Crystal babbled, 'I need an ambulance as soon as possible. It's my friend. I think she's taken an overdose. I think she's at home.' Then she reeled off Sapphire's address. 'You might need to bash the door in. She lives on her own.'

Once she had finished the call, Crystal rang Ruby and told her what had happened. 'You did the right thing,' said Ruby. 'It does sound like an overdose, you're right.'

'I can't understand it though, Rubes. She seemed fine last time I saw her. In fact, she was all excited, telling me about her new girlfriend.'

'You don't know what goes on in someone's head though, do you?'

'Aw, don't say that, Ruby. I feel like shit now to think that she might have wanted to confide in me. She kept ringing for us to meet up, but I was always too busy with the shops.'

'Don't beat yourself up, girl,' said Ruby but it didn't make Crystal feel any better.

'Ruby, I want to go and see her. Will you come with me?'

'Yeah, sure. I'll be round as soon as I can.'

Despite Ruby's words, it was half an hour before she

showed up. Crystal was going frantic with worry. What if the emergency services didn't get there in time? She'd been tempted to go on her own but preferred to have Ruby's support.

'I'm so sorry,' said Ruby when she finally arrived at Crystal's. 'I was in the middle of something when you rang but I got away as quick as I could.'

'Come on, let's go,' said Crystal who already had her shoes on.

'OK, I'll drive.'

'Alright but please make it as fast as possible.'

Janice stared at the building in dismay and checked the address again on her phone. Yes, it was the right address, but she was perturbed to find the place surrounded by emergency services personnel. She made her way to the property where there was a group of police officers and the one at the front was using a battering ram to break the door down. Behind them two paramedics waited to enter the flat.

Janice was relieved to see a policeman she knew at the back of the group. 'What is it? What's happened?' she asked.

He turned to her and lowered his voice, nervous about being seen divulging information. 'OD, we think. Young woman by the name of Sophie Tailor. Is she one of yours?'

'Was,' she said.

Then she walked away, frightened of losing control of her emotions in front of the officer. It was hard to take in. To think she'd almost found Sophie after all these years. And now she was probably too late.

*

Crystal had an ominous feeling when they arrived at Sapphire's flat over half an hour later. It was night-time by now and the place was in darkness. She took it as a bad sign that there were no lights on in the flat, but she noticed that the front door was damaged, and someone had done a rough job of securing it.

It seemed like the emergency services might have taken her advice and broken their way into the flat. Examining the door, it appeared that they had been and gone. But, despite that, she still hammered on it for several minutes. When it became obvious that nobody was going to answer, she looked desperately across at Ruby.

'For fuck's sake, Ruby, what we gonna do?'

'Where's the nearest hospital?'

'Erm, Manchester Royal, I think.'

'Right, we'll go there then. That's where they'll have taken her.'

'Yeah, if they got here in time.'

'Don't worry, they will have done. They don't usually ignore 999 calls.'

Crystal knew it would take around fifteen minutes to get to the hospital. During the journey she chattered nervously.

'I feel so bad, Ruby. She must have been feeling like shit to do something like this.'

'Stop blaming yourself. You've done a lot for that girl. Wasn't it you who helped her get a flat, and you took her under your wing when she first started out on the beat?'

'Yeah but... I can't understand it. She seemed so happy last time I spoke to her.'

'Summat must have happened. Maybe the girlfriend ditched her.'

'Would that make her decide to top herself though? I thought Sapphire was stronger than that.'

'Like I said before, girl, you never know what's going on inside someone's head.'

Crystal thought about the recent attack on Sapphire. She knew it couldn't have helped her mental state but decided not to mention it to Ruby as Sapphire had told her in confidence. Instead, she said, 'Yeah, till it's too bloody late.'

She felt the impact of her own words and said nothing further for a while. Crystal just hoped that Sapphire was OK and couldn't bear the thought of anything bad happening to her.

By the time they arrived at the hospital she was feeling really tense and the ten minutes spent circling around trying to find a parking space did nothing to ease her nerves.

'Right, let's head to A & E,' said Ruby, looking at the signs. 'They should know summat.'

'OK,' said Crystal, taking a deep breath to steady herself then following Ruby through the car park.

71

June 2017

Sapphire looked into the loving face of her mother and felt a warm glow. She seemed happy. A captivating smile lit up her features and she had her hair tied up the way Sapphire had always liked it. She looked so pretty when she wore her hair like that.

It was wonderful to see her look just as she used to before the cancer ravaged her body. She hadn't aged at all from when Sapphire had last seen her. This time there was no knife at her throat and no violence. Instead of despair, Sapphire felt content.

Her mother was beckoning her now, willing her to come and join her. She held out her hands for Sapphire who stepped towards her, eager to be wrapped up in her maternal blanket of love and warmth.

This time the dream felt more real. Her mother was actually there. It felt so good as their hands connected. At last, Sapphire felt at peace.

★

'Aw, for shit's sake!' complained Crystal. 'Where is this fuckin' A & E? We passed the sign ages ago.'

'Just keep your eyes peeled, Crystal. There'll be another sign, don't worry.'

'But it's been ages. This place is fuckin' huge!'

'Look, Crystal. Here's another sign. It's down there.'

'Shit! That means we've been going the wrong way.'

'Looks like it. Don't worry, we'll fuckin' get there.'

They walked for a minute more before they reached the reception at A & E.

'Thank Christ for that!' said Crystal before heading to the counter.

There was a queue with three other people in front of them and Crystal tapped her foot impatiently as they waited. She grumbled intermittently to Ruby who reciprocated her complaints.

Once they had reached the counter, Crystal demanded to know whether a Sophie Tailor had been admitted. The receptionist tapped away on her keyboard without making eye contact. Then she looked up at long last.

'No, we've got nobody by that name,' she said dismissively.

'But... but... there must be,' said Crystal in a panic, thinking that maybe Sapphire had been taken to the morgue instead.

'No, sorry, nothing here.' The receptionist then cocked her head to one side and shouted, 'Next please.'

Crystal felt Ruby push past her then she hammered her fist on the counter in annoyance at the woman's attitude.

'You ain't fobbing us off like that when we've been waiting in this fuckin' queue for ages! You must have some record of her. My friend here rang a fuckin' ambulance so we wanna know what happened after that ambulance arrived at her flat.'

The woman looked terrified and was just about to say something when a thought occurred to Crystal.

'Check the spelling!' she ordered. 'How are you spelling Tailor?'

'T-A-Y-L-O-R,' said the receptionist, her voice trembling.

'Try T-A-I-L-O-R instead.'

'I've never heard of it being spelt that way,' she muttered.

'Just try it!' growled Ruby.

Startled by her ferocious tone, the woman tapped her fingers quickly on the keyboard.

'Yes, yes, we have had a Sophie Tailor admitted,' she confirmed.

'Thank Christ for that!' yelled Crystal. 'What ward is she on and how do we find it?'

As they rushed through the hospital corridors, Crystal could feel her heart hammering, and she was perspiring heavily. *Please let her be OK, please let her be OK,* she kept repeating inside her head as she feared what state Sapphire might be in by the time they found her.

Ruby found the ward and a feeling of dread descended on Crystal. A nurse directed them to a side ward and, nervous of what she might find, Crystal urged Ruby to go first. Ruby stuck her head inside before ducking back out again. She nodded her encouragement to Crystal who scrunched her brow inquisitively.

Then Crystal crept forward and took a deep breath as she pushed open the door and stepped inside. But what she saw left her feeling astounded.

72

June 2017

Sapphire's eyes flickered open but instead of seeing her mother holding her hands, she saw a strange young woman. She was smartly dressed and attractive but that didn't ease the shock. Sapphire screamed and dragged her hands away. She didn't know where she was. Her throat felt sore, and she could taste vomit. There were other people in the room too, but her attention was currently on the woman.

'Who the hell are you? Where am I? What the fuck is going on?' she demanded, raising herself to a sitting position.

'Thank God you're alright. We thought we'd lost you,' said the woman.

Just then Sapphire noticed that there was a nurse by her bedside too, monitoring her, and this drew her attention away from the young woman. She was in hospital.

Her panic intensified as she recalled the last time she had been in hospital. It was when she had lost her baby. And the time before that was when her mother had been dying of cancer. But Sapphire wasn't with her mother now: she was with strangers. Then she noticed an older woman in the background and thought she recognised her. Surely, it couldn't be!

Crystal saw that Sapphire was sitting up in bed with a nurse monitoring her. She looked hazy as Crystal would have expected but what surprised Crystal was that there were two strange women in the room as well, and it seemed as though they knew Sapphire intimately.

The younger of the two was sitting by Sapphire's bedside with a look of concern on her face and Crystal wondered who she was. Maybe it was the girlfriend and she had brought her mother with her. If so, and if it was the girlfriend who had driven Sapphire to this, then she was about to get a piece of Crystal's mind.

She wasn't happy with Sapphire either. Crystal had been worried sick ever since she'd received the call nearly two hours earlier.

'You silly cow, Sapphire!' she yelled. 'What the hell did you have to do that for? Why didn't you tell me you felt that bad?'

'Shush,' said the older woman before the nurse had a chance. She walked over to Crystal. 'Can you give them a minute please?'

'And who the hell are you?' asked Crystal with attitude.

'Janice?' Sapphire asked when she realised who the woman standing in the background was.

But she didn't receive a reply straightaway as Janice was

busy talking to two women at the door, one of whom was shouting and swearing. It was only when Sapphire peered a bit more closely that she noticed who they were: Crystal and Ruby. She was just about to say something when Janice left the room, taking them with her.

Sapphire's brain was busy trying to put the pieces of the puzzle together. She looked at the younger woman again. She was so well-dressed, cultured even, and Sapphire couldn't understand what such a woman would want with her. Then she studied her features in greater detail, and she finally recognised who the woman was. Jesus! She couldn't believe it.

'Kelsey! Is that really you?'

Kelsey smiled with tears in her eyes. 'Yes, it is.'

'But how did you know where to find me?'

'It's a long story with a bit of coincidence thrown in. Janice has been helping me. It just so happens that when she turned up at your flat it was surrounded by the emergency services. Anyway, when she found out what had happened, she called me, and we came straight here.'

She then leaned over to Sapphire and hugged her. 'I-I'm sorry I freaked out when I first saw you,' said Sapphire. 'I didn't know who you were.'

'That's alright,' said Kelsey and Sapphire couldn't help but notice that her accent had changed a little since they were kids.

'You talk differently,' said Sapphire. 'Posher.'

'Do I? Well, I suppose it's been a long time. We've both changed. The Harris family were good to me. They gave me a good life and an education. I'm working as an accountant now.'

'Bloody hell! You've done well for yourself.'

'I was just lucky enough to be taken in by a good family, that's all.'

Sapphire had been tempted to say, 'not like me', but she stopped herself. How did you tell your kid sister that you had been a sex worker for the past ten years? Looking at Kelsey now, and the respectable young woman she had become, Sapphire doubted that she'd want anything to do with her once she found out the truth.

73

June 2017

Janice understood why the woman would be angry at what Sophie had done. She obviously cared a lot for her to react like that, and Janice felt she deserved an explanation. But she also wanted to let Sophie and Kelsey spend some time alone.

As she led Crystal and Ruby to the waiting room, she said, 'I'm Janice. I used to be Sophie's social worker, and the lady with Sophie is her sister, Kelsey. I take it you're a friend of Sophie's?'

She was pleased that the woman seemed to calm down once she had explained who she was. 'I'm Laura,' she said. 'And this is Trina although Saph, I mean, Sophie, knows us as Crystal and Ruby. We're friends of hers.

'I hope you don't mind me asking,' Crystal continued, 'but how come you're here now? I thought she hadn't had a social worker for years.'

'She hasn't but Kelsey approached me to help her find her sister, so I agreed.'

Janice then explained how she'd reached Sophie's flat just as the police were battering the door down, and how she and Kelsey had rushed to the hospital.

'Would you mind waiting in here for a bit?' she asked once they'd reached the waiting room. 'Only, I thought I would give the sisters a bit of time together. They've got a lot of catching up to do.'

'Sure,' said Crystal and Ruby in unison.

Janice smiled and offered to get them both a coffee. She felt in need of one herself after everything that had happened that day. First came the shock of finding out Sophie had tried to kill herself. Then there was all the tension when she and Kelsey had arrived at the hospital. Sophie had been surrounded by an emergency medical team and she and Kelsey had been instructed to stay in the waiting room.

It seemed an age before a nurse came to tell them what had happened, and she had tried her best to stay calm in the meantime and reassure Kelsey. Apparently, the medics had been successful, and Sophie was starting to come round.

They both rushed into the side ward where another nurse remained watching over Sophie who was tossing around in the bed and mumbling something incomprehensible. Eventually she had come round but her reaction wasn't quite what Janice and Kelsey had been expecting. Thank God she had eventually recognised them and then calmed down!

Janice couldn't resist a smile as she thought about the two sisters. She knew it was unprofessional to get personally involved in her cases. But Sophie's case had bothered her for years. She was so glad she'd agreed to help Kelsey find her. Sophie had obviously been through a hell of a lot but now, hopefully, everything would come right for her at last.

*

For a moment neither of the sisters spoke. Kelsey must have sensed Sophie's discomfort as she cleared her throat and said, 'Janice told me about what happened with Dad.'

'What do you mean?' asked Sophie.

'When he tried to pick you up in Manchester.'

Sophie was shocked that Kelsey knew about that, which meant she must also have known that she was a sex worker. She felt her cheeks flush with shame. 'How did Janice know?'

'Dad went to see her, demanding that she do something about it. Janice told me she was sorry she didn't do anything at the time, but it was out of her hands by then.'

Sophie was pensive for a short while, wondering how much to tell Kelsey. But it seemed she already knew quite a lot. Then she said, 'He's got a bloody cheek, hasn't he, considering he rejected us after Mum died?'

'That's exactly what I thought.'

'Oh well, now you know,' said Sophie and she waited for her sister to speak. When she didn't reply straightaway, Sophie added, 'I don't suppose we'll stay in touch after this. I mean, thanks for coming and all that. It's been great to see you, but you're not going to want anything to do with a sex worker, are you?'

'You're not going back to that,' said Kelsey.

'I've got no bloody choice.'

'Yes, you have. Do you really think I'm gonna let you go back to that life now I've found you? I'm taking you back with me, Sophie. We always looked out for each other when we were kids, and I don't see why it should be any different now. We've already lost too much time.'

'But I don't want to sponge off you, Kelsey. That wouldn't be fair.'

'You wouldn't have to. You've got money.'

'What do you mean?'

'Mum left us a bit. It was from the divorce settlement. She was using it to live off, hoping it would last till we were at least eighteen. There's a couple of thousand there. It should see you right until you find work.'

'But why didn't she tell us?'

'She intended to, apparently. She'd already told Janice that she'd put it in trust for us till we reached eighteen, but she didn't get round to telling us before… well… you know.'

Her expression became sad at the mention of their mother, so Sophie quickly moved the conversation on.

'I've done some bad stuff, Kelsey. It's been hard.'

'I know. Don't worry. We've got all the time in the world to catch up on the missing years. But I won't blame you for what you've done. I know you're a good person and if you've done bad things, it's because you didn't have a choice.'

Sophie nodded. 'Yes, it is.' Then she recalled seeing Crystal and Ruby enter the room before they were ushered out again by Janice. 'By the way, they were my friends who came in earlier. They used to be on the beat too, well, Ruby still works in the sex industry but …'

'Shush,' said Kelsey. 'None of that matters. All that

matters is that we've found each other at last and that from now on I'm gonna take care of you.'

As Kelsey spoke her lip trembled and, Sophie, seeing her sister's emotion, found it impossible to contain her own. She reached out to her and for precious moments they cried in each other's arms.

Despite her tears, Sophie was content now. She had thought that nobody gave a damn but in the end they'd all come through for her: Crystal, Ruby and even her old social worker, Janice but, best of all, her loving sister, Kelsey.

She heard the door open and looked up to see Janice's smiling face. 'Should I leave you two a bit longer?' she asked. 'Your friends are still here but they said they don't mind waiting. In fact, the one called Laura – or was it Crystal? – said she's staying here till she's seen you no matter how long it takes even if security have to come and throw her out. She's a bit of a character, isn't she?'

Sophie smiled. 'Yeah, that's Crystal alright.' She then addressed her sister. 'Are you ready to meet my friends?'

Kelsey nodded eagerly.

'OK, Janice,' said Sophie. 'Send them in.'

Acknowledgements

I have many people to thank for helping to bring this book to fruition. Whilst carrying out the research for this novel, I received help and advice in the areas of sex work, homelessness, the social-care system, and children's care homes. To start with I want to thank my longstanding childhood friend Karen Hopes for putting me in touch with a number of useful contacts. In addition, for help with the research I would like to thank the following:

- Judith Vickers from Lifeshare, Manchester for answering all my questions relating to young homeless women in Manchester.
- Janelle Hardacre of Manchester Action on Street Health (MASH) for information relating to the life of a working girl in Manchester.
- Christine Schora for information relating to children in care homes during the period in which the novel is set.
- Mary Johnson of the UK Crime Book Group on Facebook for information about the social-care system during the years in which the novel is set.
- Sarah Richards for information about the social-care system during the period in which the novel is set.

Big thanks to my publisher, Head of Zeus, who continue to give me support and backing for which I am extremely grateful. In particular, I would like to mention staff past and present including Hannah Todd for a great job on the structural edits, Vicky Joss, Nikky Ward, Lizz Burrell and my new editor, Martina Arzu, as well as Helena Newton for a sterling job with the copy edits and Annabel Walker for your excellent work on the proofreading.

Thanks also to the staff I don't often meet but who do excellent work on the PR, sales, and marketing side of things. I had the privilege of meeting some of you at a Zoom meeting earlier this year.

Thank you to my agent, Jo Bell, for all your help and advice, and to all the staff at Bell Lomax Moreton for your support.

I would like to acknowledge all the lovely readers who have followed the series so far, and the writing community including fellow authors, book bloggers and reviewers. Your help and support is invaluable.

Lastly, I would like to thank all my family and friends who have supported me throughout my writing career by helping to spread the word and just by being there for me.

About the Author

HEATHER BURNSIDE started her writing career more than twenty years ago when she worked as a freelance writer while studying for a writing diploma. As part of her studies Heather wrote the first chapters of her debut novel, Slur, but she didn't complete the novel till many years later. Slur became the first book in The Riverhill Trilogy, which was followed by The Manchester Trilogy then her current series, The Working Girls.

You can find out more about the author by signing up to the Heather Burnside mailing list (http://eepurl.com/CP6YP) for the latest updates including details of new releases and book bargains, or by following her on any of the links below.

Facebook: www.facebook.com/HeatherBurnsideAuthor/
Twitter: twitter.com/heatherbwriter
Website: www.heatherburnside.com